NO PROMISES, NO LIES

DEVILS & DARLINGS
BOOK ONE

AJ WILDING

ISBN: 979-8-9921643-3-6 (Discreet Edition)

ISBN: 979-8-9921643-2-9 (PuckBoy Edition)

Published by Rose Onyx Press

Editor: Nicole DiPatri Sheldon

First Edition, [February 2025]

Cover design by IndieInkCovers

Printed in the United States of America

Visit www.AjWilding.com for more information about the author and upcoming books

"To the ghosts who haunt us, the choices that shape us, and the love that saves us."

TRIGGER WARNINGS

This book contains content that may be sensitive or triggering to some readers. Topics include:

- Physical violence
- Murder
- Arranged Marriage
- Domestic Abuse (depicted on page).
- Emotional manipulation and gaslighting.
- Threat of sexual assault
- Kidnapping and captivity.
- Death of a loved one.
- Organized crime
- Strong language.
- Explicit sex scenes
- Home invasion

PLAYLIST

The music that inspired the story

Only on Spotify!
No Promises, No Lies

SWEET LITTLE LIES- BULOW

THE DEATH OF PEACE OF MIND- BAD OMENS

7 MINUTES IN HELL- CHRISSY COSTANZA, VOILA

GONE OR STAYING - SLEEP THEORY

LIKE THAT- BEA MILLER

BAD SIDE- JAKE DANIELS

RUSSIAN ROULETTE- NESSA BARRETT

INTO THE DARK (FEAT. KELLIN QUINN) - POINT NORTH

BODY BAG- NEONI

ONLY ONE KING- TOMMY PROFITT, JUNG YOUTH

EMPTY- LETDOWN

BECAUSE IT MATTERED- DUTCH MELROSE

TIL I COLLAPSE- EMINEM, NATE DOGG

MUGSHOT- HUDDY

CRAVEN'- STILETTO, KENDYLE PAGE

REAPER- SILVERBERG

RUNRUNRUN- DUTCH MELROSE

THE SUMMONING- SLEEP TOKEN

BURN THE HOUSE DOWN- AJR

BURIAL PLOT- DAYSEEKER

BAD THINGS- I PREVAIL

FEEL ME NOW- IF NOT FOR ME

DARKSIDE- BRING ME THE HORIZON

BARELY BREATHING- FROM ASHES TO NEW, AGAINST
THE CURRENT

HOSTAGE- MAGGIE LINDEMANN

CAN YOU FEEL MY HEART- BRING ME THE HORIZON

LIMITS- BAD OMENS

THINK LATER- TATE MCRAE

LOVE ME- SPED UP- EX HABIT

GIVE- SLEEP TOKEN

CITIES- TWO FEET & TOBY MAI

MEDDLE ABOUT- CHASE ATLANTIC

ON YOUR KNEES- EX HABIT

GUILTY AS SIN? - TAYLOR SWIFT

PLEASE- EX HABIT

NEVER KNOW- BAD OMENS

LOVELY (WITH KHALID) - BILLIE EILISH, KHALID

SLOW DOWN- CHASE ATLANTIC

WANT ME- EX HABIT

BLOODSHOT- SAM TINNESZ

WOLVES- SAM TINNESZ, SILVERBERG

DUGS & CANDY- ALL TIME LOW

THE ALCHEMY- TAYLOR SWIFT

AGAIN

RORY

"*A*gain."

Karina's harsh tone echoes through the empty arena. So loud that even though she's across the ice, there's no way I can pretend I haven't heard her.

I lay where I fell, failing again to land the triple-triple combination I'm known for.

Leaning my head back against the cold ice, I close my eyes. It's been months since the accident. It shouldn't be this hard. Cold leeches through the thin body suit of my skating dress and I soak it in. It feels good. Despite the thin material, I'm burning up after racing through my routine over and over.

A door slam interrupts the brief moment of peace.

Shit.

Reluctantly, I open my eyes to find my coach glaring down at me. The thick fur of Karina's winter coat tightly hugs her chin. Thin lips turned down in a frown of displeasure. She's painted them a crimson red, a close match to her fiery auburn hair, which is pulled tight against her skull in a severe bun.

"Get up Aurora."

It's Rory, I hiss in my head, begrudgingly pushing myself up off the ice while avoiding Karina's eyes. I busy myself brushing the snow and sleet from my velvet skirt.

I don't bother correcting her. Karina's been my coach for over a year now. She knows what I prefer—

She just doesn't care.

As the most sought after skating coach on the East Coast, she can call me whatever she pleases. She's the best in the business. And probably my last hope of making the national team this year.

"I will see it again."

There will be no argument. I'll do it again.

And again.

And again.

As many times as she wishes, I will do it. And maybe... just maybe... one of those times, I'll land it..

Jaw locked, I skate back over to the corner, settling my breath and straightening my spine. *Get your shit together, Kostalova.*

This time last year, I was the reigning national champion. I was as solid as the ice I was skating on, a favorite for this year's Olympic team. Now look at me...I'll be lucky to land the wild-card bid to even *compete* at nationals.

Karina remains on the ice this time, watching me with pursed lips and folded arms.

My music starts again—an excerpt from Swan Lake. But movement at the top row of the arena draws my attention and I miss my cue.

Far back up in the stands, in an area of the arena mostly veiled in shadow, a figure rises. The weight of his gaze heavy on me before turning away and disappearing out into the concourse.

Awesome...

"You're a disappointment." Karina's eyes have followed mine. Her words hold no emotion. She's not trying to taunt me; she's just stating facts. "Your father spending all this money for you to fail." Karina clicks her tongue in disapproval.

My cheeks burn with both my frustration and embarrassment.

"Perhaps if you would take advice and lean out more, we would see you complete rotation." Her Russian accent and stunted English do nothing but sharpen the already harsh criticism. My coach stares down at me like I'm nothing but a waste of her time. We both know my father's money and influence are the only reason she even took me on. The nineteen-year-old has-been.

I don't react and she sighs loudly. Something akin to disappointment flashes across her face before she waves her perfectly manicured hand in my direction. "Again."

The music re-starts and this time I push forward, my blades digging into the ice, gaining speed before switching onto my inside edge.

Karina's words don't bother me as much as she thinks they do. Professional figure skating is not for the soft skinned. Nothing she could say to me could get in my head. But her words echo my own self doubts, giving them fuel.

Her methods may be brutal, and her words harsh, but if anyone can help me, it's Karina Valgova.

And I need to be better.

To be the best.

Because I'm running out of time.

I fly through the complicated footwork section of my routine, pushing loose strands of hair out of my face before leaning into a crowd-pleasing cross-ice spiral.

Nailing it.

I'm barely halfway through the routine before my focus slips and my thoughts stray back to my father.

He'd been watching today. I've been skating at the Edge Arena all summer and he's never once stopped in. It gives weight to my theory that something is up. Things have been tense at home. No one has said anything, but it's in the air. Something's different. Something's changed.

The deal we made comes to mind just as I launch into the first triple. Landing it, I take off immediately into the second, thrusting my toe-pick into the ice. But I over-rotate, landing hard against the unforgiving ice, sliding across the rink until the boards stop me.

This time, I don't waste a second. I'm back on my feet before Karina can even utter a word, already skating back to the far corner.

Again.

Fear has an ugly taste. I dig my blades into the ice and start again. The stress and impact from my repeated falls kick up the familiar dizzy feeling in my head.

I grind my teeth.

Not now.

After I exit my first spin, the vertigo worsens and I stumble off a simple three-turn.

Finally, I relent. Pulling out of the routine and skating for the bench, I keep my eyes on the ice, unable to meet Karina's eye as I tear through my bag. I search for the little orange bottle of pills.

My fingers close around the bottle, and I release a breath, quickly shaking two small pills out and swallowing them with a cool rush of water. Leaning back against the bench and closing my eyes, I wait for the spinning to stop. The medicine is fast-acting but I will it to work faster.

I'm running out of time.

After a minute, Karina joins me, lowering herself gracefully onto the hockey bench. "I admire intensity but... you skate like life depends on it. Where is love, where is *passion* for skating?"

I take another long drink of water, grounding my head and avoiding the question.

I do love skating. If I didn't, I wouldn't be here every freaking day getting my ass kicked by frozen water!

But she is right about one thing: this is life or death. There is gold in my future, that much is certain. But whether it's a gold medal or a gold ring—*depends on me.*

Opening my eyes, I set down my water, the vertigo fading away. I rise on shaky knees that have nothing to do with the long-term effects of my concussion.

"Again."

2

ONCE A GOON...

RORY

Karina keeps me training until the Zamboni driver grows fed up enough to wrench open the gates. He backs the giant ice cleaning machine out onto the ice while I'm exiting my scratch spin.

Practice running late is nothing new, but now that we're training at the Breakers' practice pavilion, there are hockey players lingering on the other side of the boards, impatiently waiting for their own ice time.

I avoid their cool stares on my way back to the bench to collect my bag. As quickly as I can, I slip my blade covers on my skates and exit the bench. Karina's already disappeared, not one for post-practice words of encouragement or disparagement.

She gets plenty in during our session.

I frown at the mess of hockey players crowding around the rink's door, blocking my path to the women's locker room, still waiting on the Zamboni to finish cleaning the ice. The Breakers players laugh and shout, playfully knocking each other around like a bunch of oversized children. Some battle with their sticks over a small ball that looks to be made of tape.

I roll my eyes. As un-amusing as I find hockey players, running late also means I'm probably late for my shift at the Chill Zone. The bar on the second floor of the rink. I can't wait for them to clear out and take the ice.

Throwing my bag over my shoulder, I grit my teeth and start forward.

I'm not short—taller than your average figure skater at five-foot-five—but even in my skates, the Breakers *tower* over me.

These guys are already tall, but throw skates into the mix and most are far north of six feet.

As I weave my way through the crowd of rowdy hockey players, most of them don't even notice me. I only catch a few glares for overrunning my ice time.

Figure skaters and hockey players rarely play nice.

The team certainly wasn't happy about sharing their brand new private rink with the Boston Belles skate club, but there's a lot of money in figure skating. The Breakers are a relatively new team, still trying to establish themselves within the league. They need all the help they can get, which is also why the Breakers run a youth program at the rink as well.

While I can't understand the allure of chasing a rubber disc around the ice with sticks, the Boston Breakers are a big deal in this city. The team opened up some of their practices when they were on a hot streak last year and they've been selling out ever since. On Saturdays and Sundays, fans can come watch for a nominal ticketing fee.

Today was one of those practices. The doors have opened and the once peaceful arena now buzzes with chatter from fans hoping to catch a glimpse of some of the more notorious

Breakers players. Like Colt King, the new star center or Aidan O'Rourke, resident bad boy who racked up plenty of penalty minutes last season.

It's annoying, but it's not like I don't reap the benefits. Hockey bros are pretty good tippers. The Chill Zone cafe where I work part time offers coffee and breakfast sandwiches for morning practices, and burgers and beer for afternoons and evenings. It's also the reason I know more about hockey and the Breakers team than I care to.

A whistled cat-call draws my attention and I turn around to glare at the player responsible, which is why I don't see the hulking six-foot-three defenseman in my path—until I walk right into him.

The impact sends me reeling.

It's hard enough to walk on skates; even worse after colliding with a brick wall. I brace myself for the impact, but it never comes.

"I thought figure skaters were supposed to be graceful," the player holding me laughs while tugging me back up. He'd caught hold of my arm before I hit the ground.

I only know a couple of the players from their reputations, and what the fans talk about in the Chill Zone. Honestly, all hockey players look the same to me. With his helmet on, I don't recognize the one holding my arm. When my eyes narrow, his lips quirk up in a mischievous grin, dark green eyes sparkling with amusement.

"At least I'm graceful where it counts—on the ice. I might stumble, but at least I'm not tripping over my own ego like you." Ripping my arm from his grasp, I move to dart around him. My patience is non-existent.

But he blocks me again with his body, nearly sending me careening to the floor all over again.

"You're welcome, by the way." The asshole raises a brow at me. His infuriatingly handsome face holding an arrogant smirk.

I roll my eyes, having to tilt my chin to meet his eye. "Mmm, right, aren't you a real lifesaver? You save the girl by knocking her down first?" *God. He's massive.* "I'll try not to make a habit out of relying on you for balance. Checking people into the boards, I suppose, is far easier than actual skating." I give him a sweet smile.

The gate to the arena finally opens up and the crowd of players around us thins as the team finally takes the ice. But the defenseman planted in front of me remains where he is, grinning at me, thoroughly entertained.

"Funny." The Breakers player considers me. "Maybe you should try a sport where you get points for falling down."

He hits a nerve, and I clench my jaw. *He saw my practice.*

"O'Rourke! Get your ass on the ice!."

A quick glance back at the bench shows an irritable looking assistant coach watching us impatiently. The rest of the team is already out on the ice, warming up.

"O'Rourke." I repeat the name. Trying it out on my tongue. It's familiar; I've heard it before... *Aidan* O'Rourke, the Breakers' enforcer, frequently in the headlines for his fights and aggressive style of play. According to ESPN, he's one explosive incident from getting cut.

Turning my attention back to the hockey player, I look him up and down once more with disdain. "Once a goon, always a goon."

His smug smile fades into a frown.

I keep going. "Maybe if you spent less time in the penalty box, you'd learn a thing or two about *finesse* on the ice." With that, I shove past him. And this time he lets me.

"It's been a pleasure."

Not.

I feel his stare on my back the entire way back to the locker room.

3

HOCKEY AND CHILL

RORY

$\mathcal{I}$ let out a groan when I see the time. Seeing as how practice has already started, I already missed out on the pre-practice rush. Every minute wasted is less money in my pocket.

I rip the skates off my feet, not bothering to take off my tights as I slide my jeans on over them. Rushing now, I throw on a sweatshirt and sling my bag over my shoulder while practically running through the door.

This time, the pathway is clear of goonish hockey players; the Breakers' practice now fully underway. No one even spares me a glance as I rush for the stairs.

The arena floor itself is closed off to fans. Only the upper level stands and viewing deck by the bar are open to fans. In my hurry, I trip up the stairs, not missing the barely-suppressed snort that sounds out from behind me.

"Not a word," I growl venomously, without sparing a glance back, well aware of who's following me.

"I wouldn't dream of it," Alexei replies, though I can clearly hear the amusement in his tone.

Sighing irritably, I continue up the stairs, not learning my lesson and taking them two at a time.

By the time I push through the double doors, I'm nearly thirty minutes late for my shift. I walk out into a throng of girls that's encircling the only access down to the lower levels from the main concourse.

Two bored looking security guards stand to either side of the doors, keeping the puck bunny wannabes on the second level and far away from the players below.

A dozen sets of eyes fly to me when I appear through those forbidden double doors. Jealousy gleaming in their baby blues and greens. When I feel Alexei close in behind me, those suspicious glares disappear. Oh, they forget me *entirely* and evaporate into flirty smiles and fluttering eyelashes.

Annoyed, I push through the vapid little leeches lying in wait; all hoping to snare a player on their way out of the rink.

Alexei is no hockey player, but could easily pass as one. The man stands over six feet tall with broad shoulders, a defined chest, and thick arms. He's built like an athlete. But far prettier than any I've ever seen.

I leave my body guard behind to fend off the puck bunnies and dart into the Chill Zone.

There's not an open spot to be found along the bar as I casually slip behind it while shooting Elle an apologetic look. She's neck-deep in pouring shots of Jack.

"I'm sorry, I'm sorry, I'm sorry!" I rush out, feeling terrible about leaving her alone. Quickly, I stash my bag under the bar, not wanting to take any additional time to stow it properly in the back room.

She looks up, her hazel eyes finding me with a broad smile on her face. "It's fine. Don't worry about it!" Elle is on the Belles skating team too and all too familiar with how Karina Valgova runs her sessions.

My eyes scan the packed bar. "Where do you need me?"

Elle's focused back on her task, but cocks her head toward an empty beer glass cued up under the tap. "A lager for the green flannel," nodding again, this time in the opposite direction.

I spot the man in the aforementioned green flannel, eyeing the two of us curiously from further down the bar.

"On it." I start for the glass, but she hisses at me under her breath, looking pointedly at my sweatshirt.

"Shit. Right." I duck back under the bar, feeling for my bag, reaching in to pull out the blasted jersey but coming up empty. Besides my skates, an extra bottle of water and meds, the bag is empty.

My face betrays my blunder and Elle sighs, "There's an extra jersey in the back."

Grinning at her, I dart into the small staff room, dumping my bag on the bench of the break room where it belongs. I spot the black, silver, and green jersey hanging on a rack by the door.

I rip it off its hanger and hurriedly pull it over my sweatshirt. The Chill Zone employees wear Breakers jerseys as their uniform.

Back behind the bar and now appropriately dressed, I dive into work. I roll my shoulders in the oversized Breakers jersey as I clear glasses and pour shot after shot. Flirting with the mostly male patrons, and reaping the cash benefits.

Elle and I fall into an easy rhythm. Together we make it through the rush. The two of us clean up on tips as die hard

Breakers fans salivate over their favorite players. We're so busy, I barely have any time to notice my new favorite defenseman running drills below us.

I definitely don't notice the way #19 Asshole O'Rourke powers down the ice, sweeping up the puck and scoring top shelf from the point.

The bar clears out pretty quickly after practice ends and I feel Elle slide up next to me as I finish up wiping down the bar. She whispers once she's got my attention and looks pointedly across the room. "What's the deal with you two?"

I follow her gaze, finding Alexei at the end of it. My designated Bratva stalker is lounging casually at a nearby high top table against the long wall of windows overlooking the rink. His eyes are on the ice below and not on us.

But I know better.

I go back to cleaning, still hoping to be out of here tonight at a reasonable hour. "I told you, it's not like that."

"Mmm," she hums, her eyes on my ruggedly handsome and remarkably dangerous Russian bodyguard.

The one that could kill her six different ways without even batting an eye.

"You say that, but have you *seen* him?"

"The man follows me everywhere I go. *Of course* I've *seen* him." I look back up at Alexei, who's still pretending to ignore us from his usual spot in the corner. I catch the ghost of a grin playing on his lips. The man has ears like a bat.

I like Elle. We've become friendly over the past few months since I moved back to the city and started working at the bar, but I can't tell her the full truth. I can't tell her anything about the Bratva—or my life in it—without putting her own life at risk. All she knows is that because of an overprotective father, I have my own personal security detail.

Not that Alexei fits the mold of 'professional security detail.' He's young, only a few years older than us, and looks like a built Abercrombie model covered head to toe in tattoos.

But Elle hasn't questioned it, though I get the feeling she knows I'm holding something back and is polite enough to respect that.

Worse yet, Alexei's a charmer. He can flirt his way in and out of any situation. With his dark hair and thick lashes, he's got the jawline of a cover model and the muscles of a well-practiced athlete. Knowing who he really is and what he does for my father has me immune to those devastatingly good looks.

But one look at Elle is enough to tell me she's already fallen under his spell.

"Don't even think about it." I narrow my eyes and point a finger at her in warning.

"I thought you didn't want dibs?" she laughs and pulls her gaze—reluctantly—away from my bodyguard and back to me.

"I don't." Alexei's nothing but professional and I'm not interested in any of my father's men. "He's a walking red-flag Elle," I sigh, the day finally catching up to me. "Trust me on this one." I set my rag down to take a sip of my water.

"Whatever you say Ro." My friend continues to gaze dreamily at Alexei, who by now has noticed the both of us staring at him and heads our way.

"Nice jersey, Rory." Alexei winks at me as he approaches, mischief written all over his face as he slides his fine ass onto one of the bar stools. His dark eyes trail over my friend. "Hey Elle."

While my friend swoons beside me, I check out the jersey

I'd worn throughout my entire shift. In my rush to get behind the bar, I hadn't noticed the glaring #19 staring up at me.

I choke on my water, realizing I've had the name *O'Rourke* plastered across my back for the better part of two hours!

Alexei leans over his elbows onto the bar, showing off the brightly colored artwork that decorates both of his arms.

Elle inhales sharply, busying herself by polishing the already spotless bar top nearby.

I shake my head. He knows *exactly* what he's doing.

"Ready to go, Rory?" Alexei's dark eyes slide back to mine.

"Sure am." I drop my rag into the laundry bucket and not-so-subtly nudge my shoulder into my friend, who's still staring wide-eyed at the boy candy draped over the bar. "I'll see you tomorrow Elle."

"Bye Elle." Alexei shoots her another wink, and I groan loud enough for both of them to hear me. Blushing with embarrassment on his behalf, I grab hold of his arm, directing him out of the bar and away from my only friend.

"Don't even think about it," I warn him, too.

4

BLOOD TIES

RORY

*a*s my main bodyguard, Alexei and I spend a lot of time together. We aren't exactly what I would call friends, but he knows me well enough by now to know how to read my moods.

We ride home with the radio off.

The practice session today wore me out. Add to that, the gym workout this morning, the ballet lesson in between, plus the Chill Zone shift tonight... I'm tired and overstimulated.

I count my cash tips silently in the passenger seat. I'm not pretentious enough to ride in the back of the armored SUV alone, like my father or brother might. It was a solid shift. Two hundred more dollars to add to my stash.

I shove the money into the zippered part of my backpack, right next to my black cards.

Sure, I have access to enough money that I can *buy* just about anything I want. But it's my father's money. And easily traced. The cash is a contingency plan. If I can't remain competitive as a figure skater, I'll be married off to the highest bidder. *Or sold off, is more like it.* My athletic accomplishments were the only reason I've escaped the altar so far.

Arranged marriage. While archaic and antiquated, the practice is very much still alive in today's reigning mafia families.

Leaning back in my seat, I rest my head up against the cool window, a dull ache in my forehead. The medication from Dr. Jakes is wearing off.

By the time Alexei pulls into the mansion's gates, I'm fully ready to trade my jeans for sweats and curl up alone in my room with a good book. And maybe a steak... I'm starving.

The Audi in the driveway ruins all my plans.

Niko.

Alexei opens my door for me as he always does, but instead of trailing me inside like he normally would, he lingers by the SUV. He offers me a grim smile.

I hesitate when I reach the front door, my hand hovering just over the brass knob. The cold stone of the mansion's exterior walls looms over me. Taking a deep breath, I force down the bubbling anxiety before finally twisting open the knob and stepping into silence.

The foyer is empty. The marble floors gleam in the fading evening sunlight, well buffed to perfection.

Cautiously, I poke my head into the kitchen, finding it too to be empty and just as ominously quiet as the foyer was. *No cook to be found.* Deciding to swap my steak for a protein shake, I head for the fridge.

After retrieving the milk for my shake, I shut the door, revealing a pissed off looking Niko standing right behind it and nearly jump out of my skin.

"What do you want?" I say with far more confidence than I feel. I wish Alexei was here, even though he can't protect me from my own brother. As the son of the Pakhan, Niko outranks him.

Clutching the milk to my chest, I back away as inconspicuously as I can manage. My heart is racing.

Wishing someone else was in the room.

Anyone.

Witnesses.

Needing to put as much space between us as possible, I take the milk and my cup and circle back around the island, keeping my eye on Niko as I go. My brother's earned his reputation for being both unpredictable and unhinged; a dangerous combination.

And he despises me.

Thankfully, Niko remains where he is. He folds his arms as he leans against the refrigerator. "Well, aside from the fact this is *my* house... I can't check in on my little sister?" His eyes follow me as I move around the kitchen island, snagging on the Breakers jersey I'm still wearing.

I scoff under my breath, mixing the chocolate powder into the poured milk. "The sister you've tried relentlessly to *get rid of* since she moved back in?" I dare glare at him before quickly averting my eyes. *He's a lot scarier now than he was when we were kids.* "No."

Niko's expression doesn't change. He always looks like he's just pissed off at the world. His blue eyes watch me finish making my shake.

There's no love lost between my brother and I. He's never missed a moment to remind me how much I don't belong here. How I'm not a Kostalov. That my mother was just a gold-digging whore who *lied* to get what she wanted out of my father.

He can deny me all he wants, but the resemblance is striking. Both of us favor our father in looks. Same sandy blonde hair and steel-blue eyes. And even though my hair is a shade darker than his, there's no mistaking Kostalov-blue-eyes.

Can't say that I blame him, seeing as how our father was married to Niko's mother when he fathered *me*. Niko's hated me since the day I was born. Though I hardly see how that's my fault. It's not like I had a say in the matter.

It didn't help that we were raised separately. My mother's wish. She petitioned to keep me, *a delicate daughter*, as far from this world as she could. And even though he never left his wife for her, my father *adored* my mother and so he granted her wish.

My mother whisked me away far from the Bratva, far from Boston, and threw me into figure skating to appease my father. Niko made being here so unbearable that I hardly ever visited. This was the longest I'd been home in years.

"Since when do you like hockey?" Niko's still staring at the jersey, his upper lip curled in distaste.

"I don't." I shift uneasily, playing with the long sleeves, uncomfortable under his gaze. "We have to wear them at the Chill Zone."

He looks at me like I have five heads. "I don't get why you want to work there. You have black cards for Christ's sakes!"

So I can run away from here.

I take a long drink of my shake, mumbling something about it keeping me busy in between training sessions. Eyeing my brother warily as I do. If *anyone* suspects what I'm up to, it's game over.

An uncomfortable silence follows before Niko speaks again. "Father called me."

I flinch at the mention of the F-word. I recover quickly and hope Niko didn't notice.

His eyes narrow, telling me he did, and continues, "He wants a meeting. Both of us."

I cough, to hide my yelp of surprise. Aside from the required Sunday dinners where we sit in uncomfortable silence and discuss little other than my training and the weather, I rarely see my father, let alone *talk* to him.

"What for?"

"To discuss your *future in this family*." He frowns, his words dripping with disapproval.

Recovering from my initial reaction, I roll my eyes. "If this is another one of your attempts to get rid of me—"

"I didn't call it." Niko's jaw tightens and I freeze.

"When?" I carefully place my drink down on the counter, noticing my hand shaking.

"Now."

5

THE ARRANGEMENT

RORY

*I*ndeed, Niko wasn't playing another one of his cruel tricks...Adrik Kostalov is, in fact, waiting for us in his study. The Russian Kingpin doesn't even bother looking up from his desk at our arrival.

Niko holds the door open for me, and I shoot him a scathing look as I pass. He returns it with a glare of his own.

And then we wait.

Neither of us bold enough to interrupt the Russian Pakhan's work.

Dark wood walls surround us. The scent of leather and cigars fills my nose. I've only been in this room once, my very first day back in Boston.

I glance longingly up at the beautifully bound leather books that fill the wall behind the grand mahogany desk.

Adrik is the type of man to deal only in rare literature. There are likely many first editions on those shelves. I've long since wished to explore his collection, but never dared ask. This study was strictly off limits and to be called in here...

"Have a seat Aurora." The elder Kostalov finally looks up from the paperwork covering his desk. "Nikolai." He nods curtly at my brother behind me.

I sink slowly into one of the leather armchairs positioned in front of his desk, doing my best to act like this is normal.

Nothing about my life in the last year has been *normal.*

Adrik folds his hands in front of him, settling his gaze on me. I fight the urge to shrink back under the weight of his full attention. My father is a powerful man. Far greater men than me have pissed themselves after a single stern glance from Adrik Kostalov.

"Aurora, you look well. Despite a disappointing showing at the rink today..." I clench my jaw and carefully school my face. "Are you feeling well? Still experiencing lasting effects from the concussion?"

"I'm feeling fine Papa," I say, a little too quickly. "The new meds are working, and I hardly ever need to take them..." My eyes flicker between my brother and my father. Both watching me with the same unreadable, hardened stare. "Today was an off day. Nothing to worry about." I smile, though it doesn't touch my eyes.

My father studies me intently. I swallow the lump that's formed in my throat, not sure what he's looking for. He leans back in his chair with a sigh, "The attack on you and your mother..." he pauses, unable to go on. A brief flash of grief breaking through his stony expression.

"Have you found out who ordered the attack yet?" I ask softly

Adrik rarely speaks of my mother; the attack that killed her even less. But the question haunts me, keeping me up most nights.

Why her?

There's no question it was a mafia hit. You don't just *happen* across a car bomb placed under your car by accident. She never stood a chance. That day's images are forever seared into my brain. *I wasn't supposed to be there.* It's never made sense. She had nothing to do with this world. But no one ever claimed responsibility.

"Unfortunately, no," Adrik shakes his head, regaining his composure. The little balloon of hope deflates inside of me. "Which makes the matter of your safety even more imperative. I called you in here today, Aurora, because it's time we discuss your future in this family."

Dread fills me, knowing exactly where he's going with this. What I've known was coming since I set foot in this mansion a year ago; since he cancelled my college plans, citing *security concerns*, and dragged me back to Boston....

"Okay." My voice is small and I keep my eyes down.

"Since you've been living under an assumed name all these years, your role in this family has mostly gone unnoticed by outsiders."

I nod solemnly. *For safety reasons, or to protect Adrik's reputation?* The Bratva Pakhan has many enemies, many of whom wouldn't hesitate to take out a vendetta on the Russian Lion's only daughter.

Using my true name, Aurora Adrikova Kostalova, while powerful, would also be a death sentence. As far as the rest of the world was concerned, I was just *Rory Annabelle Collins*: *Rising Figure Skating Prodigy* from Canada.

"Understand, as the daughter of the Pakhan, there are certain—expectations." Adrik pauses for only a moment, his eyes studying me. "We've discussed already..."

We discussed *once*, and he *promised* me...

"I hope to present you *officially* as the daughter of Adrik Kostalov at my birthday party," he smiles. It's far worse than his frown.

I bite the inside of my cheek to hold in my scream. The party is only two weeks away. It will be the event of the season —Black tie—All the city's most influential members would be in attendance. My father knew how to command the under-belly of the city but also flourished and relished in the attention of the upper society.

"You are already nineteen, and nearing a birthday your-self." *I'm surprised he remembers,* though my twentieth birthday isn't exactly 'coming up.' It's still several months away.

Niko shifts from where he leans up against the window a few feet away. He opens his mouth to say something but ulti-mately decides against it—slamming his jaw shut instead with a click.

"At your age, in our—*culture*," he chooses his words care-fully, "A girl of your age would already be married. Or at the very least, engaged."

I shoot up in my chair, instantly on the defensive. "But you said—"

My father raises one hand and I fall silent. Fidgeting in my chair, I fight the urge to run screaming from the room.

"I remember what we discussed, Aurora, however..." Adrik's eyes flicker over to Niko, whose jaw stays cemented shut. My father doesn't even bother to look apologetic as he continues. "Circumstances have changed. War is brewing within the city and the Bratva—has had its own set of recent setbacks." His mouth twists with an air of annoyance. "An engagement would more than double your protections. It's a dangerous time in the city."

"Then send me back to Canada!" The words burst out of me in frustration and my father has to issue me a warning look. Doing my best to reel it back, I speak up again. "I did everything you asked! I'm on the list for qualifiers. I'll make it to nationals. I will! Karina—"

"Yes, but that was before your accident; the concussion. Karina has concerns." Adrik's frown deepens, "And from what I saw today at practice, ангел, I have to agree" I look up when he uses his nickname for me, *angel*. "It might be time to face that your skating career might be over." He looks at me with pity in his eyes.

"Karina doesn't know shit!" The words are out of my mouth before I can stop them.

His eyes harden to steel, and I can feel the mental slap against my cheek. "Manners, Aurora," he scolds, his tone chillingly cold and devoid of any compassion or empathy.

I nod, doing my best to look as contrite as possible. "I apologize Papa, but you assured me as long as I remained competitive, any *arrangement* would be postponed."

Adrik rises from behind his desk, coming around to stand in front of it. I slide back in my chair as far as it will allow.

"You sustained a major injury, Aurora. Dr. Jakes says you're still having the headaches and dizzy spells."

I look away, unable to contest facts while also adding Dr. Jakes to a list of those not to trust.

"You can't even land the triple combination!" My father throws his hands up, shaking his head in clear disappointment.

I don't dare look at Niko. Oh, how he must be *loving* this. All those years of winning gold medal after gold medal don't count for anything. If I can't be a source of pride for my father on the ice, then I'll be relegated to lining his pockets instead, with money and alliances.

Adrik waves his hand and I track the movement. "It's no matter. Things change and you are a Kostalova. There are expectations that come along with the *luxuries* you enjoy so much."

The urge to scowl at him is almost worth the slap I'm sure I would receive. *Almost.* The comment just goes to show how little he actually knows me. He doesn't allow me enough freedom to partake in any of life's *luxuries.* Everyday it's straight to the rink and straight home. That's it. Prisoners have more freedom than I do.

"An opportunity has presented itself."

I dart a glance to the side at Niko and he meets my eye, though his face gives nothing away.

"An alliance." My father puffs out his chest, proud of whatever it is he's *arranged.*

I grip the arms of my chair tightly to keep myself from bolting from the study. "But skating—"

"If it's important to you, I'm sure your future husband will allow you to continue your athletic pursuits this year. We can add it as a clause to the contract if you'd like."

I blink at him.

And there it is.

A future *husband* who will control every move I make. *Decide for me.* Just like how it is now. My temper flares and my cheeks burn with frustration. Pain emanates from my palm where I've curled my nails in, digging deep into the soft skin.

The Bratva is in trouble. I'd been kept far away from the business side of things, but even I can sense it. The war Adrik spoke of earlier was catching like embers between the major players in the city. The Italians, the Irish and the Russians. Each one claimed Boston as their own, but there can only be one king.

It isn't my war. And I want *nothing* to do with it.

"If you need an alliance so bad, why don't you offer Niko up on a silver platter?" I snap, my arm flying toward my brother. *The next Bratva heir.* "Doesn't an Italian capo somewhere have some daughters coming of age?"

Niko's familiar blue eyes, *my eyes,* flare in response to my outburst. He slowly shakes his head back and forth with a look I know translates into '*shut the fuck up.*'

My father lets out an exasperated sigh. He runs a hand down his face, letting another outburst slide. "If there were any other option, Aurora, I would take it. But I will not compromise your safety. As long as you remain unclaimed, you are at high risk."

Unclaimed. Like I'm nothing but a valuable possession ripe for the taking.

"Will I have a say?" I start, and my father's eyes narrow on me, warning me I'm pushing this too far. "In the *suitor...*" I continue, the whole idea so archaic and antiquated. "Will I have a say?" I repeat, demanding to know. One glance between the two Kostalov men gives me my answer.

"You've already chosen." There's a subtle accusation of betrayal within my tone.

"Yes, Aurora. I have chosen. The contracts are being drawn up for you to marry Matteo Carroza, Consigliere of the Italian Mafia. The right-hand man of Cole DeLuca himself."

A tense silence fills the room. I know exactly who Cole DeLuca is. *The Butcher of Boston.* The youngest Italian boss

Boston has ever seen. He secured his position with violence and bloodshed after an internal war threatened to do the Outfit in.

And Matteo is his right-hand man. There were no good options but *this*...

This was the *worst* one.

6

THE DARK SIDE OF BOSTON

RORY

a distraction is the last thing I need.

I didn't sleep last night. I just kept going over and over the situation in my mind, fortifying my exit strategy. So far, I've squirreled away a couple thousand in cash from my job at the Chill Zone.

It's not enough.

Not *nearly* enough.

If I'm going to run, I need money. *Documents*. I won't only have to hide from the entirety of the Russian Bratva, but now let's throw in the Italian Mafia for shits and giggles; an organization arguably more connected than us by far. My head starts to feel spinny.

My father has already taken it upon himself to appoint me extra guards, needing to protect his investment. *To keep me from running*. There were two armed men waiting for me outside this morning when I walked out for practice.

Alexei, noticeably missing.

My frown deepens at the sight of Petr waiting by the SUV

doors, puffing on a cigarette. One of my father's most loyal men. Of course my father would appoint Petr to the job.

It reminds me that, not only do I require the *means* to escape, I also require *opportunity*. It would be no small task to ditch the hardened Russian soldiers whose entire job was specifically *not* to lose me.

About an hour and a half into a particularly rough practice, those men my father sent to follow me around everywhere appear at the rink door, banging loudly on the glass to get our attention. Alexei was still nowhere to be seen. I've asked, but all they've told me he was *needed elsewhere* today. Petr now stands in the doorway of the hockey bench, beckoning me over to him.

Karina skates by my side. "You better go girl, that one right there is not one you want to cross." She shoots me a wry look and I make a face before skating slowly in Petr's direction, not in a hurry to find out what he wants.

Petr shouts something at Karina in Russian over my shoulder.

I whip my head back to my coach, expecting an argument, but her back is to me. She's already skating off. *What the fuck?*

Gritting my teeth, I take my time skating to the bench, where I stashed my skate guards, along with my bag containing my water bottle and phone. Petr scowls at me the whole way. A look I return, irritated when he doesn't translate what he'd just shouted at Karina in Russian. Only barking at me to *hurry my ass up* in English.

Not that I really need him to. I understand and speak

fluent Russian, as well as perfected my Italian and Spanish. A skill my mother *insisted* I learn and keep secret.

It used to grate on me to keep the secret, and I'd thought about revealing it. My father would be over the moon to know his daughter had learned Russian. Back then, all I craved was his approval. But on my brief visits back home to Boston over the years, I quickly realized there was often a discrepancy between what the men said aloud and what was subsequently translated to me. Keeping the secret had proved an advantage for precisely this reason.

Petr had just told Karina, *There was a situation, and that he needed me off the streets now, by order of the Pakhan.*

It doesn't happen often, but it's not the first time. They'll drag me back to the mansion and put me under extra guard. And we'd wait for however long it takes for the men to come home. Usually bloody.

Something was going down in the darker side of Boston.

I've only just slipped the second guard over my blade when Petr reaches across the hockey bench, yanking me roughly off the ice.

Surprised by the rough treatment, I shout out, pulling back. I try to twist out of his grasp, but he holds firm. At nearly twice the size of me, there's little more I can do to push the Russian brute off of me.

He drags me past the locker rooms, moving toward the arena's emergency back exit.

"I have to change!" I protest, pointing to the women's locker rooms as we pass, trying to dig my heels in to stop him.

"No time, *Printsessa.*" He mockingly mutters the second part, loud enough so I can hear him, but softly enough that he can still deny it if I decide to press the issue. "Move!" He barks out, losing his patience and practically shoving me through the rink's emergency door and out into the side alley.

I stop fighting, mostly because I'm still in my skates and teetering unbalanced on the uneven concrete underfoot. A black SUV waits for us, its windows tinted dark enough you can't see in.

"Get in." Petr growls at me like I'm an idiot baby whose hand he has to hold to cross the street, and I bristle at the tone.

It's considered a great honor, watching over the Bratva Pakhan's daughter, but Petr *despises* guard duty. He certainly had other ideas on how he'd rather be spending his days, and babysitting me is not one of them.

When I don't move, Petr opens the door to the backseat and begrudgingly, I hop inside, still in my skating dress, tights, and leg warmers that come up past my knees. He tosses the small duffle and backpack he swiped off the bench in after me and slams the door shut, causing the vehicle to shake. He immediately opens the passenger door and slides in. I don't even think the car door fully closes behind him before the car is in motion.

Spotting Van at the wheel is a breath of relief. He's good man, or as close as you can get to it by Bratva standards. I was friendly with his daughter Kaia before she was married off to a lower-ranking Bratva soldier out of state last year. There's no smile for me today, though. Van's expression is tense as he blows a thick cloud of cigarette smoke out the crack in his window before effortlessly swinging the SUV out of the alley and onto Main Street.

My ass slides across the smooth leather seats as he takes another particularly sharp turn down a side street.

Petr's distracted, looking out of the windows in all directions - forward, back, and to the side. And repeat.

I watch through my own window as we pass the turn leading back to the Kostalov mansion.

Not *home*—that house—would never be my *home*.

"Where are we going?" I finally get up the nerve to ask once we stop taking hard turns, accelerating onto the highway. The men are familiar, but I didn't grow up in the Bratva. And I'd be lying if I said my father's men don't intimidate the shit out of me.

With their lingering gazes and leering stares, Alexei is the only one of the lot I trust... *somewhat*.

"Your father wants you at the club," Petr clips out as if it's against his will to provide me any information before his phone rings. I grimace at the mention of Elements, the newest in a long list of nightclubs my father owns. Elements—his current passion project—perfect for laundering the money the Bratva brings in from its *extracurricular activities,* in addition to its legitimate businesses. He's really been expanding over the past year.

My attention shifts back to the duffle that has since fallen onto the floor of the SUV with Van's chaotic driving. I snatch it up, instantly disappointed to discover it's the bag I left on the bench, not the one from the locker room—the one with my *clothes.*

Sighing, I dig through the contents of the duffle, relieved to find my favorite old Vancouver Wolves hoodie I must have stuffed inside it at one point, along with a pair of warm sheepskin boots. I dig a little more, but alas, I turn up no pants.

Great.

Van has the air blasting despite the cool fall weather outside, so I take advantage of the straightaway of the highway to unhook my seat belt. I make quick work of unlacing my skates, switching over to the soft sheepskin boots. Pulling the hoodie over my head, I'm mildly reassured by the fact it's oversized and covers most of my skating dress. With the sweatshirt on, only several inches of my black velvet skirt is visible. The tights I'm wearing are thick, but offer little in the way of friction. I slide from left to right as Van weaves in and out of Boston rush hour traffic.

Petr's phone is in a constant state of ringing. He answers, each time only saying one or two words before hanging up again, only to answer another incoming call seconds later the same way. His jaw grows more and more tense and he spends longer each time looking out the rearview window. It's obvious he's making sure we aren't being followed, but by who?

The soldiers assigned to protect me are over protective for sure. My father would likely castrate them, forcing them to eat their own balls if they let anything happen to me, *but this isn't normal.*

I look from Petr's tense expression to Van's and chew my bottom lip. Turning in my seat, I crane my neck to look both behind and ahead of us, keeping up my own vigilant watch as Van speeds forward.

"What's going on?" I ask the next time Petr turns around to check the road behind us.

His eyes flicker toward me. They are such a light blue they are nearly white, unnerving when he settles them on you. "Don't worry about it," he gruffs out, looking back over the road.

I narrow my eyes at the response. When I open my mouth to argue, once again Petr's phone rings out, cutting me off. "Da?" Petr growls into it. His eyes widen at whatever comes through on the other end, and he whips back around in his seat. I can hear shouts in Russian on the other end, but not clearly enough to make out what they're saying. Petr's shouting now too, all manner of Russian expletives and swears streaming out of him. The SUV lurches forward as Van pushes down harder on the gas pedal and I look between the two of them again nervously.

Whatever's happening, it is *not* going in our favor.

The only useful thing I can discern from Petr's colorful conversation is *we weren't followed*.

That's something... I reassure myself nervously.

Petr slams his older model flip phone shut with a curse and reaches for his piece. The sight of the gun makes my palms sweaty. He flicks the safety off and turns to stare right at me. The SUV brakes to a stop and I realize we've reached our destination. The neon green light from the club's name, *Elements,* lights up both of our faces.

Those silvery blue eyes focus in on me now. "You don't look at anyone, you don't talk to anyone, and you do what you're fucking told," Petr instructs roughly.

I'm only half listening—distracted by the sight of two men materializing from the shadows of the building to stand by the car door. Both are openly armed and scanning the street for any incoming threats.

"Aurora." Petr shouts to bring my attention back to him.

"Okay!" I huff out, rolling my eyes. "It would be a lot easier if you just told me what was going on," I mutter bitterly, already scooting my ass over to the car door closest to the sidewalk.

Petr gets out of the car, while Van remains at the wheel. Petr has his gun in hand before he opens my door for me, half pulling me out.

"Do what you're told," he growls. "Пойдём." *Let's go.*

7

THE ELEMENT OF SURPRISE

RORY

$\mathcal{W}$e've no sooner entered the club before Petr's phone rings *again*. He holds it up to his ear, one hand over the receiver. "Take her up to the office," he shouts in Russian at the two guys who escorted us into the building before turning and disappearing back outside.

I stare after him. I'm immediately uncomfortable being left with the two unfamiliar men in the dark sultry light of the gentlemen's club. The sun has barely set, but business at Elements is already in full swing.

The club caters to an upscale clientele. However, it doesn't matter how much money you have—sleazy men are sleazy men. Having money just makes them more dangerous.

As we move through the busy floor, I'm instantly aware of how short my skirt is. It falls in a triangle, with the upper part of my thighs on full display. I grip the sleeves of my hoodie in my fingers and resist the urge to tug the hem down as we weave through the busy club floor.

I feel eyes on me but keep my head down, avoiding eye

contact with any of the patrons or dancers we pass. The tanta-lizing beat of the music only increases my anxiety.

Quickening our pace, we move directly for the far stairs; the ones guarded by a hulking bouncer. He nods a curt greeting as we pass him; the two men in suits leading me up to the back offices—and VIP rooms.

It's a major red flag we are here at all. I've been to Elements before to see my father, but only when it was closed or early in the morning. Never while it was open. As much effort as my father has put in to shield me from his world, being here at all suggests whatever is happening out in the city is a big fucking deal.

But as weird as the car ride over had been, everything inside Elements appears to be business as usual.

The two men ahead of me speak rapidly to each other in Russian as I follow them down the narrow corridor, passing by a series of numbered doors.

I'm quiet, listening to every word they exchange.

It's work to school my face so I don't show a reaction, but they're barely paying me any attention. I discern there have been multiple hits tonight on Bratva strongholds, all over the city, all different locations. No one knows who yet.

The hits were coordinated attacks, targeting crucial supply lines and storage facilities. I can't help the sigh of relief when they confirm that last they heard, both my father and Niko are still alive. I'm uncertain what would happen to me if they died.

"Your father is on his way." The taller of the two men turns my way, addressing me for the first time. The sudden switch over to English surprises me and I manage a terse nod in response. The men show me into my father's office before pulling the door closed behind me, remaining in the hall.

The overhead lights are off in the empty office, but flashes of light and a soft neon pink glow blankets the room. Opposite the door sits a wall of soundproof glass; windows overlooking the entire first floor of the club. I walk slowly over, my eyes widening at the scantily clad girls spinning on poles or dancing provocatively in the cages hanging from the ceiling.

I scan the crowd with a growing sense of despair. I'd always known who my father is, but it is one thing to know and something else entirely to experience it firsthand. Life within the Bratva still feels surreal. Like a bad dream from which I can never wake up. I miss the quiet, suburban life my mother and I shared. Privacy, freedom... safety.

Commotion on the floor below catches my attention. I see flashes of light and hear loud popping sounds, loud enough to permeate the soundproof glass. In a second, all hell breaks loose.

Club patrons dive for the floor. The dancers run screaming for the back room hidden behind the bar.

Men flood in through the entrance of the club, standing out in the crowd of suits with their dark colors and obscured faces as they engage in a brutal firefight with the Bratva already inside the club.

I watch, mesmerized, and still as stone, at the horror show playing out before me in muted fascination. One of the masked men in front shoots a male patron on his knees, point blank.

The man is dead before his body hits the floor. I can feel the fear and the terror coursing through me, but can't make myself do anything in response to it. Stunned, I stare down at

40

the body of the patron. Blood pools around his head, and his eyes are frozen open in fear.

Shattering glass breaks me out of my state of shock. Struck by a stray bullet, the window overlooking the floor falls before me in a sheet. The screams, the shouts, the gunshots flood in. The sounds are overwhelming alongside the music still blasting at full volume.

I hit the floor and cover my ears for several minutes until the sound of gunfire finally dies down. I jump at each *pop* I hear now, only sounding out once every thirty seconds. *They're taking care of any survivors.* Sweat coats my palms.

An eerie silence falls. Someone has finally turned off the music.

Heart racing, I tentatively lift my head just high enough to allow myself to peer down onto the floor below without making myself obvious. Men I don't recognize walk through the space. *Masked* men.

The Bratva have lost the firefight.

Not good.

Fuck.

Fuck. Fuck. Fuckkkkkk.

Panicking, I scramble away from the edge as I crawl backwards on my stomach so I'm hidden from view once again.

I'm increasingly aware of the stinging pain on my left cheek. Bringing my fingers to it, I wince at the sharp pain when I graze the wound. My fingertips come away red. I must have gotten cut when the window shattered. A couple of my fingers are bleeding too, and probably my knees, now that I think about it, from crawling across the broken glass.

Knowing I can't just sit here, I look around. I need to move, hide, *something....*

In the near silence below comes the sounds of boots crunching on glass and the heavy groaning of the door leading upstairs as it's dragged open. The bouncer is likely amongst the bloody bodies below.

My eyes fly to the office door. Closed—but not locked.

Crawling as fast as I dare to the door, I reach up, pushing in the little pin to lock it before resting my back against it. My breaths are coming fast and shallow.

It's too late to run.

The Mafia couldn't care less about fire codes and so the stairwell is the only way down. Only a small push-button lock stands between me and the big, bad men with guns.

A choked laugh escapes my lips and I look around the office again for something I can use—a weapon, maybe?

Anything.

For the office of a mob boss, it's shockingly lacking. To keep out of sight of anyone still below, I stay on my knees and crawl around to the other side of the desk, hoping to find a gun stashed inside.

I try the drawers and feel tears well up when I find each and every one of them locked. A quick perusal of the neat desk doesn't reveal a key readily accessible. Not even a letter opener I could use as a make-shift knife.

Voices carry in from the hall and I think I stop breathing, shaking violently as I turn back to face the door.

They're speaking English, but through the door they're still too far away to make out any words. What I hear is not Russian accents, nor Italian....

They're *Irish*.

8

WE HAVE A PROBLEM

RORY

The voices growing closer spurs my panic. I have to hide. Hide and hope for the best.

For the office of a nightclub, it's pretty small. There are limited options: I could duck under the desk, but seeing as how anyone who breaks in would likely go right for it. It's probably not the smartest choice.

That leaves either directly behind the door, or tucked behind the large metal filing cabinet. Neither are great options and all of them leave me exposed from one angle or another.

The door knob to the office jiggles, and my entire body seizes up. It's followed by a heavy pounding, the door shaking violently on its hinges. I trip over myself as I run for the filing cabinet, pressing myself into the small corner of space.

The loud popping sounds start again, this time, louder and closer than they were before.

Gunfire.

The office door crashes open, slamming hard into the wall behind it. I'm instantly grateful I didn't choose to hide there.

I suck in a breath, conscious of the fact that I'm no longer alone in the office.

Whoever enters the doorway does so with caution.

The filing cabinet blocks me completely from the view of anyone standing by the door. If he comes around the desk, I'll be completely exposed.

I press my back harder against the wall, hoping I could just melt into it. Maybe they'll see the office is empty and move on. Maybe they won't come all the way in. If I could stop breathing, I would, because I feel as though he can hear me.

Boots crunch on broken glass. *He's coming closer*. Just as I'd feared, he's making his way toward the desk.

A dark figure appears around the side of the desk closest to me. He's so close I could touch him as he passes by, but he doesn't look my way. His back to me now; attention fixed on my father's desk.

I bite my lip so hard I taste metal. I'm a deer in headlights. If he looks to his left, he'd be looking directly at me. But as luck would have it, he goes right for the drawers.

When he too finds them locked, he lets out a string of colorful curses. The thick Irish accent is unmistakable.

In his frustration, he slams his gun onto the desk, and I flinch. Punching down on the desk with two fists, he pauses for a moment, thinking.

I'm completely still.

Not moving.

Barely breathing.

The Irishman rips off his hood, revealing reddish-blonde hair in a prison-style crew cut. When he pushes off the black mask that had been obscuring his face, I stifle a gasp.

It's no surprise I don't recognize him. My father kept me

away from Bratva business. He's mid-to-late thirties, with cold blue eyes, and rough stubble covering his face. A faded pair of dice is tattooed on his neck.

I press harder into the wall and side of the cabinet, my eyes locked on the dangerous man before me. I want so badly to run but I know he'll see me if I do.

Angrily, he swipes the gun back off the desk, taking two steps back before firing a couple rounds into it. I have to resist the urge to cover my ears, afraid the movement alone might draw his attention. *If he looks left...*

Lowering the gun, he steps forward to inspect his progress. He's gained access to at least one drawer, having shot the lock in half.

He rummages through its contents, dumping out paper all over the top of the desk.

"Find it?" Another male voice comes from the direction of the office door, but closer—*inside* the room. I stiffen, a chill running up my spine, not having heard anyone else enter, and knowing there's two of them in here with me now. The new one's Irish accent is only slight, and mixed with something familiar. Not nearly as heavy as his buddy's.

"What do you think?" Crew Cut snaps. "It would be helpful if I knew what the fuck I was looking for," he curses again. With a rough tug, he coaxes another drawer open, tearing through it.

Movement in the corner of my eye draws my attention, as the new arrival steps up to the desk.

I freeze, but it's too late.

His eyes lock on me.

Several long seconds pass, and for a moment, nothing happens. Like the first man, a balaclava conceals his face, pulled

45

up to his eyes. Curious sea-green eyes flicker from my own eyes, to my hair, and down to linger on my mouth.

My lips part and he must assume I'm about to scream, because he lifts a single finger to his lips. His eyes crinkle with amusement before sliding back to his friend, who's finishing up with the second drawer.

I let out a strangled breath—on the verge of hysteria.

The newcomer pushes back his own hood and tugs down his balaclava. He's younger than the first, maybe only a few years older than me. He looks strangely familiar, but I can't place him. "We're running out of time," he warns the first man. As if I don't even exist.

I blink wildly at him.

"Fuck," Crew Cut runs a hand over his shaved head, visibly frustrated. "I know—I know, but he said it would be here." He's already working on the last drawer. "We still have a few minutes, check the file cabinet." He lifts his head for the first time in my direction and I swallow hard when his eyes find me.

Barely a breath passes before he's up, and I'm staring down the barrel of his gun that's pointed directly between my eyes.

I breathe out slowly. Looking between him and the gun. His face is stony—impassive—and his eyes narrow as he looks me over.

Panicking, I look to the second guy for—*help*? I don't know, but he saw me first and said nothing.

He's watching me too, his expression blank, with a slight tilt to his head.

"Oi, Ace." Crew Cut signals to the second guy, and cocks the gun he's holding. I can't hold back the whimper of fear that escapes me.

"We have a problem."

9

GOOD GIRL

RORY

$\mathcal{A}$t the click of the gun, I don't wait around. I launch myself out of my hiding spot, making a desperate attempt to reach the open door, thinking somehow, maybe, if I can make it to the hallway, I might have a chance.

I don't even make it halfway.

I meet the blockade with such force, the momentum nearly takes me off my feet. An arm closes around my middle and I'm dragged backwards until I slam against a hard chest. Adrenaline spiking, I fight, clawing and kicking, but the arm wrapped around me doesn't budge. Another hand snakes up and closes around my throat and instantly I still.

"Good girl," a dark voice whispers in my ear while adjusting his grip on my throat.

I see the gun still pointed at me from across the desk. I jolt back, only succeeding at pressing myself harder against the man who has me restrained.

My breaths are coming hard and the hand around my throat loosens a hair, but doesn't let go.

Crew Cut is talking fast, so I'm barely registering his words. The pounding sound of my heart in my ears is too loud, blocking him out. "...think you can spy on me?" Crew cut carries on, his gun trained on my forehead. I stiffen in *Ace's* hold. "How'd she even get in here? I thought we rounded up all the strippers."

My cheeks warm with both anger and embarrassment, itching to set him straight, but I bite my tongue. Better they think me a stripper than figure out who I really am.

The wail of multiple distant sirens wafts in through the office window, and the sense of urgency in the office rises.

"Time to go, Jimmy." Ace's deep velvet voice and Irish accent right in my ear earns a full-body shudder. I swear I hear the fucker *laugh* under his breath.

"Shit." Jimmy does a quick spin and scan of the office before his gun finds my face again. He waves it toward the shattered window. "Put her over there. I'll take care of it." He offers me a half-apologetic look and a little shrug. "Sorry, lass, but you've seen our faces. It's nothing personal; just business."

I stare back at him with wide eyes, processing the apology. *Nothing personal? No, it's just my LIFE.*

I dig my heels in, which only serves to push me back further into Ace's hard and unyielding chest. Almost immediately, I fling myself forward, but his arm around my abdomen holds me still, and the hand still wrapped around my throat tightens as he pulls my head back toward him.

He's tall; I notice for the first time. His chin barely grazes the top of my head. I feel it brush over me and I hear him inhale.

Did he just smell me?

48

His grip tightens again, eliciting a small gasp as my airway is restricted. I swallow hard, aware he feels the movement through his fingers.

I try to ignore Ace and focus on Jimmy. I'm still staring down the barrel of his gun. But Ace hasn't pushed me toward the broken window. *Toward my execution*. If I jump from the edge before he shoots me, would I survive the fall?

Breathing gets harder and my head feels light. Maybe I won't have to pick between Jimmy's gun or jumping because Ace might just choke me out right here. My pulse pounds in my ears and in my throat, right under his thumb.

"Stop fucking around, Aidan," Jimmy snaps, growing more agitated with the sirens closing in.

Aidan?

Jimmy can't shoot me where I stand without risking hitting his friend at my back. Rolling his eyes, he turns his attention back to the desk, reaching into one of the open drawers, and scooping bundles of cash into a black bag.

The sirens grow louder, the police closing in on Elements. I'm anything but reassured. I have little faith in the police saving me. Hell, I'd be lucky if I survive another *minute* in this room.

Ace—or—*Aidan* suddenly spins me in his grip so I'm face to face with him. I'm wide-eyed and tense as I hold my chin up to look at the man about to end my life.

He considers me. His gaze is a tangle of shadows; the green of his eyes haunting with quiet intensity as they search my face. What he's looking for, I don't know.

Aidan's eyes flash a second before his face changes, a smug arrogance taking over his features. "What a shame. She's awfully pretty." He picks up a lock of my hair with the hand he'd had wrapped around my throat, letting the silky strands run through his fingers. I lean as far away from him as I can, my lips curling with disdain. He just laughs, his fingers brushing my arm. A shiver races down my spine. I clench my jaw, willing myself to despise the way the heat from his touch lingers like a forbidden promise.

"The bitch is a dancer, Ace. I'll buy you a lap dance when we get clear of this shit. Now, let's go."

I bristle at the insult, at the way my life means nothing to these men. Anger simmers under flushed cheeks.

But Aidan still doesn't move. He doesn't blink—or look away. "We could use a hostage," He muses, finally. "Heat's coming down." As if on cue, a siren cuts through the now quiet club.

A vicious laugh rings out behind me. "The Bratva won't hesitate to shoot right through her to get to you or me. They couldn't care less about some dancer."

"No," Aidan argues, "but the cops will. Even if they're crooked, it would be hard to explain gunning down an innocent girl in public."

I swallow hard but refuse to drop my gaze. Doing so feels like losing whatever game he's playing. The corner of his mouth ticks up as if reading my mind.

"Fine," Jimmy finally relents, "But you're responsible for her. And you put a bullet in her the second we're clear, got it?" He's come closer, now within my peripheral vision, eyeing both of us warily while stuffing the rest of whatever it is he's taking with him into his bag. I watch as he scoops up the black backpack I'd dropped next to the desk at some point.

I assume Aidan nods in agreement. I don't get to see

because he spins me again, releasing me, only to grip my upper arm, pulling me along with him, as we follow Jimmy into the hall. Not sure how I feel about my death being postponed.

While a bullet to the head seemed like the worst likely scenario only minutes ago, being dragged from the room alive suddenly feels far worse.

GET ON THE BIKE

RORY

*D*espite my reservations, I don't fight Aidan as he escorts me from the office. We move swiftly through the hall, down the stairs, and zig zag our way through the club, stepping around overturned tables, chairs and —bodies.

So. Many. Bodies.

Bratva bodies and the bloody bodies of Johns lay scattered about the club floor, along with broken glass and bullet casings. I let out a choked sob and Aidan turns, observing me, his gaze hardening.

"Don't cry for them. They deserved it."

I barely have time to process what he says before we're behind the bar and through the kitchen. Cool air hits me as we exit out the back door.

The back alley is full of people. I stare out at about seven or eight guys, all either already sitting atop a motorcycle, or in the process of mounting one. Their faces are obscured.

I didn't notice, but before we exited the office, both Aidan and Jimmy pulled their balaclava back up—likely in case of any cameras.

"What's this?" The man closest to the door calls out, his Boston accent as thick as his arm when he gestures in my direction.

"A fecking hostage, what else? You idiot." Jimmy growls and shakes his head, passing by him to slide atop a sleek red Yamaha.

The image of blood pooling under shattered glass is still fresh in my mind and I feel out of sorts. Dazed. Aidan lets go of my arm for a second as he retrieves his own helmet, pulling it on. His dark sweatshirt rides up with the motion, revealing a flash of sculpted muscle.

I'm instantly uncomfortable, trying to reconcile the blood in my mind with the bike and the *muscles*.

"Mac!" Aidan calls to someone over my head, pointing at me.

A second later, a black helmet flies through the air. He catches it easily, handing it to me.

"Get on the bike."

His eyes—dark and unreadable—fix on me with unnerving intensity, but fear is at war with shock right now, and I can barely form thoughts, let alone words. I glance around nervously, considering my options. Sirens wail around us, police are closing in. Motors start up and bikes race out of the alley.

Aidan released my arm. I could run; it would basically guarantee a bullet in my head, which I might also get, if I comply.

When I do nothing, Aidan pulls out his gun, pressing the cold metal up against the tender skin behind my ear. "I won't ask again." His overall tone is soft, but holds a lethal edge.

I believe him.

I flinch when the motorcycle right next to us peels out, the engine letting out a guttural snarl, as its tires screech against the asphalt.

Hands shaking, I climb on the back of the bike, all too aware of how exposed my legs are under my skating skirt. I let Aidan slide the helmet over my head, and he's surprisingly gentle. A small seed of hope blooms at the thought of the getaway car being a motorcycle, but the beginning of a plan dies when Aidan clasps a metal cuff on my left wrist.

Instinctively, I wrench it back, but he's already clipped the other side to his belt. The chain link catches and cinches tighter, and I cry out in shock—or pain; I'm not sure. I glare at him with fury and fear.

Aidan wastes no time starting the bike. The deafening roar of the exhaust rips through the now quiet alley; just the two of us left. A raw and thunderous sound vibrates through my body.

Our bodies are too close... he's ... too close. His scent is overwhelming. I want to rip it from my nostrils. Bracing my feet on the pegs, I shimmy further up the bike, putting some distance between us.

"You need to hold on to me," he shouts over his shoulder. The bike shudders under us as he revs the engine, but we stay put.

I'm shaking my head, not wanting to touch him. I see him watching me from the side mirror. He's shouting now, because he has to, in order to be heard over the motor of his bike. It's a sleek, matte black racing bike, built for speed. "Trust me, love, falling off a bike at high speed is not the way you wanna go."

When I still refuse to move, he revs the engine again. The

bike jerks forward unexpectedly, and Aidan slams on the brakes. The sudden stop sends me flying forward, my breath catching in surprise. I slam into Aidan's back, my fingers gripping for purchase, clinging tightly to his shirt to keep from falling off.

"Hold tight," he warns. His voice is laced with a smug smirk I don't even need to see to know is there, a second before he releases the clutch.

I'm embarrassed at how tightly I cling to him, burying my fingers in the fabric of his sweatshirt with a death grip. My thighs squeeze tight against his as we veer out into traffic. We've barely hit the road before a bullet whizzes past my right cheek.

We both steal a glance behind us, finding a black SUV hot on our tail. Two guys and two guns hang out the window, shouting obscenities. *Russians.*

They fire again, not yet realizing who's on the back of the bike.

Aidan changes gears, weaving between cars like they're standing still. He zips up the ramp onto the highway, the Bratva in hot pursuit. It's rush hour, and the traffic is heavy in the city. It's not long until they have us back within range.

Gunfire sounds behind us again and I scream, but Aidan's evasive maneuvers leave us both unscathed.

Dodging bullets costs us speed, and the SUV is nearly upon us. I close my eyes, waiting for the burn of bullets riddling my back, or for the inevitable fiery crash if they get Aidan first, but it doesn't come.

Hesitantly, I peek back to find the SUV falling back, in pursuit, but no longer shooting—*someone must have noticed...* I stiffen with the realization.

Aidan seizes the opportunity and speeds up, splitting lanes

to give us some breathing room before cutting directly in front of a tractor trailer. The trucker lays on his horn, but it's barely a second before Aidan swings right, cutting across another lane and another car before narrowly catching the exit ramp.

We race around the tight exit curve, but the Bratva loses us behind the truck, passing by the exit. We're in the clear.

He zips through crowded downtown streets until he finds a back way out of the city, and we're moving steadily along down a dark suburban road.

I let out a breath, not knowing whether to be relieved or terrified. At some point, I gripped near the bottom of Aidan's sweatshirt, and now I am very aware of how my fingertips graze against the warm skin underneath.

Autumn is in full swing and the wind is ice against our bodies. With only my torn tights to keep me warm, I keep my hands where they are, siphoning off what little warmth I can.

Even though we've dodged the pursuing Bratva, Aidan hasn't slowed down, and I don't dare risk re-adjusting my grip. I turn my attention to planning what I should do when we stop.

If I can get away from him then, it might be the only chance I have.

11

NO SECONDARY LOCATION

RORY

*W*e drive for a while, at least an hour—or two—leaving Boston far behind.

I'm doing my best to keep my teeth from chattering, but it's involuntary at this point. I hate the way I curl my fingers under Aidan's sweatshirt. At first, it was to keep from falling off the stupid bike, but now it's to keep my fingers from falling off, period.

Neither of us has spoken since he forced me on the back of his bike. My nerves slide into hyper drive. Each passing minute brings us closer to what could be my final destination. *Where's the logging truck when you need it?*

I've run through over a hundred varying scenarios in my head about what to do when we finally stop. We've entered quite a remote part of Massachusetts—if we're even still in the same state. Maybe he is planning to bring me to some desolate section of woods and end it. It's not like he can dispose of a body on his bike.

A morbid chuckle escapes me at the thought. Beneath my arms, I feel the muscles in his chest tense, having heard it.

He finally slows, turning into an industrial park full of rundown, abandoned mill buildings. No other cars or people in sight. *Less than ideal.*

When we reach an area of the park containing several large garages, he pulls up close to one, killing the engine.

The sudden silence is unnerving. I look around. We're in the back-end of the park, thick woods border the darkened lot.

Aidan twists in his seat and I realize I'm still holding on to him. I release my grip as if burned. My wrist imprisoned by the cuff rebounds—still attached to his belt.

He fiddles with something and my wrist falls free. The metal cuff is still around my wrist, but it is no longer connected to *him.*

He takes off his helmet, hanging it on the handle bar before eyeing me over his shoulder. "Don't run," he warns before dropping hold of the cuff entirely. I feel the weight of the metal catch and stare at the dangling chain for a second before I put one of my plans into action.

We're still on the bike, so I use both my hands to vault myself off the back of it. I land on unsteady knees, weak from adrenaline—or the ride—I'm not sure.

I take off running. The sheepskin boots are less than ideal getaway footwear, but I keep on my toes. Wrenching the helmet off my head because it's only slowing me down. I don't even look before I whip the thing back the way I came. The resounding grunt confirms I've hit my intended target.

I smile; a small victory. *Score one for Rory.*

Uncertain about the woods, I run the length of the building, sprinting for the corner. I'm fast and in shape; I could outrun him. Not hearing any sounds of pursuit behind me, I chance a glance over my shoulder, finding Aidan exactly where I left him.

He's not even bothering to chase me. My eyes instantly drop to his hands, checking for a gun, confused when I see them empty right before I slam into *something*—hard.

The crash is so hard it sends me flying backwards, but strong hands wrap around both of my wrists, preventing an embarrassing fall on my ass. Stunned—as I'm pretty certain my brain slammed against my skull—I work to focus on who's in front of me.

I look up to find another impossibly tall, hulking male. Running into this one, built even thicker than Aidan, was like crashing into a truck.

Like a cartoon character, my feet race underneath me, failing to find traction as I squirm, trying to escape his hold. Desperate to get away. The worst is when this mammoth of a man beams down at me with the biggest shit-eating grin on his face.

He's probably one of those sociopaths who gets off on the long hours of mafia torture.

I wriggle more urgently but get nowhere; his smile only grows wider. "Where ya going, pretty?"

Terror. Pure, unadulterated *terror.*

He takes advantage of my full-body freeze to lift me—like I weigh nothing at all—hefting me up and over his shoulder. His arm closes like a vice around the backs of my legs and with no shame, I'm screaming now. He walks forward, ignoring me as I pound my fists into his back, shouting for help—for anybody —*please*!

His level of unconcerned—*concerns me.*

"This belong to you?" The man returns me to where Aidan, waits patiently. As if he has all night, he leans against his bike, watching us with his arms folded across his chest.

"Get her inside," he huffs and stalks over to the nearest garage door, throwing it open.

I fight with renewed passion.

No secondary location. That's what they always preach in all those self-defense classes I took. And now here I am, about to disappear into one.

I scream again, but it's cut off short when Aidan comes into my sights, waiting at the opening of the garage as we pass him. We make eye contact and he shakes his head with mild irritation. "That's really fucking annoying. No one can hear you, so you might as well knock it off."

I'm carried inside and the heavy metal door shuts behind us.

I stop screaming—but only because we're inside—not because he told me to. When the bottom edge of the door meets the pavement, I deflate.

"The lockers?" The guy carrying me asks Aidan, who nods in confirmation to the question but doesn't follow as I'm carried further into what appears to be a rather large abandoned mill. I stare back at him until he turns away.

Just as quickly, he stops on a dime and jerks back toward us, like he's forgotten something. "Oh, and Liam?"

"Ya?" The hulking mass under me responds, slowing so he can hear Aidan's response.

"She can keep her clothes." The shadow of a grin on the bastard's face was full of derision. "For now."

I stiffen so hard I nearly slide down Liam's chest. He lets

60

out a dark laugh at either Aidan's words or my reaction, shaking his head as he trots back off with me, "You get all the fun," he laments, before we disappear down a long hallway.

12

THE GIRL

AIDAN

*W*hile Liam secures the girl, I pick up my phone to deal with the shit show that just blew up in our faces.

The Russians are furious. Which would have been all fine and motherfucking dandy if we had gotten what we came for.

The Russians still don't know who hit them and for now, that's good news. The bad news is we still don't have the leverage we need. There was supposed to be *something* in Adrik Kostalov's office we could use to broker a deal with the Bratva Pakhan.

And the girl. The girl was going to be a problem.

No witnesses, Aidan.

I storm into my office and immediately pour myself a glass of whiskey, pounding it down before pouring out another one. I sink slowly into one of the leather armchairs. Staring at the melting ice in the snifter. Willing myself to pull out my gun and put a bullet in the girl I've got secured down the hall. *Why did Jimmy have to take off his goddamn mask?* Once she'd seen his face, her death warrant was signed.

After hanging up with one of our soldiers, I scroll down to see several missed calls and texts from the douche weasel himself. The asshole wants to know if I've secured the *loose end.* I rise, slamming the phone down hard on the desk. This got too messy, too fast.

I shouldn't even be here.

"Fuck." I punch the desk hard enough to slice up my knuckles.

A sense of awareness prickles my skin and I look up to find Liam leaning against the door frame, watching me with a lopsided grin that's just asking me to hit him.

"Any trouble?" I ask, lightly pacing behind the desk, referring to the girl.

Liam shakes his head. "She's deceptively strong for such a little thing, but it didn't matter," he smiles. "Locker 3. She's in the chair. Clothes are... on." His brow quirks up questioningly.

I let out a grunt. Reaching into my desk drawer, I pull out a fresh bottle of whiskey. Usually, when we bring guys in for *questioning,* we strip them. It serves a dual purpose. For one—practicality—it rules out if they're wearing a wire. And two—the obvious—intimidation and *access.*

I take a long drink out of the dark bottle. Dragging out another glass to pour us each a drink. Sliding the glass across the desk to my younger brother.

He shrugs off the wall, sauntering forward with an easy swagger to grab his drink and collapses into one of the plush armchairs in front of the desk. "Koen should be here soon."

I nod. The eldest of the O'Rourke clan. My hand grazes

the rough stubble on my chin—while my mind races between thoughts.

"You wanna tell me what the story is there? Why you got a *girl* chillin' in the lockers right now?"

I sigh with exhaustion, but tell him anyway. "We picked her up at Elements. She was in Kostalov's office... saw both of our faces."

The look he gives me is one of surprise, peering back toward the lockers. "*She's* a stripper?"

I take another sip of my whiskey and shrug my shoulders. She doesn't look like a stripper, but yet she was waiting in Adrik's office, wearing only a sweatshirt and a tiny little skirt. I recognized her as soon as I saw her. The spicy skater from the rink the other day. What the hell was she doing moonlighting in a Russian strip club?

"She doesn't look like a stripper," Liam muses, sipping his whiskey.

I sniff. "And what do strippers look like, Liam?" With my glass, I hide the smile playing on my lips. We are the same, he and I.

"Hell, I don't know Ace, not like *that*—" He shakes his head. "Why bother to take her?"

I sigh again, knowing I'll have to answer for it soon enough. *And not to Liam.*

Running the palm of my hand down my face, I go back over the events of the night. "Jimmy broke into Kostalov's office and once he was in there, he took off his mask..." The masks were a back-up plan in case we didn't find what we were looking for. If we'd have found it, I wouldn't give two fucks if the Russians made us.

"Fucking Jimmy." Liam huffs in his chair, shooting back

some whiskey. Very familiar with our reckless, hot-headed cousin.

"He didn't see her hiding, and she saw his face. When he found her, he wanted to shoot her right then, but I—"

"So you took her?" Liam interrupts.

"I thought she could be useful. The heat was coming down and I don't know—"

The truth is, I don't know why I did it. I turn away from my brother, glaring up at the portrait of our father on the far wall. *They'll call me weak for this.* It was imperative I play this right. I'm not weak. I have no problem shedding blood when a job requires it.

But then I saw *her*—the terror in those steel-blue eyes. Even for a stripper, she just had this innocence about her. I should've let Jimmy take care of her then, but that was before she ran—straight into my arms—and fuck if I didn't want to push her away. I drain the last of my whiskey.

"Is that why Jimmy's texting me, asking if you've put a bullet in the dancer yet?" He pulls his phone out of his pocket, giving it a little shake in my direction.

My grip tightens on the glass, and I know Liam sees it.

"What's the plan Ace? You know we got practice starting back up—"

"I know," I bite back, a little too harshly, and pour out another glass of whiskey.

I don't have time for this. Any of this. There's enough heat on me as it is without incurring the ire of the shit stain that is my cousin Jimmy Reilly. Add to that how we got no leverage on the Bratva despite our efforts. We're in deep shit.

"There was nothing in his office."

Liam's jaw clenches. He knows as well as I do what's at stake. "Could you have missed it?"

I shake my head. "No, Jimmy turned it over pretty good." I consider for a moment. "Perhaps the informant fed us bad intel."

Liam's face sours a little. "I don't know Ace, the info was pretty solid. Something important to Adrik was supposed to be in his office. It should have been obvious."

"Well, it wasn't," I snap irritably. "Now I've got no leverage on Kostalov and a party favor in the form of a stripper tied up in the back of the warehouse."

He looks thoughtful for a moment, tilting his head slightly to the side. "Maybe...you should question the stripper."

That catches my attention. "About what?"

He holds up his fingers, ticking them off. "First off, that girl is too fucking pretty to just be a stripper. Second, if she was waiting in Adrik's office, maybe she's like, for the VIPs? If she's close to him, she could know what was supposed to be in there that was so important. Or, third, if she is just your run-of-the-mill stripper, a lot of Bratva go to the club. She could still know something we could use."

I consider it, though it's unlikely. Sometimes dancers hear or see things, which can be useful. But if she had seen anything of any real significance, the Russians would have already taken care of her themselves.

My ringing phone interrupts my thread of thoughts. I grind my teeth as I look at the caller ID, bringing the phone to my ear. "What?" I bark into the device.

"I need to know you took care of the girl." Jimmy's anything but quiet, and his voice, even over speaker, carries loudly enough that, by the way Liam sits up, I know he can hear him too.

I hum softly, buying time. "I'll take care of the girl when I'm done with her." My words hold a dangerous edge, daring him to push me. I may not have been playing around with the Irish mob too much over the past couple years, but that doesn't mean I don't outrank Jimmy's ass.

Jimmy's gruff demeanor cracks with a laugh. "So that's what you're after? Alright Ace, have fun with your shiny new toy, but clean up after you break it, yeah?"

"Tell Koen to call me." I don't wait for his response before ending the call, anger a live flame under my skin.

Liam eyes me with caution, knowing too well how fast I can let the anger take control. "Now what?"

I empty my glass, slamming it back down before I straighten. "I'm gonna go talk to the girl."

"Play nice."

My lips twitch as I head for the lockers. "I'll go easy. It's not like she's Bratva. She'll probably beg to tell me what she knows." A strange thrill shoots through me at the image of the petite blonde on her knees.

I have to take an extra minute to clear my head of the image before entering the hall where the interrogation cells are. It's silent in the hall. No crying. No screaming. *Strange.*

It's a grimy little room, with cement walls and a drain on the floor in the middle of the room.

Her eyes are on me as soon as I enter. A soft blue—almost gray in this light—and I could get lost in shade of blue if it not for the overwhelming despair I see reflected in them.

She's scared of me.

Good.

She should be.

13

NO PROMISES, NO LIES

RORY

"*I*'ll tell you what, answer a few of my questions and I'll let you go." His smile was beautiful and *almost* convincing. "I promise."

My hands tighten into fists, where they're tied—a little too tightly—behind my back. "A promise is just another lie, dressed up to look beautiful enough to believe. Preying on hope." I mutter under my breath, looking away from him.

Despite my sheltered upbringing from the worst of this world, I wasn't naïve. I knew who stood before me; figured it out before he stalked back in here to question me. Aidan O'Rourke: the Irish Devil, second son of the mob, and Breakers' enforcer. He was chaos personified, a captivating mix of skill and brutality. I've seen their faces, know their names. There's no walking away from this.

Not for me.

I lean back in the chair his henchman wrestled me into and watch him study me from the corner of my eye.

"What's your name?"

"Rory."

He's silent for a long moment, trying to get a read on me. If he's surprised I answered, he doesn't show it.

"Why do you dance at Elements?"

The question is unexpected, and I can't help but look up at him in surprise. "I—I don't—"

"Don't lie," he warns sharply.

"No promises," I bite back.

He smiles. *The devastating kind of smile.* "No lies," he repeats, his green eyes darkening.

"Contrary to what you might *think*, I didn't lie," I snap back at him, although he is not someone I should be mouthing off to.

"I'm *not* a dancer." I glare at him. Getting kidnapped clearly makes me cranky.

A muscle ticks in his jaw. He still thinks I'm lying. *Whatever, screw him.*

"If you're not a dancer, then what were you doing at Elements?"

Should've been ready for that... I bite my lip to buy time and watch him track the movement. There's no way I can tell the truth and not make this situation exponentially worse. A quick bullet in my skull, as some unknown dancer, would be a Godsend compared to what the Irish would do to Adrik Kostalov's *daughter.*

Still, my competitive nature flares at this little game we've started. *No promises, no lies.* Thinking fast, I shrug, brushing him off. "I went to Elements with a friend." It's not an outright lie, although, calling my bodyguard a *friend* is stretching the truth—*frenemy*, maybe...

Aidan's face gives nothing away. "And do you usually end

up in the back office of a strip club when you visit them with *friends*?" His arched brow is dripping with skepticism and is on my nerves.

"No," I snap again, exhaustion giving way to irritation and a short fuse. "Gunshots started, and I got pulled in there." Also, technically not a lie—just *out of order*.

The way he stares at me gives me the shivers. It's intense... *he's* intense. Ever since he entered, the room feels smaller, and it's harder to breathe. I'm pretty sure he could tell if I outright lied, but skating the line between truth and lie... he doesn't seem to know what to think.

"And so what?" The way he cocks his head reeks of predatory authority. "I'm supposed to believe you just *happened,* to be in the wrong place at the wrong time? That the girl who bumped into me earlier this week at the rink is the *same* girl I find in the Russian Pakhan's office a couple of nights later? You expect me to believe that's just a *coincidence*?" He straightens from where he's been leaning against the far wall and takes a step toward me. It's an effort not to cringe back. Every instinct in my body screams *danger*.

Run.

He knows it. His eyes glitter with the challenge.

It's an intimidation tactic. Or at least it should have been since, now I'm even more determined not to react the way he's expecting me to. To fall apart into a crumbling mess where I ramble out every useless fact I can think of about the Bratva to save my own skin.

No. He can thank my brother Niko for that. Years of being bullied at his hands, and I'm unshakeable. A goddamn CIA lock box.

All Aidan's managed to do so far is piss me off. I lift my

chin and meet his eye. I was already on thin ice, dead anyway, so... *Fuck it.*

"More or less," I shrug. "Have I given you a reason not to believe me?"

He stares at me.

And damn it all to hell, I stare right back. Keeping my face carefully blank, I refuse to back down. Though, my eyes—I fear—betray me.

If I didn't know any better, I could've sworn the corner of his mouth ticks up. The alarm in my head going off once more at the faint smile. But just as he takes another step, leaning in toward me so only inches separate us, a knock reverberates off the heavy metal door.

Aidan's mouth snaps shut. Neither of us turns, not wanting to be the first to break our little stare-off.

I choke down a swallow. At least an hour has passed since they locked me in here. I've had plenty of time to take in my surroundings. This room, this *building*, all of it, serves a purpose. *No one* would hear me scream. No one heard what I'm sure were countless others screams as they met their end in this very room. I think of the drain just under my chair, but I still refuse to look away from the devil before me.

In the end, it's he who finally caves, when whoever's outside bangs once again, louder this time.

He turns back, shouting out to whoever is waiting outside, "One sec!"

I try not to flinch at the sudden boom of his voice. I refuse to be afraid of this man. I have spent every single second of my entire life terrified. At least I could say I wasn't a coward when I stared down death.

Aidan O'Rourke turns back to me, a scowl on his face. I

know he's being beckoned to go. Pissed off sure looks good on that jawline. Aidan is muscled and honed to perfection, the product of relentless discipline. With dark brown hair and piercing green eyes, he's like a beautiful storm, untamed and lethal.

He reaches again, this time into his pocket, flicking open a knife as he walks toward me. Instinctively, I lean as far back as the chair will allow, but he circles around until he's behind me. Where I can't see him.

Fuck. Not the way I'd expected to go out. I take a deep breath and close my eyes. But instead of cutting my throat, the knife slips through the ropes. With a sharp tug, I'm cut free.

Slowly, I bring my sore wrists into my lap. My shoulders ache from being stuck in the same position for over an hour. My eyes stay on Aidan, keeping the danger in my sights.

"Sit tight. We're not done here." He barely looks at me again before banging on the door. The heavy metal vibrates with the sound of his palm hitting it, reverberating through my brain.

The door slides open effortlessly to let him out before slamming shut again. The voices fade in the hall—*they're leaving.*

I look down. He didn't cut the ropes from my ankles, each still bound to a leg of the chair. It'll take ages to untie them.

I sigh, looking around. I'm in what I've worked out was, at some point, an old freezer room. And I'm good and stuck in here. He wouldn't have cut me loose if I could escape.

Reaching down, I get to work loosening the impossibly complicated knots *Liam* was kind enough to supply. I wonder what the hell their plan is. And how do I survive it?

14

MINE

AIDAN

I exit the lockers with a glare in Liam's direction, even though I know if Liam interrupted my interrogation, it was for good reason.

"Your office," Liam advises as he strikes up a guard position outside of the locker we've got the girl in.

Rory.

I play her name over and over in my mind as I make my way down the hall.

My hand balls into a fist alongside my long strides. I'm worked up. Something about the girl set me right on edge.

I don't like it.

I shouldn't be surprised to see the lean tattooed male making himself at home in the office, but my jaw clenches in irritation when I find him there.

Rory.

I wish I never knew her name.

Those blue eyes, wild and full of fear, yet, still defiant.

The smattering of freckles across a perfect little nose. *A figure skater.* What was she doing with the Russian Bratva? The question is driving me crazy. And as tiny and breakable as she is, she seems less inclined to help fill in the blanks.

I pass by Koen without a word, rounding the desk to pick up my empty glass and pour out some more whiskey.

"We need to talk." My brother's voice holds his usual tone, warning he's in no mood. He waves his glass at the open door behind me and narrows his eyes—green, like mine, but darker.

I turn, shutting the door, even though I know it's just Liam here. "So talk," I grit out, keeping a tight grip on my simmering temper, as I face him.

"Did you take care of the girl?"

My jaw flexes at the mention of Rory, but I work it into a twisted smile when I feel my brother studying me.

"Jimmy's that paranoid? He called you in to make sure I take care of business?" I scoff, crossing my arms to deal with the increasing tension I feel building up in my muscles. When will the prick learn I outrank him? I may have been away from the family business for a couple of years, but my position is still *mine.* Here waiting for whenever the fuck I want it back.

Koen's face remains unchanged. My brother is hard to read at the best of times. "She's not some damsel in distress, Aidan; she's a witness. A loose end. And one we can't afford... *you* can't afford."

I grind my teeth. It wasn't enough that letting Rory live could stir up shit with the Bratva—it could also throw a major wrench into my hockey career. I'm already skating a thin line this season, balancing the two. I can't afford a single setback.

I know this, but yet... "She's an innocent Koen. You want her blood on your hands?"

Koen laughs. It's cold, and the smile doesn't touch his eyes.

"She's a dancer at Elements, a *Bratva* club. The girl is *far* from innocent. Besides, even if you let her go, the Russians would just as soon put a bullet in her skull, assuming she either talked or turned."

I'm quiet for a moment—thinking. He's not wrong. I'm well aware Rory is a dead girl walking, whether I handle her or let the Russians clean house.

"She's a complication."

"She's *my* complication," I growl back. "*Mine* to handle." I'm not sure when I got so territorial over some girl, and the thought unsettles me. I snap my jaw shut.

Koen stares at me for a long while. I meet his eye, not yielding to his play for dominance. "The Russians are up in arms over the attacks. So far, we're in the clear. They don't know who hit them. The plan is working. But if you let the girl live, it will all be for nothing." I bristle at his words.

Like I need a reminder.

Koen stands and I straighten to my full height as he comes closer.

At six-foot-three, I have a solid inch on my older brother. Koen might be the heir, and with our father now dead, he's the new boss of the Irish. But he and I both know when it comes down to it, that means nothing to me, and nothing to him.

"Take care of it Aidan. We won't survive a full-on assault by the Bratva right now. If it gets out the Irish were behind the break-in at the club…" He trails off, shaking his head. With our father barely in the ground, Koen's rule is new, which makes it vulnerable. Not all the Irish clans in the city have bent the knee yet to their new king.

"Word on the street is Adrik has gone postal over the raid. Bratva are out there dropping Romanian and Polish Mafia left

76

and right. *Dropping bodies.* I've never seen the Russians so wound up." His ever-present frown deepens before he finally stalks past me. He reaches for the door, his hand pausing on the handle with a final look back.

"Handle it, Aidan. Or I will."

I let him have the last word and watch as he disappears into the hall. Once I hear the rumbling sound of the motor as he starts his bike, I let the sound fade away before chucking my whiskey glass at the wall. I stare at the broken shards scattered across the floor like they'll tell me what to do.

15

HOTSHOT

AIDAN

*B*efore long, Liam appears in the doorway. He looks from the broken glass and back at me with a frown. "It's four a.m."

I nod absently. One thing I love about Liam—he knows when to keep his mouth shut. "Call Ryan."

I haven't been involved with the family business for a few years. Both Liam and I have an early morning practice at the Edge. There are a lot of new and unfamiliar faces, and right now, I need someone I *trust*.

Alex Ryan and I go back—way back. He might not have the O'Rourke name, but he's as much my brother as Liam and Koen are.

Koen talks a big talk, but he won't interfere in my business. But I wouldn't put it past Jimmy and his crew to come here and take care of things themselves.

If Liam wasn't on the Breakers alongside me, I would've preferred to leave him in charge. But Ryan will do.

We make it to the rink just in time, after I made sure Ryan had explicit instructions not to go anywhere near the lockers or the girl.

Rory.

Leave it to Coach to call an early morning practice the day after an Irish raid. I've been lucky so far in that my associations haven't impeded my hockey career. While I've done my best to keep it quiet, the few guys in the league who hail from Boston know *exactly* who I am.

And what I'm capable of.

Only my reputation has kept them from running their mouths to the press, although there has always been speculation. The media may have taken a turn for the negative after last season, and if I can't turn it around, I'm facing a trade deal or worse—*no deal at all*.

While I trust Alex with my life, I put the fear of God into him before we left. No one gets in the warehouse, and no one goes out without my say-so. He doesn't even have to know why, or whom, I've got back there. Ryan—being Ryan—doesn't even ask.

The locker door is well and truly barred shut. Stronger men than *Rory* have tried, and failed, to escape the Irish lockers. She isn't going anywhere. I try to push the girl out of my head.

It's only a matter of time before Jimmy figures out exactly where I stashed the girl and takes matters into his own hands. He blew up Liam's phone until five a.m., presumably because he passed out. But I know he won't let it go. The Russians don't know who hit them, and they're pissed the fuck off about it. We can't afford any loose ends; *I* can't afford any loose ends.

Coach homes in on my distracted ass like he has a radar for these kinds of things.

"O'Rourke! Get your shit together or get off the ice!" Coach shouts as I hit the post on what should've been an easy pick up. "Run it again."

I circle back into the lineup and wait my turn to run the drill again.

"Try not to fuck it up this time, hotshot."

I don't turn around; I know exactly whose smug ass voice is in my ear. Dex Lewandroski, the Breakers' second line defenseman, has every reason to get in my head. He's been after my first line spot since he signed with the team last spring. *Not today, Dex.*

I launch forward, my blades cutting hard into the ice as I round the turn. I surge down the ice, deke past the defenders, fake out Brooks, and sink the puck top shelf, upper right corner.

Skating back past Lewandroski, I can't help but give him a little chin lift. *Fuck you, asshole.*

Through no small miracle, I hold my own for the rest of practice. I'm a mess of sweat by the time we hit the showers. I linger in the hot water, letting it pour over my head as I play back the events of the last 24 hours. Eyes heavy; I really need some fucking sleep.

I'd thought I was free of this shit, having left the family *business* behind to pursue hockey instead. But just as soon as I thought I was clear, they dragged me right back.

No one expected the hit that took out our father—and Alex's uncle—Declan O'Rourke. And no one was talking about who had done it. Nothing in this world would've stopped Liam and me from returning to support Koen and to make those responsible bleed.

No one touches family.

The hot water soothes my aching muscles, the new bruises a small price to pay. Trying to balance the family with hockey was never part of the plan, and I was already on thin ice. I need to stay focused. There are grave consequences on both sides if I don't.

Stay distracted in hockey and lose the league—everything I worked for. Get distracted in the mob—and *lose my life.*

I just need to keep my head on straight. First things first, figure out what the fuck to do with my little *complication.*

I throw open the locker door with a clang. After catching a few hours of sleep on a couch at the warehouse, I'm itching to force some answers out of Rory. I'm hoping several hours alone in the lockers have loosened her tongue. I need to know who she is and what the fuck she was doing with the Russians.

She's on the floor, knees curled to her chest. At the sight of me, she presses her back against the wall. Her eyes snap to the gun in my hand. Dark circles ring her pretty blue eyes.

Good. Easier to break.

I lunge forward, dragging her up. She tries to resist, but it's no use.

I drop her back into the bolted chair in the middle of the room. She lands with a groan and then freezes when I move in on her, stopping inches from her face. I'm so close I can smell her flowery scent, salty with the tears she's tried her best to hide from me.

I use the tip of my gun to push an errant strand of hair out of her eyes. She shivers at the touch of the cold metal against her skin. I trace the barrel down the side of her cheek and watch as the tip of it pulls against her bottom lip.

There's no crying, no pleading; she doesn't beg. My gun digs into the hollow of her cheek, and Rory just scowls at me. The blue-gray in her eyes shimmer in the bright overhead light like polished silver.

"Tie her hands."

Liam lingers in the doorway behind me. I don't need to look to know he's there. Without a word or argument, he circles around behind the girl.

To her credit, Rory doesn't take her eyes off of me or my gun when he drops to a crouch behind her. Pulling her wrists together, he pulls out a pair of handcuffs and cinches them tight. She winces as the metal pinches against the already-abused wrists.

I crouch down until I'm at eye level. "Who are you?"

She blinks wearily at me. "I already told you—"

"You told me nothing," I cut her off, scowling at her. She's got to give me something. "People don't accidentally stumble into the Russian Pakhan's office. You know something." I nudge her head again with my gun. She's afraid of it, but not *the normal kind* of afraid. Any other girl off the street would be in tears right now. Rory's panic has ebbed away into anger. Her eyes darken to a stormy grey. She lifts her chin, holding my gaze.

"Rory Collins. Grew up in Canada. Graduated from Northwood Academy. I came to Boston to train with Karina

Valgova and the Boston Belles, both of which you already know train out of the Breakers' practice pavilion. You can check it."

Her sass pisses me off. "Oh, I will." I yank her up. "But until then, we're going on a little field trip." I shoot Liam a look, letting him know to go ahead and fact check the information Rory just spat at us.

I want to push her more, but Koen called a few minutes ago. A new shipment is coming in, and the warehouse will be buzzing in only a few hours. Rory can't stay here.

A few of our guys have already arrived, prepping for the delivery.

I drag Rory out of the lockers alongside me as we walk down the hall. Her head darts back and forth, noticing the new guys. Her eyes plead with them for help, but she doesn't call out, yell , or scream, realizing too soon there's no help for her here.

They're all on the O'Rourke payroll.

We step outside and her eyes close tight against the bright sunlight. I nudge her forward, opening the door to Liam's SUV, and push her inside. With her hands bound behind her back, she has to shuffle awkwardly across the car seat.

Sliding in beside her, I watch as she stiffens in my close presence and then inches a little further away to put as much distance between us as she can.

Liam's at the wheel, and in another moment, we're on the road.

Pulling out my phone, I read over some new intel coming in after the hits we made on the Russian properties. Adrik has been rapidly expanding through the city, encroaching further and further into our territory. What we haven't been

83

able to figure out is where the fuck the money is coming from.

All signs continue to point to Adrik as the one who ordered the hit on our father. But I don't have my smoking gun yet; The one we need in order to light them the fuck up. If I can prove the Russians are responsible, there won't be a safe place in the city for them to hide.

I'll take them all out.

Starting with the Kostalovs.

My frown deepens when I read the update I get from Jimmy. The Russians have not taken our hits lying down. Oh no, quite the opposite. They've been on an absolute rampage for the last eighteen hours, forcing us to pull in most of our guys, especially since the Italians appear to be helping the Russians. An unlikely turn of events none of us planned for. And one I'm still trying to figure out.

The relationship between the major players of the city has only been growing more tense as both the Italians and Russians are making plays to expand their territories. There are no alliances. The city is on the edge of war.

Stealing a glance to the side, I find Rory staring listlessly out the window, fighting sleep. She probably didn't sleep at all in the lockers. I hold back my questions despite the prime opportunity to grill her on her story.

It's not long before we pull into the underground garage of our destination. Opening the door, I escort the little Bratva mystery to the elevator, nodding at security as we pass by. She makes eye contact with him but stays quiet.

I'm not worried. He's ours too. This entire building belongs to us.

We ride up in silence to the top floor. The private elevator opens right into the loft with a turn of my key.

Koen is lounging on the sectional. He sits up, a look of confusion on his face as I walk Rory right past him toward the bedrooms.

The loft is ours. The four O'Rourke siblings: Koen, Liam, Reagan and me.

And until I get what I need out of her, Rory will stay here.

Where I can keep an eye on her. Where she'll be safe.

Safe from everyone but *me*.

16

THE LOFT

RORY

*T*he loft is a surprise.

I expected another grimy basement or warehouse, but the space Aidan drags me through is, well, gorgeous. Open concept, with lots of natural light streaming in from the glass ceilings above. It's huge. They must have the entire floor. The charcoal paint and industrial feel should make it feel cold and dark, but with all the windows and reclaimed wood, there's an unexpected element of warmth.

It's the type of apartment I would kill to live in. Too bad it's my new gilded prison.

We enter the main living area and I balk at the sight of another man lounging on the dark leather sectional, scrolling on his phone. He sits up at the sight of us. Confusion turns to rage in a split second. I freeze under his fiery glare.

But Aidan's having none of it. He pushes me forward again, a little rougher than is necessary. He doesn't say a word to the man as we pass, but it feels as though they're communicating in silence.

After a hard stare, the man on the couch shakes his head in disapproval before going back to scrolling on his phone. His shoulders tense.

Aidan directs me down a long hallway. We follow it all the way to the end until Aidan propels me forward into a bedroom.

A bedroom.

He stops us in the middle of the room, pulling a key out of his pocket and removes the handcuffs.

The skin on my wrist is red and raw from first the ropes and then the sliding metal of the cuffs. I hold super still while he works, trying to avoid any more friction against the already damaged skin.

Aidan notices, running his thumb gingerly along the raw edges before he drops my hands. I stiffen at the gesture, confused by the gentleness of his touch.

"What are you going to do with me?" My words come out far stronger than I feel.

"I don't know yet." He shrugs while his eyes scan the room.

I stare at him incredulously. "You don't *know* yet?"

"No."

I don't know if that's good news or bad news. "And you're going to figure this out when?" I know this isn't how I should talk to a made man. Should be more careful not to agitate the man who currently holds my life in his hands, but still I hold my ground. Not sorry.

Aidan's eyes harden, and he takes a step closer, but I stay rooted in place. "Careful," he warns. His sea glass eyes are sharp enough to cut me.

Aside from revealing my true identity, I doubt there is

much more I can do that will make this situation better or worse. My fate is my fate at this point. Not willing to back down, I close what little gap still exists between us, raising my chin and straightening my spine. "If you could figure out whether I'm to live or die by lunch, that would be fantastic."

I move to storm past him further into the room, but he blocks my pass, instead, stepping closer and forcing me to yield a step backward.

"You better think long and hard on *why* I should keep you alive, *ice princess*. You *say* you know nothing about the Bratva, but you and I both know that's not true." His eyes narrow. "I have little need for a Russian stripper, unless you want to make things a little more *interesting*?" He takes a long and pointed look down my body until his eyes finally return to my face.

Feeling the blood rush from my face, I lock my glare on him, clamping my mouth shut instead of snapping back

Satisfied, he turns, heading for the hall, but not before calling back over his shoulder, "Get some sleep, Angel. You're going to need it." And then he's gone. The lock clicks into place, trapping me inside.

The large room suddenly feels stifling and too small. I try to stave off the oncoming panic attack by assessing my surroundings.

I need a weapon. Or a way out. But definitely a weapon, for sure.

I eye the bed warily. It's made up in white everything. White sheets, white duvet, fluffy white pillows. It looks clean, plush and comfortable... A shiver shakes my whole body and I back further away from it. There isn't much in the room. It's sparsely decorated. With only a simple bed, nightstand, and a dresser. A quick perusal through all the drawers turns up nothing. Empty. They're all empty. All of them.

The hall door is thick and heavy. There's no way I can bust it down, and even if I did, I'd have to get past Aidan, Liam and probably the other guy I saw earlier on the couch.

The entire far wall consists entirely of industrial style windows reaching up to the roof. *I could break the glass...* Pressing my palms to it, I peer down, praying it's not twenty stories up. I'm both surprised and disappointed when I look down into a closed courtyard garden only about seven feet down. My heart sinks when I realize it's fully enclosed.

From my perch, I can see a door leading out to the courtyard, but from this angle, there's no telling where it goes.

That's one option. We'll call it plan E or F, maybe.

I turn my attention to the two other doors in the room besides the one I know leads out to the hall.

The first door reveals only a modest bathroom staring back at me. All white, like the bed. I can't say I'm not relieved to see the toilet and sink. I quickly take care of some needs and wash my hands and face that are streaked with blood and dirt.

Staring at my reflection, I hardly recognize myself. A long jagged cut mars my left cheek, from when the glass wall shattered back at Elements. And a dark bruise blossoms under my right jaw, but I can't remember how I got it. Several shallow cuts and scrapes line my fingers and forearms. My wrists are a mess. Raw and angry and *burning*. I run some cold water over them and it helps, but still I wish I had some cream or something to wrap them in.

I finger comb my hair, using some water from the sink to dampen it down. Once again, I come up empty after tearing through the bathroom vanity. There's not even a toothbrush that I could try to whittle down to one of those shivs like they make in prison.

There's one more door, next to the bathroom. This one I open with more confidence. As I suspected, it's a closet. Walk-in with no walk-out. Bare except for a large black bag in the middle of the floor.

A small flame of hope sparks when I recognize what it is...

A hockey bag.

17

POWERPLAY

AIDAN

I don't need to be a mind reader to know Koen's pissed.

No, scratch that; Koen is fucking furious.

With Rory secured in the guest room, I stalk back out into the living room to have this conversation. I spy Liam, already sprawled on the other half of the sectional, wisely out of Koen's reach. He mouths a silent *"Good luck."* Raising his bottle of water to me.

I swipe some whiskey from the drink cart we keep in the corner and plop down in the recliner. I don't usually drink during the season but... extenuating circumstances.

Taking a long pull from the bottle, I close my eyes. I'm more tired than I thought.

Koen doesn't wait for me to talk.

His green eyes are nearly black with rage. "What the fuck were you thinking, Aidan? Why did you bring her here? If the Bratva finds out—"

"The Bratva don't know shit." I sit forward. "And why would they care about one missing stripper?"

"I thought she wasn't just a stripper," Koen hedges.

I run a hand down my face, exasperation mixing with exhaustion. "I don't know what she fucking is. None of it makes sense." *What was she doing there?* And why was she not more afraid? Rory was frightened, sure, but she still had the nerve to *challenge* me. *To fight back.*

"Whatever you're going to do with her, you better figure it out fast. Because she can't be here. Reagan..."

An image of our sister flashes into my mind and guilt sets in. Admittedly, I had given little thought to how bringing Rory to the loft could endanger my little sister.

"We should let her go. It's not worth the risk." Liam adds his two cents, his mouth a thin line.

"Are you out of your mind?" Koen's nearly shouting. "She knows too much! She's seen all our faces, Jimmy's, and she's seen the fucking loft! How long do you think until she runs to the media, with quite a tale to tell about the Breakers' defensive dynamic duo Liam and Aidan O'Rourke?" My brother glares at me. "Did you blindfold her at least before you brought her here?"

I wince, and Koen's eyes burn into mine. "There's no way she remembers." She was half out of it for most of the ride, a vacant expression on her face. A look that made me leave her alone on our ride over here. One that *almost* made me feel bad.

I take a chance and change the subject. "Are we any closer to figuring out who ordered the hit on Da'? The raid on Elements gave us nothing."

Koen narrows his eyes at me, letting me know we are nowhere near done discussing Rory, but this is important, too.

"All evidence so far points to the Russians. Fucking Kostalov."
He throws his hands up in frustration. "This shouldn't come
as a surprise. But I can't yet rule out anyone, including the
Italians."

We know it was the Russians. They'd been encroaching on
our territory for months, testing how far they could push us.
The Irish and the Russians aren't exactly enemies, but we're far
from allies.

Several recent disagreements over a couple of shipments
gone wrong, and the growing skin trade popping up all over
the city, has pushed the relationship between the two organizations nearly to a breaking point.

I nod, but stay quiet.

"Then why don't we make our move? Take out Kostalov?"
Liam asks, looking between Koen and me.

"Kostalov has too much protection." Koen works his jaw.
"Besides, the Italians have been making some unusual moves
over the past week or two."

That catches my attention. "What moves?"

"They're cozying up to the Bratva. Rumor has it the Italians have also expanded into the skin trade."

That's bad news. Da' worked hard to keep that shit out of
our city. We know the Russians are behind it, though I have
reasons to believe the Italians have now dipped their hands into
the pot too.

"I can't see De Luca signing off on that." Like us, the
Italian Capo has a hard line on that sort of business. There's
plenty of money to be made in drugs and arms without
needing to sell bodies.

Koen shrugs, "I'm just telling you what I heard. They
photographed Giovanni last week meeting with their sociopath

Carezzo." *Giovanni*... no skin deals went down in this city that didn't have his fingerprints all over it. "Our guy says the Italians are making runs for him."

I think about it for a minute.

So far, Giovanni was dealing with low level pimps and organizations. We'd done our best to stamp out the trade altogether within our territory, but that shit has a way of continuing to pop up. But if they get the Italians backing them...

"The Italians have more to gain by getting rid of Da'. Is there any concrete proof pinning it on either of them?"

"No." Koen's jaw ticks. "We need to play this carefully. If we go after the wrong crew, we end up with more enemies than we can handle."

He's not wrong. Things have been difficult following Da's death. Koen took charge, but a couple of the older members of the Irish are still holding out on bending the knee.

"Did the Russians agree to bring us in on the arms deal with the Cartel?" The deal would run in the millions. And we could use the cash. The Bratva have been fucking with Irish business and it's cost us. If we don't get shit under control, and fast, some of the remaining Irish factions might decide enough is enough.

Liam takes this one, "No, Adrik is taking his time deciding. Feels like he's playing with us."

"Even if he is responsible, we can't afford to lose that deal." I tighten my fists. "*Especially* to the Italians."

I turn my attention to Liam. "Reach out to Ryan, give him the identity of our informant. Have him lean on him. Tell him we need to meet. He can stop by tomorrow, but tell him to be careful. We need leverage on Kostalov to make this deal go through." As important as revenge is, if we didn't get the cash we needed soon to pay our guys, Koen's rule would fold before it even began.

Liam nods. "I'll make the call."

"Back to the girl."

I slide my eyes back to my older brother, gritting my teeth.

"No one knows she's here. Her presence threatens nothing." I state the facts calmly. "You're right, maybe I shouldn't have brought her here. I admit, I was just trying to keep her away from Jimmy while I figured shit out."

He nods, finally seeing reason. "We should talk to her. Find out what she knows. You do think she knows something, don't you?"

"There's something she's not telling me. I can feel it. It's also no coincidence I ran into her at the Breakers' rink, and a day later catch her red-handed in Kostalov's office."

"Yeah, a weird coincidence," Liam agrees with me.

"Fine. She stays here for now, until we know what it is we're dealing with. But if she endangers Reagan," Koen's eyes flare at me, "I'll kill her myself."

I look my brother in the eye. "You'll have to beat me to it."

18

SHARP EDGES

RORY

I tear through the bag. In it I find gloves, a helmet, skates, some gym clothes, and a couple of stinky practice jerseys. *Hockey players are disgusting.* The smell emanating from the gloves is a putrid one. I plug my nose with one hand as I dig deeper into the bag.

The sound of a key jiggling in the door sends a lightning bolt of panic through me. I only have enough time to grab the one thing I think I might be able to use before racing out of the closet, hastily closing the door behind me.

I grip the hockey skate I stole tightly in my hand, hiding it behind my back. *Shit*, I'm not ready. My mind races to formulate a plan, and I stand awkwardly in the middle of the room.

Aidan's eyes sharpen with suspicion the second he sees me. They flick around the room in a brief, deliberate sweep before locking back onto mine, unyielding and intense. I will my pounding heart to calm.

"Whatever it is you have, it's best you give it over, Angel." The Irish accent I detected earlier comes out a little stronger with his words. He holds out a hand as if I'd actually comply with that bullshit.

I take a step back, shaking my head. My eyes dart between him and the bed between us.

"You can't keep me here against my will."

Aidan's mouth curls up into a devilish smile as he slowly stalks closer, reminding me of a big cat who has its eyes set on its next meal.

"I hate to break it to you, Love, but I can do just about anything I want with you." He winks, amused.

I tighten my grip around the skate at my back. Biding my time until he's close enough.

"No one knows where you are, and *no one* is coming to rescue you. You're all *mine*." He edges closer and I take another two steps back. Not unaware that he's herding me into the corner. I force my eyes to stay on him, ignoring the door he's left open at his back. *I only have one shot.*

"You don't eat unless I allow it. You drink what I give you." His lips quirk and I swear vomit climbs up my throat at the innuendo. He stops his advance, pinning me in place with his stare alone. "And you answer whatever questions I ask you— honestly." He adds, "No lies," slowly shaking his head.

I scoff and cock my head to the side as I look him over, arching a brow. Hoping to appear unimpressed. "I'm sorry, but I'm not one of your little soldiers. Taking orders is not something I do. In fact, I barely take suggestions."

Forest green eyes darken with violent excitement and I gulp, losing some of my bravado, backing up until I hit the wall behind me. Nowhere left to go.

"It sounds like someone needs to learn their place." He comes for me. I hold back, waiting until he's within striking distance before I lash out with the skate. My fingers are tight around the boot, blade side out. Slashing at him with all of my strength. He notices the blade in my hands a second too late.

I make contact. There's a bright flash of red.

Aidan brings his arm up just in time to save his throat. His eyes flash with surprise when I cut him, slicing down his arm, blood pouring out, streaming in crimson rivulets down his wrist, and dripping down to the floor.

I falter at the sight of the damage I've inflicted. Before I can form another thought, he moves. Snatching the skate right out of my hand and slamming my back against the brick wall behind me. Curling one hand around my throat—pinning me there.

Fear coats my tongue like ash, and I meet his gaze with wide, unblinking eyes.

He tosses the skate behind him, cursing. When his bloody hand comes back in my direction, raised, I flinch, turning my cheek and closing my eyes.

Bracing for the hit.

My mind decides this is the best time to remind me of all those media articles I'd pulled up after running into him the other day at the rink, detailing the hot-head that is Aidan O'Rourke. Hit first, ask questions later. Violent, brutal and relentless. He nearly killed a guy last year on the ice. *With a single punch.*

When the strike doesn't come, I slowly open my eyes, finding Aidan staring at me stone-faced. Still as a statue with a barely contained rage burning in his eyes.

He takes in his bleeding arm. Twisting it so he can view the extent of the damage. I'm no medical professional, but even I know it's going to need stitches. "FUCK!" He shouts, his voice echoing against the loft's high ceilings.

I flinch again.

He releases me. My shaking legs are no match for my dead weight, so I crumple to the floor, sliding down the wall at my back. Both terrified and devastated that my escape attempt failed so miserably.

Aidan doesn't say another word. He storms through the room, picks up the skate, and wrenches open the closet door. He hauls out his hockey bag to take it with him, slamming the door shut behind him.

A single tear leaks down my face and I curl in on myself, feeling hopeless.

19

LITTLE LION'S GOT CLAWS

AIDAN

ory is asleep when I finally return to the guest room I've stashed her in.

She'd come close to doing serious damage, just missing the crucial radial artery in my arm and barely missing my throat. Lucky for me, Reagan had been studying to be a nurse before we locked everything down after the hit on our father. My forearm is freshly stitched up and bandaged, courtesy of my little sister. Although, I could've done without her commentary on the matter.

The feisty Russian stripper is certainly the talk of the loft tonight. I don't think I'll ever live it down, letting her get the jump on me like that.

I'm irritated, but at the same time, impressed by Rory's attempts to fight back.

Little lion's got claws.

But now, she's out cold. Exhaustion finally caught up to her. She doesn't wake when I make my way across the room. I take the opportunity to study the little figure skater.

She's curled up on the floor by the brick wall. Arms wrapped around her knees and knees that are tucked up into her chest. Exactly where I left her. A quick glance over at the bed shows it untouched. Her honey-blonde hair spills over her shoulders, curling at the ends, catching the light from the garden outside like spun gold. Framing delicate features—high cheekbones, a dainty nose, and lips that curve into a fascinating little pout that all give her an angelic quality.

But her eyes tell a different story, haunting me day and night. Steel-blue and piercing, a striking contrast to her soft features, carrying a depth that hints at shadows hiding under the surface. There's a fragility to her beauty, but also a strength, like ice that gleams in sunlight but is sharp enough to cut.

The six-inch wound down my forearm is a testament to that. She looked like an angel, yes, but not the kind that belongs in the heavens. No, there was something darker about her, a quiet defiance in her steely gaze that marks her as a fallen one. One that carries scars hidden deep under a perfect golden exterior.

She wears a worn Vancouver Wolves Hockey sweatshirt. *Was she telling the truth about being Canadian?* I haven't yet followed up with Liam. The little skirt poking out from under her hoodie has the trademarked figure skating cut to it. Her tights have little runs in them. They trail all the way up her thigh. *Interesting.* Why was she in a strip club's office in her skating clothes?

Leg warmers hug her ankles, but she shivers in her sleep. From nightmares or the cold, I can't tell.

I set down the tray of food I brought for her on the floor, a few feet from where she's lying. She'll see it when she wakes up. A sandwich, an apple and a bag of chips. Along with a couple of bottles of water. I chastise myself for forgetting until now to feed her. In my defense, we don't normally feed our hostages, but for this one, I can make an exception. I need her alive to answer my questions.

Her honey hair has fallen loose from its braid, spilling across her face. I frown at the sight of the angry-looking cut on her cheek. The edges are a little puffy and swollen. Possibly the start of an infection. She's cleaned it, but I make a mental note to provide some antibiotic cream.

The more I study her, the less sense any of it makes.

She's not a stripper or an escort. She doesn't have that vacant look so many in the skin trade get after being so ruthlessly passed around. Could she be telling the truth about the club?

How does someone like Rory get mixed up with the Russian Bratva? And with Adrik Kostalov, of all people? It was his office, after all, that I found her in.

If I can only confirm her innocence, there's no consequence in letting her go. Scare her, rough her up a little to keep her from going to the cops, sure, but if she has no ties to the Russians, there's no threat to the Irish by letting the girl live.

Still, my gut nags at me that there's something more going on with this girl. Her reactions to the situations she's lived through in the past day or so aren't typical. Any ordinary girl, plucked up off the street, would've pissed her pants in a mess of tears and screams when Jimmy pointed that gun in her face.

Rory's afraid, but she's calm, resourceful. She cut me with my hockey skate, for God's sake. Was aiming for my throat, and would've succeeded too if I hadn't thrown my arm up when I did.

And what the fuck was that reaction after I took the skate

from her? She was ready for me to hit her. Unless you have experienced being hit before, you wouldn't react that way. The terror in her eyes when she tracked the back of my hand coming toward her...

It pissed me off. *Who's hitting her?*

I step back, reaching over and pulling the thick, white knit throw blanket off the top of the bed. Gingerly, I drape it over her tiny form. She stirs a little as the weight of the blanket settles over her but doesn't wake.

As feisty as she was, it was only a matter of time before she crashed. And crashed hard. Adrenaline can only take you so far. I should use her exhaustion to my advantage; grill her until she's delirious from lack of sleep. But I back out of the room as silently as I came. Careful not to wake the sleeping skater curled up on the floor.

I'm still pissed as hell over the shit she pulled with the skate, but I'm not a monster. It's the least I can do for the hell I've put her through during her time with me. Like I said, maybe she is innocent in all of this. Caught up in the wrong place at the wrong time.

When she wakes up, I'm going to need those answers. And like it or not, she's *going* to give them to me.

20

IRISH STEW

RORY

Sunlight streaming in from the wall of windows rips me out of a dreamless sleep.

I go from barely awake to full panic mode when I catch the corner of the white blanket covering me in my field of vision. In an uncoordinated frenzy, I scramble up, forcefully shoving the blanket off, as if it bit me.

I stare at the pooled white knit, now a few feet away. *Did I grab it in my sleep?* I try to remember...

The sight of the tray of food throws all thoughts about the blanket out the window. I crawl to the tray as my stomach— who'd long since given up on hunger cues—growls menacingly. I'm just about to reach for the wrapped sandwich when an unwelcome thought pops into my head and my hand freezes.

I stare down at the food. The chips and bottles of water are still sealed shut, leaving the sandwich and apple as the most suspicious items on the tray.

Or is that what they'd like me to think?

A thin enough needle could pierce through packaging, and I'd never be able to tell.

Would they drug me?

My ravenous hunger and thirst ultimately win out over my concerns. They might have drugged the food, but not eating it won't save me. If they wanted to, they could hold me down and force a needle into my neck.

So, bottoms up, I guess...

I practically inhale the sandwich and chips. Polishing off two bottles of water. I grab the apple and stash it into one of the empty drawers for later. Who knows when the next time they'll feed me will be?

That done, I look around the room, unsure what to do with myself. I listen at the door for any sounds, but all I get is silence. Either the hall door and walls are soundproof, or there's nothing happening. The garden below the window is empty.

Feeling grimy, I head into the bathroom, eyeing the shower. A hot shower would feel so good right now. My body aches from sleeping on the floor. A second search of the bathroom turns up nothing but a little hand towel by the sink.

The thought of being naked and exposed if Aidan waltzes back in here mid-shower has me out of the bathroom faster than you can say soap.

Back in the room, I avoid the bed, circling back toward the wall of windows. As if ignoring the bed could help me avoid my fate if I were to provoke a certain male...

The words Aidan said to Jimmy back in the office haunt my thoughts. How his eyes scanned my body, the flash of desire, *his hand around my throat.*

I tuck myself onto the sill of the window, making myself as

small as possible. All the locks are sealed shut—*I checked*. Leaning my head back against the wall, I watch a little sparrow work diligently on her nest in the tree outside for a while.

I must fall asleep because when I startle awake again, the sun is gone. Instead, a gray drizzle soaks the little courtyard garden, the cobblestones slick with rain.

There's movement by the door. The knob twists, and the sound of a key in the lock has my blood growing cold. *Time to face the music*. I haven't seen Aidan since the hockey skate incident. Somehow, the anticipation of his return is worse. My fear of him has only grown as the hours have ticked by.

He must have left the food, or sent someone with it. The thought that someone was in here while I was asleep gives me chills. But the food also means they still want me alive. It would be a shame if his little prisoner died before he willed it.

I've worked out Aidan has a problem with killing an innocent. The problem is that he's almost certain that I'm no innocent.

If I'm going to survive the day, I need to do everything I can to convince Aidan I have nothing to do with the Russian Bratva, the Irish Mob nor Adrik Kostalov. That I'm just Rory Collins from Vancouver, a figure skater and nothing more.

The door swings open.

Aidan's huge frame fills the opening, as he leans against the door with his arms crossed. A thick white bandage is wrapped around his forearm. Guilt and satisfaction war within my mind.

I don't move from where I'm perched on the window's ledge.

"Good Afternoon."

I blink at him. *Good Afternoon?* I stay silent, staring.

Bracing for him to either shoot me or drag me off to his torture chamber. Anything really. He's impossible to read. I have no idea what to expect from him.

"So Liam's cooked up a proper Irish stew, we thought—we thought maybe you'd like to join us?" He rubs the back of his neck uncomfortably.

Thank God the window is at my back because I would've fallen over at how hard I jerk back in shock. "Join you?" I get out.

Aidan's chin dips slowly, his eyes never leaving mine. "Yep." He puts extra emphasis on the "*p.*"

I narrow my eyes. "I must be missing something. What's the catch?"

He shrugs, so nonchalantly I want to slap him. "No catch. Just maybe a change in tactics," he openly admits.

I consider refusing, but I'm already a little stir crazy from being trapped in this room all day. The scent of what must be the Irish stew has permeated through the open door, forcing another growl from my now empty stomach.

Hopping down from the windowsill, I mimic his shrug. "Yeah, sure, why not?"

It takes another half-second for him to react, caught off guard by my response. "Great. Let's go." He gestures out into the hall, distrust in his eyes. He'd thought it would have taken more convincing.

I force myself to walk willingly within his reach, relieved when he leads the way instead of walking behind me. I curl the ends of my sweatshirt around my fingers. Not able to shake the feeling of a lamb being led to her slaughter.

When we reach the living room, Aidan swings left, leading

us into an enormous kitchen. It's painted evergreen, like Aidan's eyes, with more exposed brick and stainless steel.

The sound of female laughter draws my eyes to possibly the most beautiful girl I've ever seen, sitting at a long table in the middle of the large room. She's laughing hysterically at something Liam said, playfully shoving another male I don't recognize in the shoulder.

It goes quiet and all eyes slide to Aidan and me as we fully enter the kitchen, and I'm instantly self-conscious. I shift uneasily on my feet under the weight of their stares.

Aidan turns, swinging his arm toward me. I hesitate, my eyes watching his hand, and he immediately drops it. A flash of *something* in his eyes. "Every—everyone, this is Rory."

"Rory, you remember Liam?" My eyes dart to the dirty-blonde, spooning heaven-scented stew into bowls on the other side of the island. I *remember* how he wrestled me into a chair back in the warehouse. The asshole has the balls to wink at me.

"Mmm, how could I forget?" I grumble, mostly under my breath.

Aidan points to the male I don't recognize. The one currently shooting daggers at me with his dark eyes. "My older brother, Koen."

I swallow hard and give him a curt nod of acknowledgement; one he doesn't return. The anxiety in my chest doubles. *Koen O'Rourke. Fuck me.* I realize he's the male I saw on the couch yesterday when we arrived. I fight through the realization that Koen O'Rourke—*who doesn't know who I really am*—already seems to hate me. There's no mistaking the disdain in his eyes.

"And this little hellion right here is our little sister, Reagan."

Reagan gives me a soft smile and a little wave I can't help but return. Out of all of them, she's the only one who looks truly "Irish." With red-gold curls cascading down her back and bright emerald green eyes that are a stark contrast against pale skin. She's absolutely stunning.

Aidan pulls out a chair and I plop uncomfortably into it. He takes the seat next to me, and I fidget under Koen's scrutiny and Aidan's proximity. *Should've stayed in the room.*

Another beat and Liam places a steaming hot bowl of stew in front of me and the sweet scent makes my mouth water.

"You can thank Reagan for the invitation. I think if Aidan wasn't successful in dragging you out here, she'd have fetched you herself," Liam jests.

Reagan laughs, "Rory here is our guest, and she needs to eat. She might as well do it with us."

I can't say I agree with her. As a matter of fact, I would've preferred to stay as far away from these three men as I can get. But at least the stew smells good. *Not a bad last meal.* I smile to myself at the morbid thought, but when I catch Koen watching me, it quickly fades away.

I busy myself with taking a bite and nearly groan at the explosion of taste on my tongue. The stew is warm and hearty, full of meat, potatoes and carrots. It instantly brings a feeling of comfort as it fills my empty stomach.

Aidan hands me a roll and I take it from him, careful to avoid any accidental contact with his fingers. The weight of his gaze is heavy as I take another bite of my stew; my eyes trained on the bowl.

The silence at the table is so loud I want to die. No, seriously, I would've preferred a firing squad over this tense silence.

Reagan senses it too and clears her throat. "So, Rory, where are you from?"

My eyes dart around the males of the table, pretending to be busy filling their own stomachs.

"Oh—um—here I guess." I stumble over my words, nerves on edge. "Boston," I clarify. "But I grew up in Canada. I only recently moved back to the city." I take another bite of stew to stop myself from rambling on.

"And what brings you back to Boston?" Koen's rough voice startles me, having not heard it before. It's deep, with a slight Irish lilt to it. Like Aidan's, but stronger. For the moment, he's stowed away his death glare, now eyeing me with cold curiosity. He takes another bite of his own stew while awaiting my answer.

"Skating," I can say without hesitation. "To skate with Karina Valgova." I look at Aidan, finding him watching me, an unreadable expression on his face.

"You skate absolutely beautifully!" Reagan exclaims from across from me.

My look of confusion prompts her to explain.

"Liam showed me some videos of your routines and, oh-my-God, you're talented. Like *really* talented," she gushes, beaming at me, meaning every word she says.

"Thank you." I choke out. Uncertain how I feel knowing Liam, and likely Aidan too, have been watching video after video of my competition film for "research."

"I wish I had learned to skate. I know enough to get by, but it just looks so freeing flying across the ice. Because of these two brutes over here," she eyes her brothers with contempt as she continues. "I only ever associated skating with hockey; not exactly my cup of tea." She holds up one hand to the side of her mouth as though she's telling me a secret. "If you know what I mean."

It brings a genuine smile to my face and I can't help the laugh that escapes me. "I do. Hockey isn't really my thing either." My eyes flash to Aidan's, and he narrows his gaze.

"So besides skating, what else do you do?" Koen asks, redirecting the conversation back to the interrogation in disguise. "Moonlight in any *clubs*?" He arches his brow and chews on his spoon while watching me closely.

I do my best to suppress the wince as I answer him, "Skating is my life. It's the only thing that matters." The truth of that statement stings. "If I'm not at the rink, I'm training. If I'm not training, I'm at ballet or at choreography. And other than that, I'm home, alone with my books."

"—Or at the Chill Zone, the bar upstairs at the Edge," I add quickly when they just stare at me. "I work there a couple of days a week."

Koen zeroes in on me, leaning slightly across the table. "Hard to believe, a pretty girl like you. No friends? A boyfriend, perhaps?" I don't miss how Aidan's spoon stills at the mention of a boyfriend. Drawing his spoon slowly out of his mouth but not looking at me.

I shake my head, forcing myself not to break eye contact with Koen. His eyes are green like Aidan and Reagan's, but darker. Almost as if someone blended green with black. "No friends. No boyfriend." I refuse to blink.

Reagan gasps at my admission. "No *friends*?"

I drop my eyes to my bowl, pushing the vegetables around. "No time." I shrug. *Too dangerous,* I correct in my head.

"Well, we'll have to change that, won't we? Once this business with my brothers is sorted out, you and I, we're getting drinks."

I look up at Reagan O'Rourke with shock. Could my salvation come from the youngest of the O'Rourke clan? A petite redhead grinning at me from across the table?

"I'd love that." My voice is quieter than it should be. Grabbing hold of my empty glass, I rise. "I'm just going to get some more water." I'm not sure if I'm allowed to get up, but I do it anyway. Feeling their eyes on me as I make my way over to the sink, and fill up my cup, gulping it down before topping it back off again.

"But you have family in the area, though, right? Seeing as how you were born here..." There's no missing the snark in Koen's tone. "Parents? Any siblings?"

I'm saved from answering Koen's dangerous line of questioning by the arrival of someone new to the loft.

"Hello?" A familiar sounding male voice calls from just outside the kitchen.

"In here!" Aidan calls in response, his eyes on me again.

"Alex!" Reagan squeals, jumping out of her chair to pounce on the male who has made his way into the kitchen. He catches her mid-jump, swinging her around in a tight embrace.

I look on with mild interest until they spin and I glimpse the man's face.

I freeze.

I'm only mildly aware of the shattering clatter my glass makes when it hits the tile floor, when I lock eyes with one of the last people I'd ever expect to see walk into this house...

Alexei.

21

THE RUSSIAN ANGEL

AIDAN

The sound of glass breaking echoes throughout the room.

Rory has gone a sickly pale, staring at Alex like she's seen a ghost.

Alex slowly sets Reagan down, who's wise enough to return to her seat at the table in between Koen and Liam. The former leans forward in his chair, as interested as I am in this new development playing out before us.

Alex is staring at Rory like he, too, has seen a ghost. He shoots nervous glances my way while an awkward silence hangs over the room.

"I thought you said you didn't have any *friends*, Rory," Koen taunts behind me.

My jaw is tense and I keep my eyes trained on the blonde who I don't think has even blinked since Alex walked in.

"I don't," she practically whispers.

"Well, it certainly seems like you know our *friend* Alex

here," Koen hedges. "Or maybe you know him by his other name—*Alexei*?"

She flinches.

I sit forward. *Oh yeah, she knows him alright.* I flex my jaw, taking in this recent development.

If Rory knows Alex as Alexei, it means she had to have met him while he was doing business with the Russians. No one other than Bratva knows him as Alexei.

The thought hadn't crossed my mind to consult him earlier. Alexei Ryan serves as one of our spies inside the Bratva. He worked his way up the ranks, and now he's working for Adrik Kostalov himself. But the question is: *how does Rory know Alexei?*

My eyes shift to Alex. He senses it and meets my gaze, indecision dancing in his dark eyes.

Rory is silent, her pleading eyes on Alexei as she slowly shakes her head *no*. Mentally begging him to keep whatever secret she's been working so hard to hide from us. *From me.*

I lean in, "Or maybe the question is, what do *you* know about Rory, *Alexei*?"

To Alex's credit, he battles with himself for only a few seconds before finally spitting it out, solidifying what we already know is true. His allegiance remains firmly with the Irish.

"Rory's a nickname—," he speaks slowly, his voice soft and apologetic. I swear you could hear a pin drop in this fucking room. Alex lets out a deep breath that sounds an awful lot like regret, not breaking his gaze with the girl frozen across the kitchen before he continues, "—for Aurora."

Koen and I exchange a look; both of us wondering why he was so nervous to tell us that.

"It's a pretty name, Alex, but it's hardly a revelation." I lean back, annoyed. Alex is practically a brother to me, but he's wasting my time. His next words stop me in place.

"Her full name is—"

"No... no... no... Alexei, no..." Rory, or should I say, *Aurora*, begs from across the room.

"—Aurora Kostalova."

He says nothing else. He doesn't have to. Kostalova... she's a fucking *Kostalova*?

Everything happens at once.

My gaze slides back to Rory, my expression darkening.

Her blue eyes rocket back to mine. If I thought I'd seen fear in her expression before, that was nothing compared to what I see there now.

I'm barely even out of my seat before she takes off. Running past Alex, racing for the elevator.

I chase after her but take my time, knowing full well she won't be able to get out of the loft. I activated the exit code myself in anticipation of a situation such as the one we now find ourselves in. "Where you running off to Angel?" I shout. "This game is only just getting started."

She slides into the door, smashing at the button with her fingers. When the code screen appears, she howls in frustration at the little screen. Smacking it several times with her palm. She sees me coming from the corner of her eye. The scream she lets out is blood curdling and I feel it under my skin.

I smile.

Rory takes off into the living room, circling around the couch. I take a shortcut, jumping clear over the sectional to land behind her, tackling her to the ground.

We fight for a minute as I struggle to get her under control.

She rolls onto her back, clawing at my face, eyes, anything she can reach. I pin her hips down under mine. It's already over, but it takes another couple of seconds for me to pin her wrists down over her head. Her chest heaves as she stills, recognizing defeat.

Koen and Alex move so they're behind me. Liam must be keeping Reagan in the kitchen, tucked safely away from the drama unfolding in the living room.

"You told him," she bites out. Her words are directed behind me at Alex, dripping with betrayal. Her eyes smolder like a storm at sea.

My friend's jaw tightens, but he says nothing.

"Cuff her," I order.

Koen hands cuffs to Alex, who bends down and slips the metal bracelets around Rory's wrists while she shoots him daggers with her eyes. He finishes binding her hands together and steps back. Watching me. I've known Alex my entire life. He's one of us, an O'Rourke—unofficially. He trusts me with whatever I decide to do, but—there's a wariness in his dark eyes.

Fuck, he cares about her.

I take hold of the chain linking the metal cuffs and drag the girl up so she's on her knees. She tries to stand up, but I push her back down with a warning glare.

No wonder she looks so familiar. It wasn't just that I'd seen her around the rink a time or two. She's the spitting image of Nikolai Kostalov. Her *brother.*

They could be twins. Hell, maybe they are.

I take my gun out and push it into her forehead. She glowers at me.

The balls on this one.

116

"No. More. Lies," I growl out, tapping her head with my gun with each syllable. I drag the gun down the side of her cheek, the cold metal lifting her chin before I drag the barrel across her lips. Momentarily distracted when the tip of the gun parts them.

"Give me one reason I shouldn't put a bullet in you right now..." I grip her chin roughly with my other hand, forcing her gaze to stay on mine when she tries to look away. "...send your little Russian head in a box to your father with a pretty bow on top?"

This fucking girl looks me right in the eye when she says...

"I can't."

Her response pisses me off. I haul her up. Slinging her over my shoulder, and I storm down the hall to the bedrooms.

Her legs kick furiously, and she beats my back with her cuffed hands. Screaming the whole way. The noise isn't a problem; we own this entire building. It's not like anyone can hear her, but it doesn't mean the sound doesn't go right through me.

"Shut. The. Fuck. Up." I smack her ass with my gun. It stuns her enough into blessed silence.

We enter the guest room I had her in, and I toss her onto the bed, her body rigid.

She was right to be wary about this bed. I'm on her before she realizes, holding her body down again with my hips, ignoring the hits she gets in with her bound hands. They bounce off my hard chest, and I laugh as I reach up and pull out the chains tucked between the headboard and the mattress, a leather cuff attached to the end of each one.

She's a whimpering mess now as I pin her hands over her head, releasing one wrist only to secure it to the bed.

"Please, you don't have to do this."

I ignore her, taking her second wrist and pulling it to the other side. She's stopped fighting me. Probably realized she's going to end up exactly how I want her, no matter how much she fights or begs.

I step back to admire my handiwork as soon as her second wrist is secured. She tests the new restraints. Her fingers curl around the metal chains attached to the leather cuffs on her wrists.

"Now here's how this is going to go," I begin, lightly pacing the room. "I'm going to ask you questions, and you're going to give me some fucking answers. Or I *promise* you, things are going to get a whole lot worse for you around here." I turn my dark gaze on her and she shrinks further back into the mattress. "And God-fucking-help you if you lie to me. Got it?"

When she only stares back at me, I repeat my question, louder this time, "I can't hear you, little lion, I said, do you understand?"

She bites her lip before she nods her head. "Got it," she replies weakly.

"Good girl." My words earn me a glare.

"You are Adrik Kostalov's daughter?" I wait for confirmation.

Her answer is dripping with resentment. "Yes."

Whatever, I'll take it. "Why didn't you tell me?"

"Because you'd kill me," she answers simply. Her eyes slide to mine.

I tilt my head to the side, studying her. *I can give her that one.*

"What is the Bratva planning?"

She scoffs, "How am I supposed to know?"

"Why are they allying with the Italians?"

Her jaw tightens before she answers, "I don't know." *Lie.*

"Is Adrik dealing in skin?"

She wrinkles her nose in disgust. "Skin? Like animal skins?"

I push on, "Did Adrik order the hit on Declan O'Rourke?"

She stills, staring at me with wide eyes.

I repeat my question, "Did Adrik order the hit on Declan O'Rourke?" Enunciating each syllable. I couldn't be more clear.

"I don't know." Her voice no louder than a whisper.

I pounce on her. "Did Adrik order the hit on Declan O'Rourke? Yes or no?"

"I don't know!" She shouts this time, pulling against the restraints, unnerved by my repeated question.

"Mmmm, nope. *Wrong* answer." I step closer to her. "I think you *do* know, *Aurora*," I taunt, tracing a single finger from her ankle to the hem of her skirt as I move closer, my threat clear. She lies perfectly still, frozen in fear. "Did Adrik order the hit on Declan O'Rourke?" I ask, softer this time.

"I don't know!"

My fingers play along the edge of her skirt and I watch as she falls apart. "I don't know! I DON'T KNOW, OKAY? I don't know!!!"

I drop her skirt and she releases a panicked breath, pulling hard against her restraints again.

"Such a little liar. Let's see what a little time does to loosen that tongue of yours." I turn, stalking for the door. She writhes on the bed behind me. I can hear the metal straining with her movements and she shouts after me.

"No. Please!!! Don't leave me like this..."

"Aidan!"

I almost turn back at the sound of my name on her lips, her desperate plea to me. But I don't. I keep going until I'm out of the bedroom and into the hall.

"I DON'T KNOW ANYTHING. I SWEAR I DON'T." She's sobbing now. "PLEASE DON'T LEAVE ME HERE!"

They're the last words I hear from her before I slam the door shut behind me.

22

KOSTALOVA

AIDAN

*M*y mind is racing, and I can feel both Koen's and Alex's eyes on me as I storm down the hall and cross into the living room. Collapsing into the recliner, I absently rub my bandaged forearm.

"This is not good." Koen's hard gaze lands on me.

"If that wasn't obvious..." I mutter. Leaning forward, I pull my hand down my face. *Fuck, I need to sleep.*

Liam pops his head out of the kitchen at the sound of my voice. "Remember, we have practice in an hour."

I let out a low growl of frustration, burying my face in both my hands for a second. "Yep—right—okay." I roll my shoulders back, like I can shake off this exhaustion, before turning toward Alex and Liam. "Let's make this quick."

I'd been out of this shit for so long I forgot how much of a toll it took on my life. I've been burning the candle at both ends over the past couple of weeks, trying to keep up with the team while dealing with all of this on the side.

The death of a boss was a dangerous time in the mafia world. A period of instability, transition of power—it was the perfect time to take advantage. After our father's death, so many things had gone awry. Shipments had gone missing, product was destroyed—raids like the one on Kostalov—gone wrong. I'm starting to think there could be no explanation other than sabotage...

"Kostalov has a daughter?" Koen asks.

I shake my head, still stunned at the development. "No wonder Adrik has his men out there, tearing this city apart after we hit Elements. We stole the man's *daughter*. We keep this in-house for now," I say, looking each of my brothers in the eye.

They dip their chins in agreement, understanding what's at stake.

"Guess you found the leverage in Kostalov's office, after all," Liam muses.

"A heads up would have been nice." I glare at Alex.

Alex's hands go up in self defense. "I sent you in for Adrik's ledger, not his daughter! I didn't even know she was missing! Adrik's had me overseeing all the new guys he brought in for the Cartel this week."

"Why doesn't anyone know about her?" I direct my question to the group, but zero in on Alex as I amend my former question. "Why didn't *we* know about her?"

"Hey, you said *need to know* only. That means intel on shipments, changes in Bratva leadership, locations and deals. If I revealed information about Kostalov's daughter, it could easily be traced back to me."

"I don't get it." Koen leans forward, his hands clasped together in thought. "Why keep his daughter a secret?"

Alex gives him a look. "Obviously, to avoid a situation such as the one she's found herself in now; to keep her from being a target—like Reagan is." We all sit a little straighter at the mention of our sister. In danger all her life for the last name she had no choice in.

Reagan *hates* the fact she requires an escort nearly everywhere she goes. But with that fiery hair of hers, there's no hiding her in plain sight.

"Find anything?" Liam had been working on fact checking Rory's original story. Back when I was still hoping for her innocence. Now that we have the new facts, I'm sure he's already begun trying to piece together the puzzle.

Liam nods, pulling out his laptop. "Aurora is the product of one of Adrik's extramarital affairs. She and Niko are half-siblings. When Adrik found out about the baby, he sent his mistress away to raise her." He pauses for a bit, reading through his notes. "In Canada. He kept them comfortable, so long as Rory took figure skating lessons."

That last bit needles me a little. Growing up in hockey, you could always tell the kids that were there because they loved it versus if their parents willed it. The videos Liam and I watched last night of some of Rory's competitions showed off her skills. Bratva princess or not, the girl was talented. But I wonder how much of a choice Rory had in it all.

"So what changed?" Koen asks, thinking along the same line as me. Something had to have changed for Adrik to expose his daughter like this after all this time. "Why bring her back to Boston? Why now?"

Liam's jaw clenches. "I don't know yet, haven't gotten that far." He types something into his computer and shakes his head again.

Alex clears his throat, earning all of our attention. His voice is low and so we all lean in slightly to hear it.

"I don't have all the details but—" he hesitates, clearly a little conflicted on sharing. "—there was a hit on the mother. The two were compromised somehow. Someone found out about them and tried to take them out. Maybe for revenge on Adrik, but no one ever claimed responsibility. Adrik moved Rory into the mansion full time a little over a year ago, for her safety."

"Shit." Liam's eyes are on the floor.

Koen's silent.

"Was she there?" I ask Alex. "Rory?"

"For the hit?" he asks.

I nod.

"Yeah, she was home from school on holiday, a couple of weeks before graduation. But she was supposed to be at the rink. It was only luck that Rory survived it. She spent weeks in the hospital." He looks between us before uttering the words, "Car bomb." My jaw clenches. Our father was killed the same way.

"That's a tough go," Liam whispers, his eyes on me.

"Yeah, but most mafia kids have similar sad tales." Koen shakes his head, reminding us not to feel bad for our enemy. "It only makes her more valuable as a bargaining chip. Adrik clearly cares for her." He levels a glare in my direction.

That's fair. "It's not like I knew I was bringing Aurora Kostalova into our family home, Koen." I turn back to Alex. "How close are she and Adrik? Would he have confided anything in her?"

It's been weeks since the hit on our father. Alex hasn't been able to turn up any concrete evidence to prove it was Adrik, other than Declan O'Rourke's death being advantageous for the Bratva. The skin trade within the city, which our father was firmly against, had exploded in the wake of his death. Hockey season's right around the corner and I need this shit wrapped the fuck up.

"I don't know." Alex shrugs. "I'm hardly ever allowed in the house and they're never out in public together. She never talks about him. They could be, but it's hard to say. Adrik's a hard guy to read."

He's got that right. Adrik's most dangerous quality is that no one ever knows how he's going to react. When you think he's going to bob, he weaves, and when you think he's about to weave, he blows all of it to pieces.

Koen stands up, checking the time on his watch. "Aidan, you keep working her over. If she knows anything, we need to get it out of her." He swings his head in Alex's direction. "It's good to finally know what the fuck you do for the Russians, Alex. But we did say 'need-to-know'."

Getting Alex as far as we have into the Bratva has been no simple task. When his mother died, our parents took him in, raising the lad right alongside us. But around the age of fifteen, his father suddenly made an appearance. Fresh off the boat from Russia, he took his son away from the Irish, ensuring the Bratva would toughen him up.

But Alex's loyalties remain with us, and he's happy to play both sides of the coin. It's a risky job, should his duality be discovered.

Koen continues, "I will see what kind of deal we might extract from Adrik using our little bargaining chip."

I nod in agreement, though my thoughts are elsewhere.

"Aidan and I need to get the fuck to practice before Coach

benches both our asses." Liam closes his laptop and starts herding me toward the door.

"No one goes into that room until I get back." I don't move until each one of them agrees.

Aurora Kostalova is *mine*.

Mine alone to deal with.

23

HELP!

RORY

I must have fallen asleep because when I open my eyes, it's so dark I can barely see. The only light filling the room is from the garden outside. The string lights scattered throughout the trees cast a soft glow through the windows.

My shoulders ache from my arms being stretched out over my head all night. I move my head from side to side as I again test out my restraints. I'd spent hours screaming and tugging on them. My wrists are raw from my efforts and I can see blood smeared across the white sheets beneath them. The slight spinning sensation in my head as I move has me instantly on edge.

No.

The stupid headaches have plagued me since my concussion last year. I can't get a migraine now, not while I'm stuck on my back on this mattress. There isn't enough slack in the chains to fully roll from one side to the other.

Lifting my head, I let out a groan when my vision suddenly

dips and rolls. The vertigo quickly worsens. The room spins around me, and I choke on a stifled sob.

"Help." My little plea is far too soft for anyone to hear. Not that anyone would come, anyway.

I shut my eyes tight, but the sensation of moving follows me. It's work to clear my throat enough to try again, fighting a cotton feeling in my mouth, my throat hoarse and scratchy from hours of screaming.

"Help." My cry is a little louder this time, but nowhere near loud enough. Swallowing hard, I lift my head and project my voice, this time achieving the volume I need. "Help, someone, please!" I call, a newfound desperation in my voice.

When my stomach rolls, another sob escapes me, along with a few tears. They stream down my cheek and into my ear. Lifting my head again costs me. The spinning worsens, and nausea becomes a brand new concern.

I need my medicine. I *need* it. Ever since the accident, I carry it with me always. A grade 3 concussion can fuck with you long term. The migraines are one of the *complications* that have lingered. They've improved, but I'm fairly certain stress is a trigger. *And I'm fucking stressed.*

My meds are in my backpack. I don't know where it is now but I know I saw Jimmy pick it up when they took me from the club. It's a long shot it's even here. Probably tossed out when they found nothing of value inside. It's an even longer shot if I can convince Aidan or one of his brothers to give it to me.

The world tilts again and a familiar metallic taste floods my mouth. I squeeze my lips shut and try breathing deeply to will away the nausea. *I will not throw up. I will not throw up.* My skin is hot all over, feverish. Another violent lurch of vertigo and the tears are in full-on stream mode. *I'm going to throw up.*

With the last of my strength, I let out a scream of fear. "Aidan! Aidan, *please!*" I hate how desperate I sound, but it's the truth. *If he doesn't help me...*

My eyes fly open at the sound of the door opening. Squinting through tears, a wave of relief rolls through me at the sight of Aidan's irritated face illuminated by the soft light of the hall.

"As much as I love hearing you beg, Kostalova," he drawls, "some of us are trying to sleep."

I blink at him, my head spinning too much to form any of the words I need to say.

The annoyance on his face only grows, and he turns to leave, his hand on the door as he starts to close it behind him.

No.

"Stop. Please *Aidan...*" My voice is shaking with fear. I'd like to think the emotion in it appeals to his better nature, but his face is stone cold when he turns back around to face me.

"I swear to God, Rory, don't make me gag you—" He takes a few steps into the room, coming closer.

"My—my pills. I need my pills. *Please.* Backpack. Orange bottle." I rush the words out, no longer capable of full sentences. My head is in full spins now, stomach rolling violently; the metallic taste in my mouth growing stronger.

He stops in the middle of the room, studying me. His eyes narrow into a glare of suspicion. "I don't have time for this—" He turns back toward the door...

That's when it happens. I lose the vice grip I have on myself and have just enough time to throw my head to the side before my stomach empties itself. All over the bed. All over me. I forget all about Aidan, choking on vomit while trying to get much needed oxygen into my lungs.

There's a brief reprieve before it starts again. I inhale sharply, my throat burning with acid.

Suddenly, there are hands in my hair, pulling the strands away from my face. I heave again and my entire body shakes from the violence of my sickness. One of my hands is freed and then the other, and next thing I know, I'm being rolled onto my side.

I have a vague sense of Aidan's voice shouting in the background, but it's as if I'm underwater, unable to make out any of the sound. I only hear muffled noises that seem so very far away. My vision fades in and out of black and I pause, my entire body trembling, while I wait to see if I'll be sick again.

"Breathe. Deep breaths," Aidan instructs. His voice is soft in my ear, his hands still in my hair. One hand holds it away from my face while the other gently strokes the strands, almost soothingly.

"Liam!" Aidan turns toward the door before shouting again toward the hallway. I flinch at the rise in volume and feel him pause.

"I got it, I got it—" Liam hurries into the room. His eyes are wide as he takes in the sight of me before dropping them back to the black backpack he's holding in his hands.

I blink at the familiar bag while he rummages through it. Another wave of dizziness hits me and my body tenses as I brace myself. Aidan stiffens beside me.

"C'mon man," Aidan mutters impatiently.

"Okay, I think this is it—here—" Liam thrusts something at Aidan. I exhale in relief as the rattling sounds of pills bouncing around a container hits my ears.

Aidan takes the bottle, quickly skimming over the directions before popping off the lid and dumping two small white pills into his palm. I want to reach for them but can't seem to make my arm move.

He leans in. His gaze holding mine as he gives me a slow nod. "Bottoms up, Kostalova." I open my mouth, letting him drop the pills inside. He follows up with a few sips of water. I swallow deeply. My body shivers with relief, as if it knows help is on the way.

We wait in silence for several long minutes. Liam must have slipped out of the room at some point.

My rapid breathing finally evens out, body relaxing as the vertigo ebbs away. The meds provided quick relief.

"Better?" Aidan asks, the sound of his voice only slightly jarring in the tense silence.

I look up at him, nodding hesitantly. Uncertain what happens next.

"Good." His green eyes are bright in the warm garden lights, right before he strips off my clothes.

24

DON'T OVERTHINK IT

AIDAN

I'd thought she was faking it. I'd tried ignoring her when her cries for help woke me from the first couple of hours of sleep I'd gotten in days.

The second time I heard her call out, I sighed begrudgingly, pushing back the covers. I took my time and stopped by the bathroom to splash some cold water on my face, noticing the dark circles ringing my eyes. Physical proof of my exhaustion.

The sound of my name from down the hall elicits an unfamiliar physical reaction deep inside me, a twisting feeling in my chest that leaves me anxious. I don't understand the reaction and so it pisses me off. I stomp down the hall, fully prepared to tape *Aurora's* pretty little mouth shut so I can get some sleep. Until I lay my eyes on her...

She's pale. *Deathly pale...* Her eyes shut tight, exactly where I left her hours ago.

Something's wrong.

When she expels the contents of her stomach, I rush to her side, pulling her hair back to keep it out of the mess and turning her head so she doesn't aspirate. I shout for Liam, knowing Alex had gone back to the Bratva and Koen's out overseeing the latest warehouse shipment.

She mumbles something about pills in her backpack in between heaves. It's here, I remember it. I gave it to Liam when we were trying to figure out her connection to the Bratva.

My brother appears in the doorway, his hair tousled from sleep but his face alert. His eyes scan the room, looking from me to Rory. I explain what I'm looking for and he nods once before disappearing again.

I skim the label on the bottle: *Take two pills as needed for migraine.* Together, we get the pills into her and as soon as they are down her throat, her body sags with tired relief.

When I think she's through the worst of it, I get to work. I slide her little velvet skirt off and almost get her tights halfway to her knees before she realizes what's happening. She lets out a little scream and weakly tries to kick at me.

I level her a look saying *knock it off,* and she quits fighting. She shrinks back but lets me tug the tights the rest of the way down her legs, leaving them bare. She curls them back under her, trying to sit up to get enough leverage to propel herself away from me, but she falters, too weak to manage it.

I curl my fingers under her sweatshirt.

Rory slaps at my hands. "What are you doing?" The pure fear in her voice gives me pause. My hands close around her wrists as she tries to push me away. I wrap them slightly higher up her arm to avoid the raw and bleeding marks she's given herself by tugging against the cuffs. She's so weak she's shaking from the effort to fight me off. I reach again for the bottom of her hoodie, trying to tug it up and over her head. It's a struggle to work it off of her while keeping her pinned.

"You're covered in vomit. Stop wiggling." I growl out my frustration, shifting so I'm straddling her now, trapping her legs under me and pinning her hips to the mattress. She doesn't listen, and continues squirming beneath me until she grinds up against something hard.

She stills.

Her eyes go wide, which elicits a little smirk out of me. "Or by all means, keep wiggling around, Angel. I'd be happy to darken those white wings of yours. Though I imagine those fallen feathers have already turned black."

She grits her teeth but remains still, giving me the opportunity to tug the hoodie and her tank top off. They're tossed to the floor. She trembles under me, now only in her bra and underwear. White and lacy. Perfectly accentuating her toned, athletic body.

God help me.

Rory lets out a sigh of relief when I swing my leg off of her, only to let out a squeak of surprise when I scoop her up. She goes rigid in my arms when her bare skin hits my chest. I'd slept shirtless. My skin burns in every place we touch.

Too weak to fight back, she keeps her eyes on me, while I keep mine trained forward. Her pretty blues are too cloudy with anxiety.

"Don't overthink it, Kostalova. You can't stay here. Both the bed and you are a mess."

She looks away; her pale cheeks flushing pink with embarrassment. She shouldn't feel embarrassed about anything. It's not like she got sick on purpose.

I carry her out of the guest room and into the hall, unsure of where exactly I'm taking her until we end up in my room.

I make a beeline for the bathroom, nudging the soft overhead sink light on with my shoulder. I avoid the harsh overhead light so as not to trigger another migraine. It casts a warm glow around the room. I set Rory down gently on the wide edge of the tub, supporting her weight until I'm sure she's stable.

My private bathroom is far more accommodating than the one in the guest room. It's large and open, with a breath-taking view of the night sky through the glass ceiling. The best part about this room is the large jacuzzi tub sitting to the left of a huge walk-in shower.

Reaching past her, all too aware of our proximity, I twist the knob until steaming hot water pours out. I dump in a few sweet smelling oils I must have stolen from my sister at some point.

Soothing vanilla and cinnamon scents swirl with the steam rising off of the bath.

Rory shifts uneasily where she sits on the edge of the tub, gripping the edge as if she's teetering on the edge of a high-dive. The sound of running water fills what would be an awkward silence. She seems lost in thought, and I let my eyes roam over her body.

She's perfect.

At first glance, she appears thin and delicate. She's tiny and was swimming in the oversized hoodie she'd had on. But underneath, her body ripples with toned muscle and definition. *An athlete.* Like me, she's spent hours working on this body in pursuit of her sport. Pushing it to its limits and then some.

She catches me checking her out and gives me an icy glare.

My mouth twists into a sly grin. Fire lights behind those blue eyes and I can't explain how good it makes me feel seeing the fight spark back to life inside her. She'd looked halfway to death when I'd found her in the bedroom.

Rory's gaze flickers anxiously between the water and me. The tub nearly full," she whispers, "I can't bathe with you in here."

I lean casually against the cool stone of the bathroom wall, crossing my arms. "And why not?" I ask, not able to resist the opportunity to fuck with her.

"Because... you... I...," she begins, stumbling over her words. Her eyes drop to her nearly naked body, already on full display from where she's perched on the tub wall.

"Can you get yourself into the tub?" Doubt is evident in my tone, but I also throw in a single eyebrow raise.

She opens her mouth with a quick retort, but snaps it shut, suddenly unsure herself. There's a couple of feet between where she currently sits and the water. I can still see her body trembling from where I stand across the room.

I nod to myself in confirmation and step forward, easing her gently into my arms again before she can protest and walking her over to the water. Slowly, I lower her down, her body relaxing once submerged in the water's warmth. I threw some magnesium salt in there too, for good measure. She could use it.

She leans back in the tub as the water's warmth floods her senses. Eyes closed, she lets out a soft moan of pleasure. And fuck if I don't need to leave this room right now. At risk of developing a hard on at the sight of the Russian angel, clothed in scraps of white lace and soaking wet in my bedroom's bathtub.

Rory's eyes fly open as if remembering where she is.

I do my best to hide the smile tugging at the corner of my

mouth by opening the cabinet to my left and pulling out a thick white towel. I place it within her reach.

"Clean yourself up, remove those..." I gesture to her bra and panties, which are unfortunately still attached to her body. I pull my gaze back up to large, stormy eyes. "Pull the drain and use the towel to dry yourself off. Let me know when you're done and I'll come back to help you out."

She doesn't say anything, sitting very still. Considering me. Apprehension and a few other emotions dance in her eyes.

Reluctantly, I tear myself away and leave her to it, leaving the door open a crack behind me so I'll be able to hear her if she calls.

Back in my room, I release a slow breath, not quite sure what to do with myself. I change into a clean pair of shorts and sink down onto the bed, resting my elbows on my knees, and wondering what the fuck it is I'm doing.

Rory is a Kostalov. I remind myself.

Regardless, I need her in good condition in case Koen decides on a good trade with the Bratva.

That's all this is.

25

IF YOU TOUCH ME, I'LL KILL YOU

RORY

*T*he warm water is heaven on my aching body. I slip off my underwear with reservation, uncertain if Aidan will stick to his word and stay out of the bathroom. He'd left the door open a crack when he'd left, and I keep one eye on it as I sink deeper into the water.

When he doesn't stick his nosy head back in after several minutes, my shoulders sag in relief, the tension finally easing out of them. The medicine got to work quickly and the dizziness and vertigo have finally cleared and, with it, the awful nausea.

I soak for a while, pushing the limits of his generosity, letting the sweet scent of vanilla and cinnamon seep deep into my pores. The scent is far more feminine than masculine. I can't help but wonder why Aidan has it.

Does he have a girlfriend?

He's a made man. He could be married for all I know... Aidan O'Rourke, second in line for the Irish throne now that his brother has taken over as boss.

I look around for other feminine traces. The room is neat and clean, which isn't what I'd expect from a single Irish hockey player in their early twenties. Though I'm fairly certain the room belongs to him.

It keeps with the industrial theme of the entire apartment; metal accents, and gorgeous reclaimed wood floors. Aidan might be an ass, but he has good taste in decor.

I allow myself a few more minutes to enjoy the warm water before sitting up. I'm feeling a little stronger, but there's a lingering pounding in the back of my head. The meds have a tendency to make me drowsy. The need to sleep is hanging over me like a dark cloud.

Reaching down, I pull the tub stopper, letting the water drain out. I use the thick, warm towel to dry myself off, wrapping myself carefully in it once finished. Realizing I can't put my soaked undergarments back on, I stare at the door with uncertainty, feeling awkward about calling Aidan back in here.

The walls of the tub are high, higher than your average bathtub. I contemplate whether or not I can get myself out. My legs quiver at the thought.

Aidan must sense what I'm thinking, because the sound of his voice outside the door nearly sends me jolting into the metal water spout.

"Finished up in there, Angel?" he calls through the crack.

I frown at the name he's tacked on there with a slightly mocking accent. "Yep." My answer is short and clipped. I ensure my towel is well and truly secured before bracing both of my palms on the edge of the tub. As I pull myself up, my muscles protest, screaming out as I push them, my body still overwhelmingly weak and shaky.

Aidan pushes the door open in time to see what I am up to,

just before my legs give out. He catches me before I hit the tub floor, showing off his sheer strength when he deftly swings me up into his arms, like I weigh nothing at all. He shoots me an irritated look that I give right back to him before he carries me out of the bathroom.

Looking around, I find myself in a large bedroom. The high lofted ceilings and exposed brick give it the illusion of being even larger than it is. Wood furnishings warm up the industrial space and Aidan's decorated the walls with a few black and white abstract paintings.

A couple of older framed photographs sit atop his dresser. I scan them as we pass by, recognizing one where Aidan stands with the rest of his siblings—Koen, Liam and Reagan—next to an older man I don't recognize. He wears a broad smile and has an arm wrapped around both Liam and Reagan. He must be their father, Declan O'Rourke. *Could Adrik really have killed Aidan's father?*

I'm too preoccupied by my thoughts to notice we aren't leaving the room. No, instead, Aidan is heading directly for his bed. The second I realize his intentions, I let out a shriek of protest, kicking my legs right before he drops me unceremoniously onto silky black sheets.

I stare up at him, all too aware how only a towel separates our bodies. But as soon as he drops me, he turns away.

My heart is racing in my chest and while keeping my eyes on Aidan, I grope around blindly, trying to get ahold of a blanket, a sheet—anything to pull over me.

Aidan spends a moment rummaging through his closet before finding whatever it is he's looking for. He heads back in my direction and I desperately try to catch a glimpse of what he holds in his hands, fearing more chains or ropes or *worse...*

"Arms up."

I shake my head weakly in protest, unable to fight the tears from welling back up in my eyes. He sighs impatiently before lifting them himself. My eyes shut tight and I bite into my lip. I know I'm too weak to fight him off, to stop him from taking whatever it is he wants.

Soft fabric against my skin is a surprise. Aidan works the oversized hoodie down my arms and over my head before letting it drop, covering the rest of my body. It's soft and warm, in the way only an old, well-worn hoodie is.

I blink back up at him in surprise.

He points at where the hem of the sweatshirt falls on my thigh. "The towel..." He motions with his hand that I should give it to him. Awkwardly, I shimmy the towel down and hand it over to Aidan. While the hoodie covers all the important bits, I still feel exposed with nothing under it.

He tosses the towel in a hamper by the door and opens one of the dresser drawers. Grabbing a pair of black boxer briefs, he tosses them at me. Stunned, they catch me right in the face. He offers no explanation before he disappears out into the hall, giving me privacy, I realize.

Not trusting him for a second, I eye the door warily while doing my best to tug on the boxer briefs as fast as possible. Once I have them on, I feel slightly better now I'm fully covered. The briefs are too big for me, but after a few rolls of the waistband, they stay up on my hips all on their own. *He wouldn't have given me clothes just to rip them off again...right?*

Aidan returns a few minutes later with a couple of bottles of electrolyte water he must have on hand for hockey. He tosses one to me. This time I catch it, before he cracks open his own and downs it in one go. While he hydrates, I have an uninhibited view of him. Warm light seeps into the bedroom from the open bathroom door, which only helps to highlight the rippled masterpiece that is his body.

I would expect as much from any serious pro athlete, but the sight of Aidan's bare chest, covered in dark ink, has my mouth running dry despite the water. And as much as I want to, I cannot tear my eyes away. They trail over chiseled abs and a sculpted chest, to his firm jaw and piercing green eyes. Green eyes watching mine, a slight trace of amusement in them.

Aidan smiles over the water bottle in his mouth and points down. I drop my gaze to find the water bottle he gave me still unopened in my hands. Feeling my cheeks flush red, I busy myself twisting the cap and take a drink. The cool water is a sweet relief against my sore throat. Between the bath and the water, I'm feeling much better.

Clutching the plastic bottle in my hand, I sit stone still atop the bed watching Aidan move around the room, nervous about where we go from here. My body stiffens even further when he suddenly plops down on the mattress beside me, sliding beneath the sheets.

"What are you doing?" I squeak out at a far higher pitch than normal.

"Well, I *was* trying to go to sleep..." Aidan answers pointedly. He rests the back of his head in his hands, his arms spread out across the pillow.

"Not here?" This time, my panic was much harder to hide.

"Yes, here." He rolls onto his side so he can see me. I'm still sitting up on the bed, fisting the sheets tightly in my hands. "It is *my* bed after all."

"Okay...well, should I go back to—" I start shifting out of

the bed and freeze when I feel his hand close lightly around my arm, stopping me.

"Kostalova," he says my last name as though exasperated, "you're sleeping here—" He gives a light tug and I fall back on the bed beside him. "—Where I can keep an eye on you." He pauses, regarding me. "Well, that... and you threw up all over the only guest bed so..." He shrugs and releases me, re-assuming his previously relaxed position, stretching out across the mattress. The enormous bed shrinks dramatically with him inside it.

We lie there together in dark silence for a few minutes. "You're not going to tie me back up?" The question practically bursts out of me and I could kick myself for saying it aloud. But despite my exhaustion, I'm on edge and there's no way I'll be able to sleep if I don't find out.

It's quiet for a beat before Aidan responds, "Do I need to?"

I open my mouth, but then realize I don't have a good answer. Do I want him to? *No. Of course not.* Should he? *Probably.*

Aidan lets out a little chuckle as if coming to the same conclusion. "The exits are code entry only, we're twenty stories up and you can barely walk after what I'm guessing was a massive migraine attack. I'd say have at it princess—*or* we can call a truce for the night. And both get some much needed goddamn sleep."

I turn to my right to find him watching me. Searching his face, I try to decipher if this is a trick, or he's trying to lull me into a false sense of security. But I either can't find anything or I can't read him.

He's right about one thing, I *am* exhausted. My eyelids are growing heavier by the second. I curl my fingers around the long sleeves of Aidan's hoodie and settle deeper into his bed. His very comfortable and very *soft* bed. Making my decision.

Aidan's right, I'm not going anywhere in this condition. Might as well bank some sleep and see what opportunities might present themselves tomorrow.

"Fine." I fight the sleep dragging me under like a riptide, struggling to keep my eyes open. "But if you touch me, I'll kill you," I mutter with as much conviction as I can gather. My words fail to have the impact I wish them to.

Another low laugh escapes him. "Fair enough, little lion. Fair enough."

26

TOP SHELF

AIDAN

*T*hese early morning practices are killing me.

They're nothing new. Hockey is a sport filled with a lot of early mornings and late, late nights. But I'm not usually also a current reigning member of the city's dark underworld during the height of the pre-season.

My work with the family over the last few weeks since Dad's death has really been taking it out of me. Both jobs require my full focus and in trying to do both, I can't help but feel like I'm coming up short—on both sides.

Colt cuts down the ice at a blazing speed, flying past our offensive line as if they're standing still. I clock Liam to my right, ready to engage should Colt go his way.

But I know he's coming to me.

King attempts to fake me out. His eyes read right and so do his shoulders—for a moment. But at the last second, he dekes past Liam, surging toward the goal from the left. But I read him like an open book back on the blue line and knock the puck away from him with a simple poke check.

He doesn't expect it, and sails past me, leaving the ice wide open. Picking up the puck Colt lost, I fly for the opposite end. The opposing team is in the middle of a line change and so I only have to stick handle past two of them in order to sink the puck top shelf into the left corner.

West, our starting goalie, shakes his head at me before reaching out to give me a fist bump as I circle their net. "Respect."

"You're still a brick wall Cavanaugh; that one just slipped through." I tease him with a little wink and a smile on my face.

Coach blows his whistle, and everyone heads for the bench, circling up on the ice.

James McIntyre. One of the best coaches in hockey right now. Tough but fair, difficult to read because he hardly ever shows emotion. Personally, I prefer his level head to a coach who blows his top after every goal against or player mistake. McIntyre's cool gaze trails over the lot of us. His silence builds anticipation before his gaze finally settles on Colt.

"What the fuck was that, King? You make that mistake in a game and you'll find yourself benched for the rest of it." He frowns before giving a disappointed shake of his head. "Cocky and arrogant. O'Rourke had your number from a mile away. *Anticipate* that." Then he turns to me. "Nice goal, O'Rourke. Let's see more of those."

"Yes, sir." I grin, letting it widen when I catch Colt glaring at me. I raise my water bottle to him in a fake "cheers" before pouring the rest of it over my sweaty face.

Hockey is a dog eat dog world. But it's important we have trust within our team. Since the Breakers are a new team, we've yet to establish any. This year's Breakers are far from it.

For whatever reason, Colt King decided he hated me day

one. And Reid Kincaid and Colt go way back. My relationship with two of the major players on the first line offense has been frosty at best. With only a few short weeks remaining until our season opener, we have yet to work out our shit and it shows.

Still. I've been nothing short of civil to the guy. It's Colt and Reid with the problem. A problem they need to work the fuck out.

Coach talks for a few minutes more about a few upcoming pre-season games and events before releasing us for the day. I take a turn for the locker rooms, but I stop when I hear my name called out.

"O'Rourke, hang back a second, eh?" McIntyre's thick Canadian accent showing.

He waits while the rest of the team clears out. Liam gives me a side glance before disappearing down the tunnel to the locker rooms. I shift restlessly on my skates. I'd left little Kostalova asleep in my bed this morning and need to get back to the loft to figure out what the fuck to do with her.

"Today was better, but I still get the sense you're distracted..." Coach's eyes narrow on me like he's trying to read my mind to find out exactly where the block is.

I try to refocus my attention on my coach. *Me? distracted? Nah...* Couldn't have anything to do with the fact I woke up this morning curled around a little Russian angel, nose buried in long, golden hair. I can still smell that heavenly scent. A mixture of vanilla and cinnamon from the bath, mixed with something else... something purely divine and innately Rory.

"Sorry Coach, I'll have my shit together before the Falcons game," I promise him. Our first pre-season opener is against our bitter rivals, the New York Falcons.

"See that you do, O'Rourke." He pauses, studying me with

an unreadable expression on his face. "I know the recent loss of your father has been hard on you and your—family." I do my best to keep my expression blank. Coach is well aware of my roots, but seeing as how both Liam and I have stayed out of the family business the past few years, it's hardly been an issue.

"Don't let yourself get distracted from what matters. This season's make or break for you... My recommendation only goes so far."

It's a contract year and I'm on the chopping block. Some of it is warranted, but most of it's not. The team owners don't like me. I know Coach has my back but like he said—*his recommendation only goes so far.*

"I need you focused, Aidan. No distractions." His hazel eyes flash with a warning.

I give him a stiff nod to let him know I've heard him. Everything I've ever wanted is almost within my grasp. A contract with the Breakers keeps me in the city for the next few years. It's all I want.

I *need* this business with the family wrapped up so I can get back to the life I've worked so hard to carve out for myself. I'd chosen hockey over the mob a long time ago, and my family supported my decision. My *father* supported my decision. Claimed Liam and I had a gift and it would be a "damn shame" if we let it go to waste.

"No distractions," I repeat, reminding myself as much as affirming my coach.

A certain Russian princess flashes into my brain as I speak. Now, more than ever, the little angel needed to *go.*

27

DON'T FEED THE CAPTIVES

RORY

I wake to an empty bed.

Blinking against the bright light of the morning, streaming in from the many windows in the room, I realize I slept in.

After having early coaching sessions for almost as long as I can remember, I'm usually up before the sun every day.

If the clock in Aidan's room is to be believed, it is 9:45 a.m.

Sitting up, I shift my feet to the floor. Taking it slow, in case of any lingering vertigo. Once I realize I'm no longer dizzy, I breathe out a sigh of relief. Only a mild headache remains— like the kind you get when you've cried too many tears.

Looking around, I can see the bed is not the only thing empty. I'm alone in Aidan's room.

It's peaceful. The warm sun of the late morning streams through the glass ceiling and windows, the sounds of birds chirping from the courtyard below. I notice Aidan's room also overlooks the private garden.

The light of day reveals a surprisingly neat bedroom. Decorated in dark greens and charcoals, it reminds me of the man who calls it home.

My stomach growls, reminding me that basic needs exist. Glancing around the room, I don't see a tray or any food left out; only a bottle of water by the bed. My attention slowly slides to the hall door. It's closed.

I chew my bottom lip and stare at the door. It's probably locked. But before I lose my nerve, I slowly cross the room to test the handle.

Unlocked.

I suck in a breath and blink at the door I've cracked open in disbelief. Opening it just enough to poke my head out, I find the hallway empty, and the rest of the loft quiet. Except for the distant drone of a tv further down the hall.

Where is everyone?

Aidan told me the exterior doors are code locked, and we are twenty stories up. *Does that mean I have free rein in the loft?* Though dressed in only Aidan's sweatshirt and boxers, I'm not too keen on leaving this room and strutting about the O'Rourke family stronghold.

Maybe he didn't mean to leave this door open... or think I'd have the balls to leave it.

My stomach growls again, and either way, I'm not about to look a gift horse in the mouth. I step over the threshold and pull the door shut behind me, deciding just as my heart threatens to pound right through my chest.

Escape is on my mind, but my stomach growls again, and food becomes priority. My stomach—and a newfound defiance I didn't have last night—propel me forward. As I tiptoe down the long hallway.

Should I stay in the room like a good little captive and wait to see what the Irish have planned for me? *Probably.* Was I going to? *Nope.*

The sight of Koen on the couch nearly sends me running straight back to Aidan's room. Though smaller than his brother, something about Koen is far more terrifying. I can't quite put my finger on it, but I'm pretty sure it's the complete lack of emotion he shows on his face. A sociopath if I've ever seen one..

I pull back so I'm out of sight, pressed against the wall, listening.

Nothing.

Before I can think better of it, I peek out again at the eldest O'Rourke. He's sprawled out on the sectional—his attention solely focused on the phone in his hands. The TV flashes from above the fireplace, airing the latest hockey highlights.

There's only a couple of feet I need to cross out in the open. If he doesn't look up, I might pass through the room without being caught. *But that's a big if...*

One foot after another, I'm staring so hard at Koen he might just look up from the invisible force of my gaze alone. I swing into the kitchen, nearly collapsing with relief, pressing my back against the wall separating the eldest O'Rourke from me. Clinging to it like it's a lifeline. I don't dare peek out to see if he saw me. Instead, I close my eyes and listen, trying to hear over the sound of my panicked heart's beating for any movement in the living room.

When the sound of Koen storming across the room doesn't come, I open my eyes. Nearly letting out a scream at the sight of the smiling redhead right in front of me.

I have to clasp a hand over my mouth to keep quiet.

Reagan.

My eyes dart around her, taking in the space. Momentarily relieved to find it empty, except for the youngest O'Rourke grinning at me. I can handle Reagan, I think.

She must see the fear in my eyes because she moves slowly, careful to keep her hands where I can see them. Like she's interacting with a wild animal. She touches a single finger to her lips before motioning with the other hand for me to follow her deeper into the kitchen.

Green eyes, so much like her brother's, sparkle with mischief.

I hesitate, stealing a glance behind me at where Koen still lounges out of sight.

Reagan shoots me a reassuring smile, and even though I'm still apprehensive, I follow.

Worst case scenario... She's smaller than I am. I could probably take her if she tried anything...

Reagan leads me past the island, down a half stair and out a gorgeous set of French doors. Right out into the beautiful little garden I've only seen from my window. She shuts the doors behind us carefully before speaking.

"Hungry?" She points to a long wooden table. Nestled in a little grove of climbing roses and set full of delicious looking breakfast options.

My mouth waters at the sight.

"C'mon." She motions me over and I follow obediently. "Help yourself." She takes a seat at the middle of the table and hands me an empty plate.

I take it and plop my ass in the seat across from her, wasting no time loading up on delectable looking French toast and eggs. There's also bacon, hash browns, a few large crumbly muffins and a pitcher of juice, along with a large carafe of coffee.

The first bite of the fluffy French toast nearly sends me sliding out of my chair. It's so damn good. Reagan smiles knowingly, taking a bite of her own.

"Oh my God, this is amazing!" I get out between bites, practically shoving it in. Afraid someone might take it away before I can get enough of it. "Did you make this?"

She grins at me. "Me? God no, I'd sooner burn the house down trying..." She laughs like it's the most ludicrous thing in the world.

Recovering, she tucks a red strand behind her ear before schooling her face. "No, I'm not the domestic type, this—" She gestures to the food, "—this is all Koen."

I freeze mid bite, nearly choking on what's already halfway down my throat.

"*Koen* cooked this?" I stare at the piece of egg on my fork with newfound suspicion.

Reagan shrugs. "Yeah. He can cook like... anything."

I force a swallow, gathering up my nerve. "And—where is everyone else this morning?" I ask, cautiously.

She taps pretty gold painted nails against her chin, thinking... "This time of day? Aidan and Liam are usually still at the rink, but they should be back any minute. Koen usually has breakfast ready for when they have early skates. They're pretty ravenous after practice."

The idea of Koen, a hardened Irish mob boss, cooking up a five-star breakfast to keep his hockey-playing younger brothers fed is a strange thought.

153

"And what about Alexe—err—Alex?" I correct, eyeing the garden doors warily.

Reagan is focused on pouring herself a steaming hot cup of coffee. "Back with the Russians, I think." She waives the carafe at me. "Coffee?"

I nod absently, lost in my thoughts as she fills the mug. When she comes back into focus, she's studying me. Close up, her green eyes are lighter than her brothers, with more hints of amber and gold mixed in.

"Are you really the Bratva Pakhan's daughter?" she whispers like the words themselves are dangerous. The youngest of the notorious Boston Irish family is looking at me with a mix of curiosity and fascination. Not a trace of hatred or ire in her expression.

"Unfortunately," I mumble, cramming in another bite of eggs while keeping a watchful eye on the door.

Reagan raises two perfect eyebrows at my response before letting out a little sigh. "Sounds like being the Bratva princess is about as much fun as being the Irish one..."

Taking my eyes off the door, I study her again.

We're about the same age. Unlike her brothers, an overwhelming sense of goodness surrounds her—warmth. Uncommon in this world we were born into.

"I suppose so," I say, agreeing with her, feeling a tentative bond forming between us as we find common ground. I take a sip of my coffee and my shoulders sag in relief. The dull pounding in my skull lessens as I fill my stomach with food and caffeine.

Very few people could understand the way I was raised and the lifestyle I was compelled to follow. While it had been easy to make friends while I was away at school, I couldn't keep up with them. Couldn't visit friends or have them come to me. Not without putting their lives at risk. The danger was too great.

After a while, I slowly started isolating myself. Aside from Elle, Alexei, and my coaches, there are very few people I interact with daily.

"To mafia bullshit!" Reagan raises her coffee mug, a little smirk on her face. Dimples apparent on her lightly freckled cheeks.

I let out a laugh despite myself. "To the bullshit!" I clink my mug against hers and we both laugh a little harder.

The conversation between us flows from there. I fill my stomach and sit back, enjoying the warmth of the sun on my face, the fresh air, and Reagan's smart mouth. She's unassumingly funny. I liked her immediately. Growing up in the mob hasn't yet tainted her with its dark, ugly claws.

Not like me.

Hanging out with Reagan almost makes me forget the personal hell I'm trapped in.

The sound of a throat clearing has both our heads whipping around, falling silent. Even the birds have the good sense not to chirp under Aidan's predatory gaze.

He stands in the doorway, furious green eyes locked on me.

Nope. Definitely wasn't supposed to leave the bedroom...

He does a quick pass over Reagan, as if checking to see if any harm has come to his little sister by my hand. "What the fuck is this?" He finally fumes after confirming Reagan appears just fine.

I'm rigid in my seat, but Reagan leans back in her chair, the picture of nonchalance, rolling her eyes at her brother.

Aidan's own eyes narrow at his sister. "Where is Koen?" he demands, his voice loud enough to summon Koen himself. The eldest O'Rourke's confused expression hardens as he takes in the sight of the two of us sitting together in the garden.

"What the fuck is this?" His Irish accent is the strongest I've heard it. Seeming to come out of the O'Rourkes more so when they're angry.

"Asshole number one already said that," Reagan points out, and I stare at her in horror. Shocked by the boldness of her attitude. Thinking of all the ways Niko would have killed me dead if I ever spoke to him like she just did. "Would you guys like to join us for breakfast?"

"Reagan, for God's sake," Aidan lets out, pinching his nose, clearly exasperated. "Get away from her." He motions to me, but I narrow my eyes, stealing a bit of my new friend's attitude.

Reagan sinks deeper in her chair and folds her arms across her chest. "You guys act like you have a Bratva soldier in this house." She shakes her head and her eyes lock on mine. "Rory's a girl. She didn't choose to be born to the Russian Mafia any more than I want to be part of the stupid Mob."

Both brothers stare at their little sister, rendered speechless. Both of them watch me with a warning in their eyes and so I sit *very* still. Fearful the slightest little movement from me might end with a bullet in my head.

The two brothers fall forward unsteadily as someone pushes through the middle of them.

Liam strolls in, head held high, taking in the tense scene in the garden before shooting me a wink. "Rory, good to see ya."

He struts forward, dropping into the seat next to Reagan and reaches for some French toast. He eyes the red little minx next to him with feigned disappointment. "Reagan, Reagan, Reagan, didn't Aidan and Koen ever teach you not to feed the captives?" He mocks, grinning at me.

28

MADE MAN

AIDAN

The panic I initially felt in my chest seeing Reagan alone with Rory slowly ebbs away as I sit and listen to my sister carry on in that carefree way only she can about everything and nothing all at the same time. As if the O'Rourke family casually having breakfast with a Kostalova is a normal, everyday occurrence.

I learn Reagan and Rory have quite a bit in common. I guess I shouldn't be surprised. They're around the same age; both girls grew up carrying the weight of their family's sins.

Rory's nervous. Her eyes keep flitting to mine before she responds to my siblings' questions. She's constantly taking my temp, gauging my reaction, even though she's the subject of Koen's hard stare from across the table; he's pissed she snuck right past him. When my sister takes a wild turn into the latest drama on this season of The Bachelor, I put Rory out of her misery.

I stand, the movement drawing the attention of everyone at the table. "As much fun as this has been Rae, breakfast is done and we have business to attend to. *Rory*, if you don't mind accompanying me back to my room?"

I don't miss the slight flash of fear in her eyes before she buries it away, steeling her spine and rising gracefully from the table. Even pushing her chair neatly back in.

"Thanks for the company, Reagan." Rory offers a tentative smile toward my sister, who beams back at her. *Fuck, that's going to be a problem.* But before circling around to my side, Rory turns to face Koen. "That was the best French toast I've ever had. Thank you for cooking."

Koen looks up at her with an odd expression on his face, not sure how to react to the girl we're holding captive in my bedroom thanking him for the food. He finally settles on a small nod before his eyes slide to meet mine as Rory passes between us. We exchange a look before I follow her silent form down the hall to my room.

She hesitates before entering, as if afraid the room might swallow her whole. But she lifts her chin and steps inside, walking a few feet before turning to face me.

I shut the door behind me and watch as she takes another step back, creating more distance between us. The sight of her in my old Breakers hoodie is something else, and I can't tear my eyes away from her if I wanted to.

"So, where do we go from here?" she asks, a slight waver in her voice. She's nervous as hell, but she's trying not to look it.

"I'm not sure..." I tell her honestly, crossing my arms and widening my stance. After everything that happened last night, I'm not sure I can bring myself to chain her back up in order to torture the information I need out of her. "How often do you get migraines like that?"

Her face pinches, and she looks uncomfortable. "Not too

often—it's worse when I'm stressed... a side effect of the concussion..." she trails off, breaking our gaze. *From the car bomb*, I finish her sentence, having read through Liam's research thoroughly. Rory had been fifteen feet away when the bomb went off, killing her mother instantly and nearly killing her. She'd been lucky to walk away...

Her eyes linger on the photo frames I have sitting along my window sill. She's staring at one in particular; the one of my siblings and me with our dad. The last one we took, in fact. When she speaks, her voice is quiet, tired even, "I don't know if my father had anything to do with your father's death." She peeks up at me.

I stay quiet, letting her continue.

"I stay far away from the—from the family business." She says, carefully reading my face. Tensed like a deer in the sights of a wolf. Ready to bolt at the first sign of danger.

I nod, "I should've known as much." In my anger over finding out who she actually was, I hadn't considered what information she may or may not have access to. Seeing her with Reagan at breakfast got me thinking. We keep our sister as far away from the family business as we can.

The way she's looking at me... Koen and I need to rethink our play here. I know without a doubt, I will not be able to put a bullet in this girl. But using Rory to leverage a deal with the Russians may only alienate the Irish further. We need to be working on alliances, not pushing the Russians further into the Italians' hands.

There's a knock at my door. Both of us turn right as Koen bursts in, not waiting for a response, Liam close behind him. I can tell by both of their faces something's happened.

"What is it?" I push off the bureau I was leaning against and see Rory, skirting toward the left side of the room, putting me between her and my brothers.

Interesting.

"Alex's been made."

Everything stops. My blood goes cold. "Where is he?" I pray for the slight chance he escaped before the Russians could get a hold of him.

"The Bratva have him." Koen's face is grave as he confirms my worst fears, a tortured look in his eyes. It's rare for my brother to show emotion, but the Russians have Alex.

"Trade me." Her voice startles me. Startles all of us. I'd almost forgotten she was in the room after Koen's news.

All eyes turn to Rory. Worry clouds her blue eyes. Her mouth tightens into a thin line. "The Bratva will trade Alexei for me—Alex," she nods, certain of her words, "but you need to make the call now before..."

All of us know what the Russians do to traitors. The same thing we would. Admitting to stealing the Russian's little angel may kick off a new war between the Irish and the Bratva, but it's likely Alex's only chance.

Koen looks to both Liam and me before stalking out of the room, his phone in hand.

"Looks like you found your ticket home, princess." There's a slight resignation in my tone. I don't know why, but I have an overwhelming urge to lock her back up in my room and never let her go. I shove it away, focusing on my worry for Alex.

Rory frowns, her eyes trailing over to my wall of windows and she stops at the one looking out over the small courtyard garden. Her fingers clench and unclench at her sides several times before she lets out a steadying breath and turns to face me.

"When do we leave?"

29

DON'T EVEN THINK ABOUT IT

RORY

*L*iam drives while Koen makes call after call, rounding up everyone he can on such short notice.

He got through to the Russians right away. Koen had my father's full attention once he learned they had his daughter currently in their possession. They arrange a trade immediately to get Alexei out of the Bratva's hands before more damage can be done. So far, all we have is my father's word Alexei is still alive.

Aidan is like a live wire beside me in the back of Liam's SUV. I'm aware of every little movement. The rise and fall of my chest, the slight ticking of his jaw, my heart racing a little faster each time he shifts slightly closer to me.

It's good news Alexei is alive at all. I might not know a lot about the inner workings of this dark world, but even I know what they do to traitors.

Alexei may be one of the Irish, but for the past couple of months, he had become someone I could trust. He didn't leer at me or crack lewd jokes when my father wasn't watching. He was respectful, protective, and he was *nice*. The thought of Alexei enduring any of what the Bratva is capable of has my stomach rolling.

I shift anxiously in my seat. The movement catches Aidan's attention and our eyes meet. I don't know what it is I see in those deep green pools, but it only fuels my lingering confusion.

The Irish shot up the club, stole me. They chained me up, interrogated me, but somehow I'm more reluctant to go home. If anything, the O'Rourkes have opened my eyes to how isolating and depressing my life had become.

No friends, no boyfriend, no fun. Just training and reading alone in my room.

I need to work harder, keep fighting, and escape my fate before I'm shackled to it by my ring finger.

Liam steers the SUV behind a couple of abandoned warehouse buildings. We're close to the docks and the smell of salt and low tide is heavy in the air. A somber standoff awaits us on the loading dock.

I lean forward to get a better view, searching the line of suits for any sign of Alexei. Not caring that it puts me right across Aidan's lap. He stiffens under me.

It's easy to tell the difference between the Irish and the Bratva. The Irish seem to prefer dark hoodies and leather to suits, and bikes to cars. The Irish half of the circle is full of motorcycles, except for Liam's SUV.

There seems to be a competition over who could bring a bigger show of force. Even with so many men on the dock, it's easy to spot my father and brother. My father is wearing his usual dark suit. My brother is next to him, looking far more imposing than I've ever seen him, a murderous expression on his face that sends a shiver through my body. But there's still one person I don't see...

Aidan lays a reassuring hand on my hip. I twist to look at him.

"He's probably still in one of the cars." His attention is on the Bratva outside.

I nod, unconvinced. I wouldn't put it past my father to double cross the Irish, even at my expense. Sitting back, I twist my fingers anxiously, fidgeting with the sleeves of Aidan's hoodie I'm still wearing.

We pull to a stop, and my father's steel gaze finds me. Letting out a gasp, I scoot deeper into the car seat.

Aidan notices, his already tight expression dipping into a frown. "He can't see you." He wraps a knuckle on the glass window. "Mirrored glass."

Koen speaks up from the front seat. My eyes fall to the black gun he holds in his hand, the other on the door handle. "Rory stays here."

I look at him in surprise. *He used Rory, not "Aurora."*

He waits for both Aidan and me to nod in confirmation before stepping out of the car in unison with Liam, shutting the doors behind them. Aidan's gaze falls back to me, an unreadable expression on his face before he too exits the SUV, joining his brothers.

The three of them walk together, out on the dock. A formidable sight. Aidan and Liam fall back slightly to flank Koen at the center. They stop only once they've closed the distance between the two antagonist groups to about fifteen feet. My father and Niko remain where they stand.

I'm pressed up against the window, scanning, trying to watch all of them at once.

165

"Koen O'Rourke," Adrik dips his chin with a poisonous smile, greeting the eldest Irish son. "I didn't know we were making this a whole family affair," he gestures to Aidan and Liam. "Nice to see Ace and Liam around again. I thought they'd left the *family* business." The smile creeping across my father's face is snake-like.

It's a smile Aidan doesn't return. He's busy keeping his eyes trained on my brother. The latter watches the Irish enforcer with a death glare.

"What my brothers do or don't do is none of your concern." Koen looks around pointedly. "Where's Alexei?" The malice in the Irish boss' eyes might just set the Russians on fire. Koen didn't come to play.

Adrik's eyes slide from Aidan and back to Koen, his smile fading. "He's here," nodding to a nearby SUV. "Where's my daughter?" he counters sharply.

Niko steps forward, his eyes still locked in a contentious stare off with Aidan. He crosses his thick arms across his chest, giving everyone a good view of his piece held tight in his grip.

Koen merely nods, ignoring my brother, his expression unchanging. "She's here. But first I want to see Alex."

Adrik narrows his eyes to thin slits, displeasure playing at the corner of his lips at Koen's assertiveness. I've never seen anyone talk to my father that way—making demands. What's even more shocking is my father relents. He signals with his hand to two Russians standing guard by the SUV and they open the door. I recognize the burlier one as my father's right-hand man, Petr. *So he survived Elements, did he?*

Seconds later, they drag Alexei from the vehicle. Dirty, bloody, and barely recognizable. I can't hold back my sob, holding a hand to my mouth, tears in my eyes.

The O'Rourke clan collectively stiffen at the sight of their adopted brother.

Adrik smiles, delighting in the pain he's causing. "You sure you want the little rat back? We weren't exactly done playing with him."

Alexei struggles to support himself as the Russians drag him roughly forward. He's so pale. Fresh blood drips from so many places it's impossible to count the number of wounds. His face is so battered, his left eye swollen shut. I might throw up.

There's no stopping the tears. They flow freely down my cheeks at the sight of my bodyguard. I don't know how Alexei is even alive...

"Let's get this done," Koen growls out, maintaining his cold and impassive mask. But even from inside the car, I can feel the eldest O'Rourke's wrath simmering. Alexei may not be blood, but from what I've witnessed over the past couple of days... it hardly matters.

Koen and Aidan share a look, and Aidan turns, starting back toward me. He wears the darkest expression I've ever seen, and it makes me want to crawl deeper into the car. After seeing Alexei, I bet the Irish wish they'd roughed me up more.

Frantically I wipe at my face, doing my best to erase my tears, but it's no use.

The door opens and I'm looking up into Aidan's cold eyes. They scan my face—seeing my emotions. His dark expression softens for a moment.

He grabs hold of my upper arm and tugs gently. I step willingly out of the car. All eyes are instantly on me. Aidan walks me over to stand with his brothers, keeping a light grip on my arm. And suddenly, I'm faced with the realization I'm still wearing only Aidan's sweatshirt and rolled up boxer shorts.

I can't look at my father nor my brother. Instead, I keep my gaze trained on the ground, occasionally peeking up between my lashes to check on Alexei. He spies me looking and winks with his one good eye.

Fresh tears leak down my cheeks, dripping off my chin. I give him a soft smile in return. He gave me up to the Irish, but he still doesn't deserve this.

Movement out of the corner of my eye has my gaze snapping to Niko. He walks aggressively toward Alexei and points a gun at his head.

I'm vaguely aware Aidan's gun is in his hand, threatening, but not quite pointed at me. Aidan and the O'Rourkes have had me for days. *Days*. The Bratva had Alexei for *hours*. Hours, and the harm they'd inflicted....

"Aurora," my father has to call my name twice in order for me to finally tear my gaze away from my bodyguard and direct it onto him. "Aurora, они тебя трогали?" *Did they touch you?* My father knows I know at least enough Russian to understand his question.

My gaze wanders to Aidan before I slowly shake my head, staring up into forest-dark eyes. "No."

Aidan's brow lifts only slightly, not understanding Adrik's question.

My father nods in what looks like relief. "Well," he says, clapping his hands together, savoring this torturous moment far more than anybody else, "Ladies first?"

Koen's jaw flexing is his only tell as he dips his chin in agreement. "Send her over."

Aidan takes a few steps forward, bringing me with him. I

only resist a little, shaking in his light grip. I see a question enter his eyes and he looks between my father and me. We're halfway and Aidan stops.

This is it.

But instead of letting go, Aidan's grip tightens on my arm. The sudden anchor behind me forces my attention back, confused.

Aidan's eyes are a blaze of fire as his stare penetrates mine. Full of anger, malice and something else—*confusion? Regret?* I can't know for sure.

I blink up at him, the intensity of his stare holding me in place, more so than the grip he has on my arm.

I nearly jump at the sound of Niko's deep voice. "Don't even think about it, O'Rourke." Both Aidan and I turn to see Niko pushing the barrel of his gun roughly against Alexei's skull. "Let her go," my brother threatens, shoving the gun into Alexei's temple. His finger grazes the trigger. "Now."

My eyes plead with Aidan. Another moment passes, and he finally releases me.

I don't know what to make of it, but I *need* to get Alexei back to the Irish. He desperately needs medical attention. The amount of blood he's had to have lost by the state of his body alone... It's a miracle he hasn't bled out already, standing before us in his state.

My walk across the remaining space is slow but determined. I'm hyperaware of the powder keg I'm currently in the heart of. One wrong move from anyone and we're all dead.

When I'm nearly to the Bratva side, Petr shoves Alexei forward. He stumbles past me. Our eyes meet, and he gives me a small reassuring nod. I open my mouth, unsure of what to say with everyone watching us. But I'm cut off when Petr extends his arm. He grabs hold of my sweatshirt and forcefully drags me the rest of the way towards him.

A low growl sounds to my right, and suddenly I'm pulled into a different hard chest: Niko's. He wraps one arm tightly around me, the other holding the gun steady and trained on Aidan. The Irish defenseman remains right where I'd left him. Murder dances in his eyes.

Eyes that are focused over my head, on my brother. I hold my breath until Alexei reaches him, nearly collapsing onto the Irish enforcer. Aidan supports Alexei's weight, but he doesn't take his eyes off Niko, as he backs away slowly until he reaches his brothers. Liam takes Alexei's other arm over his shoulder.

We stay and watch the Irish load up. Tensions are still high as both the Irish and Russians eye each other with mistrust. Some guys look like they're itching for a fight. I spy crew cut —*Jimmy*—from the club, watching me with a narrowed expression.

"That's enough, Nikolai." My father's voice to our left startles me and I flinch in surprise. Niko's arm tightens around me, but he finally lowers his gun. Aidan gives me one last hard look before disappearing into the SUV behind Alexei. The Irish pull out.

"It's over Aurora. You're safe now." My father strokes my hair in a loving gesture that doesn't match his expression. "Take her home," he advises to Niko coldly before stalking off, forgetting about me entirely and conferring intensely with Petr and another one of his men.

The words *safe* and *home* circle through my mind.

Numbly, I climb into Niko's car, barely aware of anything he says to me. Not at all eager to get back to the life I'd left behind.

30

ICE TIME

RORY

"*So are you ruined?*"

My father's first question to me. I'd no sooner walked through the mansion doors before I found myself in my father's office. I was grilled for hours about my time with the Irish. Niko stayed too, though he remained mostly silent, lurking in the back corner with his arms crossed and an extra pissed off expression on his face, even for him.

I clench my fists just thinking about it. No, "*are you okay?*" Or "*what can we do?*"

Nope. Why am I not surprised his primary concern is the status of my virginity?

Not that I am a virgin—but I certainly haven't told *him* that. A tiny little rebellion in a world where I've had little choices. My father couldn't exactly control *everything* while I was away at boarding school...

After what seemed like hours of reassuring him that the Irish hadn't touched me. He finally allowed me to go up to my room, with orders to remain there until further notice.

Restricted to the property. The thought of missing even more training... I begged him to reconsider.

All I need is some ice time. I need to *skate*. All it got me was a backhand smack to my left cheek, reopening the healing cut I suffered from the glass window shattering at Elements.

Wiping the blood away with my sleeve, I stomp up the stairs. I throw myself on my bed, fuming over being forbidden from leaving the house.

National qualifiers are four weeks away! *I don't have time for this.*

After one week stuck in this house, I'm on the verge of madness.

I spend most of my days downstairs in the mansion's gym, working out and practicing off-ice jumps, but it's not the same. I can't take it anymore... The need to get on the ice consumes me. The ice has always been my safe place, the only outlet I've ever had in my lonely little world. Being away from it for this long has me on edge. I've felt different ever since I'd arrived home. Since my time with the Irish, I'm desperate for a taste of the familiar.

The clock on my bedside table reads precisely four-thirty a.m. when I carefully slip out of my bedroom door. Clutching the skate bag I have slung over my shoulder, I walk down the hall on near-silent toes.

Niko's gone back to his apartment in the city, and my father has his own wing on the opposite side of the mansion. While there are always soldiers on guard duty at the house, it's lighter than it should be. At this hour, there are probably only one to two guys on duty. And they usually stay outside.

My father's ego might be the death of us one day. Niko's been on him for months to beef up security at the mansion, but Adrik refuses. So sure no one would dare strike him here, arrogant is what it is. The Irish shot up Elements only two weeks ago and blew up a couple more warehouses full of inventory.

This isn't the first time I've snuck out for early ice. Sometimes a girl needs to leave her house alone without the escort of a six-foot-tall armed Russian. Having every move of mine watched and reported on is incredibly draining. And I can't say I don't get a little thrill whenever I steal a chance to be on my own. Free to do what I want, where I want. It's a silly little novelty, but I live for these moments.

I'm careful to stay far away from the back end of the house. Since Sasha is watching the front, whoever else is on duty should—*in theory*—be out back.

I clear the house without incident, slipping out the side door, conveniently out of range of view from the guardhouse down by the road. Creeping forward, I'm careful to stick to the shadows looming from the high walled fencing on the property, keeping my eye on the guardhouse.

Sasha's head is bent over, the bluish glow of a screen lights up the little room. I wait, checking my watch and digging the toe of my sneaker nervously into the deep gravel, all while scanning the nearby area for any threats. *Sasha should be taking his bathroom break any minute now...* I'm dressed all in black. The hood of my sweatshirt pulled up to cover my light hair. It would be next to impossible to spot me where I'm hidden, if you weren't trying.

Just as I worry Sasha's bladder schedule has changed, he rises with a loud hacking cough. *Yeah, years of smoking will do that to you.* He steps out, suit unkempt, tie hanging round his neck, and shuffles out of the gatehouse toward the garage housing my father's fleet of fine vehicles, as well as the guard's office. The desperate moaning and squeals from the porn he's clearly in the middle of watching fades away with him.

I make myself wait for another entire minute after Sasha closes the door behind him before making a mad dash for the gate. Until I make it outside of the compound, I'm exposed. So the faster I am, the better. The gravel crunches softly under my sneakers, and I breathe a sigh of relief when I hit the wrought-iron fence. Off to the side is a pedestrian gate, so I don't need to draw any attention by hitting the button for the main gate.

In seconds, I'm through. I meet my Uber a couple of blocks over, far out of sight from the house.

Sneaking out is definitely easier than *sneaking back in,* but that's a Future Rory problem.

Until then, the ice awaits.

31

MY PROBLEM

AIDAN

*A*lex is expected to make a full recovery. But it doesn't change the fact the Russians fucked him up. Multiple broken ribs, a swollen eye, and a few broken fingers are the worst of it. The rest of him is just bruised up real good.

He got lucky.

Real lucky.

He's staying with us at the loft until he recovers and it is super important he lies low. The Russians don't easily forgive and they're not ones to let traitors live. If we didn't have the Pakhan's own daughter to trade, Alex would never have survived.

Aurora Kostalova.

Rory.

The little lost princess hasn't shown up to the rink all week for practice. Not that I'm looking... but the terrifying Russian lady she trains with was quite loud yesterday when Rory missed practice yet again. Her private session is right before the Breakers' afternoon practice. Several times a week...

I can't complain, Rory not showing up means extra ice for the Breakers. And the more ice time, the better.

Which is why I'm at the rink again at the ass crack of dawn. I haven't been sleeping well and getting a little extra puck time is better than staring up at my ceiling for another couple of hours.

As soon as I enter the rink, I realize someone's already beaten me to it. The main lights are off, and shadows cover half of the arena. But loud music echoes through the large space: angry rock guitar sounds and heavy drums. I recognize the band, Collateral Damage.

I expect to see one of my teammates, perhaps having had the same idea as me, but instead, a single skater tears up the ice, drawing my interest. This type of music isn't the kind you'd normally hear the figure skaters prancing around to.

I move closer, so I'm lingering halfway out of the tunnel, still mostly out of sight. I've yet to see her face, but I don't need to because I already know...

It's *her*.

Rory's movements are sharp and she's skating with a fierce determination, matching the aggressive beat of the music. Even as I descend the steps to the arena, she doesn't notice. Too lost in the music and her routine or whatever it is she's working on.

Her jumps are explosive, defying gravity as she rotates at breakneck speed high above the ice. I watch transfixed as she launches into a series of spins, changing levels and increasing speed so fast I don't know how they don't make her sick. Especially given the little migraine condition she has.

She's dressed more casually today, but still hot as sin. All in black. Tight high waisted leggings cling to her hips and a black sports bra that criss-crosses across her spine, revealing most of her back and a sliver of her toned stomach.

I think back to how sick she got the other night... how can she do what she does on the ice with that kind of ailment?

The Rory on the ice today shows no sign of imbalance, gliding smoothly out of a death spin with a flawless transition. The routine she's working through is nothing like the fluffy little ballet crap her coach usually has her on.

I scan the arena seats for any sign of a guard, but other than the two of us, the arena is empty. Something tells me the little princess finally had enough of missing practice and snuck out.

Smiling to myself, I duck into the nearest locker room before she spots me, fully aware I'm about to ruin her day.

I lace up my skates in less than a minute, forgoing the pads, opting for my gloves, stick, and my old beat up baseball hat.

Rory's head whips around at the sound of the heavy rink door slamming shut behind me. The sound echoes around the empty arena. She's about halfway up the ice from me. "Hey!" she shouts, annoyance with a hint of apprehension in her voice. *Maybe ditching your body guards wasn't the best idea today...*

I skate forward, bending my knees to sink deep into the ice. Head down, cap pulled low over my face, pretending I don't hear her. I tug on my gloves and drop a puck to the ice. Stick handling it expertly down the back end as I take a lap.

Out of the corner of my eye, I see her check her watch. I'm closer now, lazily pushing the puck down the ice, warming up.

"Hello?" she calls again when I don't acknowledge her. "I have it for twenty more minutes you need to—" her voice cuts out and the corner of my lip curves up, knowing she's recognized who it is she's trapped on the ice with. I drop the pretense and swerve in her direction, gliding into a neat t-stop only a few feet away from her.

Her face betrays her fear. She looks so tiny standing there in front of me in her tight little skating clothes. *So breakable.* She glances nervously around while keeping me in her sights.

I lean casually on my stick, "What is it I *need* to do, Angel?" Tilting my head to the side as I check her out. She's even hotter up close.

Rory is as white as the ice beneath her feet. But to her credit, she holds her ground. Clearing her throat, she forces her gaze to mine as she says carefully—sternly, "You need to leave."

I slowly circle her. "Do I?"

She swallows hard, her eyes darting to the nearest exit. She spins on her blades, keeping me in sight. Not letting me get behind her.

"And who's going to make me?" I lift an eyebrow, checking her up and down, "You?"

Her cheeks burn pink.

"Cause it looks like you're all alone out here..." I marvel at the empty rink, shaking my head and clicking my tongue before gliding to a stop with a little spray of ice. I've positioned myself right between her and the closest exit, edging closer, turning my hat from front to back. I swear I can hear her heart pounding from here.

"I'll scream—" she warns. As if that's supposed to phase me...

"Go ahead." My grin is slow and dangerous, focused solely on her. "There's no one here."

She stares at me for half a second before she takes off, racing for the gate on the opposite end of the rink. The move catches me by surprise so she gets a couple strides head start.

I'm quick to give chase. Dropping my stick on the ice with a clatter. Catching up to her easily. Just as I come within reaching distance—Rory cuts on an angle. Dodging my arm and taking off in the opposite direction before I can stop.

She's nearly at the gate by the time I catch her again, but I'm too close. If she stops to open it, I'll have her. Forced into a split second decision, she flies by the gate, shooting me a frustrated look.

I'm hot on her tail. The unexpected challenge and chase awakening something primal. Every nerve in my body seems to snap to attention, ignited by a single, undeniable spark. I'm fast, but she's nimble. Each time I get too close, she twists or twirls right out of my reach. When once again she evades me by a hair, I release a low growl, frustration settling in.

Falling back, I study the little Russian skater. Reading her body, putting my defensive skills to work. The next time she pivots, I'm ready for it. She doesn't have enough time to react before she skates right into me. She lets out a little shriek of terror when I wrap an arm around her middle and scoop her right off the ice. It's unexpected, and she freezes long enough for me to pin her body up against the boards. Careful to keep my knee tight across her legs, not wanting to catch a skate blade to the shin. The slice down my forearm is a reminder of the little lion's bite.

She wriggles against me, trying desperately to escape. I lean on her a little harder, using my weight to keep her in place. *Fuck, chasing her turned me on.* Both exciting and pissing me the fuck off.

"What are you doing here?" I demand. She shouldn't be here. *Alone and unprotected.*

She scoffs, "*What am I doing here?* What are *you* doing here?"

"You're lucky it's me and not Koen, or worse, Jimmy Reilly..."

My cousin still wants Rory dead. Probably more so than he did before, anxious she'll rat him out to Adrik for what he did to his desk.

Her blue eyes flash in recognition, but she shrugs it away. "Do your brother and your cousin frequent the ice rink at dawn?" she asks dryly.

"No," I admit.

Rory lifts her chin, proud of herself for proving her point. "Then I don't see the problem." She pushes at my chest. For such a little thing, she's stronger than she looks, moving me a couple of inches. I smile at her just before I shove her back against the boards with one hand, reminding her she might be tough, but she's no match for me.

Her breath catches from the pressure. "Fucking hell, Aidan, what is your problem?" she fumes. I delight in the anger I've stirred up in her eyes.

"My problem?" I turn it back on her, "What's *your* problem?" I'm both irritated and turned on by her bratty attitude.

"My problem is you!"

I push her up against the boards again, leaning in close so I can feel her warm breath against my face. "Exactly," it comes out as a growl. "Your problem is *me*. And it's going to keep being *me*. So I suggest you stay behind your little guards, safe and sound in your pretty castle if you don't want to end up as collateral damage, *Kostalova*." I practically purr her name before darkening my tone, "Stay out of my way, little lion."

I expect my words to scare her, but they do the exact oppo-

180

site. Her little hands ball into fists while a storm rages to life in her eyes.

"It's old news, Aidan. I don't care about your sociopath brother or your little cousin with anger issues or *you*. You gave me back, remember? In a deal to save your little traitor friend." Her words are bitter, but she can't hide the emotion in her eyes when she mentions Alex. "I'm no longer your problem. Now Let. Me. Go."

I stare at her as she holds my eyes, tilting her chin up with an air of defiance.

My hands release her just before the crashing sound of a door slamming draws our attention. Both our heads whip back toward the main gate.

"O'Rourke." My name rolls off the tongue of one of the last people I want to see. I roll my eyes into the back of my head and look toward the roof. "Rory," Colt nods impassively at the tiny skater next to me.

That catches my attention. *How the fuck does he know Rory?* Drawing myself up, I turn to face him, stepping in front of Rory as I do.

"King," I offer a cold greeting, crossing my arms and sizing up the new Breakers' center, warning in my eyes.

"Everything okay?" He looks past me to where Rory stands. No longer pinned against the boards, but still leaning against them. Uncharacteristically quiet for once.

I open my mouth, but it's Rory who responds. Her voice surprisingly level given the little exchange, Colt just interrupted.

"Yup. In fact, I was just heading out." She knocks into my shoulder as she brushes by me, gliding to the door, and exiting the rink behind Colt without sparing me another glance.

He watches her pass him and my jaw tightens along with my fists.

"Remember what I said," I call after her, ignoring Colt's hard stare. The brief pause in her step is evidence enough she hears me, though she doesn't turn around.

What Colt makes of it, I don't care because I'm already skating across the ice, picking up the stick and puck I'd abandoned earlier, and in a couple of strides, I sink it into the net from the point.

This is far from over.

BETROTHED

RORY

By the time I get myself back into the mansion, I'm ready for a nap. Between going over my routine, running into Aidan, and climbing the freaking wall to get my ass back into the mansion undetected, I need to check out.

Easily dodging security, I made it to the East wing in the clear. I'm in my room with the door shut behind me before I sense him.

Caught red-handed, I linger by the door, staring across my bedroom at my brother.

Niko watches me from where he sits, shadowed from the sunlight streaming through my window in my plush reading chair, like some kind of vampire. Casually flipping through one of my books.

I tense, checking to be sure it's not the one I hollowed out to stash my escape fund in.

"Where were you?" He doesn't even look up, his eyes still scanning the pages.

"Around." I wave my hand noncommittally, still working on how to play this off.

My brother lifts his head, raising a brow as his gaze drops pointedly to my skate bag—still hanging off my shoulder. I drop it at my feet and kick it a little behind my hamper.

Niko's face remains unchanged, and it's next to impossible to read his mood.

"How did you get out of the compound?"

"I didn't," The lie comes out too quickly. I'm already on edge after my encounter at the rink with Aidan and Niko's always made me feel unbalanced. He hates me. And he's never wasted an opportunity to remind me. But I double down. "I was down on the synthetic ice..." *It's a lie. We both know it's a lie.* But I have plausible deniability...

My brother rises slowly, setting the book down on the chair as he stands to his full height. Towering over me, he casually buttons his suit jacket. This gives me pause and I take him in. Our father wears a sharp suit every day, but Niko... Niko usually prefers dark jeans and t-shirts. "Father sent me to find you," he says, and my eyes snap up.

"What for?" My voice is quiet. Nothing good ever follows those words.

There's a bored expression on Niko's face as he turns his attention to the books I have lining my shelves. "The Italians are coming for brunch." He says it like that's a normal, everyday occurrence.

"And what does that have to do with me?" I am well aware that when father takes meetings at the mansion, I'm to stay quiet and out of sight in my room. Niko's eyes slide to mine. "You're coming."

I blink back at him in confusion. That is until it hits me...

"Matteo?" My voice weak, remembering the discussion we had with our father before the Irish took me.

Niko gives a slow nod before passing by, pausing for a moment on the threshold. "One hour. Put on something nice and don't—" he looks at me with narrowed eyes, "—be late."

As soon as he's gone, I crumple to the floor. Hugging my knees to my chest, wondering how I fell so quickly into this mess and how the hell I'm going to survive it.

An hour later, I'm walking down the ornate stairs of the foyer dressed in a simple black dress with a flared skirt that sits just above my knees. Funeral colors seemed the most appropriate for the day I officially meet my *fiancé*.

"Here she is," Adrik's voice booms as I enter. My heels click against the cold marble floor. He beckons me closer and pulls me into him in a loving gesture before he spins me to greet his guests. "Gentleman, I'd like to introduce my daughter, Aurora Kostalova, at last."

I look up to find two very Italian—very *attractive*—men looking at me.

"It is a pleasure to meet you, Ms. Kostalova." The taller of the two men steps forward with a pleasant smile on his face.

I smile politely back as he takes my hand in his and deposits a light kiss atop it, his face carefully blank. What I see in his dark eyes reveals his true depth, as though he can read my soul. "Cole DeLuca," he says, introducing himself.

My body instantly tenses at the realization the man standing before me is the notoriously ruthless Italian Capo. "It's a pleasure to meet you, Signore DeLuca," I stutter out.

185

I know Cole is the youngest capo in the DeLuca family history, but I'm still shocked to see just how young he is. He appears to be around the same age as Niko, and well... Koen O'Rourke, for that matter, too. My father is the last of his generation to hold a boss seat in the city.

Cole's lips twitch. "I assure you, the pleasure is all mine." He still holds my hand, looking at the man standing next to him, he transfers my hand to his. "Aurora, allow me to introduce my cousin, Matteo Carroza."

Matteo steps forward and I take in the man I am to marry. While not as tall as his cousin, Matteo's still over six feet. Dark hair, slicked back in the Italian style, falls to his collar, neatly highlighting his tan skin and sharp features. Caramel brown eyes smile down at me. "I'm so happy to finally meet you, Aurora."

I'm tempted to ask him to call me Rory, but I know my father won't like it.

"Aurora has talked of nothing else all week!" my father gushes.

I have?

"We're so glad you could both join us for lunch today. I had the chef prepare an Italian special!"

I catch Niko's eye and he raises a single brow while I tilt my head in confusion at our father's lie. It's the closest to sibling camaraderie I think we've ever come. I notice Cole's eyes on me as he turns for the table, his lips tilted up in a faint smile.

Oh yeah, this man doesn't miss a trick.

Matteo gallantly pulls out my chair, and I sink daintily into it. He takes the seat next to mine and I remind myself to not fidget. Which means I'm probably sitting too still now... Everything feels wrong. The fit of my dress is off. My heels pinch at my toes and one curl keeps falling relentlessly into my face, no matter how many times I try to tuck it back behind my ear.

The men chat for a bit as our cook serves the food. Small talk about the weather and horse racing—one of my father's favorite past times. I know better than to interrupt, so I wait to be asked a direct question, pushing the leaves of my salad around my bowl.

"We were disappointed last week when we had to reschedule our initial meeting. I heard Aurora had quite the run in with some Irish recently?" Matteo smiles at me, but directs his question to my father.

Adrik chuckles in response, laughing off the building tension in the room. I don't miss the way he and Niko exchange a quick look. *The Russians had hoped to keep my kidnapping quiet from my future fiancé.* "That she did. And we got her back, no worse for wear." He takes a sip of his wine—looking uncomfortable.

I don't know why, but it grates on me to hear my father taking credit for an exchange I orchestrated. They didn't even know who had taken me until Koen called to propose the trade for Alexei.

Matteo moves his hand to cover mine and I nearly jolt at the surprise contact. His hand is icy cold. "Still, it must have been horrible to endure. The O'Rourkes are nothing but a bunch of savages. A bunch of heathen devils." He squeezes my hand, and I give him a tight smile.

"You know the O'Rourkes?" I ask carefully, taking a casual sip from my wine, jumping into the conversation for the first time.

Matteo scoffs, sitting back in his chair before looking across the table at his cousin. "I don't know Cole, do we *know* the O'Rourkes?" My eyes dart between the two Italians.

"Oh, we go way back," Cole muses darkly. There's a quiet danger in the way the man talks and moves. Like a big cat, coiled up and just waiting to be set loose.

"Koen only hopes he and Cole never end up in the same room together is all I gotta say..." Matteo takes a sip of his own wine, his caramel eyes dancing maliciously. I draw back from him. "Don't worry Aurora, the Irish will pay for thinking they could touch you." He raises his glass at my father, who returns it with a tight smile.

"They didn't touch me."

Silence falls over the table at my sudden words, spoken in clear confidence. I clear my throat, "What I mean to say... is they... didn't hurt me."

From across the table, Cole eyes me with curiosity.

"Maybe not, but we'll make them bleed for it, anyway," Matteo boasts, pumping out his chest.

"Salud!" My father raises his glass up, higher this time, in the Italian style cheer, and Matteo cheerfully clinks his glass.

I don't miss the subtle glare my father gives me as he drinks from his glass, reminding me to mind my place.

33

ICE GIRL

RORY

*A*fter our "successful" lunch with the Italians, my father reluctantly agreed to allow me to resume my normal schedule once Niko offered to stand in as my guard. That is, until father can choose a replacement for Alexei.

I'm not sure why Niko volunteered. But as I steal a glance at my brother lounging in the stands above, feasting on popcorn from the Chill Zone, I'm sure it was to get out of some other Bratva duty he just didn't want to do.

The topic only came up after Matteo offered to assume responsibility for my guard until the wedding, but neither my father nor my brother seemed to care for that idea very much and politely declined.

Today, it's back to the drawing board on my plans to avoid this arranged marriage. I only have about three thousand dollars saved up in cash tips from the Chill Zone. All of it hidden inside a hollowed-out book on my bedroom shelves. It's not enough money to run on... *I was supposed to have another year.*

A surge of anger leads me to bobble the landing of another jump, and Karina's sharp reprimand bounces off my mind. I ease back into the zone, but once again, my mind drifts, this time to my mother.

My mom did everything in her power to keep me away from this life. *From this fate.* Before I was even born, she convinced my father that for my safety, we should live separately. In different houses, different states, different *countries*.

Things haven't been the same since her death. I miss her so much. And I hate that things were tense between us, at the end. We'd been fighting a lot. She'd stay up worrying about me if I missed curfew, tried to keep me close to home... I'd thought it was because I was leaving for college soon, which confused me, seeing as how she'd always pushed so hard for me to apply to college and for scholarships to pay for it. Colleges far away from Vancouver and even further from Boston.

But I knew my father had begun to have other ideas about what was next for my future. I had overheard heated conversations between my parents on one of his brief visits just before Nationals last year.

Anonymity was my protection. I lived under a fake name, with fake friends and a fake life. Only facing the horrors of my real life a few times a year when holidays or events forced us back to Boston.

But Niko... This hell was his everyday reality. And he seemed to blame me for it. Raised by the Russian Lion, he was a loose cannon himself, bloodthirsty and chaotic. And he utterly despised me. The little sister from his father's mistress, an insult to his mother. Niko made sure to be unnecessarily cruel at every opportunity.

And as a result, I did everything I could to stay far away from that house—from Boston.

But when my mother died, so did her protection.

I enter my scratch spin and let the world blur around me, blur out the thoughts clouding my mind. Spinning faster and faster... controlled chaos.

My father promised—*He promised.* As long as I was skating competitively, I was supposed to be left alone. Safe from the constraints of an arranged marriage.

He lied. And I was the idiot who believed him.

I only just realized there was never any escaping my fate. It was always to be this way. My only value in this world was as a pawn in the bloody games of men.

I slam my toe pick into the ice, ending the spin with an abrupt stop. Lifting my chin, I skate back to the bench where Karina watches in silence. Uncapping my water bottle, I take a deep drink.

"It was better. Still needs work, but... better," Karina frowns.

I nod in acknowledgement. Coming from Karina... that's just short of a glowing review. I still feel her eyes on me and brace myself, knowing something else is brewing behind that contemplative look in her Russian blues.

"Qualifiers are in three weeks' time. You still very rough on the edges. Injury and all..." Her fingers dance around her head and I narrow my eyes. Besides that one hiccup before I was kidnapped, I haven't had any episodes. The concussion symptoms seem to finally be fading away. "You have not performed in over a year," Karina shakes her head, clicking her tongue. "This is no good. So—" she looks at me, a devious smile in her aging eyes, "—I have taken liberty to sign you up for Belles."

My mouth just about falls open. *This has to be a joke.* "The *Belles*?" I repeat, hoping I heard her wrong or something got lost in translation.

She nods, pleased with herself, "Yes, the Belles... skate club."

I know who they are. I shake my head. "I can't skate with the Belles, I don't have time!" I protest, thinking of any and all excuses I can use to get me out of this. "Training is more important."

Karina purses her lips, looking me up and down. "You know routine. Routine is not problem... Confidence is problem. You need to learn to perform again. Smile again..."

I feel my cheeks heat at her assessment. I continue to shake my head no, but Karina is not having it. "No discussion. You skate with Belles or you don't skate in qualifiers. Understand?"

Fuck.

The Boston Belles were like hockey cheerleaders—ice girls for the Boston Breakers. Responsible for hyping up the crowd during home games and promo events. Smiley... pretty... cheerleaders.... Next to marrying Matteo, it's probably the *last* thing I want to do with my time.

Karina takes my silence as my agreement and gives me a sharp nod of approval before gathering up her things, since we've reached the end of our ice time.

"Excellent. You start tomorrow."

Wait, what?

34

PRETTY, PEPPY, POISON

RORY

The only upside about having to join the Belles is the fact that Elle is on the team. And she just about goes berserk when I tell her what Karina's forcing me to do.

"We're going to have so much fun!" The curly-haired blonde is practically bouncing with excitement.

I blink back at her before burying my face in my arms atop the bar. It's a slow afternoon at the Chill Zone. Unfortunately for me, my ice time is right before the Breakers' hockey practice and the Belles' practice is right after that. Which means I'm trapped at the rink in between since there is not enough time to go home, or anywhere else for that matter.

At least joining the Belles means more time away from the mansion... *Upside?*

Time is moving monotonously slowly and I'm doing everything in my power to avoid looking below us, where the hockey team is running practice drills. Knowing I'll see *him*.

Ever since that last run in with Aidan on the ice, I've done about everything in my power to avoid running into the Breakers defenseman. It hasn't been difficult—he might be avoiding me, too. But Niko keeps me on a tight leash and I've been careful not to over-run my ice time. Not wanting to know what might happen, were the two of them to square off. So all week, I'm off the ice and out of the rink before the Breakers even start trickling in.

I don't even want to think about what it's going to be like at their games. Forced to watch and cheer them on while dressed in ridiculous ice girl attire.

"Are you sure your brother doesn't want anything?" Elle's words force my head up. She flicks concerned eyes in Niko's direction. He sits as far away from us as he can, lurking in the back corner of the bar, preoccupied with his phone.

"I'm sure." I turn my head on its side so my cheek is resting on my arm. I'm tired and sore. After the gym and ballet this morning, plus practice with Karina, I'm peppered with a couple new bruises and aching muscles. Skating with the Belles too is really going to put my endurance to the test.

Elle's still looking at my brother, uncertainty dancing in her sky-blue eyes. "I'm just going to go check."

I open my mouth to stop her, but she's already halfway across the bar. I watch with morbid amusement as she pries my brother's cold gaze up with her bright smile and incessant chattering, listing the daily specials. He shuts her down pretty quickly with a firm and sharp, "No," as he turns his attention back to his screen.

Elle's smile wavers slightly, and she gives him a shaky little nod before turning away.

As she turns, Niko runs an exasperated hand down his face before calling out to her, halting Elle in her tracks. "Fine. I'll take an IPA, any IPA..."

Elle flashes him an excited smile and scurries away to get his beer, winking conspiratorially at me.

I raise an eyebrow, and Niko scowls back at me before turning his attention again to his phone. *Hmm... Perhaps metal man has a heart, after all.*

Elle's back at my side after delivering Niko his beer with another dazzling smile. Honestly, it's impossible to be mean to her. She practically radiates sunshine.

An influx of girls coming into the empty bar draws all our attention. Elle waves them over excitedly and I remind myself to play nice as I push up off of the bar top. "Liv, Sadie over here!"

A gorgeous girl with long dark hair and equally dark eyes heads our way along with her friend, a shorter girl with olive skin, curly caramel hair and honey eyes. They both check out my brother on their way in.

Elle is practically vibrating now with her excitement. I paint a smile on my face for her benefit. "Rory, I want you to meet Liv," Elle gestures to the dark-haired girl, who gives me a small smile.

"Hi."

"—And Sadie," motioning to the smaller girl next to Liv, who offers a little wave in response.

"You're the new girl who's joining the team?" Liv asks. I notice the subtle drawl of a Southern accent.

I take a deep breath. "That's me."

Sadie shoots me a sympathetic smile. "It won't be so bad. We have a lot of fun. Karina's my coach too." She gives me a knowing look. *Perhaps I'm not the only skater Karina's conscripted to the Belles...*

I have to admit, it's a relief they're nice. The cheerleading team from prep school was a completely different beast...

"We should head down," Liv reminds us, hefting her bag higher on her shoulder and shooting another curious look at Niko, who's studying the new arrivals from his corner with interest.

Elle and I grab our bags and open the door into the now quiet ice rink, the Zamboni having already finished its rounds. "The Breakers have their opening pre-season game next weekend," Sadie fills me in as we make our way down the steps. "It's kind of a big deal. And on top of it, they're playing their rivals, The Falcons. But don't worry, we'll have you up to speed in no time."

I nod nervously. As much as I don't want to be a Belle, I also don't want to be embarrassed as one.

"Stay clear of Natalia," Liv warns, holding the door for us to pass into the Belles' private locker room.

"Natalia?" I ask, not sure if I've heard Elle mention her before.

"Mmm," Elle confirms. "She's.... Well, she can be a little intense."

"What Ellie-baby means to say," Sadie chimes in, "is Natalia can be a total bitch... And given your reputation... Little Miss National Champion..." she waves at me, "she is going to *hate* you."

"Perfect," I roll my eyes.

Indeed, it's a frosty welcome from Natalia when she finally arrives. A couple more girls trickle in and after introductions, I'm feeling a little better about the situation. Do I still want to do this? No. But at least the girls make the situation more enjoyable than I thought it would be.

As we head out on the ice for warmups, I feel a gentle touch along my arm. I spin around to find Elle at my back. "Remember not to take it too seriously... We're here to have fun."

"And for the hockey players, of course." Liv keeps pace with us. "There's nothing more thrilling than watching the Breakers *break* their opponents." Her dark eyes flash with violent excitement, grinning before skating off. "And they look *really* good doing it." She flips her long hair while pretending to swoon.

Elle and I exchange a look and break into laughter. We finish up warm-ups before the Belles' coach signals for us to circle up.

I fall easily into learning the routines and by the end of practice, I start to relax and, dare I say... even have fun.

Natalia's definitely giving me the stink eye, but it's easy to ignore her. The rest of the girls have been super nice and help-ful. *Maybe this won't be so bad...*

35

LET'S FUCKING GO

AIDAN

The locker room is a mixture of nerves and excitement. It might only be pre-season, but the first game always comes with a potent rush of adrenaline. For some guys, this is their first game playing on the professional level. And for the veterans like me, it's the start of feeling like a god again.

There's nothing that compares to that feeling.

Sitting next to Liam, I lace up my skates, headphones in, slipping into the zone. The one where nothing else matters but this team, the puck and hockey.

I'm ready.

Over the last two weeks, I've buckled down, putting in the work at practice and it shows. Since everything went down with the Russians, things have been quiet on the family front. Koen handles most of it on his own, allowing Liam and me to focus on the team. *On hockey.*

My relationship with some of the guys isn't what I would

call *friendly*, but at least we're no longer on the verge of killing each other...

I look up from my skate, locking eyes with Colt across the room, and I raise my chin at him in acknowledgement. Fresh out of juniors, it's his very first game with the league, and no matter how much I can't stand the guy, I understand the pressure he's under.

His dark eyes flash with a hard intensity, but after a moment, he dips his chin in return, before going back to securing his elbow pads. At least we can both respect the fact that, in order to win this game, we need to have each other's backs. We don't have to be friends.

Coach gives us a pep talk, complete with a look that says, *don't fuck this up, boys,* before we head into the tunnel together.

The Breakers are still a new team working to establish themselves in the league. Hockey is an expensive sport and eventually the team needs to make money. And money comes from filling the arena with fans. From the sounds coming from above, it looks as if the promoters have done just that.

We wait just out of sight as the arena lights dim. Our team's hype music blasts over the speakers as the announcers ramp up the crowd for the start of warmups.

I catch glimpses of the Breakers Belles racing around the arena, their glittery pom-poms flashing with green and silver lights in the dark rink as they work to drum up the already excited crowd.

Our assistant coach gets the go-ahead through the radio to release us and we surge out of the tunnel. Rez takes my side, the two of us co-captains for the team. Together, we lead the team out onto the ice. When the Breakers circle around our end, the crowd goes crazy around us. I don't think I've ever seen the arena so packed... and for pre-season at that.

A couple of girls in the front row just behind the goal bang wildly on the glass, trying to catch our attention. Colt passes by extra close, giving them a devilish smile along with a wink, living up to his image as the team's puck-boy.

On the other side of the rink, the opposing team does the same, while the cheerleaders twirl and jump in the middle. Some of the other guys smile and wave at the fans, even toss out pucks to some kids, but not me—I'm dialed in and focused.

Soon enough the ice clears, and it's time for puck drop.

It's Liam and I, along with our starting offensive line: #6 Reid Kincaid, left wing; #89 Rez Tyler, right wing; and 1st line center, #21 himself, Colt King. King is the only recent addition to the first line this season, fresh off the junior hockey circuit. Since the draft, the sports reporters have frequently been referring to the Breakers starting line as the "Dream Team." Guess we're about to find out how true that statement is.

Colt wins the face off and we're flying down the ice together, crossing into the Falcon's zone. Reid has the puck and fakes a pass to Rez before sailing it back over to Colt, who's snuck right past the Falcons' defenseman. He one times it through the five-hole to put the Breakers on the board in the first minute of play.

"Hell fucking yeah!"

Colt drops to one knee, sliding across center ice, holding his stick like a bow, drawing one arm back as if firing an arrow. The arena eats it up. The fans go nuts and we all rush Colt into the boards in celebration before high-fiving the bench.

Let's fucking go!

By the end of the second period, I'm flying high. The Breakers are up 3-1 and we've got the Falcons on the ropes. They've resorted to dirty plays in an attempt to knock us off our game. But the only thing they've succeeded at is landing two of their own players in the sin bin. The Breakers will start the third period on a power play.

I'm slow getting off the ice before heading back down to the locker rooms for the period break and that's when I see it... A very particular shade of honey-blonde hair. Narrowing my eyes, I study the passing Belles as they race around the rink, pumping their arms to the beat of the music, and twisting and spinning in perfect unison. My gaze stops on the little Belle crossing center ice. She's facing away from me, but the way she skates... I already know.

Rory pulls in, tucking her right leg close, gathering power before throwing herself up and into the air. Her legs extend past her ears in an impressive split jump before she lands effortlessly back on one blade.

I'm the only one left in the box. I'm supposed to be below with the team, but I'm frozen in place. Our assistant coach holding the door shoots me anxious glances, but I ignore him. My eyes fixed on the girl I've worked all week to get the fuck out of my head before this very game, and here she is, front and center in all her glittery glory.

Why didn't I know Rory was a Belle? She wasn't last season... I'm sure of it.

She wears the Belles uniform, a cropped version of the Breakers jersey: black with elements of green and metallic silver stripes. The words Boston Breakers are scrawled across her chest, right over the silver shamrock. The sweater hugs her torso, showing off her lean, sculpted abs. She's painted a shimmery green shamrock just over the waistline of her too-short pleated skirt. The pleats fly up as she races backwards across the ice, showcasing shimmery green hot pants and her remarkably toned ass underneath. I grip my stick a little tighter. Leg warmers complete the look, rising over her knee with classic hockey stripes in green and silver, pulled over figure skates made to look like hockey skates.

My initial surprise quickly turns to annoyance and I squeeze my stick so hard it's a wonder I don't snap it in half. *Who does she think she is joining the Belles?* The sight of her in that revealing little uniform has thrown me so far off balance. I shake my head in an effort to clear out this mental image I know will replay in my mind—probably forever.

How dare she infiltrate this space? I've worked hard to separate my family life from my hockey life. Seeing her here brings up complicated emotions that will only serve as unnecessary distractions. Anger flares and I have half a mind to rip her off the ice right now.

Adding insult to injury, Rory skates with infuriating confidence. A radiant smile on her face as she relishes in the cheers from the crowd. And they *love* her.

Alongside my rising anger is an unwelcome rush of desire. I can't deny how captivating she looks—I'm unable to look away. Little Kostalova skates the rest of the routine with a combination of strength and grace. And unlike when I've spied on her practicing her competition routines, she genuinely seems to be enjoying herself, the usual cold intensity missing from her beautiful face.

Rory stops on the blue line closest to me, raising her shimmering pom-poms to the sky, looking up to the crowd above. My eyes trail over the defined lines of her abs, the way her pleated skirt swirls about her legs. The heat rising deep within me has nothing to do with anger... This infuriates me even more and I glare at the little Belle, who spins around oblivious to the daggers I'm shooting her way. Giving me her back. Too absorbed in her routine and her job, eyes on the crowd. The number 21 flashes across her back in metallic silver embroidery. She tosses her hair and reveals the name *King* scrawled across her shoulders.

It's instant rage at the sight of Colt's name written on her body, with an unexplained craving for it to be *mine*.

Loud whistles draw my attention across the rink to the Falcons' bench. A couple of their players have hung back as well, watching the Belles' routine. I recognize one of them as the Falcons' starting left wing, Logan Pierce. The piece of shit leans over his bench, trying to slap Rory's ass as she skates past them.

At the last minute, she spots him and veers sharply to the left, just missing his hand. Her smile falters for a moment before she recovers, though looking a little unnerved.

My fists tighten at my side, and I grind my teeth.

By now, Assistant Coach McKinley's anxiety has propelled him forward, eyeing me nervously as he gingerly pushes me toward the tunnel. I should be down below, listening to Coach's second period speech. Reluctantly, I allow him to herd me down the tunnel, tearing myself away from the sight of Rory on the ice.

I stalk into the locker room with a slam of the door. The room is silent. All eyes are on me and I shoot Colt a dark glare before plopping down next to Liam, who gives me a curious look.

Shaking my head, I push him off. Not wanting to explain my newfound mood. For now, I need to channel all these complicated emotions into hockey. I can't afford any distractions. I can't let *her* distract me. The wild emotions inside threaten to spill over, and maybe I'll let them—on the Falcons' offensive line.

Pierce is gonna get it.

If there's one thing hockey's good for—it's an excellent outlet for pent up aggression.

36

THE VIBE IS SLUTTY CHIC

RORY

*S*kating for the Belles tonight was nothing like what I expected it to be. I'm grinning from ear to ear when we finally make it back to our locker room after the game. High on an adrenaline rush from the crowd, the performance, the win—everything.

The Breakers entered the third period with a 3-1 lead, but a couple of unnecessary penalties and bad plays allowed the Falcons to tie up the game 3-3.

Aidan O'Rourke came out for blood in the third, earning his reputation—and time in the penalty box for a major penalty—after charging the Falcons' #25 Logan Pierce five minutes in and starting a fight.

The most rabid Breakers fans cheered while the rest of us watched in apprehensive fascination as Aidan punched the grin right off of Pierce's face. Logan's blood drips all over the ice, which leads to an unexpected break in play while the officials cleaned it up.

Not usually a fan of this violent side of the sport, I had to hide my grin. Pierce deserved it, especially after what he tried during the period break.

Unfortunately for me, the Irish Devil's spot in the penalty box put him right next to the platform the Belles dance on throughout the game. By that point, I'm sure he'd noticed me and whatever his feelings were on it, I didn't want to know. Throughout his entire sentence in the box, I could feel the heavy weight of his gaze on me, but I refused to acknowledge it, keeping my eyes fixed firmly on the game.

That part aside, cheering and skating with the Belles tonight had turned out to be way more fun than I ever could have expected. I wasn't about to let Aidan O'Rourke ruin it.

In the end, #19 made up for it by sinking a buzzer-beating goal just out of reach of the Falcons' goalie to secure the win and avoid overtime.

"Rory," Liv's voice pulls me out of my head as I slip off my last skate and shove it into my bag. I notice most of the team looking my way. "You down?"

My eyes dart around the small room, hoping to pick up some context clues, but I come up with nothing. "Down for what?" My cheeks heat slightly.

Elle elbows me in the side teasingly, "The team's all going out to Last Call tonight to celebrate the first win. It's a sports bar close to the rink. You in?"

I catch the little side look she gives me. She might not know the reason, but she knows it can be... difficult for me to go out and do things like normal twenty-year-olds do, with how strict my security detail can be.

I nod, knowing full well agreeing to go out with the team means sneaking out of the mansion tonight... I'm sure Niko's already pacing the halls of the family area. He hates hockey. It was work enough to talk him into allowing me to do the games at all. There's no way he'd be down for an after party... *Engaged Bratva princesses have no business being in clubs.*

"Yeah, I just need to run home first, shower and change..."

"Okay, great. Text me your address and we'll pick you up in like an hour?" Liv calls on her way out of the locker room, bag already slung over her shoulder.

"The vibe is *slutty chic*," Grace, another girl from the team, laughs from across the room.

"Sounds good." I'm still riding high on the adrenaline shot this game gave me. And I use it to fuel my confidence to even attempt going out tonight. It might be a risk, but knowing my father pushed up the marriage timeline with Matteo, it might be one of my last chances for a girls night out.

And I have just the outfit in mind.

Niko is more than happy to drop me off at the mansion after the game. Like I suspected, he's eager to be free of me. But as I'm exiting his car, I stop, turning back around and making eye contact with my brother.

"Move it along, brat." He taps the steering wheel impatiently, making what I'm about to say even harder.

Niko didn't have to agree to this. I could still be confined in the house right now—or worse—dealing with Petr or another one of my dad's guys, who would absolutely not be willing to wait around the rink for hours.

Hesitating, I bite my lip, losing my nerve after seeing the sharpness in his icy eyes.

"I don't have all night, *Aurora*. What is it?"

"Thanks for tonight, Niko." My words come out in a bit of a mumbled mess, but by the way he stiffens, I know he got the gist. "I know you have better things to do, but tonight was a lot of fun and, well... thanks for making it happen."

My brother's mouth tightens, but he doesn't say anything. I shut the door before he has a chance to ruin it and head for the house. By the time I reach the steps, his Audi is long gone.

Just over an hour later, I'm clean and squeezed into my *slutty-chic* outfit of choice. Honestly, it's more clothing than I've had on all night, but somehow feels ten times as scandalous. If I get caught out in this outfit, I might not need to worry about my future at all.

Elle lent it to me the last time we tried to go out, but I never made it. My father ended up dragging me to a never-ending dinner with a couple of insufferable politicians he had in his pocket. Both of whom made me feel incredibly uncomfortable all night with their *wandering* eyes.

The structured black shirt caps on my shoulders and clings tightly to my upper body, leaving the tiniest sliver of skin above the short gold sequined mini skirt. I left the holographic green shamrock Liv painted on earlier this evening visible. She sealed it with like eight coats of clear coat and, even after hours of skating and a shower, the thing hasn't budged.

The three-inch thigh high black suede boots give my legs the illusion of length. I leave my hair down. I refrained from washing it in the shower and the now loose curls from being shaken out all night cascade in a 'messy sexy' way down my back. In a rush, I add a quick, bold red lip and dark eye makeup to complete the look.

Not wanting to leave anything to chance, I escape the

house with the maid's three level step stool. Bypassing the gate entirely and climbing over the side wall instead.

It's no trouble at all escaping the house tonight. Both Niko and my father are out, and security seems lighter than usual—if that were even possible. Which is good for me, since I'm already running late. Liv and Elle texted me they were *here* at least ten minutes ago.

I'd given my teammates the address for the house a block over. With *explicit* instructions to wait for me in the car.

I'm flushed by the time I burst from the yard belonging to our neighbors behind us. The crisp night air prevents me from sweating, but I'm breathing hard by the time I slide into the back of Liv's Highlander.

"You good, Collins?" Sadie arches a brow, a concerned look on her face from the seat beside me.

"Yep," I push out, breathless from both nerves and excitement, but grinning. "Let's do this."

37

LAST CALL

RORY

*L*ast Call is absolutely packed by the time we arrive. The popular sports bar is on the prime strip between the ballpark, the Garden and the Breakers' arena. The line to get in nearly wraps around the next block.

When I make a start for the end of the line, Liv links her arm through mine, rolling her eyes before leading me right past club hopefuls until we reach an unimpressed looking bouncer who's armed with a radio and a clipboard.

"Name?" He looks between the four of us with a bored expression.

Liv breaks out one of her signature dazzling smiles. The stunning white is a sharp contrast to her jet black locks. "Olivia Sinclair and the Breakers Belles."

He doesn't bother checking the list in front of him, waving us through.

The Last Call is a luxury high-end sports bar and the girls half drag me through the entrance when I try to stop to admire the dark decor. The bar is huge and packed tight. High top tables and plush black leather couches adorn the lounge area. One wall is basically a large projection television, with highlights from the Breakers game tonight currently on the screen. And for those not wanting to watch the games, there's a massive dance floor across the bar. Already packed with people moving to the music pumping out from the neon flashing DJ's booth.

"There's the team. C'mon" Liv shouts above the loud music, taking my hand in hers. I snatch Elle's, dragging her behind me as we weave through the packed crowd. "What do you think, guys?" She angles her head back to us when we're almost through the crowded floor. "Do you think I have a chance with Colt tonight?"

Colt?

"Colt King?" I ask for confirmation, bewildered. Though it makes sense, now that I think about it. Liv nods before turning her attention back to parting the crowd.

Wait—if Liv is *trying her chances* with Colt tonight, that means the *team* she is referring to is...

Oh no.

My suspicions are confirmed when the crowd finally tapers off and reveals a roped off platformed VIP area packed full of Breakers players.

We stop momentarily for Liv to rise onto her tiptoes, whispering into the VIP bouncer's ear.

"You didn't tell me '*the team*' meant the *hockey* team," I hiss at Sadie and Elle behind me, narrowing my eyes accusingly.

Elle shoots me an apologetic smile while Sadie replies, "Well, I mean all the Belles are here, too," She shrugs. And sure enough, mixed in with the hulking hockey players are the rest of the Belles skating team. Natalia's smile drops to a frown the second she spots us.

I shut my eyes tightly as my friends push me against my will into my VIP version of hell. *Maybe he won't be here... He hates people. Why would he be here?*

Tough luck. My eyes fly open, locking immediately onto Aidan's. In the neon glow of the club lights, his green eyes are brighter than I've ever seen them. The second he recognizes me, they darken to green flames.

"Welcome, ladies." Colt King wraps his arms around Liv's shoulders and mine, drawing me unwillingly further into the team's center and closer to my *favorite* Irish defenseman. Aidan's eyes flash with unmistakable violence as we get closer and I force myself to look away. Someone hands me a beer and I take it, needing something to do with my hands.

"You know, my last team didn't have a cheer squad." Colt looks between Liv and me, batting his long, dark eyelashes. "I'm looking forward to working alongside you ladies."

A few of the guys shout their agreement and raise their glasses.

"Ain't that right, O'Rourke?" Colt shouts over to his teammate. I laugh nervously, finding it hard to tear my eyes away from the simmering glare Aidan is shooting at Colt and me. Colt is all too aware of what he's doing, smirking at Aidan —actively trying to rile the enforcer up.

Sensing my discomfort, Elle tugs me out of Colt's grip. He doesn't seem to mind. He wraps himself closer around Liv, who fawns under his undivided attention.

"Wanna dance?" Elle's eyes shoot toward the dance floor, giving me a much needed out.

I nod, a little too exuberantly. I take a long pull of my beer as we sneak away, Sadie trailing after us.

One song and one more beer in, I've almost completely forgotten about the brooding Irish enforcer back in VIP, mostly thanks to Elle. The girl is absolutely magnetic to be around. She's like the sun, extending her rays of sunlight to everyone around her. She and Sadie have me laughing to the point of tears as we compete in an impromptu dance-off to see who can come up with the most ridiculous dance moves.

Our fun does not go unnoticed, and soon I find myself with a tagalong. When the music takes a turn into a sexier beat, I feel him slide up. I let him grind up against me for a few minutes before spinning around to put a face to the firm body pressed up against mine.

A slow smile creeps across my face at the sight of the attractive blonde whose hands are on my hips. The way he's dressed, his moves, the look on his face, all of it screams *player*. I'm hardly looking for a boyfriend, so what do I care? *He's perfect.*

Reading my look of approval, my dance partner slithers closer. His warm breath tickles my ear when he leans in. And despite holding a glass of what looks to be alcohol, I don't smell alcohol on his breath. "What's your name, gorgeous?" He pulls back to flash me an overly whitened smile while he awaits my answer.

I have to tip onto my toes to get close enough to his ear, wrapping my arms around his shoulders for stability. "Rory," I tell him with a smile on my lips, still vibing to the beat of the song. "Rory Collins."

He beams in response before giving me his own name, "Cameron—Cam Reeves."

"Nice to meet you, Cameron—Cam Reeves," I repeat with an amused smile, and he laughs.

Cam notices my empty beer bottle. "Need a refill?" he asks.

I follow his gaze to the empty bottle and shrug my shoulders. "Sure, why not?"

He wraps his hand around the neck of the bottle, taking it from me. "Be right back." With one last wink in my direction, he disappears into the thick crowd surrounding us.

Almost immediately, I feel hands on my hips, spinning me around. Sadie and Elle's excitable screams force me to cover my ears.

"Oh-my-God, he-is-gorgeous," Elle rushes out, straining to follow Cam's trail through the crowd.

"Agreed, Rory. You should totally tap that." Sadie sips on her glass of clear liquid, smirking at me.

I laugh at my friends' assessments, because I plan to do exactly that. Cam looks like he's the type who wouldn't mind a quickie in a back alley or bathroom.

A deep voice clears its throat behind me and I spin around, expecting Cam. The smile fades from my lips when I lift my chin, coming face to face with my *favorite* Breakers' player. His towering height makes him look distinctly out of place on the dance floor. That, and the fact he's standing completely still in a sea of dancing bodies.

"What do you want?" I narrow my eyes at him, trying to look past him for any sign of Cam. hoping to get away from Aidan as quickly as possible.

"Are you having fun?" I don't miss the subtle look of judgement in Aidan's cool green eyes.

"I *was*," I shoot back, looking him up and down pointedly.

Cam chooses the perfect moment to reappear, two glasses in his hands. I raise a confused brow at the sight of the hard liquor, but brush it off, reaching to take the glass he's handing me.

Aidan shoulders his way between us, knocking my hand and sending my glass careening to the floor where it shatters.

I squeak out in surprise when the cool liquid and bits of ice splash up against my leg.

"Dude, what the fuck?" I catch a flash of pure rage in Cam's eyes before it's gone again, giving me pause. He's laser focused on Aidan beside me.

Aidan turns to face Cam, wedging himself further between Cam and me in the process, and inadvertently pushing me behind him. He towers over Cam by at least four inches and sends a look promising death toward my dance partner.

"Get the fuck out of my club, Reeves." Aidan signals to the nearest bouncer, pointing at Cam.

Cam's light eyes darken, becoming almost unrecognizable before he sneers at Aidan. "You know what... fuck you, O'Rourke." I watch their exchange with wide-eyed surprise. Clearly, they know each other.

Cam shakes his head in frustration, but stalks his way through the crowd, pushing a couple of girls out of his way as he passes by.

Okay, maybe there were some red flags...

"What the hell, Aidan?" I practically shout, shoving him hard from behind and forcing his gaze back to me. A quick glance around me turns up no sign of Elle or Sadie; the thick crowd must have separated me from them at some point.

He looks down at me with an infuriatingly bored expression, as if he can barely stand to *talk* to me after going out of his way to cock-block me. "Your father wouldn't approve." He gives me a casual shrug before he looks away, scanning the crowd of dancers around us.

"Puh-lease," I scoff, folding my arms across my chest, "like you give a shit." His excuse for ruining my night is lame, and we both know it. But I don't have the time or the bandwidth right now to work out Aidan's true motivation. It's at that moment his previous words sink in. "Wait, a minute..." I wobble slightly on my heels, the result of both alcohol and the raucous crowd moving around us. "You *own* this club?"

He gives me a hard look, like it should be obvious.

"Of course you do," I mumble, nearly under my breath. I pull out my cell and check the time. It's nearly one. A quick glance over to the VIP area shows the Breakers and Belles in full party mode.

I spy Liv, half deep into a mojito, still wrapped around none other than Mr. Colt King himself. I heave out a small sigh. She's not leaving anytime soon...

I look up to find Aidan still watching me. "Well, as much fun as this has been... I'm out. Have the night you deserve, Aidan." I give him a little salute because... of course I do... and spin on my heel. For good measure, I shout back over my shoulder, "Don't follow me."

I leave him with my best withering stare, and make a beeline out of the bar.

38

GIVE. ME. BACK. MY. PHONE.

RORY

*S*torming out into the cool night air, my cheeks heat with both rage and embarrassment. The line waiting outside the club is still long despite the late hour, so I take off in the opposite direction down the sidewalk. I need to get away from the crowd.

The heels on my boots click against the concrete while I unlock my phone to pull up the ride-share app.

There's no way in hell I'm waiting around here for a ride home with Liv. The way she was curled around the Breakers' center... I'm not sure she's planning on taking us home at all.

The sound of heavy footsteps behind me has me instantly on edge. I feel fine—a little buzzed—but, I've still got my wits about me.

I pretend to bury my nose in my phone as I walk, subtly fingering the hemline of my skirt, just below where I've strapped the small knife I started wearing after everything went down with the O'Rourkes. I still need to convince Niko to get me my own gun.

The footsteps grow closer, moving fast as if they are trying to catch up to me. When a hand lands on my arm, I'm ready. I snatch the knife from its sheath and spin around, pressing the knife right up against my attacker's—*Aidan's*—throat.

"Aidan?"

Of-fucking-course it's Aidan. I have one hand against his hard chest and the other hand gripping the knife tightly and pressing it purposefully against his throat. The cold steel glints in the dim glow of the streetlight.

His hand is no longer on my arm. Instead, he has them both raised up, palms facing me in surrender. The initial wide eyed shock I saw on his face has morphed into a wicked smile. "Little lion's got claws."

"Don't call me that." I drop the knife from his throat, knowing full well he could take it from me in a second if he wanted. "What do you want Aidan?" *Honestly, hasn't he done enough?*

He looks around at the deserted sidewalk. "How are you getting home?"

The question's unexpected. I sigh, lifting my phone and giving it a little shake, showing off the half-completed ride request.

"Seriously?" His eyes narrow on my screen. "Absolutely not." He crosses his arms and gives me a stern look. *Where does he get the nerve?*

"What, did you think I was going to call Niko to come get me?" I give him a long look. "Do you think I have a *death* wish?" I turn and continue down the sidewalk, away from the bar and *away* from Aidan. I look around for a street name to enter into the ride-share app.

Aidan's hand comes down over my shoulder, plucking the phone right out of my hands.

"Hey!" I leap after it, clawing for the device. But he uses height to his advantage, easily pulling the phone out of reach. Grinning down at me, he's clearly amused.

It's enough to make me explode. I punch him, hard, catching him by surprise. Shock and delight dance in those emerald eyes. "I didn't take you as one who likes to play dirty Kostalova." he laughs.

"Give. Me. Back. My. Phone." I seethe, contemplating pulling out the knife again.

"No." The smirk on Aidan's face is enough to make my blood boil as he slips my phone into the front pocket of his jeans. Taunting, dismissive and utterly infuriating. My eyes track the movement and as soon as he deposits it, I make a dive for his jeans.

He easily fends me off, trapping my wrists in his rough hands and pulling them away from his groin. "Easy there love, didn't know you were so eager to get into my pants." *Again with that damn Irish accent.* He winks at me and I crinkle my nose in disgust.

I open my mouth to give him an earful, but I'm cut off as Aidan scoops me up and throws me over his shoulder. I kick my feet and beat my fists into his back. "What are you doing?" I shout, looking around for any bystanders who can help. But the side street I've walked us down is completely deserted. "Put. Me. Down." A closed fist hit to his lower back accompanies each word.

"No thanks, kitten. Someone's gotta make sure you get home safe and stay the fuck out of Cam Reeves' bed."

The nerve of this guy. "Not your job," I point out. "I can sleep with whatever asshole I want to."

He jostles me on his shoulder, and I let out a grunt. He repositions me so he can wrap his biceps around my flailing legs, pinning them down against his chest. "That *asshole* has a reputation for drugging his little conquests. *I thought* I was doing you a favor. Unless unconscious non-con is your flavor of choice?"

I still in his arms, processing the words.

"Yeah, that's what I thought."

"Fine," I huff out, letting my body deflate and giving him the win. "But I want to go home." But Aidan is carrying me back toward the bar.

"Where the fuck do you think we're going?"

He comes to a stop, sliding me down his chest until my feet are firmly planted back on the ground. I'm calmer now—still digesting what he just told me. Aidan gestures to the left of us and I look over to see we're standing on the curb right next to an awfully familiar matte black bike. I recognize the little holographic green shamrock on the fuel tank. It's the same one I have painted on my stomach.

"No."

"Yes."

He steps away to retrieve the helmet he has hanging on his handlebars, keeping one eye on me, as if he expects me to bolt.

I haven't ruled out that very possibility myself... "*You're taking me home?*" I eye him warily before looking around for potential witnesses to another Irish kidnapping. The line outside of Last Call has finally filed through, but there are a few people still milling about.

The wind picks up and I shiver, noticing the cold for the

first time. Both my anger, and the warmth Aidan had unintentionally provided, ebbing out of me.

The Breakers' defenseman looks me over, the amused smirk on his face turning into a frown. He reaches over, grabbing his motorcycle hoodie off his bike and offering it to me.

Weighing my options, I glance between him and the sweatshirt. I'm not getting very far in my skirt and heels without my phone. I could go back in the bar and find the girls, but he'd only follow me inside.

Letting out a defeated sigh, I take the hoodie, shrugging it on. It's heavy, armored and black, the color I've come to associate with Aidan. I roll my eyes like it's an inconvenience, but relax into the warmth of the sweatshirt. Next, I take the helmet and pull it over my head.

Aidan pulls a matching one over his own, disappearing behind a blacked out visor before mounting the bike. The engine rumbles to life under him. He swings his head back, looking at me expectantly. "Get on the bike, Kostalova."

I look to the stars, swearing under my breath, as I climb on the back of Aidan's bike.

My already short skirt rides up with the motion and I scoot closer to Aidan so no one can see between my legs. As soon as I wrap my arms securely around him, he takes off, forcing me to cling even tighter as he leans into the first turn.

The sight of the pavement rising to greet us has me squeezing him tight. Once we level out, I feel a reassuring hand graze my thigh. He leaves it there until my body relaxes and the death grip I have on his shirt loosens. Aidan brings his hand back to his handlebars, focusing on the road ahead.

It's a short ride back to the mansion and before I know it, Aidan's hitting the kill switch. I'm almost disappointed. He pulls off at the end of my street. I'm off the bike as quick as I am able, nearly falling off in my haste. I pull the helmet off my head and hand it to him before pulling his hoodie off, too.

He watches me and takes the jacket back without a word, putting it on. An expression I can't even begin to decipher forms on his face.

I rock impatiently on my heels and hold out a palm to him. "My phone," I huff out when he still doesn't move.

"Right." Aidan reaches into his pocket, and slides out my cell. He holds it up to my face, front camera out. I watch my phone unlock.

"Hey..." I reach for it, but he pulls it back, typing something into it. I strain to see around his shoulder, watching as he hits the green call button. His own phone vibrates in his pocket, and he pulls it out before handing mine back to me.

I take it. Displeasure pulls at the corners of my lips, when I realize he just gave himself my phone number.

"Text me when you're inside the house."

I roll my eyes.

"Text me Kostalova." His eyes flash dangerously.

"Why do you even care?"

"Because kidnapped Russian angels are bad for business." His left eyebrow lifts and he sits back on his bike, arms folded, watching me with an air of expectation.

"Fine." I grip my cell tightly in my fist and stalk off down the street. I'm fully aware Aidan's eyes follow me the entire way. I might swing my hips just a little more than necessary just to fuck with him. When I finally reach the gate, I slow down, raising a middle finger to the sky before hearing a bike rev to life and slowly fade away into the distance.

39

UNKNOWN NUMBER

RORY

I'd planned to scale the wall again, but when I attempt to sneak past the gate, I notice the guard house is empty.

According to my watch, it's barely two a.m. Unusual—but I'll take it. Anything to avoid climbing the eight-foot wall again in these heels.

Pushing open the gate, I scurry up the driveway before Sasha returns, cringing at every crunch of gravel under my boots.

As expected, the side door's unlocked. I enter the dark and silent house, but as I start down the hall, an overwhelming sense of unease creeps into me. Nothing appears to be amiss, but the mansion seems darker than usual, and there's an odd smell in the air. I can't quite pinpoint what it is, but it just smells... off.

Keeping my heels off the floor, I cross on hurried tiptoes across the parlor to check the back terrace. The lights are out, but after watching for a minute, there's no moving shadow of a guard out there.

My father has been keeping security light, but this isn't right. For *both* guards to go missing from their posts?

I stand awkwardly in the shadows of the darkened parlor— unsure of what to do. I should go right up to my bedroom, lock the door and hide under the covers until morning, but I just can't seem to move my feet.

The vibration of the phone in my pocket nearly scares me to death; my heart hammers in my chest. *Calm down, you're probably freaking out about nothing...* I tell myself as I peer down at the text. It's from an unknown number.

Unknown: "Home safe?"

It has to be from Aidan, but before I can type out a reply, loud voices carry in from the direction of my father's study. *Angry* voices.

Swallowing hard, I pocket my phone and slowly creep closer to the hallway to make out what the voices are saying. I don't recognize them. The man is shouting in Russian, demanding payment for something. A glass breaks and I flinch so hard I nearly fall over. A few dull thumping sounds follow the crash, each one accompanied by a groan or pained grunt.

Did Papa bring someone here to get money out of them? He has places for that...

Why would he bring them to the mansion?

After a few more of those thumping sounds, I gather up the nerve to peek around the corner; immediately pulling back, heart pounding harder at the sight of two armed men, dressed in black, standing guard in front of the study door.

And not all black designer suits like my father prefers; all black *tactical gear*. Military raid style.

Chest heaving, I press myself up against the wall, biting my lip. After a minute, when no one comes looking, I shakily back up a few feet. Freaking out again when I pass by the front window, spotting at least two more men—dressed the same as the two in the hall, conversing with each other out in the driveway.

I scramble away from the window, then completely freeze in panic when the angry Russian man shouts again. This time, I'm close enough to hear him.

"It's very simple Adrik—"

My throat catches, realizing the man shouting is addressing *my father*.

"—you knew the terms when you borrowed the money. Pay up and we can be done with this ugly business."

For the first time, I hear my father's voice, sounding more pinched than I've ever heard it, "I just need a couple of weeks. Let me talk to Ronan. We can work something out."

The sound of what I've realized is another fist hitting flesh has me chewing the inside of my cheek. They're hitting him— hitting *my* father.

"Who do you think sent us, Kostalov?" The Russian man laughs sadistically. I take a step back out of instinct. "You should know better than to make a deal and not deliver."

I rack my brain for the name *Ronan*. When you're quiet, you hear more than you should and I have a small bank in my head of my father's contacts: friends and foes. But I don't think I've ever heard a Ronan mentioned before...

"Fuck you, Ivan and fuck Volkov too," my father hisses.

My blood turns to ice.

I may have never heard of Ronan, but I certainly know *Volkov*. *What the fuck is Adrik doing pissing off the Russian wolves?* My father might control most of the East Coast but the Volkov control *all* Bratva business.

More shattering glass and the sound of something wooden breaking... "That's a real shame Adrik, are you sure you don't want to reconsider? I have it on good authority your daughter is upstairs right now, asleep in her little bed. Shall we go fetch her?" I can hear the malicious smile in Ivan's words.

A string of expletives stream out of my father, but I don't wait around to hear the rest. Remembering the Russian wolves out front, as quietly as I can, I fly down the hall, veering away from the stairs and heading for the kitchen and the back door.

At the last second, I think to check before racing around the corner and pull back in horror when I spot more of those armed men by the kitchen door.

Shit.

Back in the foyer, the study door crashes open behind me and I don't think. Instinctively, I scamper up the stairs—the only option left to me—tripping over my own feet in my haste.

I run past my room—not even an option since that's where they're headed—and pace frantically up and down the hall, trying to think where else to hide. An idea pops in my head and I open my room, locking the door before shutting it again. *Maybe that will buy some time.*

Still in the hallway, the sound of boots on the stairs sends me flying into the closest door, the guest room next to my own. I eye the bed but end up jumping into the small closet.

Heart racing, I pull the closet door closed, leaving a crack open so I have a clear line of sight to the hall door. There isn't much in the closet, except for a few old fur coats that smell like they might date back to the Russian Revolution. I press as far back as I can, but if someone opens the door—it's game over.

Sinking down, I curl up in a ball, wrapping my arms around my knees and trying to calm myself down enough to think. Remembering the knife I still have strapped to my thigh, I pull it out, gripping it tightly in one hand. The door to my room shakes violently as someone tries forcing their way in.

"Aurora?" Ivan sing-songs my name with false sweetness. "Aurora darling, open up. Your father would like to see you in his study."

I tremble, almost dropping the knife, thinking about what would have happened if I'd actually stayed in bed like I should have tonight.

"Aurora?" Ivan tries again, sweetness gone. When he receives no answer, he barks out, "Get it open."

The sound of someone attempting to kick the door down fills my ears. The mansion is old and well built; my door is constructed of thick and heavy wood, but even I know it won't last long against these guys.

My forgotten phone rings, the vibrations shattering the quiet, and I curse, fumbling with the device, scrambling to silence the call. Even on vibrate, the sound seems so loud. I hold my breath once I've silenced it, waiting to see if anyone else heard it...

They're still loudly working on breaking down the door. And by the sounds of splintering wood—they're almost through.

My phone is still in my hands when it goes off again, and I stare blankly at the device. An unknown number appears on the screen.

Carefully, I slide my thumb across the screen to answer the call, eyeing the hall door through the crack in the closet as I do. "Aidan?" I whisper as loudly as I dare.

It's him alright. Aidan's voice blasts through the speaker, "Kostalova, why the fuck didn't you text me when you got home? I told you—"

I swallow hard, only half listening to him rage on the other end, the crashing sounds coming from my room distracting me... they've broken through. For once, Aidan isn't my biggest problem.

"You better have a damn good reason for not sending that text, love, or trust me when I say there will be consequences."

Despite everything going on, my stomach does a flip at the thought of what Aidan's *consequences* might be... Just then, something crashes hard against the wall at my back. My muscles lock up, tense and rigid. Shouts in Russian come through the wall and the crashing sounds intensify as furniture and other debris fly around the room as they search for me. I choke out a sob, slamming my hand over my mouth to keep quiet.

There's silence on the other end of the phone.

"Rory?" The sharpness of Aidan's voice refocuses my attention, and I remember I'm on the phone.

"*There's someone in the house,*" I get out, hoping he can decipher my terrified whispers.

His voice cools to something frigid, "Who?"

"*I don't know I—*"

"Your father's men?"

I shake my head before remembering he can't see me. "*No,*" I answer him, "I-I heard them mention Volkov..."

Aidan curses.

"Aurora, come out, come out wherever you are," Ivan sings through the wall and my breath catches. Something else crashes down hard in my room, sounding an awful lot like my bookshelf collapsing.

Aidan's quiet for a moment and I check my phone to see if he hung up, but the screen still shows us connected. "Aidan?" I whisper, panic in my voice, though I don't know what I expect him to do about it. Hell, he's probably enjoying this, putting me on speaker for the O'Rourke clan to hear.

"Where are you?"

I stumble over my words, trembling at the sounds of boots in the hallway. "Hiding. In one of the guest room closets..."

"Don't let them find you." The line goes dead and I stare down at the phone...

He hung up.

My fingers tighten around the phone.

He hung up on me... *I can't believe he hung up on me.*

With the Russians tearing through the bathroom across the hall, I regroup, scrolling through my contacts until I find my brother's name. Niko's phone goes right to voicemail. *No, no, no...* I go back through my contacts, but there's no one else... and so I try Niko again.

By now, Ivan and his men have left my bedroom. A couple of them thud back down the stairs, but at least two stay back, searching the other rooms.

Someone pushes the guest room door open and I hold my breath. My finger slides across the red bar, ending my call. My body trembles with adrenaline. I don't dare move as he enters the room and looks around. "I know you're in here, doll," Ivan's voice croons.

My mind races to come up with a plan, any plan, but before I can come up with anything, a shadow blocks out the light illuminating the closet.

"Found you," The Russian sneers, wrenching open the closet door and dragging me out by my hair.

"Let me go!" I struggle against him, but he's got a solid grip and tears stream down my face from the burn in my scalp. He shoves me toward the bed, thankfully releasing my hair, but there's nowhere to go—nowhere to run. He's got me cornered.

"So, this is the little Russian angel everybody's talking about?" He leans in, his breath a mixture of cigarettes and vodka. "The one whose hand will pay off all of daddy's debts?" He looks me up and down and bile burns the back of my throat when his hand grips my hip, tugging it closer.

"Don't touch me," I bite out, still able to find some defiance in my terror.

He just smiles, and I recoil from his cold eyes. "Daddy should've paid his bills... Don't think you'll be worth very much once I'm done with you. You know what they say about putting all your eggs in one basket..."

I let out a strangled scream as he grabs hold of my hair again, hurling me onto the bed. Stalking after me and unbuckling his belt, his lips curl up, showing off a yellow-toothed grin. But my eyes go to the dark shadow closing in fast behind him.

Ivan's smile fades a second before his head twists violently, a little too far the right. A shiver runs through my body and I push myself as far back as I can go on the bed. Watching as Ivan falls to his knees, the light gone from his eyes, dead before his face hits the ground.

Shaking uncontrollably, I stare up at the dark figure standing feet from the side of the bed. Two familiar green eyes stare back at me. My heart is pounding with a mixture of relief and disbelief.

Aidan.

He came.

40

NO LIES

AIDAN

"*D*id he hurt you?" I have to ask twice to get a response. Relief courses through me when Rory slowly shakes her head no. Her blue eyes—wide and full of terrors—are fixed on mine. I look down at Ivan's body with an overwhelming desire to kill him again.

She's lucky I was so close. After dropping her off, I pulled off down the next street, waiting for her text before leaving the area.

Gunshots ring out from the floor below and she jumps.

"Stay behind me," I order. I hold out my hand to help her off the bed. Trying to keep my eyes on both her and the hall.

She hesitates for a moment, staring at my hand and back into my eyes before taking it.

I pull her up, keeping her behind me while not letting go of her soft hand. Moving cautiously back toward the hallway.

The shouts and gunfire exchange continue from the first floor as Koen takes on the rest of Volkov's men. I'd heard their bikes arrive right before I found Rory in the guest room.

"Follow me and stay close."

Her hand tightens around mine as I take us down the hallway, stepping around the body of the other Russian I took out before Ivan. The gunfire from downstairs has quieted.

When we reach the top landing, I peer over the edge.

"Koen?" I shout into the dark silence.

The familiar deep cadence of my brother's voice yells up, "It's clear. Come on down."

I relax, turning back to face Rory. A mix of shock and confusion mar her beautiful face.

"Are you okay?" I ask, unprepared for how close to me I find her.

She nods her head quickly, her eyes darting around as she surveys the empty foyer from the upper landing.

I grip her chin, and she freezes while I bring her gaze to mine. "No lies," I remind her.

Her eyes well up, but she blinks away the tears before shaking her head slowly back and forth.

With my free arm, I wrap it around the back of her and pull her into my chest, keeping her there until her breathing finally levels out.

"Aidan?" Koen calls up and I peer over the railing, spotting him at the bottom of the stairs watching us.

"C'mon," I say to Rory, reluctantly releasing her from my hold. She follows silently behind me, pressing closer as we go to pass Koen, who motions toward the kitchen.

Various bodies lie strewn about the foyer, forcing us to step around them. Blood stains the polished marble floors. As we enter the kitchen, we find the rest of Koen's men waiting around along with a bloody-faced Adrik Kostalov, standing over two men. Both are dressed in black tactical gear, hands zip-tied behind their backs, kneeling at the Russian Pakhan's feet.

Adrik's eyes snap to Rory before sliding over to meet mine. He gives what looks to be a nod of gratitude before turning his attention back to Volkov's men at his feet.

Blood coats his face, soaked from a particularly nasty gash to the side of the head. Still, he's on his feet, with his gun pointed square between the eyes of one of the Russians.

The gun goes off at the same moment Nikolai and a few of his Bratva cronies burst through the patio door.

Rory's hand tightens on mine, fear of the shot or her brother, I'm not sure and Koen steps forward, angling himself between the newest arrivals and Rory and me.

"What the fuck is this?" Niko asks, raising his gun and looking between Koen and me, not quite sure where to point it.

"It's all under control," Adrik waves his son down. "It only takes one to tell a story." The Russian Pakhan's gun moves from the body to the man now pleading in what must be Russian at his feet.

Niko looks around wildly, taking in the bodies by the back door and the sight of the Irish standing around his kitchen. His gun is still pointed at me, but there's uncertainty in his eyes. Koen rustled up quite the crew with next-to-no notice. Besides myself, it's Liam, Jace, Mac, Jerrad and Garrett standing around the room, outnumbering the Bratva 2:1. We're lucky that they were all at Last Call for closing time.

When Niko's eyes catch sight of his sister at my side, they harden and he takes a step forward, forcing me to straighten my shoulders. The rest of the room grows tense with the movement.

"Take this one to the basement," Adrik orders, oblivious to everything playing out around him, and Niko freezes. "I think what he has to say will be *very* enlightening."

Niko gives me one last glare before following his father's orders. He sends his men in with a nod. They pick Volkov's man off the floor and drag him off to the Kostalov basement from hell. What goes on down there... Of course I've heard the stories. I wouldn't wish it on my worst enemy. I don't know of anyone more *creative* than Niko Kostalov.

The elder Kostalov holsters his piece and straightens, adjusting his suit that's in quite the state of disarray before addressing both Koen and me. "The Bratva owes you a great debt for coming to the aid of both my daughter and me."

He beckons for Rory to come to him.

With a moment of hesitation, Rory detaches herself from my side. She releases my hand and walks on wobbly legs to stand beside her father. Her chin is held high despite what almost happened in that bedroom.

Adrik places a bloody hand on her shoulder and she stiffens from the contact.

"We hadn't heard from you regarding the Cartel deal... Figured we'd stop in." Koen steps forward with a casual shrug, moving to lean against the kitchen island with his arms folded across his chest. "Looks like we had good timing." He looks around with a pointed expression. "What did you do to piss off Ronan Volkov?"

I swear Adrik's skin pales at the mention of the Volkov name, but it's gone in an instant, the mask dropping into place while waving his hand flippantly through the air. "A misunderstanding. I'll call Volkov up tonight and clear this up in minutes."

Koen's frown deepens and we exchange a look.

"I'm sure you know we are having a little party next week," Adrik starts.

Little?

Kostalov's birthday party has been the talk of the town for weeks. He's made certain the city's most influential players will all be in attendance. "I'm hoping you can come? We can discuss the terms of bringing the Irish in on the Cartel deal over a cigar, perhaps?" He smiles, though it doesn't touch his eyes.

"We'd be honored," Koen says as he straightens to his full height, pushing off the counter. "I look forward to discussing terms." He steps forward, offering Adrik his hand, forcing Adrik to release his grip on his daughter in order to shake it. "Rory." My brother offers her a cordial nod, which she returns before her eyes find mine.

I don't say anything, and neither does she, as I follow Koen and the rest of the Irish out the door, her damn steely blue eyes telling me everything I need to know.

41

DANGER & DIOR

RORY

I barely slept—even with Niko and his crew patrolling the halls—I couldn't do it. Jumping at every little noise or sound while curled up in the guest room's bed, not the best place to be either, but my room had been absolutely destroyed by Volkov's men last night.

When I came downstairs the next morning, I was surprised to find no trace of the events. Staring down at my reflection in the foyer's gleaming floors. Not a trace or smear of blood remained from the bodies that lay here just hours before. It only unnerves me more, what these men are capable of.

I suppose I should be grateful no one noticed my clear lack of pajamas and obvious club attire with everything going on. Or, at least my father didn't.

Niko, on the other hand, has been nearly impossible to shake. We're back to business as usual, but with a drastically shorter leash. Niko's taken to watching every move I make. He's even moved back into his old room, the one right across the hall from mine.

My brother's new habit of dropping by my room at random times of night to make sure I am in it has led to me expanding my vocabulary of expletives as I brainstorm new and exciting ways to expel him from my space.

It's unnecessary.

Following the Volkov attack on the mansion, my father finally ramped up security. It's practically Fort Knox now. And while I'm reassured no one is getting in, unfortunately, it also means no one is getting out.

The Breakers are on a bye week after their win over the Falcons. I should enjoy the time off, but all it does is increase the intensity the black cloud of misery that is my impending nuptials. Skating is both my distraction, and my outlet, and without it, I'm left to stew in my anxiety over marrying someone I don't know.

The increased security and lack of ice time is probably the only reason I'm actually looking forward to the party tonight. Niko and my father will be plenty distracted by all the guests. I might be able to slip away without their knowledge.

The last roadblock in my way is Matteo.

Father informed me he will be my escort to the party tonight. I haven't even seen my *intended* since our first meeting over brunch a couple of weeks ago. But Niko was kind enough to inform me the other day the contracts have been drawn up. It's only a matter of setting a date.

All week, I've tried to pry information about my fiancé from anyone I could corner; my family, the cook, my guards, and even the maids. I quickly came to the conclusion, from all of their tight-lipped replies, that either they know very little of Matteo Carroza, or they don't want to tell me what they do.

He was pleasant enough at brunch, and it's my only hope

that he's nice, because my father has decided; I will marry Matteo, and it won't matter whether or not I want to. In the Mafia, marriage is for life. Divorce will not be an option.

Perhaps I can coax some more details out of the man himself tonight. Maybe I won't have to run away after all. He was nice enough the other day. Sure, he was preoccupied with talking with my father, but it's hardly enough information to decide whether or not to marry the guy. But we are grasping at straws here.

That was until he sent the dress... A sense of fashion? Check no on that one.

I stare at the dress laid out on the bed. It's gold. And not in a shimmery, pretty, polished-gold way. It's gold in a gaudy, tacky, *look-at-me* kind of way. Short too... Almost indecently so, seeing as we're attending a formal black-tie event where I'm to be paraded about in front of the Bratva and other made men. Our engagement will be formally announced. *Why would Matteo want me to wear this?*

I chew my lip and glance toward my closet, at the dress I'd originally planned to wear tonight. The red color makes it a little ostentatious for my taste, but I couldn't help but fall in love with it the other day when Elle forced me to try it on. The material is soft satin, with a structured bodice that dips down into a deep V, held up by thin straps before tightening at the waist and flaring out at the hips. It's elegant, sophisticated, and, most definitely, the dress I'm wearing tonight.

My mind made up, I stride across the room, pulling out the dress before I can talk myself out of it. Matteo won't care. He's a man. He probably won't even notice, I even pair it with gold, strappy heels and dainty gold teardrop earrings for my fiancé's benefit.

Pulling my long hair half back, I leave a few curled tendrils out to frame my face. I keep my make-up light, with only a little mascara, a brush of blush, and soft pink lips.

I smooth the skirt of my dress and take a few steadying breaths before braving the foyer.

Taking my time, I descend the staircase, hoping Matteo's only just arrived and I'm not running late. But when I reach the midpoint landing of the stairway, I freeze.

Because it's not Matteo Carroza standing at the bottom of the steps below...

It's Aidan O'Rourke.

42

THE BRIDE WORE RED

RORY

The last person I ever expected to see tonight leans casually against the railing of the stairwell, waiting —but not for me.

I see him before he sees me—paused on the landing, frozen at the sight of him. A quick glance around shows the foyer empty besides the two of us.

No one else around...

My pulse races when our eyes connect, and for a second, I consider turning tail and running for my room. But some unknown force propels me forward, moving my feet as I descend the rest of the stairs. My hand glides gracefully along the banister as I go. Each step brings me closer to him.

Aidan's green eyes follow me down.

I search his face for the usual arrogant smirk—noticeably absent. In its place, an unreadable expression—an unfamiliar softness in the dark pine of his eyes. They trail down my body from my eyes to my gold painted toes. He pushes off the banister when I finally reach the bottom, straightening to his full height.

"Gorgeous," he murmurs, just loud enough for me to hear.

I blink back in surprise, searching his face for any trace of sarcasm, but I don't find it. The raw vulnerability I see in his eyes is a direct line to the warmth I feel spreading across my cheeks, and something deep inside me twists.

The silence stretches out between us. All the air feels like it's gone from the room, forcing my breaths to quicken. What air remains feels supercharged—crackling with something unspoken. Or maybe this dress is just too tight...

Just as I open my mouth in response, voices drift in from down the hallway—from the study. My father appears, wearing a politician's smile, followed closely by Niko, Matteo, and Koen.

Koen?

The group halts, the conversation falling to a noticeable stop at the sight of us and I... I'm increasingly aware of the proximity between myself and the younger O'Rourke with every second that passes.

Sure enough, as soon as my eyes lock on Matteo, his expression darkens, sizing up Aidan beside me.

Remembering myself, I straighten my shoulders and take a few timid steps toward my fiancé. "I was looking for you—" I say hesitantly, thrown off a little by the way Matteo is glaring at me. "What are they doing here?" I look to Koen, who's watching me with an unreadable expression not unlike his brother's. His mouth tight, something like resignation in his eyes. I tilt my head in confusion.

It's my father who finally breaks the uncomfortable silence,

"O'Rourke and I had business to discuss." He turns to the newly appointed head of the Irish mob, "We'll see you boys at the party."

Koen gives a curt nod to my father and another to me before striding out the front door, taking Aidan with him without another glance back in my direction. I stare after them, feeling completely thrown off my axis.

"Aurora?"

I turn, surprised to find Matteo now just inches away, looking at me expectantly.

"What?" I glance between him and my father, realizing I've missed something.

"I said, are you ready to go?" He speaks slowly, with marked annoyance in his tone. I've only met the man twice and already I've managed to piss him off.

"Yes," I agree, nodding my head a bit too exuberantly.

We arrive at the Royale, one of the Bratva's elite hotels. Matteo opens the door, even though he hasn't spoken a word to me the entire ride. Too busy making endless polite conversation with the rest of the Kostalov family.

Surely he can't be mad at me for standing in the foyer of my own house next to Aidan, can he?

My anxiety hits its peak as we walk through the lobby on our way to the ballroom, like we're in some kind of royal procession. Matteo walks at my side but doesn't take my arm, staring straight ahead. I twist a strand of my hair between my fingers, stealing anxious glances up at him every few minutes.

A nervous attendant informs my father it'll be a moment

before they'll announce him into the party. Live music and the sound of voices carry through the closed doors ahead of us.

My father waves him away, "Fine, fine."

The attendant scurries away, grateful to be dismissed.

"I'm going to get a drink," Matteo announces out of the blue, adjusting his suit jacket, a deep navy.

My father nods, turning to discuss something with Niko.

Matteo starts back toward the lobby, and I feel the weight of his gaze. His eyes narrow, darting in the bar's direction before coming back to rest on me.

Oh, he means for me to accompany him. It's a bit of a shock seeing as how he's practically ignored me all evening. I look to my father and Niko, but both are still fully engrossed in whatever it is they are discussing. I take a few cautious steps toward Matteo. Once he's confirmed I'm following him, he stalks off toward the lobby and it's a struggle to keep up with him in my heels.

I've just about caught up to him when he suddenly takes a sharp left turn down a service hallway. I follow him, confused, since we're no longer headed for the bar. About halfway down the hall, he whirls on me.

I nearly stumble back in surprise, and he catches my arm before I fall, using his grip to shove me hard into the wall and hold me there.

Stunned, I stare up into cold, brown eyes, fixed on me. When he drops them to my chest, my breath catches and I try to squirm away, uncomfortable under his close gaze. "Nice dress." The dangerous sarcasm in his tone sends a shiver racing down my spine.

Is that what this is about? Is he mad I didn't wear the one he sent?

244

I struggle for a response, for anything to say, too surprised and distracted by the pain his hand is causing my arm. He tightens his grip, his fingers digging into my skin. The more I try to pull away from him, the tighter he grips, so I stop moving.

He smiles.

My heart drops.

His smile is unnerving. Nervously, I look around for anyone—but the hallway is empty. Matteo brings his other hand up to tuck a stray curl behind my ear. I flinch at the sight of his hand so close to my face.

He *laughs*, invading my space more now that he knows I dislike it.

"I don't want to see you anywhere near Aidan O'Rourke ever again. Do you understand me?" Every syllable is enunciated.

I clench my jaw but refuse to answer, my temper rising.

Matteo moves fast. His fist is in my hair before I can dodge it, forcing my head in an up and down motion. "Yes, Matteo, I *understand* Matteo," he seethes under his breath. I can tell he wants so badly to scream the words at me, but we're still so close to the lobby. My eyes flicker in that direction, willing someone, *anyone,* to walk by. His grip on my hair is punishing. Tears spring loose and I can't hold back the whimper of pain.

"Say it."

"I understand, *Matteo*." I force the words out. His eyes are on my face and so I clench my fists. Spite coating my words. He narrows his eyes, but after another terrifying moment, he finally releases me. Stepping back, he fixes his suit while I take in a few shaky breaths, held up only by the wall at my back.

Matteo takes off back down the hall, but I linger, holding onto the wall like it's my lifeline.

"Aurora," he says my name, sharply enough to get me to move to meet him where he waits for me.

Shaken and dazed, I follow him, like a lost puppy. Rubbing my arm while blinking away tears.

"Put a smile on your face before I give you something to cry about." His words cut through me like a knife and I flinch again. His caramel eyes harden and I swallow a lump in my throat before turning the corners of my lips into a forced smile.

He grips my wrist and tugs me closer to him. "You're going to have to do better than that," he snarls under his breath. We've just about reached my father and brother, and at the sight of Matteo and me, my father gives the go ahead to the attendant to open the door.

Matteo switches on a dazzling smile, and I stare at him in horror, realizing just what type of man I'm set to marry. He half walks/half drags me into the room. Someone announces the man of the hour, his son, and *"the happy couple."* Adrik's very own daughter Aurora; and Matteo Carroza, Consigliere of the Boston Outfit.

My father has spared no expense on this party. The ballroom is full of finely dressed attendees. I move in a daze, retreating into myself, amidst the shouts and cheers for the newly engaged couple.

Someone thrusts a glass of champagne into my hand. I drain it before the toast, catching sight of a familiar shade of green as I bring my glass back down.

Quickly, I avert my gaze. I force my attention anywhere but on the imposing hockey player whose eyes I can still feel boring into me from the back of the room.

I flinch at Matteo's touch when he goes to move us through the crowd, guiding me to our seats. I stare out into nothingness as the toasts begin, a stupid smile plastered on my face. Playing my part as the doting daughter and perfect fiancée until my cheeks hurt.

43

COULDN'T SPRING FOR A RING?

AIDAN

*E*ngaged?

And to Matteo Carroza, of all people!

My brother tenses beside me when they make the announcement. This is news to us both. Watching the newly minted couple parade about the dance floor, I can feel the wheels turning in his mind from here.

A marriage between Matteo and Rory is a big deal.

A big fucking deal.

And not a good one for the Irish.

Somehow, things went from already fucking bad to way fucking worse. I go back over the conversation I had with Koen on the ride over here.

"I don't trust him."

Koen grunts beside me, zipping through cars on the highway like they're standing still. "Me neither."

One of my favorite things about my brother and me is we always seem to be on the same page. The two of us have always been able to know what each other is thinking without words. And right now, we're both thinking Adrik Kostalov is a snake.

The paperwork the Russian Pakhan had drawn up today... The cut was generous—too generous. That was only the first red flag. Adrik is getting sloppy in his old age.

His proposal: the Irish will supply muscle and ammunition to support the Cartel's cargo drop and subsequent transport. For our efforts, we'll receive a thirty percent cut.

A substantial amount of cash.

It reeks of a trap. Should've left the Russian piece of shit to die the other night.

Adrik's reaction to Koen wanting to think it over before signing... even more so. No wonder the Russian bastard didn't want me in the room. I would've told him where he could file that contract.

"This thing between you and the girl..."

"Rory."

He pauses for a long while, the silence heavy. "Rory," he corrects. "Caring for her complicates things."

"I don't care about her." Another heavy silence... followed by a sigh. I'm grateful when he lets it go. "Let's get through this fucking party, take stock of who shows and regroup."

I nod, agreeing. Leaning forward in my seat. Eager to get this done.

"How long do you think they've been together?"

Koen doesn't need to ask to know who I'm talking about. He looks up and studies the "happy" couple for a moment. "Probably not long... You know how these things go."

I wonder if she had a choice. The fiery little lion doesn't strike me as an ideal match for a traditionalist such as Matteo Carroza.

Another lie of omission? Rory never mentioned him when she was with us, but we're not exactly besties. But I know I would have noticed if that trash had been hanging around the rink.

I keep my eyes locked on the Bratva princess. No longer a secret, claimed publicly by the Pakhan just in time for a speedy engagement. *Convenient. Especially seeing as how Adrik must owe a ton of money to Ronan Volkov for him to send his men in after him the other night.*

The man of the hour beams under all the attention. Always showing off. Image is everything to a man like Adrik Kostalov. I spy him shaking hands with a few men I recognize as city officials while puffing on a large cigar, fully in his glory.

I turn my attention back to Rory. *I saw her see me.* As soon as she walked in, as if she knew exactly where to look. She hasn't looked this way since... And I haven't been able to look anywhere else.

A radiant smile graces her face, but it's not fooling me. The smile doesn't reach her eyes. Eyes that are disturbingly vacant, devoid of the emotions she's playing on her face. Her body is stiff in her fiancé's arms, stealing every opportunity she can to put space between them.

Matteo's irritation is clear in the way he keeps pulling her back to him. He's all over her, almost as if he knows that if she were to get free of him, she just might bolt.

Rory remains stuck to her fiancé's side for most of the night. All the way through dinner. That is, until after dessert, when Matteo leans in, speaking low into Rory's ear. She nods, and he turns on his heel and leaves her standing there.

Alone.

Her shoulders fall forward, exhaustion clear on her face, finally out of the spotlight for a brief reprieve.

"I'll be right back," I say to Koen as I rise from my seat.

My brother just shakes his head, leaning back to fold his arms across his chest, the ghost of an expression on his face.

I follow Rory at a distance to the far corner of the room, where she picks around a dessert table.

I sidle up beside her. She's unaware of my presence until I take her left hand in mine, lightly caressing the bare finger, the one second to the right. "What, he's too cheap to spring for a ring?"

Rory freezes, her eyes on our interconnected hands before peeking up through her lashes to find my face. She rips her hand out of mine like I'd burned her with it. Her eyes scan the nearby area, nervous and frantic. Whatever she's looking for, she doesn't find it because she visibly deflates with relief. "Don't touch me," she hisses, eyes still scanning the room.

"You failed to mention your betrothed during our little adventure a few weeks back." I move closer and she visibly stiffens.

"Adventure..." she scoffs. "Is that what you call it? Cause I can think of a few other words." Her eyes finally slide back to mine and she lifts her perfect little nose in the air. "You never asked." She goes back to searching the party until her eyes find her fiancé.

I follow her gaze to Matteo across the ballroom from us, engaged in deep conversation with Boston's police commissioner.

"Right." *Does she want him?* It has to be arranged. The way they keep her locked up... But she could still want it. Carroza's a terrible human, but busy with the Mafia. He'd hardly ever be home; for some Mafia wives, that's goals.

I start to touch her arm and she flinches violently away from me, a wild look in her eyes.

I straighten to my full height, peering down at her. She's not looking at me. "What's wrong with you?"

"Leave me alone, Aidan. I'm not your business, and I'm not your problem, okay?" Her eyes flare with blue fire before she pushes past me, knocking into my shoulder in her hurry.

I let her go. I spot Koen lingering by the exit, watching, waiting on me. I join him, and once we're outside, I tilt my head, checking who else might be in listening distance before speaking. "Carroza has gotten a little *too comfortable* in our city. It's time the Irish give him the welcome party he deserves."

Koen nods in agreement. A rare smile graces his sharp features. "It has been a little too quiet around here. Time to do what we do best and fuck some shit up."

44

THE SIN BIN

RORY

*N*ational qualifiers are in two days. I need every second of ice time I can get. We're set to fly out first thing tomorrow morning.

It's late, and Karina's long gone. I just finished another run-through of my routine, failing once again to land the triple-triple combination that's thankfully toward the end of my program. And now I'm wiped after running it too many times to count. I don't bother getting up this time. Half the lights are off in the arena, leaving half the ice in shadow.

I lay back, letting the cool ice calm my heated body, closing my eyes, trying to get my head right. The pressure of the competition, and my family's *expectations*, are getting to me.

"You dead, love?"

The deep tenor of a male voice startles me and I scramble up from where I'm lying, vulnerable, on the ice. No one else should be here... I rented *private* ice time.

I peer up and some of the tension ebbs away when I realize who stands over me.

"Go away, Aidan," I groan at the sight of the Irish enforcer standing over me, dark hair falling into his face as he studies me at his feet. He's dressed for a practice in his jersey and pads, leaning on his stick, cocky grin and all.

Determined to ignore him, I lay back on the ice and shut my eyes, hoping he'll take the hint.

"Did you fall?"

Now I know I'm imagining the trace of concern in his tone. My eyes fly open. Frustrated at the interruption of my mini meditation session, I push my body up off the ice. Getting my skates under me, I huff "I was taking a *break*—" I glare up at him before sighing irritably, "which is *clearly* over now..."

Aidan helps me to my feet, hooking a hockey glove under my arm. I wince, and quickly pull away, when he brushes against a sore spot. The dark bruises Matteo's fingers imprinted there last weekend are well hidden by my long sleeve top.

Aidan furrows his brow, reading pain on my face.

"Just sore... training," I mutter lamely, working my rotator cuff to better sell the lie, eyeing him warily. *The Breakers practiced this morning...* I remember the busy shift at the Chill Zone for their packed open practice. "Why are you here?" I fold my arms across my chest and look him over, doing my best to ignore how attractive all his hockey gear makes him look. "Or do you not have anything better to do than follow me around?"

"Don't flatter yourself, love," he hums, "you're the one on *my* ice." He drops a puck at his feet, deftly stick handling it back and forth, his hands moving impossibly fast to keep it well under control. "I suggest you get off of it before you get hurt." He shoots me a look, suggesting he might enjoy that, before he takes off.

Leaning into the ice, he takes long, powerful strides around the rink. Switching from forward to backward with a smooth motion, effortlessly crossing over with footwork that could give any figure skater a run for their money.

I catch myself gawking and shake my head to clear it. The exhaustion is clearly getting the better of me. *Don't even go there, Rory.*

"Actually, you're on *my* ice," I shout after him as he passes close to me. A few pieces of hair have come loose out of my ponytail and they fly back as he whips by a little too close. "I have the ice until nine-thirty."

Aidan laughs, carrying on with his warm-up, ignoring my protests. "It's past ten, Angel."

"*What?*" I left my phone in the locker room instead of keeping it with me and the Zamboni driver switched off the scoreboard clock when he left for the night hours ago.

"By the way, your guards are top tier." Aidan almost looks angry as he talks, "enjoying the latest pornos out in the parking lot."

I curl my nose in disgust. Niko's been busy this week, preparing for some big delivery the Bratva has coming in. And so Sasha's been appointed to accompany me to and from the rink. He waits outside while I practice. Honestly, I couldn't care less about what he does. I prefer the freedom. So long as he doesn't touch me. Some of my father's other guys... I wouldn't put it past them.

Aidan slows over by the far end of the rink, dragging a hockey net out onto the ice. I linger in the center circle, watching him. I don't know why I do. It's late. I should already be home, sleeping or mentally preparing for my competition. But for reasons unknown, my skates are frozen in place.

Aidan notices me staring and the corner of his lip ticks up into a knowing smile. "Give me a hand with this." He motions to the heavy goal post he's trying to set on its peg.

I start toward him, but halfway there think better of it. I come to a stop, warring with indecision. I really shouldn't be alone with him. *He did already steal me once.* He sighs, setting down the net. "Come on Rory, I promise... I'll only bite if you ask me to." His green eyes sparkle as he shoots me a smug little wink.

My immediate reaction is to roll my eyes, but in truth, I'm stalling, hesitating for a whole new reason. *He said my name.* Out loud. I can't remember if I've ever heard him use my name before... And the way his faint Irish accent curled around the R's... Not to mention the *words* that followed my name...

Aidan raises his eyebrows, and I flush. Keeping my eyes on my skates, I finally skate the rest of the way over to help with the post. Dropping to one knee, I raise the goal peg that had fallen over. Aidan lifts the net, deftly dropping it into place and setting the goal.

I rise slowly. He doesn't back away. I catch a whiff of his now familiar scent. The amusement in his eyes fades into something more serious. I can't look away—lost in darkening pine green. Out of nowhere, I'm hit with an overwhelming urge to kiss him.

"Your competition's Saturday, isn't it?" His voice interrupts the intrusive thought.

"Yes," I say, surprised he knows. Distracted while chastising myself for that last thought.

"Still having trouble landing that combination?" My cheeks heat with embarrassment. *He's been watching me.* It's a sensitive subject, and I'm instantly defensive. *I've landed it.* I

256

just *don't* more often than I *do*. Jaw tight, I avoid looking at Aidan.

"You're in your head."

I bristle at his observation; Not because he's wrong. On the contrary, the asshole is dead on. Karina still says I'm trying too hard. My fixation with perfecting the combination keeps me from landing it. A glorious paradox.

"I know," I admit softly, still avoiding his gaze, "it's hard to find my way out..." *Skating is different than how it used to be. Before mom and the accident. Before the Russians, Irish and Italians. It used to be fun, but now...*

I can feel the heat radiating off of him, both of us surrounded by the icy chill of the rink. When Aidan says nothing for several breaths, I chance a look up at him through my lashes.

His eyes, dark and intense, are locked on me. And once my eyes meet his, it's impossible to look away. He glides forward slowly, closing the already too small gap between us. My breath catches, inhaling a warm, heady, vanilla scent I recognize as his. Aidan's gaze drops to my lips, and he leans in.

"What are you doing?" Suddenly nervous, I back away, but his glove catches the back of my neck, halting my retreat while invading every single one of my senses.

"Getting you out of your head," he murmurs softly before he closes the gap.

His kiss is tentative—gentle. Nothing like I would expect from the rough-cut Breakers defenseman—or the Irish Mob's enforcer.

I don't kiss him back; too stunned to react properly or push him away. The tip of Aidan's tongue traces along my bottom lip, as if asking permission. He increases the pressure of his lips on mine and I fold, opening for him.

That's all it takes for him to consume me entirely. My lips move alongside his, his tongue searching my mouth hungrily. His gloves find my hips, pulling my body against his.

And I let him, my skates gliding on the ice.

I don't know what I'm doing. It's bad—It's bad for so many reasons. But I don't want to stop—*can't stop*—physically *unable* to stop—and work out the exact reasons why. A familiar heat sparks, growing in intensity and I press my thighs together, needing the pressure.

Aidan breaks our kiss, pulling away, and I chase after him, my eyes fluttering open.

"Patience," he chides, his dark smile igniting every nerve ending straight down to my core. I'm breathless, though it's only been seconds. He nods behind me. I didn't realize he'd pushed us across the arena. My back is almost up against the door to the penalty box.

With his eyes locked on mine, Aidan takes the hockey stick he's still holding in his hand and reaches behind me, shoving the end into the door latch, opening it.

Need and anticipation, mixed with fear and second thoughts, cloud my mind. I open my mouth to stop this before it's too late, but get nothing out because he bends down, scooping me up. My traitorous legs wrap around him as he carries me into the box.

Slamming the door shut behind us.

Once inside, his mouth is back on mine. I'm caught between the glass and him and it's overwhelming. I am aware of every inch of my body that touches his. Rationality melts away, replaced with an all-consuming need to be *closer*.

Aidan's mouth leaves my lips only to find my neck. I arch into him, curling my fingers in his hair. When he grazes my ear with the tip of his tongue, tracing along the sensitive cartilage, I let out a shaky whimper. A bone shaking shiver tears through my body.

He chuckles, the warmth of his breath ghosting my skin. It's too much, and I rock my hips, grinding into his leg, needing his attention lower—*so much lower.* Aidan's eyes meet mine, darkening with desire. He's tossed his gloves. His bare fingers find the little sliver of skin across my stomach. His touch sets my skin alight, sending tiny electric shocks directly to my core. I'm already a trembling mess before his fingers dip below the waistline of my leggings, playing along the hem.

Aidan's green eyes never leave mine, searching them —*asking.*

I bite my lip—faced with a decision. Tense and bristling with anticipation, a deep ache intensifies low in my belly. The sweet pressure building with every second his hands are on me.

Subtly, I dip my chin.

That's all he needs, driving in and taking my mouth in a fierce kiss. His fingers slip into my panties and when they find that little bundle of nerves—I go feral. My breath quickens, scattered between soft moans and gasps. I feel his smile against my lips as he explores further, discovering the slick evidence of my desire.

Soaked.

"Melting for me, ice princess?" Aidan's finger moves in agonizingly slow circles and I might convulse from the intensity of the pressure he's building low and deep. He relinquishes my mouth, flicking my ear with his tongue on his way to my neck just as he slides one of those sinful fingers inside. A strangled scream escapes me.

Aidan presses the palm of his free hand against my mouth, letting out a groan of his own when I arch into him, forcing his finger deeper. "Fuck, you're so tight."

I'm shaking—on the verge of exploding. I reach for him, pushing his jersey up—finding bare skin. My fingers trace over ripples of hard muscle and he sighs, resting his forehead against mine in a move that somehow feels far more intimate than anything we've done so far.

When he slips a second finger inside me, I cling to Aidan's jersey for dear life. He keeps up those agonizingly slow circles with his thumb. My desperate whimpers are muffled by his hand over my mouth.

And I do melt for him—in this moment I think he could ask me for anything and I swear, I would do it. I'm entirely at his mercy, a trembling mess in his arms, starving for his attention.

He pumps his fingers faster, but it's when he curls them inside me, a sudden jolt of sensation explodes out, radiating heat, unlocking a wild and uncontrolled pleasure. I come apart, shattering completely on the fingers of the Breakers' star defenseman. Aidan fucks me with his fingers through an orgasm that seems to go on forever, all while I scream into his palm.

I've never come so hard. Never felt *anything* like this, this level of intensity. It's like I'm high, slowly coming down from the sweetest of hits. My body responds to him in ways I didn't know were possible.

As I'm coming down, the reality of what just happened slams into me as hard as if he checked me into the boards.

Aidan sets me back on my skates, the blades protected by the black rubber flooring lining the penalty box. Quickly, I disentangle myself from him and he takes a step back, putting space back between us. I fight the urge to pull him back, missing the heat of his body on mine. Both of us breathing hard.

I'm absolutely panicked for a moment, wondering if he expects—

But that characteristic smirk is back on his face. The arrogant prick is so pleased with himself, leaning against the wall at his back, the two of us still too close in the small space, crossing his arms and watching as I spiral into crisis, confusion and regret at the forefront.

The penalty box is too small... He's still far too close... His scent is all over me.

"How did it feel?" His eyes sparkle knowingly. "Letting go?"

If my cheeks weren't already on fire, they're a bloody inferno now.

"That... shouldn't have happened." I tear my gaze away from his, adjusting my clothes. Needing out of this box.

I don't know a lot about Aidan, but I know his type. I know hockey players. A hook-up like this might just be another Thursday night for a guy like him. There's no lack of stories about Belles hooking up with one player or another. Maybe he does this all the time.

"It doesn't mean anything." *And there it is.* Aidan's tone is cool and casual as he unwittingly confirms my theory. His words shouldn't cut into me as much as they do.

I keep my face carefully blank. "No, it doesn't," I agree, my voice coming out far steadier than I feel. "Let's just pretend it didn't happen. *No one* has to know." I add the last part in a rush, eyeing him warily. A terrifying realization rooting into my mind. I don't think he would tell my father or Matteo what we did. But I did just hand Aidan an Ace, one that should he choose to play, would have *devastating* consequences.

"Fine by me."

"Great." I put far too much enunciation on the "t."

Aidan pulls up the bar on the door, swinging it open. "After you, princess."

Straightening my spine, I step back out onto the ice, feeling entirely different from the girl who stepped off. I'm aware of him at my back, following me out. I don't turn around as I head straight off the ice.

"Hey, Kostalova," Aidan calls after me. *And it's back to Kostalova now.* I look back over my shoulder, still moving steadily toward the exit. "Next time you need out of your head, you know where to find me." I can't mistake the playful edge to his voice.

That ache, which I thought was well sated, flares back to life deep within me and I feel feverish. Maybe I'm coming down with something—the flu? Perhaps... *Yes, that could explain the momentary lapse in judgement.*

"In your dreams, O'Rourke," I quip back with a little smile. Proud of myself for the quick comeback.

A beat passes, and then another before he responds, "More like in yours."

I choke at his response. But by now, I'm too far away for him to hear it.

Aidan picks up his abandoned hockey stick and resumes his drills like nothing happened.

All while I walk on shaky legs back to the locker rooms, fighting the overwhelming urge to run as fast as I can.

45

FUCK AROUND AND FIND OUT

AIDAN

*I*t's nearly three a.m. I drum my fingers idly on the dash of the SUV. My thoughts drift back to the penalty box and Rory Kostalova.

"It's getting late," Liam grumbles from the backseat where he sits next to Alex. "Are we doing this or not?" He repeatedly loads and reloads his gun, growing antsy.

I can't blame him. We've been staking out this warehouse now for hours with nothing to show for it.

"Not yet," I reply. We need to confirm there are girls inside. One wrong move could spook the traffickers and we could miss any actual shot at throwing a wrench into their new, lucrative Boston operation. A reliable contact pinpointed this warehouse in particular as a temporary holding area they take girls, before auction. But there is no sense in storming the place if they've already moved them.

We know we have the right place when a nondescript white delivery van rolls up to the side door of the warehouse and a variety of suits step out. Suits strapped with AK-47s. Their attention is on the van and not scanning the surrounding area for potential threats. *Arrogance like that gets you killed.* It also points to inexperience.

I sit forward. Koen's fingers curl around his gun, dragging it off the dash. He snaps his fingers to get Liam and Alex's attention in the back seat. The mood shifts from bored to lethal in a few quick seconds.

A burly looking fellow steps out from the passenger side door. A cigarette hangs out of his mouth as he barks orders to the others. Two more armed guards appear from inside the warehouse.

As the back door of the van opens, the men haul out more than a few scantily clad women. The girls cower away from the men, their hands restrained in front of them. The men rush the girls along, herding them through the warehouse door.

One girl has to be dragged from the back of the van. A dark-haired beauty. She puts up a fierce fight. At barely five-foot-three she doesn't stand a chance against the two Italian mafioso who wrestle her out, shoving her toward the others. One by one, they disappear into the warehouse.

My grip on the steering wheel tightens when the burly fellow steps forward, plucking one girl out of the group as they pass by him. He wrenches her arms with such force it nearly takes her off her feet. To no one's surprise—it's the little dark-haired girl.

The man hauls her backwards, slamming her back up against the side of the van, catching her before she slides to the pavement. Tenderly, he strokes the hair out of her face before burying his fist in it, wrenching her head to the side. She fights him, not giving up, but with his full weight pressed against her, there's little she can do.

I watch as he takes the cigarette out of his mouth and presses it down on the soft, exposed skin of her neck. He covers her mouth when she screams and laughs at her pathetic attempts to wriggle away from him.

I click the safety off my gun, reaching for the door, but Koen's hand on my upper arm stops me.

"Not yet," Koen repeats my own words back to me, his mouth in a tight line.

He's right; attacking now would jeopardize the entire plan. And it's only because I see the promise of death in his black eyes that I drop my hand from the handle with a low, frustrated growl.

The pathetic excuse of a man finally releases the girl. She immediately spits in his face.

I spy a small smile pulling at Koen's deep frown at the balls on her. The mafioso backhands her for it. The force of the hit takes her down to the ground.

Two of his guards pick the girl up by her arms and practically drag her into the building as she continues to struggle against them, desperately fighting being taken inside. Once they all disappear, I look to Koen.

My brother tightens his grip on the handle of his gun in his hand with grim resolve on his face. "Ready?"

I nod, checking with Liam to see if he's ready—but he's already halfway out of the car.

Together, the four of us move swiftly and slowly. The building has cameras, but they do not properly account for the shadows created by the building. There is no moon tonight and we're dressed all in black. Balaclavas and hoods obscure our faces and we move strategically through the camera's blind spots until we reach the door. It's unlocked.

Arrogance.

Koen leads us through it. They have one guard manning the entrance. He's dead before his body hits the ground. But the gun shot announces our presence to the rest.

Wooden crates are stacked high, reaching as far as the eye can see. Narrow aisles in between. The crates are haphazardly placed, with no rhyme or reason or sense of order. *Fucking Italians.*

A nearby container is open, its lid leaning against the side of the crate. Liam reaches in, pulling out a sharp looking military grade rifle. I lean forward, recognizing the Kalashnikov seal on the gun's barrel. A Russian manufacturer. Koen and I exchange looks. *Interesting.*

And definitely something to discuss later.

Gunfire sounds ahead of us. Gunfire Alex quickly returns, providing us cover.

Koen motions for us to separate into two groups. We peel apart, using the crates to conceal our movements while the Italians continue to unload on the area we were just in.

Liam and Alex get off a couple of shots as they dash to the left while Koen and I proceed silently to the right. Alex takes one guy down with a clean head shot while Liam catches another fucker in the leg and he falls, his gun slides across the concrete floor.

A few more steps and we have a clear view of the main area of the warehouse.

There are three Italians left on their feet, two of whom are currently engaged in a firefight with Alex and Liam, facing away from us. The third, closest to us, stands guard over a girl at his feet.

I recognize the hell-raising brunette from the parking lot.

She's on her knees, clothes shredded—nearly naked. Rope binds her hands and feet together. Blood runs down her back from several raw breaks in her skin. I do a double take, spotting the whip still clutched in the burly guard's hands. *They were punishing her.*

Koen acts before I can, standing up from where we are crouched behind the crates, moving quickly and completely exposed. His gun is trained on the man closest to the girl. I swear under my breath, scrambling to cover him. He lets loose two shots, hitting the man in both the knee and the hand holding the whip. He collapses to the ground, howling, cradling his bleeding hand into his chest.

The commotion draws the last two Italian's attention, giving Alex and Liam an opportunity to take them both out. Then it's just the big burly fellow, currently sneering up at Koen's gun from where he sits on the floor.

The furious look in my brother's eyes gives me pause. It's rare to see Koen's emotions so plainly. No matter the situation, Koen always manages to remain focused and unfazed, always doing what needs to be done with cold, calculated precision. "Tie him up," Koen growls before lowering to one knee and tending to the trembling girl on the concrete floor.

Liam and I heave the man up, shoving him into a nearby metal chair. He attempts to fight us, but injured as he is, he's no match. I smile when my fist makes contact with his jaw. The satisfying crack of bone is music to my ears.

"You're dead men," He spits at us when Liam finishes securing his hands and feet to the chair. "You don't know who you're messing with."

Slowly, I pull down my balaclava and lower my hood, cocking my head to the side as I peer down at him. "The South

268

Side is Irish territory," I say, letting my lilting accent loose with my words. "And you don't sound too Irish to me, do you now?"

The man has the good sense to shut his trap. His face pales.

"Call for backup," Alex calls, returning from the back office areas. "There's at least thirty girls back here."

Liam swears, pressing his phone to his ear.

My blood is boiling with anger. It only grows hotter as I watch Koen help the girl to her feet, sliding his sweatshirt over her shaking, bloody body.

Grabbing a metal folding chair, I slide it around in front of the Italian, dropping into it so we are eye level. His eyes dart wildly around, searching for help that's not coming. "Look, man, I—I'm just a hired gun," he jumbles out. "I only do what I'm told."

"And who does the telling?" I play with the gun in my hand, re-loading the cartridge.

His mouth snaps shut, a look of unease on his stupid face.

"Plot twist: it gets worse for you." I click the safety off my gun. My eyes flick to his, trying not to smile at the growing look of dread spreading across his face. "Whatever comes out of your mouth next determines how much worse."

He licks his lips.

"Whose warehouse is this?"

My man doesn't miss a beat when he gives his answer, "Matteo Carroza."

Pleased with the confirmation, I straighten, holstering my gun, and reaching for the baseball bat Liam found lying around somewhere.

"Wait, wait!!" The goon panics. His eyes flash between my face and the bat in my hands. "I have more—more information, please!" I let the bat swing in my hand. Round and round it circles; the Italian's eyes watching apprehensively as I step closer to him.

"I'm waiting..." I tilt my head, watching as the man's pants darken in his seat.

He looks between me and Liam, a pained expression on his face.

"Times up," I grin, winding up the bat one more time.

"No!" The man screeches. "I know who ordered the hit on Declan O'Rourke!"

The bat freezes.

"It was the Lion, the Russian Lion—Adrik—Adrik Kostalov." He nods furiously. "He put the hit out that left old Dec' dead."

I stare at the floor, processing the words. He could be lying, but all of us have been waiting for this smoking gun. We know he's not. There are so many repercussions to the Italian's statement, but only one question comes to mind; *Did Rory lie to me?*

Slowly, I raise my head. And I bury the bat in that motherfucker's skull.

46

I EXPECT PERFECTION

RORY

J stop walking at the sight of Matteo waiting for me at the arrivals gate. The rest of the Belles continue past me, none of them catching on to my immediate distress.

All of them—except for Elle. She slows, turning back to check on me, following my gaze to Matteo, who stands, waiting for me a couple hundred yards ahead. A quick scan shows he brought at least four men with him. I can make out the guys he has stationed around the perimeter.

Elle circles back to stand in front of me, cutting off my view of Matteo. I release my first full breath since laying eyes on my fiancé. *What is he doing here?* Concern draws both of her brows in. "Are you okay?"

It's a severe shift in mood. I was flying high, coming back from Cincinnati. I skated a clean program and took the gold. The medal still hangs from my neck. Karina insisted we wear them off the plane. Proof I've earned my spot to compete at Nationals, the last leg before Olympic team selection.

My vision blurs and I blink a few times to clear it, keeping my eyes on Elle's face until she comes back into focus. I haven't confided in her... not about my family and definitely not about Matteo.

Not because I don't trust her—I do. I would give anything to confide in her, but telling her the truth only puts her in danger. And if Elle ever got hurt because of me...

"Everything's fine." I try my best to mean it, but my voice is an octave too high and my eyes are tight. She gives me a little nod, seeing too much... "Is he your new bodyguard?" Her eyes dart in Matteo's direction without turning around.

"Something like that..." I mutter before repositioning the strap of my backpack slung over my shoulder before taking a step forward, resuming our procession.

"You're late," Is Matteo's only greeting when we're close enough to be within earshot.

"Like we can control when the plane lands." Elle's laugh is light as she attempts to lift the tense mood with humor.

Matteo's cold, dead gaze slides her way. Sizing her up. I don't like it.

I loop my arm through his, drawing his attention back to me. "We should get going."

"Yes, we should." He gives a tiny, almost imperceptible nod and one of his guys steps forward out of the crowd to take my bags. Matteo turns and strides for the door.

"I'll be fine." I mouth to Elle with a little cringe and hurry after my fiancé, since he's not waiting for me.

When we slide into the back of the town car, I immediately feel underdressed in my hoodie and leggings. It's the first time I notice Matteo's wearing a tux. He sits opposite me, scrolling through his phone as the car pulls out into traffic. "Did you have an event tonight?"

"*We* have an event tonight." He doesn't look up from his phone, gesturing absently to a black garment bag hanging behind him.

"Wait, what?" I ask, confused. It's seven p.m. I just got off a flight after two grueling days of competition. I am in no mood to go to a party.

"The police commissioner Marc Robbins' fundraiser, is tonight. We're going." He finally glances up to look at me.

I blink back at him. "I don't—Where's my father? Or Niko? I want to go home. I'm... tired." My words are careful and I speak them slowly, not trying to set Matteo off. After our last encounter, I don't think it would take much.

His mouth tilts up in a small smile. He would be handsome if it weren't for those empty eyes of his. "Since we're getting married next weekend, your father agreed it would be best if I assumed control of your security until then. You'll be staying with me. We'll go home together after the party tonight." He eyes me over his phone.

A wave of dizziness washes through me at his words—processing them. *Next weekend?*

Gathering myself, I sit up a little straighter. My mind goes to the cash I have stashed away in my bedroom bookshelf. "But... I'll need my stuff," I stutter out, "I have to go home and pack."

Matteo sighs, his patience wearing thin with my questions. "There's no need. It's already done."

I swallow hard, nodding before trying again. "But, surely there may be a few things I should still—"

He slams the phone down and I jump. "You will have everything you need. There is no need to return to the Kostalov compound. You belong to me now."

I shrink back in my seat, feeling trapped, an overwhelming need for space arising.

He smiles. This time, he looks like he's truly taking pleasure in the discomfort he's causing. "You will accompany me to this fundraiser tonight. As my fiancé and soon-to-be wife, it is your duty. You will smile, you will laugh at my jokes and you keep your pretty little mouth shut unless told otherwise. Am I being clear, Aurora?"

Tears well up in the backs of my eyes, but I don't dare let them fall. Silently, I agree, avoiding his gaze. If I don't go back to the mansion, I won't have access to any of my money.

Seven days.

In seven days, I'm expected to marry this jackass. Panic stirs and I have half a mind to throw open the door and tuck and roll onto the highway. I have to get away—*Run.*

But how?

The entire ride to the fancy hotel where the fundraiser is being held, I work on the problem.

When we arrive, Matteo's guards open the door for us and he hands one of them the garment bag. "You can change upstairs." I nod, absently climbing out of the car, but he stops me.

His icy hand wraps around my upper arm and I stop, turning my head slowly to face him. "I expect perfection, Aurora," he warns. "I will accept nothing less."

It's no surprise the dress Matteo picked out for me to wear tonight is gold. The shiny fabric is actually pretty, unlike the last dress that was a little gaudy in my opinion. My only issue with this dress is it's short.

Indecently so.

I spend most of the night uncomfortably tugging at the hem to keep it from sliding up my thigh. Which it does just about every time I move.

Matteo drags me from table to table. I meet so many businessmen and contacts I can't possibly remember all of their names, their faces blurring together after so many hours.

I vaguely remember eating dinner. I'm dead on my feet by the time I bump into Cole DeLuca close to midnight. The party wound down ages ago, but Matteo insisted on staying to schmooze a few more associates. My cheeks hurt from the fake smile I've had plastered on my face all night. When my shoulder catches the Italian Capo as I pass by him, I wobble, unsteady in the high heels Matteo brought me—half a size too small.

Cole reaches out, offering his arm to help steady me. His dark eyes slide from me to his consigliere behind me. "Your fiancé is tired, Matteo. You should take her home. Call it a night." The young Italian Capo smiles kindly down at me and I'm grateful, but I still eye him with caution. The man is not known for his kindness.

He's unsettling. Power and influence rolls off of him in waves. The type of man who enters a room and everyone notices.

Matteo quickly agrees, "Yes, Signore DeLuca. Of course." He bows his head slightly in deference and offers me his arm; the picture of a gentleman.

With only a few seconds' hesitation, I accept it, which

elicits a frown from Matteo. He nods goodbye to his capo while guiding me gently toward the exit.

"Oh, and congratulations on the gold, Miss Kostalova," DeLuca calls out from behind us. And I know he isn't talking about the dress. "Quite the accomplishment."

I swing my gaze toward his, meeting his dark eyes. "Thank you," I breathe. And I mean it. I have no idea how he knows about it, but Cole DeLuca is the only one to mention my competition in Cincinnati all night.

At Matteo's urging, I bid DeLuca farewell and we make our way out to the waiting car.

I'm grateful for the silent ride home, utterly exhausted after the long day—and even longer night. We pull up to the unfamiliar dark Victorian located far outside of the city. I follow Matteo out of the car, and up the stairs, and through a very large and overly ornate foyer. I only assume I'm supposed to follow him since he hasn't actually said anything to me since we left the venue, and he hasn't directed me elsewhere.

When we reach what must be his study, Matteo closes the door behind us. The silence I'd previously felt refuge in, feels dangerous all of a sudden.

I wait awkwardly by the door, teetering slightly on my heels. Eyes watching Matteo as he paces the length of the office. Normally, I would have slipped them off by now, choosing to ride barefoot in the car. But Matteo strikes me as someone who prefers propriety in all aspects of life.

After several long, drawn out minutes, he stops behind his desk, gripping the back of a leather armchair. His gaze, when it lands on me, is volatile. I straighten up under the weight of it. The anger in his eyes awakens my fight or flight.

"You embarrassed me tonight."

I shift uncomfortably on my heels, confused. I'd done everything he asked. "I thought it went well..." He cuts me off with a shake of his head.

"A wife's duty is to her husband. To make him happy. Serve him. But you—" a maniacal look enters his eye, and he resumes his pacing. I move in tandem to keep the distance between us. Matteo's words and movements grow increasingly angrier as he carries on. "—You," he shakes a finger at me, "embarrassed me in front of *my* Capo."

I'm shaking my head at him, unsure what to say to avoid what I think is coming.

I see the moment his dark mania settles into cold absolution. "As a result, you will be punished." He states the words simply, taking a calm and measured step toward me. "Consider this a learning experience, Aurora."

Dread fills me and instinctively I look for an exit, a means of escape, but there is none. Matteo's standing between me and the only door. The fact he is calm only makes him that much scarier. He isn't threatening me from a place of rage like my father always did—unable to control his own temper.

Matteo is making a choice.

He comes for me and I can't help but back away. He smiles, delight and satisfaction in his eyes at the fear he's caused.

I slap him when he gets too close.

It's the wrong thing to do, but I don't care. He can't make me regret it, not even when he slaps me back. Twice as hard. And not even when he let loose a sharp punch to my ribs, taking my breath from me. A second punch takes me down to my knees.

He's strategic with his hits. Clinical even. Hitting... kicking... where no one will ever see. My stomach, back and legs are all fair game. But he avoids my face... my arms.

It's over quickly and I don't cry, despite the searing pain in my ribs. I don't.

He's sadistic enough to offer me his hand to help me off the floor. I consider refusing it, but he'd probably punish me for that, too. Reluctantly, I take it and he pulls me up.

He mistakes my shaking hands for fear and strokes my hair almost lovingly, like I'm a naughty puppy who's misbehaved. But I'm not afraid; I'm angry. Angry at him for what he just did. *Angry at myself for letting him.*

"Now off to bed. We have a long week ahead. As discussed, the rehearsal dinner is on Friday." It's a little glimpse into what life will be like as his wife.

"I shouldn't be here. We aren't married yet—It isn't right." Suddenly I'm nervous for a whole new reason.

"The contracts have been signed. I already own you," Matteo urges impatiently, leading me out of the study and toward the grand stairwell at the front of the house. "The wedding is merely a formality. Not to mention, given your father's abysmal situation and lack of his own security, you're far safer here."

Somehow I doubt that.

I don't have a response. Too busy taking in Matteo's "security." And it is extensive. Armed soldiers stand guard throughout the house, and even more are outside. I can see them patrolling through the windows. He has all the exits covered. My hope of escape dims.

"That being said," Matteo continues, "I have assured your father everything will be above board." He straightens his tie. "I will not touch you until the bedding ceremony on our wedding night." I wince, briefly recalling the Italian tradition of displaying bloody sheets for all to see as proof of the bride's purity and consummation of the marriage. *Bloody sheets we won't have...*

His phone rings, and he answers it. His eyes widen before darkening as he listens to the deep rumble of someone on the other end. He replies sharply in rapid Italian.

"Your room is upstairs, the last door on the left. Sal can show you if needed. I have business to attend to." He points out a nearby guard, who I'm assuming is Sal, before stalking back to his study, screaming into the phone before disappearing with a door slam.

I stand lost on the marble tiles of the grand foyer, too aware of the guard's interest on my over exposed legs.

Seven days. I look around the dark house.

I have seven days to escape this fate.

47

STICK TO MY HEART, BLADE TO MY THROAT

RORY

*M*atteo only allows me to leave his house for private sessions with Karina and for Belles practice. He forced me to tender my resignation at the Chill Zone. And he thwarts my attempts to return to the Kostalova mansion at every turn.

He's also monitoring my phone. He replaced my cell the very next day with one of his own that I know he's bugged.

Dark circles ring my eyes. I haven't been sleeping well. The purple and blue bruises on my ribs make it hard to get comfortable. At least they are fading from my skin. Hopefully, the pain fades soon too.

Without the cash I have saved, I don't know what to do. I'm pissed off at myself for not seeing the ambush coming. I should have kept it on me, or in a locker at the rink. Along with the go-bag I have hidden, currently tucked deep in my closet at the mansion. I didn't have much saved, but I was sure I could stretch it if I was frugal. *Really frugal.*

Using my cards is out of the question; they can be traced in a second. And any cash withdrawals require a signature from my father.

It's a long shot either way, but I *need* money if I want to have any kind of chance. It's imperative I get away before Matteo and I are married. *Before he legally owns me.*

Seeing him all buddy-buddy with the police commissioner the other night didn't settle my nerves any either. I know once I run, I'm on my own. Neither my family nor the police will help me.

I'll also never skate again, I know the only reason Matteo's even allowing me to practice right now is because we aren't married yet; needing to appease my father. But once we are, all bets are off. Bye-bye Olympics. It's a hard reality to wrap my mind around, though strangely, I think I'm more distraught over losing the Belles.

It's stupid, but skating with the Belles, and for the Breakers, has reminded me how much fun skating can be. I love being part of the squad, part of a team, and sort of having friends for the first time.

I've been looking forward to the game tonight all week. It will be my last one. Either I'm already gone, or Matteo will make me quit the second we say "I do."

Sitting in the locker room, listening to the other girls excitedly chatting, is bittersweet. I'm quiet; more so than usual. Focused on lacing up my skates. There's no chance for escape tonight. Though, I've considered it—slipping away mid-game. But Matteo has five of his guys on me tonight. I've got a better chance of getting struck by lightning—inside the arena.

"Rory." Shelby, the Belles' coach, calls me over from her office at the other end of the locker room. "A word?"

"Yeah?"

"Liv twisted her ankle in warmups."

I wince. Sucks for Liv, but Shelby's looking at me expectantly. "Okay..?" *Not quite sure why she's telling me...*

"I need you on the ice for the Anthem and coin toss with Elle."

"Oh, I—Umm...." Each game, the two cheer captains accompany the two Breakers captains to center ice. Liv is a captain, alongside Elle.

"You'll be fine," she reassures me. "Just follow Elle. She knows what to do." And then she trots off, already decided.

"C'mon, c'mon, c'mon," Elle urges, running up to me, clearly already briefed by Shelby on the change of plans. "We need to be on the ice like *right now.*"

Quickly, I tie off my skates and take one last look in the mirror before we race down the hall into the tunnel, rubber guards protecting our blades.

"Rory, Rory wait!"

I skid to a stop, spotting Shelby racing after us. Elle bounces from one foot to another impatiently beside me.

"Shelby, what?" I blurt out, half turned to keep running down the tunnel with Elle.

"Your jersey!!"

I look down to see her waving another Breakers jersey at me.

"I... okay." I thrust my pom-poms into Elle's hands. I quickly strip off the cropped jersey I'm wearing, and take the one from Shelby, sliding it on over my sports bra.

"Now go-go-go!" She half shoves me up the tunnel ramp like she wasn't the one to delay me in the first place. We make it to the ice gate just in time. Elle jumps in next to Rez Tyler, the Breakers' co-captain, leaving me next to—*oh fuck.*

Aidan glances down from where he stands to my left. His eyes are cold and unfriendly. The chill in his expression cuts straight through me, and I almost shiver. I haven't seen him since... the penalty box.

"Hi..." I say, hesitantly, testing the waters.

His eyes darken and a muscle tightens in his jaw, but he doesn't return my greeting. Instead, he steps out onto the ice without me.

I scramble to follow. "I'm filling in for Liv." I have to work to catch up to him. Confused, since we're supposed to skate together.

It wasn't exactly the greeting I expected after what happened between us in the penalty box last week, but alrighty then. I don't waste another breath on the surly Breakers defenseman as I take up my spot next to him at center ice; Elle and Rez to our right as we wait for the other team's captains to take the ice.

"You're wearing my number." He sounds... *Pissed*? Yes, that's definitely irritation I'm sensing radiating in my direction.

His comment takes me by surprise since I thought he was ignoring me. I feign being preoccupied with the pom-poms in my hands, covertly scanning my eyes over the #19 patch on the shoulder of the jersey. I must have missed it when Shelby shoved it at me a few minutes ago. "Not my first choice." I look away before closing my eyes at the realization that I have Aidan's name and number scrawled across my back. *Awesome. Might as well put "puck bunny" on the ass, too.*

The refs are still over by the bench, discussing something with the other team's coaches. The arena is full of noise but yet the silence between Aidan and me is deafening. I shuffle my skates back and forth on the ice, anxiously playing with my pom-poms, willing the refs to move their asses and get this coin toss over and done with.

This is stupid. I'm engaged and actively planning a runaway attempt. Fully aware nothing could ever—and should never—happen between Aidan O'Rourke and me. But still, his obvious rejection stings. I chew my bottom lip to keep the hurt from showing on my face. It was just a hook-up. But we—and I —what we did... I can feel my cheeks heating up. *Maybe he was just messing with me the whole time...*

The refs finally get their shit together and the Anthem plays. The song is far longer than I remember. I shift my weight on my skates, eager to get this over with and get far away from Aidan.

The Irish Devil himself seems to sense this and leans in closer. He chuckles darkly, "Do I make you nervous, Kostalova?" There's a bitter edge to his voice, and he's using my last name again.

I mumble something noncommittal, keeping my eyes straight ahead, fixed on Rez as he steps forward to make the call for the coin. I can feel Aidan's gaze burning into my cheek.

"I have a fiancé," I blurt out. *Granted, not one I want, but all the same...* I don't want him to think I'm going full puck bunny on him. Just because we hooked up once doesn't mean he has to be a colossal dick about it.

"I am aware." Aidan's tone is even icier, if it was even possible.

"Well, then...good." His stare burns through me, intense and consuming, like standing too close to an open flame.

Rez calls the coin flip. I don't hear the outcome. The surrounding crowd erupts in cheers and music blasts out through the surrounding speakers. I lift my pom-poms, faking the smile on my face, following Elle's lead, all while counting the seconds until I can escape out from under the scrutiny of the devil beside me.

The second she turns, I high tail it for the bench, pulling Elle with me, but we're stopped by one photographer blocking the gate. "O'Rourke! Tyler!" He shouts over our heads to get the attention of the two Breakers captains. "A photo?"

The boys oblige, and Elle and I try to sneak around them.

"Girls too!" The photographer blocks us with his arm, motioning for the two of us to join the guys where they're posed.

Elle and I exchange a look before skating to either side, with the guys between us.

The photographer quickly snaps a few shots before peering at us over his lens, groaning. "C'mon, guys... like you like each other..."

I glance nervously at Elle, unsure what the photographer wants us to do, but then I feel a heavy weight circle around my neck. I stiffen with the contact. A jolt of something indiscernible shoots through me at the sound of Aidan's dark voice in my ear. "Smile for the camera, Angel," he purrs softly.

I land a sharp jab of my elbow in between pads and smile big at the resounding grunt above me. "Speak for yourself, puck boy."

I'm out from under him the second the camera snaps its photo. I shove past the photographer and flee through the gate. A prickle of awareness tingles along my spine. *He's following me.* Aidan is hot on my skates, following me down into the tunnel.

"Did you know?" he calls from behind me.

I slow, turning with a slight attitude, "Know what Aidan?" I'm so over whatever the hell this is. I just want away from him.

Aidan's hand wraps around my upper arm, and I find myself redirected into a tiny alcove. There isn't a lot of space, so he pushes me up against the wall. He releases my arm, only to lean in, both hands pressed against the concrete at my back—caging me in.

Back on the rink, the Breakers' hype music signals the start of warm-ups; warm-ups we should both be on the ice for. But Aidan doesn't even seem to notice, his eyes nearly black when I finally look up into them.

"Adrik Kostalov ordered the hit, killing my father... Did you know?" His dark eyes search mine with a deep intensity, and my breath stutters as I play catch up. "This whole time... Did you know?"

I take longer than a second to find my voice, held captive by the murderous expression in Aidan's eyes, but he's already shaking his head.

"I—"

"You know what? Save it." He pushes off the wall and out of my airspace. My lungs take in their first full breath in at least a minute. But I'm still pinned to the wall by his glare alone, even as he backs away. There's a cold and distant look in his eyes that makes the hair on the back of my arms stand up.

"This is war, Kostalova. *War*." And then he turns and disappears down the tunnel.

My deep breaths level out and I sink with my back against the wall, my entire body shaking.

I didn't know. *I didn't.*

And why do I care so much that he thinks I did?

48

CALL IT OFF

RORY

*T*he anxiety attack Aidan set off in me before the game only grows worse throughout it. All at once, it feels like everything is spiraling out of my control. The walls are closing in. Aidan's threat, and the Matteo situation—on top of an already impossibly intense training schedule for Nationals.

Deciding to stick out the game tonight was a mistake. I'm stressed—tense. And it shows. I miss cues, messing up the opening routine in brand new and special ways. As much as I try to ignore Aidan, I'm hyper aware of his presence both on and off the ice. And he's out for blood tonight.

Which is bad news for the Sharks because no one's been able to get past Aidan all night. The Breakers lead 3-0. In the second period, Aidan delivers a brutal hit on the Sharks' left wing, Jack Kane, hard enough to shatter the glass. Ten feet from me. Our eyes meet as the refs drag him off of Kane and into the penalty box.

I fall during the third period ice dance, over-rotating on the simple double lutz. I recover quickly and finish out the routine, but my hands are shaking by the end.

Even though, through it all, Aidan pretends I don't exist. Aside from his glance during the incident with Kane, he doesn't even look my way. It has me so on edge. I'm no longer sure if him ignoring me is a good thing or a bad thing.

Of course, I can't keep my traitorous eyes off of him. As much as I try not to, I'm constantly finding my gaze inevitably drawn right back to the Irish Devil, whether he's on the ice, on the bench, or in the box.

That damn box. I swear to God he's doing it just to mess with me.

He's playing really well tonight. *Violently.* The Breakers' defenseman has spent *a lot* of time in the penalty box tonight, racking up the penalties. I almost feel bad for the Washington Sharks. Their offensive line has taken quite a beating.

With two minutes remaining on the clock, the Breakers are up by five. Aidan slams Marcus Powers into the boards, this time right in front of me. The force of the hit pushes the glass outward.

Mouth wide open, I look up to find myself the focus of Aidan's furious glare. Green eyes blaze with something that looks an awful lot like betrayal. The intensity of it leaves me breathless. Giving Powers one last shove, Aidan releases him to skate off the ice—finally thrown out of the game for charging.

I watch him go. Discomfort settles deep in my gut, setting loose a wild storm of emotions I can no longer ignore. He's pissed at me. He's pissed *at me* for what my father did to him—and rightfully so.

The second the game is over, I race down the tunnel to the safety of the locker room, tearing through my bag to find my new cell phone. I know Matteo is monitoring it, but right now, I don't care.

The rest of the girls trickle in behind me and I dart back out into the hall, phone in hand. I walk through the tunnels of the arena until I find a quiet place, then I dial my father's number. My hands are shaking so badly, it takes three attempts to get the digits right.

I chew on my nail as I listen to the ringing on the other end. "C'mon, c'mon, c'mon," I urge my father to answer. When it goes to voicemail, I almost lose it. But I take a deep breath, steadying myself once more before dialing the number a second time.

This time, he picks up. "Aurora? I am busy." He's irritated. I press on quickly before he hangs up on me.

"Papa, can we talk?" I hover in the empty hallway. "It's important," I add, biting my lip. I can almost feel his glare through the phone.

"Fine, Aurora. What is it?"

I choose my words carefully. I only have one shot at this. "I was hoping to speak with you about the engagement."

The silence on the other end of the phone carries on so long I'm tempted to repeat myself.

"What about it?" my father asks sharply, his voice cold and measured.

"I'm not sure Matteo is—" *I have to be careful here,* "—the right man for me..." He doesn't interrupt, so I continue talking rapidly, needing to get this out. "You see, at your party, Matteo, well—" I pick at my fingertips, "—he laid his hands on me."

Nothing.

I go on, my voice shaking a little to match my hands, "And the other night—he *hurt* me, Papa." Tears rise in my throat and

I struggle to keep them at bay, digging deep to find some more courage. "Please don't make me marry him. He scares me," I beg, my voice finally choking up. "I think it would be best if we called off the engagement."

And there it is. *I did it.*

"Aurora," my father pauses, and I can't tell by his tone which way this is going to go. "Your engagement to Matteo is of critical importance to the Bratva." My heart falls. "This marriage will solidify our position in the city and allow us to expand operations in brand new ways. It is crucial you make him happy, ангел. This union *must* go forward."

Silent tears stream down my face and I can't muster up even a half-hearted reply to Adrik's cold and critical response to what I've just told him.

"I'm sure this is all a misunderstanding. Are you certain you didn't cause him anger? You can be quite trying, Aurora. Matteo will need time to learn how to deal with you."

Deal with me? If there was any part of me still holding out any hope that my father genuinely loves me—it's gone.

"I will ask some of the Bratva wives to reach out. They will have good advice to share with you. How you can make him happy. It is your duty, ангел. You are a Kostalov." He speaks the words with pride.

When I still don't respond, his tone grows firm. "Do you understand Aurora? I'm sure it will get better. You just need to learn how to make Matteo happy. You must."

I want to vomit. "Yes, Papa." My words are soft, barely audible.

"Nikolai and I look forward to your wedding. You will be so beautiful, ангел."

"Yes, Papa."

"Now go and make amends with Matteo. I'm sure it's all just a misunderstanding. Do you want me to call him?"

"No," I rush out. In no universe would my father calling Matteo *help* my situation. If anything, it would only make it far, far worse. "No—I'll handle it Papa."

"Good." He sounds pleased, despite my broken words. I'm not even bothering to hide my complete loss of hope. "I will see you at the rehearsal dinner." The click in my ear tells me he's disconnected the call.

Taking a minute, I rub away the tears on my cheeks, stealing into a nearby bathroom to splash some cold water on my face to cool my burning red eyes before heading back to the locker room, my mood somber.

When I run, I will leave *nothing* behind.

49

LESSONS

RORY

"Oh, you're going the wrong way. It's a left on park," I call out to Sal, my driver for the evening.

The Belles are all going out to Lolita's bar for post-game dinner and drinks. Even though I'm exhausted, I agreed to go. That is, after I verified no Breakers would be in attendance.

"Apologies, Signorina." Sal peers at me through the car's rear-view mirror. "I have orders to take you straight home."

I sigh, frustrated, crossing my arms and slouching down in the leather seats of the town car. *Of course he does.*

Matteo's waiting for me when I arrive. "Leave us," he orders Sal, who turns and exits the room without a second glance. Antonio, a guard I've noticed, usually posted by the front door, also leaves with Sal.

Once they've gone, Matteo's eyes narrow on me. "Aurora, follow me." He turns and stalks off toward his office, a room I already hate.

I consider not doing as I'm told.

"Now, Aurora!" Matteo's shout elicits a jump. Against my will, I follow.

He holds the door for me, pointing at the chair. "Sit," he commands, like I'm a dog.

The door shuts behind me, and the air seems to thin inside the office. Slowly, I sink into the chair.

Matteo leans back against the front of his desk, his dark eyes ablaze with something like rage, and also maybe a little excitement. "Confess your sins, Aurora." He studies me. "I'll give you this one chance. Come clean, and I'll go easy on you."

My heart races, and my eyes dart around the study. No idea what I should be confessing to. "W-what sins?" I ask, unable to hide my nerves.

He clicks his tongue. My mind goes to Aidan and the penalty box last week, but there's no way Matteo can know about that... *right*? I eye my fiancé warily, doing my best to look as innocent as possible.

When I only blink up at him, Matteo sighs, pulling out his phone. A saccharine smile on his lips as he scrolls, pulling up an entertainment news article. He shoves it in my face. "Explain this, Aurora."

It's a photo of me from the game tonight. But I'm not alone... Aidan's got one arm wrapped around my shoulders and I'm leaned up against him. The photographer, or magazine, conveniently cropped Elle and Rez out of the frame. The headline teases at a possible relationship between player and cheerleader.

It's... not good.

Matteo slams the phone down onto his desk, and I flinch.

"O'Rourke?" he demands. Every alarm in my body goes off, screaming at me to run, run, *run*.

I press my lips together.

"You let a dirty Irish O'Rourke touch you *again*?" he screams, his face so close to mine spittle sprays across my cheek. The back of his hand follows it. I brace myself on the arm of the chair to keep from being knocked out of it.

Taking his time, Matteo reaches over me. He picks up my skating bag and rips it open. I hold my breath as he pulls out my custom skates, holding them by their laces. "You mock me, Aurora." The skates spin slowly in his grasp.

My hands come up in defense. "No, I'm not—I didn't *do* anything! He put his arm around me! It was a PR photo. I'm sorry!" I'm practically begging. The light from the fire in the hearth glints off my skate blade as Matteo moves closer to the fire. "Please, don't!" I plead with my eyes, my bottom lip quivering, and not for show. *The skates... the last pair my mother bought me just before...*

"You make a fool out of me." He shakes his head, pissed, but with a cruel smile on his face. *He's enjoying watching me beg.* "You're not sorry, but you will be." He tosses my skates into the fire.

"No!" I squeal, diving after them. But Matteo grabs hold of my hair and drags me back, throwing me headfirst into the far wall of his study. I collapse onto the floor. Flashes of light blur my vision. The metallic taste of blood in my mouth. Before I can get my bearings, he comes after me again, wrapping his hand around my throat and hauling me up by it.

I scramble to get my legs under me, his grip punishing. Panicking, I claw at his face, aiming for his eyes—desperate for oxygen. He curses as I drag my fingernails down his cheek. He drops me and I inhale sharply, my lungs screaming. Pain and fear are second to my growing rage. "I won't marry you! You can't make me!" I shout at him, once I have recovered enough breath. My voice hoarse. I'm sure I'll have bruises on my throat tomorrow.

I expect him to lunge for me, but he doesn't. Instead, he straightens. Adjusting his suit, he tugs up the hem of his pants as he lowers himself to my level. "Oh, you'll marry me, Aurora, if I have to tape your mouth shut and say "I do" for you." Matteo's lips curl up into a sadistic smile. "Or your father will do it for me."

I blink up at him, feeling a fleeting moment of satisfaction at the angry claw mark marring his left cheek. "What's the matter, Aurora?" he taunts, "You thought you could refuse me?" His laugh is bitter. "You can scream, cry, throw a tantrum in church on Saturday... It won't change a goddamn thing. The *wedding* is just a formality. You will be my wife. You *belong* to me. Nothing you can do will change that, so get used to it."

He kicks me. His designer dress shoes knocks the breath from me again with stabbing pain. I curl in on myself in an effort to protect my body. His next kick is stronger than the first, catching me in the back this time. A whimper escapes me, and I bite down hard on my lip to keep in my scream, hard enough to draw blood. I refuse to give him the satisfaction.

The fire flashes brighter and I look over just in time to catch sight of my skating boot flare as the fire engulfs it fully. A tear runs down my cheek before a surge of anger overtakes it.

I kick out with my feet when Matteo comes closer, intending to kick me again. The back of my foot catches him behind his knee and he falters, falling back onto the wooden coffee table. It splinters with a crack as he crashes through it.

Despite the pain screaming from my ribs, my lips twitch up

in a faint smile. Anger I've never seen before flashes in his eyes when he sees it.

He's on his feet faster than I could have ever anticipated, hauling me up roughly. "You bitch! I'll fucking kill you." He winds up, and his fist coming toward my face is the last thing I see before everything goes dark.

50

CHAMPAGNE PROBLEMS

RORY

"To the happy couple!" Sal Santorini, Matteo's uncle, raises his glass of champagne. The room is full of guests following suit, beaming at Matteo and me.

I sit, with a painted smile, in the middle of the fancy Italian restaurant, lifting my glass before taking a small sip of champagne. I move with practiced indifference. Barely conscious— my body might be here, but my mind sure isn't.

The Italian Capo, Cole DeLuca, rises, next up to deliver what is sure to be another eloquent toast to the blushing bride and happy groom on the eve of their wedding.

Thick and clever makeup covers the dark bruising by my eye and jaw. But nothing can hide the still raw and bloody cut on my lower lip. It draws the attention of well-wishers. Their eyes trail over it, widening at the sight. But then, just like those before them, they quickly avert their gaze, complimenting my dress or my hair.

My father's gaze has been heavy on me all night. Coupled

with the suffocating presence of my fiancé at my side, I feel as though I'm drowning. I sit stiff in my seat, barely uttering more than muttered thank-you's at those congratulating us. Matteo keeps his hand over mine, appearing to everyone around us as the doting fiancé. In reality, it's a subtle reminder of the control he has over me.

There's silence, and a sharp pinch on the underside of my arm brings the restaurant back into focus. Expectant eyes are on me. Robotically, I raise my glass and more shouts fill the room as our guests dip their glasses back. The Italian made men in attendance are more exuberant following the congratulatory words from their capo. *"Salud!"*, *"Tanti auguri!"*, *"Congratulations!"*

Downing my glass, I lower it only to lock eyes with Niko. I hold his blazing gaze for a moment before dropping my eyes and pushing around some vegetables on my plate. The five course meal, my last before I'm sacrificed at the altar of my father's quest for power.

My ribs hurt from sitting in this chair all night, still sore from the beating I endured from Matteo a few nights back. I try to ignore the pain. Disassociating further into the dark daydream where I drown to death in a room full of people. The crowd laughs and sips on a-thousand-dollar-a bottle champagne, ignoring my collapsing lungs and screams for help. Help that never comes.

After dinner, we make our rounds, greeting countless more guests I don't know, the same lines on repeat. *"I'm so excited. The wedding will be beautiful. Yes, I'm so lucky to have Matteo as my husband-to-be."*

A couple hours in and I don't know how much longer I

can do this. I stare off despondently as Matteo schmoozes some big name politician—and his wife—who showed up late, tuning back in just in time to hear Matteo promising to have them over for dinner soon before excusing us from the conversation.

My husband-to-be walks me back toward our table, glancing around first to check if anyone's eyes are on us before tightening his grip on my arm. I wince. His fingers dig into my skin, already bruised, courtesy of him. He leans in, increasing pressure on my ribs where he knows a dark bruise, black and purple, mottles the skin.

Reluctantly, I force my eyes to his.

"Smile, Aurora," he warns, his tone low so only I can hear him. Brown eyes threaten violence. "I don't think I need to remind you what will happen if you don't." He shoves two fingers hard into my ribs and I flinch away as far as the grip he has on me allows.

"Am I interrupting something?"

Both Matteo and I whip our attention around to find Niko towering over us both—wearing his usual expression of bored malevolence. Matteo visibly relaxes at the sight of my brother, knowing he's no ally of mine. He straightens, breaking into a broad smile before clasping Niko on the back. "Not at all. I always have time for my new brother-in-law."

Niko's eyes narrow on my fiancé. "Not yet," he growls before his eyes settle on me, "I need to borrow Aurora for a moment."

Matteo appears caught off guard. His smile remains, but it no longer touches his eyes. I can tell he's reluctant to agree, but Niko wasn't asking.

My brother reaches out, linking his arm through mine and tugging me toward him. A move so unlike Nikolai, I make no move to resist. He ignores my stunned expression as he drags me away from my fiancé. "Carroza," he gives a respectful nod to the Italian Consigliere before stalking off through the room and dragging me with him.

A quick check over my shoulder shows Matteo standing right where we left him, not trying to follow, though his expression has darkened severely. I try not to tremble at the sight of the dark promise in his gaze, turning back before I trip over my heels, scrambling a little to keep pace with Niko.

My brother doesn't spare me another glance, his eyes fixed forward. I nod politely at guests as we pass, some of them trying to start a conversation with me, but Niko isn't having any of it. He power-walks me through the bar and out onto the back terrace, right out into the intricately maintained garden the restaurant overlooks.

We're well out of sight of anyone before I finally dig my heels in, wrenching my arm from his grasp. "Nikolai, what in the—"

"Go."

I freeze, staring up at my brother. "What?"

Niko stands, his size and figure a menacing sight in the shadowy garden. He's lit only by the glow of string lights as he points in the direction he was taking me before I stopped him. I follow his finger to a black wrought-iron gate at the back of the garden.

"Go," He repeats, folding his arms.

I stare at the gate, my brain trying to compute. I look back at Niko. "I don't understand."

"He hurt you."

I furrow my brow, truly looking at my brother for the first time all night. The expression he wears on his face is murderous.

"Matteo—" Niko's jaw clenches as he speaks the name, "he hurt you." His eyes roam over the well-hidden bruises and marks as if he can see them.

I nod, a slow understanding mixed with disbelief and suspicion.

"You don't want to marry him."

It's not a question, but I answer it anyway, "No." My voice is no louder than a whisper. But he hears me and nods, looking over my head back the way we came, checking to ensure we're still alone. Matteo hasn't followed.

"You're letting me—go?" I ask the question, my eyes going back to the wrought-iron gate barely visible in the shadowed corner of the garden.

My brother's eyes soften when they meet mine again. "I never wanted this for you. Father—" he shakes his head, anger filling his eyes again, "—I thought he would leave you alone. Honor his *promise*..."

So did I. Tears burn at the back of my eyes. This time I do not stop them as a few break free and trail down my cheek, so tired of pretending.

"I thought if I made being home horrible for you, you would stay away. Prep school, college, skating... Far away from this life and this burden." He shakes his head, "I was wrong." His blue eyes meet mine. The sadness in them is unlike anything I've ever encountered, and my initial suspicion disappears. "I'm sorry. I can't go back and change it—the things I did—said." He swallows, running a hand through his blonde

301

hair, out of its usual knot at the back of his head. "But I can try to make it right."

Niko turns, striding the few yards to the gate standing between me and freedom? My mind spins. He unhooks the latch, swinging it open. "Run," he says, his face serious.

"Run, Rory, and never... never look back."

51

BREAKAWAY

RORY

I walk numbly through the gate—still waiting for the other shoe to drop. Waiting for all of this to be just another cruel trick or a trap. I half-expect Matteo to be waiting outside, but a quick glance back-and-forth shows the alleyway is empty.

I pause, turning back and wrapping my arms tightly around my brother. Nikolai stiffens under my hold, but then wraps his own arms tightly around me, pulling me in close to his chest.

"Go," he urges, gently pushing me away from him and out of the garden.

With one final look back at my brother, I disappear into the night, finding myself in a narrow alleyway meant for deliveries. The high walls of the garden at my back hide me from view. My heels click loudly against the pavement as I run down it.

Free of Matteo, and free from my father, I follow Niko's advice and I run, slipping off my heels to move faster.

Bare feet on pavement, I run with no direction—no plan. The desperate need to escape spurs me forward—to anywhere —as long as it's the opposite direction of the hell waiting at my back.

I don't have any money. No phone. Hell, I didn't even think to grab my purse when Niko steered me out of the banquet room. I can't risk going back to the Kostalov mansion for my stash of cash. I can't even risk stopping...

Niko said he would do what he could to stall them, but within minutes, Matteo could have his dogs hot on my trail. I picture my father assembling the Bratva to back up the Italians. *Fuck*. Would I even make it out of the city?

I hesitate on the street corner, hands trembling, unsure which way to go. I look nervously in every direction. Every man looking my way—Bratva; every black car—Mafia.

Feeling too exposed, I duck into a darkened alley and lean up against the brick wall. My chest rises and falls with rapid breaths. *I need to get off the streets.* The white taffeta mini dress I'm wearing sticks out like a sore thumb on the dark city streets.

Thunder rumbles in the distance, electrifying my nerves.

Think Rory, think, think.

I need somewhere safe... Somewhere I can hide.... To lie low while I work out a way out of the city *and what to do after.*

All of my plans require *money*—papers, documents, plane tickets to distant lands. I not only need to escape the Bratva but also the whole of the Italian Mafia. Matteo, I'm certain, won't ever let me go. And to fail... and have them drag me back... I would rather be dead. My whole body shudders at the thought.

And for those same reasons, I can't go to Elle or any of my

prep school friends. Not without putting them at risk. It will be the first place they look. A police cruiser creeps by and I mentally scratch them off that list, too. With so many of them in Russian or Italian pockets, I'd never know which ones I could trust. I'd just left the police commissioner himself behind at my rehearsal dinner.

Lightning illuminates the sky, and in that moment, I know my destination. Leaving the alleyway, I take off running across the street, horns blaring as I dodge oncoming traffic. Heavy Boston accents shout obscenities after me. But I'm already gone, certain of my destination, and racing away from any second thoughts that might try and talk me out of it.

The rink is quiet this time of night. I don't dare enter it. Too risky. Instead, I lurk outside in the shadows of the nearly abandoned parking lot. My eyes fixate on a single matte black bike, still parked in the second row.

Rain pours in sheets from the sky, unleashing with a vengeance as I was halfway here. Washing away the tears stinging the cut on my cheek, and the smell of Matteo on my skin. The rain soaks my white dress, and I shiver as a powerful gust of wind hits my face. It is rapidly dropping in temperature. *God, I wish I had my jacket...*

Keeping my eyes on the bike; I wrap my arms tighter around myself, teeth chattering as I keep up my silent vigil.

Movement at the rink's back door immediately has my attention. I straighten at the sight of a hooded figure exiting out into the rain. He jogs toward the bike and I watch cautiously. From this distance, I can't make out his face, but the familiar swagger of a certain arrogant six-three defenseman has me breathing a little easier.

I haven't moved an inch yet, but he stills. Tilting his head in awareness, eyes scanning the shadows of the parking lot. *He knows someone is watching.* His hand drifts slowly to the gun strapped at his waist, pausing the moment I feel his eyes on me.

I'm caught, ensnared by the weight of his gaze, and, like a moth drawn to a flame, I move forward on hesitant steps, holding his gaze until I'm only feet away. Aidan hasn't moved. The rain drips off his dark hair, running down his face, but he doesn't seem to notice.

I break our stare to scan the parking lot—anxious— exposed. Standing here in my white dress, in the middle of the empty lot. I'm sure, by now, both the Italians and Russians have deployed their forces to hunt me down.

"What are you doing here?" He growls, his voice low and dangerous. "You know this is Irish territory."

Our last conversation comes to mind... *his threat...* I keep my arms folded tight across my chest, teeth chattering involuntarily, my gaze on the pavement when I speak for the first time. "I—I didn't know where else to go..."

Forcing my eyes up, I find Aidan's familiar burning stare. His dark green eyes harden, a flicker of something dangerous, and I realize, only now, how stupid I've been. The daughter of the Bratva standing before the Irish Devil, disheveled and shivering, trusting him... *trusting Aidan O'Rourke.*

The Irish enforcer. The very one who declared war to my face just last week. I can honestly say I don't know what I was thinking when I came here... looking for him. *Clearly, I wasn't thinking at all.* Aidan's stare is colder than I've ever seen it. Chewing my lip, I take a hesitant step back, debating whether I can still make a run for it. Feeling like a deer caught in the sights of a very large and very *unpredictable* wolf.

Aidan remains silent, feeding my anxiety, but steps closer. I force myself to hold my ground as he closes the space between us. He's so close I can feel the heat radiating off of him even in the rain. It becomes harder to breathe.

Looking up, I search his eyes, desperate in my attempt to read him, but his gaze is piercing, intense, a rage in his eye burning hotter the longer he looks at me. Eyes trail up my body —taking in the sight: my bare feet, soaked dress, the wet hair clinging to my face. His perusal halts at my mouth. The evidence of Matteo's hit from the other night, on full display, make-up washed away.

I run my tongue over the rough edges of the cut and his jaw flexes, eyes darkening. Bitter hatred burns in them, and my blood turns to ice.

I drop my stare, wanting nothing more in this moment than to disappear. "I'm sorry, I'll—"

Warm fingers cup my chin, holding me in place before gently tilting up. I lift my gaze to find a stormy sea of green— Aidan's eyes brimming with raw fury. The intensity in them sends a shiver racing down my spine.

His hand moves to my waist, pulling me against him. And maybe it's the fact I'm freezing, or maybe it's something deeper, that keeps me from resisting. I should push him away, should run while I still can. But instead, as starved for warmth as I am, I melt into his embrace. The heat of his body radiates through me, chasing away the cold.

There's a lethal undertone in his voice when he finally speaks, "He's a dead man."

52

HE'S A DEAD MAN

AIDAN

Rory watches me like a deer in headlights. Frozen in fear or panic. Torn between staying and fleeing.

I catch her before she can run, pulling her close and caging her in my arms. Ensnaring the fallen Russian angel before the shadows can swallow her again.

I can see on her face she thinks about resisting, but puts up little-to-no fight. And once I have her in my arms, I hold her stiff body tight to me until she relaxes. Her skin is ice, and she trembles lightly against me, soaking wet. Her white bandage dress, sleeveless, offers her little warmth. *How long has she been outside? Out here?*

And to think I've been inside running drill after drill for hours, trying to get this very girl out of my fucking head.

She flinched.

She flinched when I reached for her just now. Blue eyes flashing with fear at my sudden movement. Full of apprehension and panic since I caught her hiding in the shadows. I take advantage of her proximity to further inspect the purple bruise high on her cheek. Her busted lip is out of my current line of sight.

Grinding my teeth, I have to resist the overwhelming urge to hop on my bike and pay the Italian Consigliere a much overdue visit. I need to torture him until blood drips from every inch of skin and he's no longer able to beg for mercy. I do the next best thing. I offer her my dark promise.

"He's a dead man."

Something went down. My strong, defiant little ice princess is a shivering mess of fear and anxiety as she stands before me with uncertainty shining in the gray of her eyes. Uncertain if she can trust me.

Releasing her, I rip off my hoodie and pull it over her head. It's wet but not yet soaked through. The hem of it falls to her knees. *Good.* It'll at least help block the wind.

"Get on." I swing my leg over my bike, revving it up.

Rory's slow to follow, still second guessing her decision to run *to me.*

I pull out my phone and type out a quick message before sliding it back into my pocket. The way we left things earlier this week... *the way I threatened her.* She must be desperate to come here, to come to me... Still, she climbs on the back of my bike, wrapping her arms around my middle, awakening every nerve through my thin, wet t-shirt.

I do a cursory sweep of the lot. It's empty, but the way Rory's eyes keep darting wildly around tells me we need to get off the streets. It's not like I don't know she's supposed to marry the Italian Consigliere tomorrow...

"You ready?" I ask, my hand on the throttle. "If you do this —there's no going back." And I'm not talking about her family, or the Italians, for that matter.

"I know." She tightens her hold on me, her fingers twisting into my t-shirt. I'm hyper aware of every point of contact between us.

"Hold on tight." Rolling back the throttle, we take off into the night. Rain pelts my face. Normally, I wouldn't risk putting her on the back of my bike in this weather, but the rink isn't far from the loft. And something tells me we don't have any time to waste.

After a few minutes on the road, Rory's grip relaxes a little, and she rests her head against my back. A wave of unexpected warmth surges through my soaked t-shirt, sending a jolt through my body and quickening my pulse. Despite the way the wind from the storm whips past us, and the darkness chasing her, there's a calm in the way she's holding on to me. Her body relaxed against mine. *Trust.*

When I'm sure we weren't followed, the parking garage offers a welcome reprieve from the relentless pelting rain and rolls of thunder. We're both drenched. I don't bother parking my bike, instead pulling it right up to the curb by the private elevator.

I hold out my hand to help Rory off the bike. The nerves are back. She's anxious. Trembling fingers meet mine and my eyes catch again on the bruise just under her eye. I have to suppress another surge of rage meant for the man who's done this to her.

She's quiet—in shock, maybe. Her blue eyes are glazed over like frost on glass. Once she's off the bike, instead of letting go of her hand, I lace my fingers through hers and tug her along with me. "C'mon," I move us toward the elevators. She trails behind me, her fingers closing around mine. A flash of hope in her eyes. *Hope that I won't betray her.*

"Ace." The guard at the desk offers a nod of acknowledgement, his eyes flicking to Rory for half a second before turning the key to unlock the private elevator.

We step inside and Rory attempts to let go of my hand, but I keep hers hostage. My gaze on the doors, watching the lights as the elevator ascends to the top floor.

The doors open up to a very pissed off Koen. His hard gaze lands on me before dropping slowly to Rory. She tries to take a step back, to retreat further into the elevator, but I take this moment to tug her into me, wrapping an arm around her protectively.

I see the moment Koen's eyes notice her split lip, following it up to the dark mark marring her cheek, her red-rimmed eyes... His gaze softens. We exchange a long look.

"Is that Aidan?" Liam comes around the corner, his phone pressed up against his ear.

The phone in my pocket has been going off nearly non-stop.

"What the fuck?" Liam glares at me, coming to stand beside Koen. "You can't send out an SOS text and then STOP responding..." He notices Rory at my side for the first time, and his steely expression changes. "Oh, hi, little Kostalova."

I turn toward her. "Do you remember where my room is?"

Rory nods, looking nervously between my brothers and me. I nudge her forward, to the far hall and the bedrooms. "Go. I'll meet you there in one minute."

"Okay," she answers quietly, letting go of my hand. I resist the urge to pull her back. Watching until she disappears down the darkened hallway before turning my attention to Liam and Koen, who are watching with rapt attention.

"Call Alex."

"I already did. He's five minutes out," Liam confirms.

"Good." My face twists, the anger I've been holding onto finally burning through to the surface. "He doesn't live to see sunrise." I stare down both my brothers.

Koen and Liam straighten, their faces serious as they exchange glances. They know exactly who I mean.

A dark smile appears at the corner of Koen's mouth. "The cars or the bikes?"

"The bikes." My jaw flexes.

"I want him to hear death coming for him."

53

DON'T WORRY ANGEL

RORY

*S*leep won't come. My mind keeps circling... How did Matteo react when he realized I was gone? *How did my father?* Would they think to look for me here? Would the Irish cut their losses and send me straight back? Was Aidan already working on brokering the best trade deal for the Bratva Princess?

No.

I push back against the intrusive thoughts.

Helping me gains Aidan and the Irish nothing... and he has every reason to give me back. But somehow... I know he won't. I trusted him in blind faith when I jumped on the back of his bike. And again hours ago when he handed me a dry Breakers hoodie and some boxers before he disappeared. *"I'll be back."*

He's not here. In the loft.

And neither are his brothers.

I know, because somewhere around three a.m. I gave up on sleeping. I wandered through the quiet loft until I found Reagan curled up on the giant sectional in the living room.

The Irish princess sits up, pausing her movie when she spots me hovering in the hallway.

We stare at each other for a few seconds before she cocks her head. Lifting the edge of her blanket, a silent invitation. I crawl into it, thankful for the company. What starts as quietly watching a movie quickly devolves into me unloading onto her everything that's happened with Matteo. Needing to get it out.

"I hope Aidan doesn't send me back." I wrap the blanket tighter around myself. "If my father doesn't kill me... Matteo will. He'd have the right, after what I did... Or maybe Aidan will save them the trouble and finally kill me himself."

Reagan shakes her head, adamant. "Not even on the table. Even when he *hated* you—*a Kostalova*—he couldn't do it. Now—" she trails off, a little smile playing on her lips. "I think if anybody so much as looks at you the wrong way, he might drop them off the French King Bridge."

I sigh. It's what I want to believe, but Aidan took off so quickly after we got here... I haven't talked to him about any of it. Or confessed that I don't have a plan in place yet. It's not like we're exactly—friends. *I don't even know what to call what we are.*

And it might not even be Aidan I need to worry about. Koen's the boss. And the eldest O'Rourke has little love for me. If he wants me gone—I doubt Aidan would stand in the way.

Reagan yawns, settling deeper into the plush cushions, and both of us quietly return our attention back to the movie.

Minutes later—she's asleep.

But I'm still too keyed up... The boys have not returned. After Reagan caught me keeping a vigilant watch on the elevator doors, she assured me we were safe here. "If all four of them had to step out, there's no doubt a small military presence, at the very least, is on the other side of that door," she laughs.

Just before dawn, I retreat into Aidan's room, hoping maybe laying in bed might help sleep come. I've just settled under the covers when I hear them... The deep tenor of male voices fills the loft.

Suddenly nervous, my heart threatens to pound right out of my chest. I'd spent the entire night wishing Aidan would come back so we could talk, but now...

I twist my fingers in the comforter while keeping my gaze fixed on the bedroom doorway. But nothing could prepare me for the sight of him when he rounds the corner...

Blood.

Blood everywhere... splattered across his clothes, his face... a mosaic of crimson.

Is it his? I rise, trembling, from the bed. Concerned. Taking cautious steps closer. There's too much blood for it all to be his. He wouldn't be standing... Aidan remains half in the hall, leaning on his shoulder against the door frame, watching me. A wild and dangerous look in his eye.

I stop. Barefoot on the hardwoods. Not daring to go any closer. Scanning his blood stained fingertips.

"It's not mine." The sound of his voice pulls my gaze up. His eyes finish the rest of his sentence. Relief sweeps through me for not one, but two reasons.

"Matteo?"

Aidan dips his chin in a slow nod of confirmation, watching my face carefully, searching my eyes for a reaction. A beat passes between us.

"Good."

His eyes flash with surprise, brows lift slightly.

"He deserved it." I hold his eyes.

Something flickers in them and whatever it is seems to propel him forward. Before I know it, I'm in his arms. Aidan's kiss is hungry—starving. But he pulls away just as quickly. "I'm sorry," he says, shaking his head and turning away.

I tighten my grip, stopping him. Aidan looks down at me with confusion.

I rise on my tiptoes, gently touching my lips to his, tugging him closer to me. Not caring when some of that dark blood smears across my arms—my face.

There's no hesitation. He comes as I call. His lips crash against mine, punishing in their desire, as if he's devouring me whole.

Picking me up, Aidan carries me through the bedroom, past the rumpled bed and into the bathroom. He walks us straight into the shower without breaking the kiss.

When my back hits the smooth tile wall, he reaches down and twists the knob.

Water rains down on both of us and I shiver, the freezing water heating fast. Aidan sets me down under the stream and rips off his shirt. The water falling from him is tinged red, washing away Matteo's blood as it streams down the hardened muscle. Aidan steps into me, green eyes locked on mine, fingers finding the hem of my borrowed sweatshirt.

Slowly, he peels the soaked fabric up and over my head. A feral gleam enters his eye when he slides the boxers down over my hips and I kick them away.

My back is to the shower wall again before I can form another thought. His fingers trail south over my bare skin, finding a nipple and gently pinching it until it hardens, and I release a soft moan. He deepens the kiss, tongue sweeping into my mouth as he explores my body. The feel of his hands on my skin is like a hit of the sweetest drug.

I can't get enough of him. With my mouth still on his, I reach down and unhook his jeans.

He stills, breaking our kiss for the first time. His eyes scan mine, a question in them.

I answer it by pushing down on his jeans until they're off. Until the only barrier between us is the icy wall I have built around my heart. But the heat Aidan draws out with every touch is wearing that ice thin.

He reaches up, brushing a lock of my wet hair behind my ear. Following the strands down, his fingers trace around the curve of my breast. This time, the shiver shooting through my body has nothing to do with the cold.

He explores further, running his fingernails over the ripples of my abs, *where he hesitates.*

His body stiffens and I look up, confused, but Aidan stares at my ribs. More specifically, on the dark purple bruises from Matteo that have barely faded. A symbol of the punishment I endured for allowing Aidan to touch me.

"I killed him too quickly." His voice is haunting as he stares at the marks—finding more.

I drag his chin up, tearing his eyes away from my skin. "It's okay," I reassure him. "It doesn't hurt," I lie. It hurts. But only if someone touches it and God, if I don't want Aidan to stop touching me.

He shakes his head. "It's not okay," his jaw tightening, "No one will ever touch you like that again." The dangerous edge to his voice ignites a spark deep inside me, only making me want him more. "If they do—they die." Aidan's pine green eyes are

317

nearly black when they finally meet mine. I see nothing but unquestionable certainty in his dark gaze. And I... *I believe him.*

I showed up at the rink today, tail between my legs. Scared, alone, practically begging for his help. He could have laughed or sent me right back where I came from. But—he didn't. Aidan could have hurt me, or worse. But I knew. *Knew.* He wouldn't.

Weeks ago, he pressed his gun to my forehead, demanding I give him a reason not to do it. Not to kill me. Something passed between us at that moment. Something I can't explain... I looked into his eyes and my tortured heart saw his, and I just knew he wouldn't do it.

Aidan didn't even ask a single question before pulling me onto the back of his bike. Bringing me here... to his home. Where he knew I would be *safe.* And then he left. He went back... And he eliminated the threat. The Irish Devil made Matteo Carroza pay.

"He will never touch me again because of you, Aidan." I reach up, cupping his face in my palm. The Irish enforcer leans into my touch, his eyes closing at the sound of his name on my lips. "You—your brothers..." I hang my head, no longer able to meet his gaze. "I don't know how I'll ever repay you."

He grips my chin, jerking it up. "You owe us *nothing.* Do you hear me?" His eyes blaze as they hold mine. "I don't know when it happened or how, but—you're one of us now. And we protect our own."

"I can't let you risk—"

"You're *mine*, Rory. My complication, my problem, my *angel, mine* to protect."

I think I stopped breathing. Hearing his words—the corner

of my mouth twitches up. Aidan's eyes drop to my mouth and he lets out a groan, "Do that more often." And then his mouth is on mine again. His hand travels down, down until—I hike up a breath, shuddering when his fingers find my clit.

He pauses there—a single finger moving in slow, gentle circles—waiting. I bite my lip and dip my chin, knowing exactly where this is going and wanting it more than I've ever wanted anything. Aidan's green eyes sparkle. His slow circles drive me mad, building up a delicious tension that runs deep, low, and wild.

I raise my hips, searching... no, *needing* more.

Aidan's other hand explores the rest of me. Fingertips trailing down my arm, leaving a tingling warmth in their wake. Jolts of electricity ripple through my body at each point of contact, sending little shivers down my spine and building to an impossible intensity deep within my core.

Hot water streams down my chest, further fanning the heat from the flames that Aidan continues to stoke. As he increases the pressure, a whimper escapes. He swallows the sound with his mouth, again running his tongue along my lip until I open for him.

He rewards me, shoving his finger inside me and curling it up against a spot I don't know if I knew existed.

I see stars.

Arching my back against the glass, I beg him for more. When Aidan adds a second finger, my knees nearly buckle, but he holds me in place. His fingers slowly pumping in and out, fucking me nearly to climax. The fire in my core becomes inescapable, consuming every thought.

I squirm in his arms. Aidan's hand closes around my throat to keep me in place. His hold is firm, but gentle. Reminding me of the first time we met, I feel the tension in his grip all the way through my core.

He withdraws his fingers, and I let out a whine of protest, "No—"

"Don't worry Angel," he assures me with a devilish wink, "I've got something better."

I swallow hard. He feels the movement under his palm. The hunger in his eyes sharpens into something more serious as he stares deep into mine. "Are you sure?"

Not breaking our gaze, I dip my chin. A little smile on my lips. Aidan leans forward, hot breath from his mouth right up against my ear, leading to a full body shudder.

"Not good enough—I need to hear you say it, baby." The contrast between Aidan's velvety voice in my ear and his firm grip around my throat... the way his hardened body presses me against the shower wall, has me spiraling toward the edge

"Fuck me, Aidan O'Rourke. Fuck me, how you think I deserve."

He drops to his knees.

Surprised, I try to follow, but his hand holds firm on my throat, holding me back, and that's when I feel it... Aidan's tongue trailing up against my clit. My entire body quivers while I twist and squirm. The feeling is too much... overwhelming me. I want to both run and submit to it all at the same time.

He increases the pressure, slipping two fingers in while he sucks my clit. Working me closer and closer to the edge. I throw my head back, my body going taut, so close to unraveling. When Aidan's teeth graze the little bundle of nerves, I'm done for. Screaming as I come. Exploding like a rocket. He finger fucks me through my orgasm until I go limp in his arms.

Rising, he kisses me roughly as I come down, my knees shaking as he slips his tongue into my mouth.

"Don't get weak on me now, angel." He lifts me up into his arms and I wrap my arms around his neck. I still, when I feel the length of him push against my entrance.

My eyes go wide and I keep them locked on Aidan's. Slowly, ever so slowly, he slides me down onto him. I gasp when he pushes further still. He lets out a groan and I feel myself tighten. My breath catches as he stretches me. I shudder when he pushes even deeper.

"Fuck, baby," he breathes. His mouth is against my neck—still for a moment while I adjust to him inside of me, filling every inch. Slowly he starts to move, in and out. Each time exploring deeper—pushing harder.

My nails dig into his back, pleasure growing as I chase a second orgasm. My hands find his hair, holding on for dear life as Aidan plows into me. Clinging to him. Letting him take whatever he wants. He fucks me fast and hard and my eyes roll back when he shifts slightly, hitting just the right spot. He senses it and his hands tighten on my ass where he holds me against him. The way he's making me feel is immaculate. I release little whimpers as I get close.

The hot water streams down over us and Aidan's voice in my ear nearly does me in. Eliciting shivers through my body. "Come for me baby," he kisses my neck. I can feel the tip of his tongue graze along my skin. "Come for me again."

And then he bites down.

I'm done for.

Releasing a scream, I tighten around him, convulsing with the sensation shattering all my barriers, breathless as he fucks me ruthlessly through my second orgasm. Drawing it out until he comes alongside me, his breath ragged.

By the end, we're both a panting mess against the shower wall. Water pouring down over us, streaming down my face.

Aidan reaches down, turning off the water with one hand, the other keeping me from collapsing. Opening the shower door, he retrieves a towel off the hook.

I'm exhausted, fully sated, and limp in his arms. All defenses obliterated. Aidan could do just about anything he wanted to me right now and—I'd probably let him. Especially if it felt anything like what we'd just done.

Aidan carries me to his bed, gently lowering me down and wrapping me in a soft towel.

He disappears again into the bathroom, emerging a half second later with his own towel wrapped around his bottom half.

Aidan's body is truly a masterpiece. Every bit a professional athlete, his body a testament to years of training and pushing himself to the limit.

But it's the tattoos that set off a fresh jolt of electricity through me. Covering nearly every inch of his upper body, dark ink snakes across his skin. Intricate designs I want to trace with my fingers. They tell a story I don't understand. The ink distracts me from the myriad of scars covering his skin, faded white lines and jagged marks which could have originated from either side of Aidan's double life. My gaze falls to the green Breakers shamrock inked over his heart and the green roses along his neck.

He notices me staring and walks slowly toward the bed. I push myself up, but Aidan clicks his tongue, "Don't even think about it." Confused, I look up. He points at the pillow behind me. "Sleep."

Seeing the uncertainty on my face, Aidan frowns. The mattress dips under his weight when he climbs into the bed. Joining me.

Next thing I know, there's a hand wrapped around my middle, tugging me back down and holding me flush against Aidan's hard chest. I'm stiff in his arms, anxious over what we did and how I'm supposed to act.

Again, I hear Aidan's voice, a soft whisper against my ear, "Don't overthink it, ice princess. Just sleep." His arm tightens around me and I let myself sink further into him. The warmth radiating from him spreads into me. My body relaxes despite my mind still reeling. "Sleep, baby. Where it's safe."

I play the words over in my head. *Safe?* With *Aidan?* This should be the last place I should consider safe. Not long ago, he'd held me hostage in this very room. But yet... wrapped in the arms of one of the Bratva's greatest enemies, I finally feel the elusive pull of sleep. My eyelids grow heavy, a feeling of calm settling over me.

Safe.

Aidan weaves his fingers through mine, drawing lazy circles along my palm. I have my answer moments later when sleep finally drags me under.

Safe in the arms of the Irish Devil who stole me.

54

THE PROMISE

AIDAN

*T*he slightest creak in my bedroom floorboards wakes me.

I'm up and out of my bed, gun in hand and pointed at... wide eyes. More gray than blue today. Full of guilt, and rimmed with fear. She's halfway to the door, looking like someone caught stealing from the cookie jar.

"Rory," I lower the gun the second I see who woke me, dropping it back into the side drawer beside the bed. "What are you doing?"

She follows the movement with her eyes. "I'm sorry, I thought it would be easier this way—wait, was that there the whole time?"

My smirk is answer enough and the corner of her mouth ticks up, if only slightly.

That's when I notice a pair of gym sneakers on her feet. My gym sneakers. Entirely too large. How she's even got them to stay on, I don't know. I make a mental note that Rory needs clothes...

"If you think you're heading out into the city alone, you've got another thing coming..."

"Well, I thought with Matteo dead—"

"With Matteo dead, shit only gets messier." I rise, pushing the hair out of my eyes, now that it's clear that we're starting our day. I pull open the dresser in search of a shirt. "It's not safe for you out there."

"Why do you even care?" she snaps, shifting anxiously on her feet. The question comes out as spite, but I can hear the underlying stress and uncertainty. It hangs between us. The bubble we existed in last night has popped and reality has set back in.

"Why did you help me last night?" she demands, her nostrils flaring, teetering on the verge of hysteria. "You killed him. Killed Matteo. And brought me here." She waves her hand around my bedroom, but my eyes stay locked on her. "The last thing you said to me at the Breakers game the other night was you knew my father killed your father. You wanted *revenge*." She takes one step toward me—I haven't moved. "Is that it then, *Ace*? Am I to be your revenge?"

In truth, I don't know what I want from her. There are several members of my family who would certainly love the answer to that very question. But I don't have one... I just know I want her here. *With me.* And far away from that fucking family of hers. Since the moment I first had Rory in my arms, back at the club, her rapid heartbeat fluttering against the palm of my hand... She became my fixation.

My obsession.

I tried to stay away. Distanced myself from her, both physically and emotionally. But it didn't work. Aurora Kostalova still consumes my every thought. Every time I look into those salt blue eyes, I feel a pull so powerful it defies logic. Defies explanation.

I've found myself trapped within her gravity—it's intense and it is dangerous. Her presence alone is enough to throw my entire world off balance, tilting to her as if she was the damn sun itself, threatening to burn through the cold exterior wall of ice I'd carefully constructed.

Inside, a battle waged. Could I use her? Yes. *Absolutely.* Having Adrik Kostalov's daughter in my possession meant I could have the Russian Pakhan by the throat. But could I give her up again? Or—if it came down to it, could I put my gun to her head and pull the trigger?

My need for vengeance is at war with something far more dangerous. The answer should be yes. I should tell her she's nothing more than a means to an end—a pawn in the same deadly game we were both born to play.

I should lie.

But I can't lie... Not to her... Not about this.

Clenching my jaw, I step closer. She holds her ground. Defiance flashes in her eyes, though still alight with fear. Part of her wants to run, yes, but the other part—the other part is *curious.*

"Revenge? No, Aurora Kostalova," her eyes harden when I use her full name, "You're not to be my revenge—but you may just be my salvation."

I'm close enough to touch her and, like a shadow reaching for light, my hand rises. Fingertips trace down the side of her face. Her eyes close. Her breath quickening, catching when I hit just the right nerve. *So responsive.*

"I can't be your hero." Reluctantly, I drop my hand and

take a step back from her. "I'm no one's hero." The things I've done... The dark things I've yet to do... she has no idea.

Rory's eyes flutter open, peering up at me, looking just as confused as I feel. My angel is teetering on the edge of a fall, the cracks in her halo splintering further every second she's with me.

"But if you don't want to go back... I won't let them take you. Not this time."

I lower myself slightly so I'm holding her gaze, searching her eyes and letting her see mine before I say what I'm about to say. Everyone who was supposed to protect her let her down... Time and time again. I want her to see that I mean what I say. And despite all the reasons she shouldn't—she can trust me.

Rory's eyes soften as they stare up at mine and she closes the gap between us. Both of us caught in each other's gravity. On an inevitable collision course of desire and destruction. Her pretty white feathers, once pristine, now brushed with the faintest traces of shadow, touched by the edges of darkness. *A fallen angel.* I pull her into me, unable to resist it any longer, wrapping my arms tight around her and resting my chin atop her head.

"You are safe with me, Rory. I *promise.*"

55

WEDDING BELLS

AIDAN

Koen appears in my doorway. His eyes drop to the little Russian in my arms.

"Family meeting."

Rory startles at the sound of his voice, pulling away from me.

"Both of you," he says, before disappearing into the hall.

Solemnly, I reach down, taking Rory's hand in mine. "Come on," I tug her after me, but she's apprehensive. "It's okay," I reassure her, squeezing her hand to remind her of the promise I made.

Still unsure, she allows me to tug her down the hall, her hand gripping tight to mine. We walk out to find both of my brothers, Koen and Liam, on the couch. Alex is holding up the far wall with his back, and Reagan is even present, curled up in the armchair by the window. Rory stiffens at the sight of her former bodyguard.

"The Bratva know the Irish have Rory."

"Jesus, Koen." I run a hand down my face. "Good morning

to you, too." I find a spot on the couch and tug Rory down next to me.

Koen ignores me, "Adrik has spun a story claiming the Irish kidnapped his daughter and murdered her fiancé." He frowns. "If it wasn't war already... It is now. The Mafia is all fired up over Carroza."

I nod, well aware of the shit storm about to come down on us. Only accelerating the inevitable war with the Bratva and Mafia with my actions last night. Throwing gasoline atop the flames of an already roaring fire.

"Nikolai Kostalov has promised to inflict a slow death upon all the O'Rourkes unless his sister is returned immediately and unsullied." Rory's eyes widen, shocked or afraid by her brother's proclamation—I can't tell.

Koen's eyebrow raises when I let out a laugh, leaning back further into the cushions. "Well, I don't think it's a secret that quite a bit of *sullying* went down last night."

Rory stiffens beside me at the same time Koen's gaze hardens, and Liam grins, shooting me a sly wink.

Reagan winces across the room, "Gross."

Clearing his throat, Koen attempts to rein this conversation back in. "You know I have your back, no matter what..." His eyes drop to Rory at my side, our hands still linked, before returning to mine, and I nod.

"We all do—" Alex adds from behind us.

"All that is to say, a war is coming. The Irish are fierce and they are loyal and will fight to the death to protect their *own*." Koen's eyes bore into mine, full of unspoken words. The silence drags out as I tumble over them. My jaw works as I try to think of any other way...

"I don't understand," says Rory slowly, looking between Koen and me.

"There's no other way?" I ask.

My brother slowly shakes his head.

Rory watches our silent exchange anxiously, and it's me who answers her, "He means the Irish won't protect you—*us*... We have to get married."

"No—" Panic breaks out instantaneously across Rory's face and she pulls away from me, pleading with Koen—with me. Scooting further down the couch. "No, please. Don't make me—I don't want to get married..."

"We won't make you do anything you don't want to do." Koen's jaw is tight and his eyes don't leave Rory. I'm watching the two of them carefully.

She's quiet for a moment, coming to the same cool realization I did only moments earlier. "But if we don't... it'll endanger everyone in this room."

Koen confirms with a dip of his chin.

She lets out a shaky breath, avoiding my gaze before launching to her feet and backing down the hallway. "I just—I need a minute," she mumbles, disappearing toward the bedrooms.

After fifteen minutes pass with no sign of Rory—at Reagan's urging—I go after her. Finding my little Russian angel perched crossed legged on my bed, eyes boring down into the chestnut hardwoods.

I join her. The two of us sit in silence for I don't know how long.

"I don't want to get married," she whispers quietly, her eyes glued to the floor.

I look up at the sound of her voice. "Neither do I."

She looks my way, and I sigh, running my hand a few times through my hair. "Look, your father is dead set on marrying you off, Rory. If he gets his hands on you—*again*—that's exactly what he'll do. Likely to the next in line after Carroza. It could be better, it could be worse..." I search her eyes, trying to guess what she's thinking. "They're going to keep coming."

She closes her eyes, looking an awful lot like she's going to be sick. Suddenly I sit up. "Do you need your medicine?" Concerned her spiraling might lead to an attack...

Her mouth tightens. "No," is all she says.

Another tense moment of silence passes before I try again. "I can give you money—ship you out of the country. But this is the Russian Bratva we're talking about here... Not to mention the Italian Mafia think they have some sort of claim on you as well..." My words end in a growl and Rory looks up. "It's not a matter of if they'll find you—it's when."

"I know," she concedes, sighing softly.

"There are few things the Mafia respects, loyalty, power and family. If you become family—their claim on you dies. You'll be Irish. One of us. They will have to respect that. Marriage is sacred in the Mafia."

"They won't just let it lie..."

"No, they won't," I admit, because she deserves the truth. "They'll still come for me, but we'll have the full weight of the Irish mob at our backs. Their claim on you will die. No one can touch you once you belong to me." Her steely gray eyes soften for the first time, but she shakes her head.

"I can't be the reason for a war between our families. What

if something happens to one of your brothers because of me? What if something happens to you?" The anxiety and distress melts what's left of the ice wall around my heart. *She's worried about me.* My family. Wanting to put us first, even if it compromises her own safety.

I cup her chin, bringing her head back up. "The war is already here. They're coming for us either way. It's time to choose a side princess. Will you stay the Russian Angel? Or will you trade in your halo for the Irish Devil?" I smile softly.

Rory still looks undecided, so I change tactics, ignoring the fact I'm trying to convince her to *marry* me.

"You want to skate."

Rory looks up, confused by the subject change. "Of course I want to skate, obviously! What does that have to do with—"

"I want to play hockey," I cut her off, "Keep playing in the league... A nice, *long* career. You want the Olympics. Neither of us wants this life. I was already out, I was—" My jaw clicks as I think about how many more times the Irish will draw me back in. *And what it might cost me...*

I reach out, taking her hand in mine, running my thumb over the little silver scar she has across the back of her left hand.

"Marry me, and I will keep you safe. I will get you out. And when we're free and clear and past this, we can go our separate ways, get a divorce—" Her eyes widen in shock. "—If that's what you want. I'll give you that."

"But a *made* marriage is forever..." She repeats the words quietly, words I'm sure she's been told a thousand times. *'Til death do us part.*

"The Irish... we do things a little bit differently." I'm *lying* and I wonder if she can tell. I don't even realize it until the words are out of my mouth. But that's only when I realize once

332

I make this girl mine—I don't know if I can ever let her go. I might also be lying when I tell her I can let her go. I'll divorce her—if that's what she wants... but even if we're living apart, I'll always look out for her. She'll always be *mine*.

Rory chews on her bottom lip, her eyes conflicted.

I release her hand and stand, backing away, toward the door. "Think on it. Stay the night. The guest room is yours, though I think you know where I'd prefer you." My eyes flicker over the bed she's still sitting on. I can't overlook the fact that when she ran, she ran to *my room*.

"You don't have to decide anything right now."

She nods, hearing me, but she's deep in her thoughts.

When I reappear in the living room, everyone is exactly as I'd left them. I crash back down on the sofa, my hands locked over my head, staring up at the ceiling.

"Well?" Koen asks after several minutes of silence passes. I can feel the weight of all of their eyes on me.

I blow out a breath, slowly dropping my gaze to his. "She's going to think about it overnight."

Koen works his jaw and slides a look over to Liam, whose jaw tightens but remains shut. "I want you to know, no matter what, we're here for you, but if she doesn't marry you..." He shakes his head, concern flickering in his eyes as he runs them over Reagan. "It's going to get ugly. We should take some extra measures..."

I nod. Extra measures like securing our sister, so should anything happen to us, they won't be able to get to her. "We'll do what we have to."

"That won't be necessary." The sound of Rory's voice has everyone on edge. I twist in my seat to find her standing at the entrance to the living room, her eyes on mine.

333

"I'll do it. It's the best chance we have... I will marry Aidan."

Shouts and excited cheers rise around us from everyone but Koen. Ideas for the wedding ceremony come tumbling out of Reagan's mouth and it's clear why she's been so quiet this whole time. She's been busy making plans.

Liam stands, sweeping Rory up into a crushing hug, swinging her around before setting her feet back on the floor. "Welcome to the family, little Kostalova."

Alex finds her next, her eyes watering a little as the two come face to face. Her former bodyguard nearly fully healed from what he suffered at the hands of her family. He smiles at her reassuringly, "You're making the right choice Ro. Aidan—the O'Rourkes..." he trails off, but Rory nods in understanding, wrapping her arms around him.

"I know." She lets out a breath, putting on a brave face, though I know she's terrified. She steels her spine, releases Alex and looks around at all of us. "What now?"

With his phone already pressed to his ear, Koen is halfway out of the room as he says, "I'm ringing Father Lucent, he'll be here within the hour."

Rory pales, looking a little like she's going to be sick. "An... *hour*?" She swallows hard, her eyes darting to mine. I try my best to give her a reassuring smile. It's all moving so fast.

"Can't afford to waste any time. Let's get you two married and everyone out of the city while we plot out our next move. Before the Russians and Italians make theirs." Koen's face is grave. "I suggest everyone start packing."

"I think I have a dress you can wear," Reagan offers, moving to sweep Rory up. "It's not much, but it's better than Aidan's stinky boxers." She sticks her tongue out at me as she

334

pulls Rory away with her, and I return it with a face of my own.

"You sure you're ready to be one of us?" Koen asks, watching the three of us. His question directed at little Kostalova, an unexpected softness in his hard eyes.

If Rory's startled by his sudden question and the fact he stands only a few feet from her, she doesn't show it. Instead, the corner of her lips tilt up in the slightest hint of a smile. "I think there are worse things."

56

LOVE, LOYALTY, FRIENDSHIP

RORY

"*I* don't have any white dresses, I'm sorry!" Reagan tears through her closet once more. Articles of clothing fall to the floor the more fiercely she looks through them.

"It's okay," I reassure her, but she won't be diverted from her task. "I can wear this."

Reagan freezes, turning slowly, with a slow perusal of my body from the bottom up. I cringe when her eyes finally lift to mine. I'm completely aware that I'm still in Aidan's boxers and faded Breakers sweatshirt.

"We may be under the wire, but we're not desperate, Rory," she huffs, turning back to her closet and pouting at it.

A knock comes at the door and I can't help but jump, the tension in my body coiled tight.

"Not to rush you ladies, but Father Lucent is waiting." I recognize the sound of Liam's voice through the door.

Reagan swears, diving back into the growing chaos that is piles of expensive fabrics. "Okay, we'll be just a minute."

"Reagan…" Liam warns, his tone skeptical.

"Like ten more minutes tops!" she shouts. Lifting a shimmery silver fabric high into the air with a broad grin on her face, she adds, "Maybe less!"

After what seems like well over an hour, I'm squeezed into Reagan's dress, a glittering silver tea-length cocktail dress with thin straps and a sweetheart neckline. My hair is curled, the front pieces braided away from my face.

Picking at the leaves on the single white rose Liam gave me to hold, I pace the small room I'm to wait in that looks very much like a study.

But unlike Papa's or Matteo's, this study isn't dark or imposing; it's cozy, filled with warm light from the setting sun. The loft's floor to ceiling windows see to that. The books lining the oak shelves aren't fancy or leather bound. Instead, they're beat up, with crinkled spines and some even missing covers. Well-read and well-loved.

A handful of couches and wide arm chairs are scattered about the space nonsensically, as if frequently pushed around and moved. I eye the thick blanket draped over the back of one of the couches, resisting the urge to wrap myself up in it and hide for the rest of my life.

I still at the sound of a knock at the door, and am momentarily relieved at the familiar sight of Alexei's head poking through.

"Ready Ro?"

I swallow hard, a lump forming in my throat. Dipping my chin, I clutch the rose stem as I walk forward, relieved when my former bodyguard links his arm through mine. I lean on him for support as he escorts me to the courtyard garden where the wedding will take place. Nervously chewing my lip. Thankful for the clear bit of gloss Regan brushed over them.

The late afternoon sun casts a golden hue over the private garden, the string lights making up for the fading light glowing softly overhead like little stars.

I freeze under the attention of so many people. I knew Koen had put a call out to the Irish underbosses, needing witnesses for the ceremony, but I never expected so many to come with such short notice.

Muscle-bound tattooed bikers, dressed in various cuts of leather, line the ivy covered brick walls of the garden. There are a few disgruntled glares, but most of the men look on curiously. Forcing my gaze past them, I follow the cobblestone path to find Aidan at the end.

When his green eyes find mine, I forget everything else. My trembling hands steady for a moment under his gaze, something unspoken passing between us.

Alexei nudges me forward and I take my first step down the make-shift aisle, noticing Aidan's brothers standing stoically by his side, all of them dressed to impress. My heart does a flip at the sight of Aidan in his tailored suit. The rough-cut Irish Devil certainly cleans up nicely.

When I reach the end, Reagan reaches forward from my side, plucking the rose out of my hand before it's replaced by Aidan's hands, pulling me in closer to him. I inhale sharply, my eyes wide as they stare up at him. Alexei joins his brothers, taking up his place next to Liam.

Father Lucent clears his throat, pulling my attention away from Aidan as he addresses the gathering. His voice is commanding, with a thick Irish lilt, and he doesn't waste any time with pomp and circumstance, going straight into the vows. He nods at Aidan to begin.

Aidan turns slightly to his left, receiving a small ring from Koen, who stands beside him, before facing me.

"The Claddagh is a traditional Irish ring," Aidan says as he slides the tiny circle, heart facing in, down my left ring finger. Holding my trembling hand steady, he continues, "The heart symbolizes love." I swallow hard, unable to look away from Aidan's steady gaze, the only thing anchoring me from running for my life. "The hands represent friendship," he smiles, "and the crown—loyalty." His smile grows serious. "I, Aidan Patrick O'Rourke, take you, Aurora Adrikova Kostalova, in the spirit's name of God that lives within us, by the life that courses within my blood, and the love that resides within my heart and my spirit, to be my chosen one." He looks me in the eye, lightly squeezing my hand as he continues, "I pledge to you my living and my dying, each equally in your care. I shall be a shield for your back and you for mine. I choose your strengths and weaknesses, and I offer mine to you. I will choose you, above all others, every day for all the days of my life."

His words elicit a surge of emotion, and a tear escapes my eyes. I want so badly to believe them, but know he's only putting on a show for our witnesses, for the collection of underbosses Koen pulled together at the eleventh hour. The ones we have to convince to protect us. I can feel Jimmy's eyes burning into my back. I blink the rest of my tears back, doing my best to maintain my composure as I repeat Aidan's words back to him, solidifying our vows to each other.

With his ring firmly on my finger, Aidan leans forward, leaving a chaste kiss on my lips. I close my eyes. When I open them a second later, it's over. Our small little gathering claps—even Koen—as the priest pronounces us man and wife.

Aidan takes my hand, squeezing lightly while lacing his fingers with mine reassuringly. And just like that, my fate is now firmly entangled with his.

57

CLADDAGH

RORY

*M*arried.
         I stare at the ring on my finger as miles of endless trees pass by us. *I can't believe I'm married.* We left the city immediately following the ceremony, all of us—but in different directions. Aidan and I drive alone—in deafening silence.

It's possible he's sensing my mood. It's not exactly like I'm trying to hide it... Sitting in the front seat of the SUV with my arms crossed, staring sullenly out the window.

After putting on a brave face for the O'Rourkes, their Irish priest, and myself, I don't have it in me. Emotionally drained, I sit curled up in my seat, spinning the white gold ring on my finger, chewing my bottom lip. I'm not sure what surprised me more, that Aidan could produce a ring with less than two hours' notice, or how much I'd like it.

A crowned heart, held by two hands.

Married.

The wedding was hours and miles ago. It all happened so fast, it doesn't even feel real.

Almost immediately following the ceremony, the Irish got word the Italians had attacked one of their warehouses, firing the first shots of the war that's been brewing for months. Koen ordered Aidan and me out of the city until things died down. Alexei and Reagan are somewhere in another car. I don't envy him. Reagan was not too keen on the idea of lockdown.

Until we were clear of the city, and Aidan was certain we weren't followed, we had one of Aidan's men tailing us.

Now we're alone.

Koen pushed us out of the loft so fast I'm still wearing the dress Reagan insisted on giving me. The matching heels had been only a smidge too small. I kick them off onto the SUV's floor and pull my legs back up and wrap Aidan's suit jacket tighter around me.

"Cold?"

My head whips in Aidan's direction at the sound of his voice. Having given me his jacket, he's loosened his collar and tie. I squirm in my seat. We've been in this car alone together for hours, so why do I suddenly feel nervous?

Aidan reaches for the temperature controls, raising the heat inside the vehicle.

"N-no. Just getting comfortable..." I blurt out.

"We're almost there." Aidan turns his eyes back to the road.

"And where is *there* exactly?" I finally gathered the nerve to ask the question I've been milling over since we left Boston.

A small smile appears on Aidan's face, and I ignore the way it makes my heart flip flop. "The cabin."

I stare at him, waiting for more of an explanation, but it never comes.

It makes sense a few seconds later when Aidan pulls off the curvy country road and onto a dirt one. After several minutes of rough travel, lights come into view. I feel relief at the sight of them. I don't think Aidan will hurt me, but I still haven't entirely ruled out the possibility. He *did* threaten my life only a few short weeks ago, after all....

My jaw drops slightly at the sight of the wooden cabin sitting in front of an endlessly black expanse. Even in the dark of the night, it's beautiful. A soft orange glow seeps out from behind the closed curtains.

When the car comes to a stop, I step out and stare out across the dark void behind the cabin, my breath visible in the freezing air. It takes a moment for my eyes to adjust, and the frozen water comes into focus, barely lit by the tiny crescent moon in the sky tonight.

"The lake," Aidan explains, following my gaze.

"Right." My mood darkens at the sight of the ice.

"I picked the cabin because I thought if we stayed here, you could at least still train..."

I don't look at him—I can't. I keep my eyes out on the lake. "I'm tired," I say finally, as I shift uncomfortably on my bare feet, having abandoned Reagan's heels in the car.

Aidan's quiet for a half a beat, but then I hear the crunch of gravel under his boots. "This way."

I follow. He pauses for a moment and I half worry he's about to scoop me up, but I rush past him, doing my best not to wince at the sharp gravel stones stabbing my feet.

I let out a sigh of relief when I reach the soft wood of the porch, waiting for Aidan to unlock the cabin door. The lock clicks and the door swings open. I've barely taken a step toward it before I feel his arms around me. And then my feet are off the ground as he swings me up, carrying me across the threshold.

Irritation finally snaps the last thread of my patience, and I kick my feet, punching his chest with my fists. "Put. Me. Down," I demand.

My struggling barely fazes him, but once safely inside, Aidan kicks the door shut with his boot and sets me gently back on my feet.

"What the hell?" I hiss at him.

He just shrugs, heading toward what looks to be the kitchen. "It's tradition, isn't it? Seemed like bad luck not to—"

I blink at him.

"You know?"

"No, I don't know," I snap. Though he might have a point —I don't need any more bad luck than I already have.

The O'Rourke cabin is surprisingly warm and welcoming. Similar to the loft the siblings share back in the city, it's tastefully decorated, but not cold like you would expect from a family in their line of business. Designed for comfort. Someone's come ahead of us and already lit the hearth. The crackling fire is the only sound in the entire place while I glare at Aidan moving around the kitchen.

The initial nerves I felt about being alone with Aidan have only intensified now that we're *here*. Uncertain of his *expectations*. It's our wedding night, but does it still count if it's a fake wedding? I know we've already slept together once, but that was *before*.

Before the vows and my newfound status as his *wife*.

I'm not unaware of how *alone* we are. My initial nervousness is only intensified now that we've reached our destination.

The anticipation of what might be expected tonight is

causing my stomach to knot up with pressure. I'm on edge, wound so tight I'm seconds from spiraling—and spiraling hard.

"Hungry?" I tear my gaze away from the fire I'd lost myself in to find Aidan pulling open the refrigerator. A quick view of the open fridge shows someone has also been by to stock up the food.

"No," I lie. Or maybe I'm telling the truth. I haven't eaten in forever, but I don't think I could eat even if I wanted to right now. "Where can I—" I trail off when I accidentally meet the green of Aidan's eyes watching from across the room. "—sleep?" I finish, desperately keeping myself from chewing my lip, my anxiety eating me alive.

"Upstairs," Aidan replies calmly, eyeing me as if I'm a frightened deer who is seconds from bolting. "First door on the left." He lifts his hand toward a stairway tucked into the corner of the house.

I'm halfway to the stairs before I remind myself to slow my pace. I linger awkwardly on the landing, turning slowly back... "And you'll—"

"First door on the right."

I release a breath, not having realized I'd been holding it.

"If you need anything," he nods slowly, unspoken words written in his eyes.

"Ok." I turn back to the stairs. "Thanks," I add as an afterthought.

I climb slowly, unsure about what, or who, might be upstairs and also listening to the sound of Aidan in the kitchen to ensure he isn't following me.

Ducking into the room, I close and lock the door before pacing the small space for several minutes, debating how much noise dragging the heavy-looking dresser in front of the door might make. Doubtful I even have the energy required to move it, I sigh, leaving the dresser alone before stripping down to my underwear and climbing into the soft bed. Leaving the shimmery silver dress in a pile on the floor. If Aidan wants in—he's getting in, dresser or not. The man throws pro hockey players into the boards for a living.

As exhausted as I am, I toss and turn, too keyed up to sleep. Huddled under the thick, white comforter, feeling naked and exposed in only my underwear. Alone with my thoughts in the early hours of the morning has me questioning my decision to trust Aidan.

We're alone. Not even his brothers are here... and I'm terrified Aidan might change his mind and charge through that door, insistent on claiming his right as my *husband*, but it never opens.

He never comes.

WIN-WIN

RORY

*T*he silence is unnerving.

I've been up for hours, sitting cross-legged on my bed, hesitant to leave the room. Too afraid to face my *husband*.

After turning the room over, I was incredibly disappointed to find all the drawers and closets empty.

I'm fairly certain I heard Aidan leave his room a while ago. Which means it's likely empty... I have the option of either shrugging my shimmery dress back on or darting across the hall to raid Aidan's room for another pair of boxers and t-shirt.

Could I just ask Aidan for some clothes? Yes, but something changed when we made those vows and I feel—I don't know how I feel. And maybe that's the problem... What was light and easy all at once became heavy and hard. I don't know how to act around Aidan. We said this marriage was paper only, a temporary solution to a mutual problem—but it doesn't feel that way... At least not to me.

The past 48 hours are catching up to me and I'm anxious. I

have nothing else to do but think about it. *Did I make the right decision?*

Hunger eventually drives me from my room.

I turn the knob carefully to not make any noise, cringing at the loud whining sound the door makes when I drag it open. I'm too busy looking between Aidan's closed door and the stair landing for him, that I don't see the bags until I'm tripping over them. Luckily, I catch myself with my hands before face planting into the rich mahogany hardwoods.

Frozen for a minute, thinking for sure Aidan would've heard me wipe out. I don't move. When he doesn't come running, I release a sigh and push myself up to my knees to inspect what exactly it is I've tripped over.

Several paper bags of various colors lay now scattered across the hall, thanks to me careening into them. I steal a peek into the closest one and a spark of hope blooms in my chest at the sight of women's clothing.

Gathering up the bags, I drag them all back into my room. I kick the door shut, locking it, and dump the contents out across the bed I made hours ago—out of boredom.

I stare wide eyed at my haul.

Sweatshirts, leggings, t-shirts and tanks. All brand new and my size. Styles similar to the clothes I'm used to sporting at the rink. There's even a small bag full of lingerie. Nothing too crazy, but it's all soft and lacy and feels nice on my skin.

I can't help but notice Aidan's included a fair bit of Breakers gear in the haul: a black beanie with a green shamrock and a hoodie with the Breakers logo. There are also two Breakers' jerseys—home and away—*with, of course, O'Rourke #19 on the back.*

I fold everything up and carefully put each item away in the drawers of the bureau or hang it in the closet. I select the buttery soft, sage green sweat set to wear for the day, along with a pair of thick woolen socks. The cabin is warm enough, but it's still winter, and the floors are ice cold against my bare feet.

I eye the Breakers gear hanging in my closet. It definitely raises the question of what exactly Aidan's going to do about hockey? He can't just disappear from the team. He has commitments, practices, games... and from the media reports, his spot on the team this season is tenuous at best...

The Belles have a bye this week because the team is away, but Aidan's supposed to be in Toronto for an away series the day after next.

Hockey brings my thoughts around to my skating career and instantly sours the good mood the new clothes have inspired. I knew when I ran from the Bratva I was lighting a match to my career. There's no way it will ever be safe for me to compete again. I try not to think about the Belles. It's a loss I haven't yet mourned, so I shove it away, still not yet ready to face that particular consequence for my actions.

As if on cue, the distinct sound of a stick and puck on ice catches my attention.

It draws me to my window, where I finally locate Aidan, gliding across the frozen lake, close by the house, making quick movements with his hands. The dark circle of a puck flashes between the cage his stick creates until he winds up and slaps it hard. It clinks against the beat-up looking metal post of the goal he's dragged out there.

I watch him for a minute. He's dressed only in sweats, gloves, skates, and a backwards baseball hat. Then I realize... if Aidan's on the ice... the house is empty.

I slide across the bedroom floor on my slippery socks and

I'm out the door and down the stairs faster than you can say hockey. I go straight to raiding the kitchen for anything to soothe my roaring stomach.

The premade protein shake in the fridge with my name scrawled across the bottle is a surprise. So is the stack of pancakes next to it, waiting for me in a glass container.

I down the shake while heating the pancakes in the microwave. It takes a minute to find the plates and silverware. The shake is so good. The thick chocolate coats the inside of my stomach and eases the nauseous feeling not eating can bring about.

When the pancakes are ready, I debate running back up to my room to eat them, but I can still hear hockey sounds coming off the lake and so I slide onto one of the kitchen island's stools. As I eat, I watch Aidan practice from afar through the large windows that look out over the most amazing view of the lake and snow-capped mountain in the distance.

Once finished, I rinse off my dishes and load them into the dishwasher before exploring the cabin a little.

The O'Rourke cabin is large, but most of the downstairs is open-concept. In the light of day, it's bright and sunny. The entire back end of the cabin is made up entirely of windows, offering a picturesque view of the lake outside. Having spent most of the day sequestered in my room, the sun has already begun to set. The beautiful orange and gold light reflects off of the snowy surface of the lake and the effect is breathtaking.

I freeze at the sight of the cluster of lights at the far end of the lake. *A town.* It must be a town. The sight of it gives me an idea...

Now that I'm out of Boston, it would be much harder to

track me. If I can make it to that town and beg a ride to the nearest bus station, I could be *anywhere* within a matter of days.

I sit up a little straighter as I work out the details of my getaway plan. The thought of ditching Aidan and the O'Rourkes leaves a pang of guilt deep in my gut, but I reason it away with the fact that I barely know them. And if I just so *happened to disappear*, it might be best for everybody...

The Bratva and the Italians would no longer have a reason to wage war on the Irish. It's a win-win.

Now all I have to do is run...

59

THE BOLTER

RORY

*A*t first light, I'm out of my room.

My heart is beating hard enough to wake Aidan through his own door as I tiptoe past it, holding my breath the whole way down the stairs and through the living room.

While running under the cover of darkness would've offered more protection and more of a head start, the night brings with it a whole new host of threats, and being so unfamiliar with the area and the house itself, waiting until dawn seemed like the better option. If all goes well, I'll be out and across the lake before Aidan even wakes up.

Every little sound—every creak in the floorboards—seems amplified by a thousand. I breathe a little easier once I reach the mudroom. I chose a white hoodie and a soft pink, almost purple, set of leggings, hoping it might help me blend in more out on the snowy lake than my usual dark colors would.

I'll have to make do without a jacket, but the thick hoodie should be warm enough to get me across the ice.

I estimate it's about a mile from here to the town across the lake. I should be able to make it in only a few minutes on skates if I push it... And I need to push it. I will be exposed the entire time I'm crossing the lake. But going around could take days...

The sight of several pairs of hockey skates lying on a mat by the door is a relief. I was too afraid to venture out here yesterday and so I wasn't sure where they kept them.

I check a few sizes until I find a pair close enough to mine. It snowed a little last night and the light dusting coating the yard outside glitters in the rising sun. I slip on a pair of what must be Reagan's snow boots to get me from here to the lake's edge. There's already about a foot of packed powder on the ground outside.

Double checking my ears for the diamond studs my father gifted me last year and my wrist for my gold circlet I'd worn to the reception, I take a deep breath before I pull open the garage door. I might not have cash, but those two items would at least get me a little ways just as soon as I find a pawnshop to trade them in.

I toy with the ring on my finger. The Claddagh ring is old and likely pure gold, seeing as how Aidan already had it prior to us getting hitched. Perhaps a family heirloom... But the thought of trading the ring doesn't quite sit right with me. It's probably best I hang onto it, and if things get bad... it will make a good backup.

The space between the garage and the lake offers no cover as I sprint across it, my hair streaming out behind me. I slip coming down the hill and slide almost the rest of the way to the icy edge of the lake.

Heart racing, my breath comes in shallow bursts as I swap out the boots for skates. My trembling fingers make tying the laces difficult, and I try not to think of my own skates, destroyed by Matteo, while anxiously stealing glances back toward the house. It feels like I have eyes on me, but not even the birds are awake yet...

It's now or never.

I lock eyes on my target across the frozen expanse before me as I step out.

The rough texture of the lake nearly puts me on my ass at first, but I steady myself. Using a couple of slow strides to catch my bearings. Skating on a lake is nothing like skating on a rink, but the ice smoothes out the further away from the shore I get. The sound of the blades cutting across the rough surface seems to echo across the frozen expanse and has a smile growing across my face.

The lake ice is rough around the edges, but I like it more than I care to admit. Taking in the surrounding sights: the rising sun paints everything with an orangey glow, the majestic feel of the mountains in the distance. It's just me out here on this impossibly wide expanse of ice. I throw my arms out, savoring this feeling. The bitter wind sharpens my senses as I dig into my blades; like a bird in flight with freedom in its sights.

The chill that goes through me at the sound of his voice behind me has nothing to do with the icy wind whipping across the lake. I freeze, spinning back around in time to spot Aidan racing down the hill, skates in hand, shouting out words I'm too far away to hear.

I lose precious time to my shock. He's got one skate on before I'm able to react.

I bolt, taking off in a mad dash for freedom across the ice.

It's nonsense to run and I don't know why I do it, but something inside me snaps. I've got the taste of freedom on my tongue and I'm desperate to not give it up. My fear of being used again propels me forward. The memory that he is faster than me prevents me from even looking back.

A deafening crack rings out. It's loud enough to be a gunshot and for a second—I think it is. Flinching hard, I nearly fall, spotting a web of cracks spidering out all around me. A second loud crack, and the ice below me shifts and groans. I stumble, but remain upright, spinning slowly back around to find Aidan stopped about fifty feet away, unmistakable fear in his eyes. The words hidden in his shouts finally register with me.

"Stop."

"Rory, no!"

"Thin ice!"

"Not safe!"

"Don't move!"

60

THIN ICE

RORY

"Careful," Aidan warns. There's a raw edge to his voice, and he seems torn between staying where he is and skating to me.

He's shouting instructions, but fear has a hold of me and it's buzzing in my ear as I stare down at the splintered surface beneath me. Dark water streams out through the cracks below, spilling across the icy surface. A strong current churns underneath. If I fall in—I'm *gone*.

Aidan shouts again, drawing my attention and bringing him back into focus. "Rory, you have to trust me."

"I DON'T trust you!" I snap back, my body shaking uncontrollably. "That's the problem." Fear and panic bypass my filters, the truth spilling out.

"You were running."

It's not a question, but I answer it anyway. "I can't stay— It's only a matter of time before you or your family use me too." I'm frozen in place, unsure which way to go... While it's true no matter which way I choose, I could fall through. If I go further out where it's likely to be more unstable, it's a risk... but then again, going back the way I came seems dangerous too... Considering the agitated Irish enforcer waiting for me...

Danger either way... I look anxiously back over my shoulder, weighing my options.

"I promised to protect you, Rory." The raw emotion in his voice pulls at my heartstrings and I turn to face Aidan with wide eyes. "If you wanted to leave... all you had to do was ask." There's a sad expression on his face and he looks like he might take a step toward me for a second before deciding against it. His gaze hardens. "Where?" he asks.

I stare back at him, mouth open, but my voice fails me.

He tries again. "Where do you want to go? Where will you finally feel safe?" He adjusts the hat on his head and a lock of his hair falls partially out of the front. "Wherever it is, I'll take you there." His eyes find mine. "I promised I'd protect you, and I will. I keep my promises, Rory." He exhales sharply, frustration evident in his gaze.

My mind races as I study his eyes—his face. Even from this distance, I can see the hurt he's too panicked to hide flashing in his green eyes that shine bright against the endless white surrounding us. "What do you want from me, Aidan?" I ask the question almost too quietly for him to hear me.

"I'm the second son of the Irish, heir to a legacy of blood. An enforcer both on and off the ice. I'm no stranger to violence. I've killed before and I'll kill again."

I see emotions in his eyes—fear, vulnerability perhaps— that I've never seen before. It's unsettling, but I can't look away...

"I stole you...Tied you up... Threatened you..." *All true.* I wrap my arms tighter around myself. The feeling of a phantom gun tracing along my jaw sends a chill through my body. "I let you go—physically," he nods, his eyes never leaving mine. Both of us stuck out here in the middle of this icy lake, neither of us able to go forward nor backward until we have this out. "But I couldn't get you out of my mind. I tried distancing myself—I tried to stay away, but no matter what I did, I couldn't. And when that bastard hurt you..." Pure rage replaces fear and his fists tighten at his sides. "He died too fast—deserved far worse than what I gave him. I would burn that city to the ground if it would keep you safe. I'd *never* hurt you, not when I—" he stops, his eyes going to the sky while running a hand down his face. "Since the moment I first saw you. Those steel-blue eyes of yours wide with fear... Oh, I hated you," an echo of a smile graces his lips.,"but I *wanted you*, nonetheless."

"You're lying," I bite out, but the words come out weak —uncertain.

"Am I?" Aidan asks, tilting his head as he studies me, his expression unreadable. "You've felt it too, haven't you? This... whatever *this* is between us. Look me in the eye and tell me you haven't."

The urge to run is so strong and I would—if it didn't mean falling to an icy grave. So instead, I bite my lip, fighting the truth. His gaze is intense, like a magnet, the relentless force that even now draws me toward him. I've felt it since the moment we first crossed paths. Even when he threatened my life, held his gun to my head—I felt it. And hated myself for it. A connection that defies logic and defies loyalty. I open my mouth...

The ice cracks again. This time I feel the shift and I let out a little scream, falling to my knees.

"Spread your weight out," Aidan urges, still obviously torn

between remaining where he is and racing for me. But he's nearly twice my weight and if he does, he'll doom us both.

Shakily, I lower myself to the ice's surface and reluctantly push out my arms and legs.

"Good. That's good. Deep breaths, Rory," he encourages and the ice quiets again. "Now crawl." I start forward. "Slowly, slowly." His voice rises in pitch when the entire area groans under my movements.

I let out a slow breath before I put one palm forward and push myself with the opposite leg, moving *inches* at a time, painfully slow.

All the while, Aidan paces the safe zone like some kind of caged animal.

I'm about ten feet away when my skate lands a little too heavy behind me and a shudder rings out in a ripple beneath me. I only have one second, which I used to find Aidan's eyes before I feel the bottom give out from under me and I scream. But the six-foot-three defenseman dives forward, his hand wrapping around mine and hauling me towards him. I fall hard against his chest and he pushes us both back from the icy edge, putting a safe amount of distance between the two of us and the dark water visible now through the wide, gaping hole. All that's left of the ice that seconds ago I was lying on.

"Are you okay?"

"Yeah," I breathe out, absorbing his warmth. I lay on his chest panting, struggling to catch my breath. The relief I feel in his arms. *Safe.* I can't bear to let go of it yet and so I cling to him. He lets me. Running his hand down my hair, gently caressing the strands to calm me. "Yeah, I'm okay."

I don't miss the way his own hands shake.

"I don't want to let you go," he admits, and I still. His heart beat in my ear while I listen to his words. "I know we said this was temporary—a paper marriage. And we would play pretend just until the dust settles... I can't do anything more to convince you that you're safer with me."

I push myself up so I can see his face, pale even in the rising golden sun.

"I won't let anyone touch you, not your family, not the Italians and not the Irish." He'd stand up to his own family —*for me?* "I promised to protect you until my last breath, and I'll uphold that promise." His face drops and he speaks the next few words as if against his will. "Even if it's me you wish to run from, if you want to go... Rory, I won't stop you. I'll take you anywhere you want, anywhere, just — tell me." Aidan's arms tighten around me before letting go entirely. *Releasing me.* "Even if—even if I don't want you to go..."

My resolve crumbles the longer I stare into his eyes. At the raw, unfiltered emotion I see staring back. Everything Aidan hides from the rest of the world. I have no words—my thoughts are still a tangled mess, so instead I lean forward, pressing my lips to his in a kiss that's both soft and fierce, pouring into it everything I can't put into words. I feel the ever present tension in my body melt away when one of his hands finds my hips, pulling me closer, his other hand gently cupping my face.

Both of us are breathless by the time we pull apart. I look up at him from beneath my lashes. "So don't."

He stares down at me, searching my face before his lips crash down on mine again. He flips us and the cold ice at my back is a sharp contrast to the heat at my front as Aidan claims my lips as his. His kiss is raw and desperate. I realize I'm as lost in this as he is, and whatever happens next, we're in it together. Our skates tangle up beneath us.

I let myself fall, and Aidan swept in and caught me. In him I feel something I haven't felt in a long time. Safety, warmth, *love*.

"I'm done running." I pull away just long enough to utter the words before he presses another hungry kiss to my lips.

"Good. But I'm not done chasing you."

61

TRUST. ME.

AIDAN

I scoop my wife into my arms and carry her off the ice, trying not to think about how I could have lost her—was seconds away from losing her.

My Wife.

She keeps her head pressed up against my chest and her arms wrapped around my neck as I carry her all the way to my second-floor bedroom and deposit her onto my bed.

The sight of my angel, stretched out across my bed in hockey skates, nearly does me in. The only thing hotter might be if I ever found her wearing my jersey—*and nothing else.*

A slow, predatory grin spreads across my face, and she narrows her eyes at me.

I pick up her skate and she goes to jerk her leg back, but I hold tight—loosening the laces. "Careful now. Wouldn't want to cut me with that blade." I peel the first one off, tossing it over my shoulder.

Her smile is dark when her eyes drop to the long smooth scar that runs the length of my forearm. "No promises."

I peel off the second skate, clicking my tongue. Taking her chin in my hand, I tilt it up, "No lies."

There's a flash of vulnerability in her eyes. I push her gently back down on the bed until I'm kneeling over her, trailing feather light kisses down her neck as I slowly strip her clothes, tracing my fingers across bare skin as I work. Rory's breath quickens, eyes closed. She arches her back, searching for more contact—searching for *me*. When she's fully naked, my mouth hovers over her ear, *"Do you trust me?"*

She tenses, blue eyes flying open.

Her response is instant, my finger setting her nerves on fire, and she squirms beneath me, letting out a quiet whimper. I lean back in so my voice is low in her ear, *"I said,* Rory, do you trust me?" My fingers stop, just above and to the right of her hipbone, moving in slow, light circles. She bites her lip, deciding.

Finally, she utters out the three words I've been waiting to hear, "I trust you." Her eyes are hesitant, cautious, but she's decided, exposing her neck and waiting to see if I'll tear out her throat.

I press a kiss to her lips, dropping my fingers until they graze her inner thigh while I reach over her head with my other hand, feeling around the back of the mattress until I find what I'm looking for. *What I set up last night.*

I break the kiss and quickly reach over, slipping the leather cuff over her wrist and tightening it before she can rip it away.

Panic takes over, and she thrashes under me, trying to throw me off of her. But I have her trapped between my thighs as I secure the buckle. I look down at her calmly. Her chest heaves, nipples tightly pebbled. I have to fight the urge to take one in my mouth.

Rory reaches for the buckle, her fingers fumbling to undo it. I grasp her free hand and throw it back to the other side of her, pinning it to the mattress above her. But I don't bind it—not yet. Instead, I stare into the fear clouding those beautiful blue eyes. *She's shaking.* I speak slowly, keeping any movement controlled to not alarm her further. Leaning forward, I lightly touch her lips with mine, only to withdraw and gaze into her wide eyes.

"Trust. Me."

I don't move until she responds. I can feel her heart racing under my right palm just over her chest, holding her to the bed. Her eyes search mine, looking in them for an answer to a question only she can ask. With one more fearful look at the cuff already around her wrist, she returns her gaze to mine and shakily dips her chin in a slow nod.

I release her left wrist. She leaves it where I pinned it to the mattress. Breathing hard, Rory watches as I reach over and pull out a second cuff, trembling when I close it around her wrist and tighten just enough so it doesn't hurt, but she won't be able to slip out of it.

And then I leave her there, swinging my leg off of her naked and quivering body. I'm still fully clothed, meandering to the foot of the bed. Without warning, I reach out and tug at her feet, pulling her down until the chains on the cuffs grow taut. The little squeak of fear she lets out travels straight to my cock. I flash her a dark smile before I strip off my shirt.

Her eyes follow me as I move to my dresser drawer, pulling something out, careful to keep it concealed in my palm.

"Aidan?" she questions, her voice a mixture of fear and hope—hope that she hasn't made a mistake in trusting me.

I circle her slowly, flicking on the little device I ordered especially for her when I ordered her lingerie. She can hear it vibrating in my palm and looks at me in confusion.

"Have you ever used one of these before?"

She hesitates but dips her chin almost sheepishly in admission.

I shake my head, "Nothing to be ashamed of, love." I take in the sight of her beautiful body, stretched out and waiting for me. *Mine.* Her legs pressed firmly together. "Have you ever used one of these with a partner?"

She shakes her head slowly. Her answer makes what's about to happen next all the sweeter.

"Good girl," I praise and she shivers, her chains clinking softly. Lying down beside her, I study every inch, exploring her body with my hand. When I roll her nipple between my two fingers, she quivers, pulling on the chains that hold her hands stretched out above her head.

I bring the little device closer. She eyes it warily. I lay a kiss on her stomach in reassurance as I work my way down. "Your safe word is *offsides.*" I hold her gaze, my face serious. "If you don't like something. You use it. Got it?"

She stares at me, her eyes going back and forth between the toy and me. I pinch her nipple roughly to bring her attention back to mine. She lets out a yelp. "*I said*, do you got it?"

"Yes," Rory says clearly this time. Still wary, but there's a spark of excitement there as well.

I explore her first with my fingers, running the back of my hand between her breasts and down the length of her. She expected the toy, so her initial flinch was an overreaction. I let out a dark chuckle, slowly circling her. She's already dripping, her pussy pink and perfect. I stroke her gently.

"So wet," I hum with approval. "My girl likes it a little

dark?" I grin deviously before slipping a finger inside, smiling wider as she arches back. With my other hand, I press the toy to her clit, switching it on. She screams out in surprise, which graduates into a moan of pleasure as I move the toy around her most sensitive area.

She struggles against her restraints, overwhelmed by the sensation yet craving more of it. I swear I could come from the sight of her writhing at my hand alone. I turn up the intensity on the toy, circling it around her clit, teasing her to the brink of orgasm. Just as she's about to go over the edge, I pull the toy away.

Rory lets out a strangled whine, eyes opening, hips lifting —searching for contact.

I reach up and pinch her nipple, rolling it between my fingers while I move to the side of her, away from her spread legs. She pulls helplessly at her restraints, squirming below me, wanting my attention lower.

"You want to come, love?" I ask her with a dark smile.

"Yes," she whispers, hesitantly, her eyes watching mine.

I continue to play with her nipple, then switch to her other breast, and she lets out a gasp. "You ran from me." I abandon her breasts, slowly tracing my fingers across her stomach, but not close to where she wants me. "You think you deserve to come?"

She bites her lip, watching me for a moment before slowly shaking her head.

I click my tongue, slowly working my way back to where she wants me. From my back pocket, I pull out a second toy. This one is long and thick. Without warning, I thrust it inside her. She lets out a scream. When I turn it on, her eyes roll back in her head, her back arching off the mattress. Body shuddering from both the vibrating penetration and the sucking stimulation of the first toy I've pressed back up against her clit.

She fights against it, squirming away, trying to escape the sensations overwhelming her until she surrenders. I edge her until she's panting, so close. The sounds she's making...

I pull away again and the chains clink as she pulls against them, trying to follow. A frustrated growl escapes from low in her throat.

I chuckle at the sight of her little pout, inching up closer to her head.

"Please..." she begs, circling her hips.

"You want to come, baby?" I ask again, and she nods eagerly, biting that damn lip.

Sliding down my joggers, the corner of my mouth twitches up when her eyes go wide at the sight of my cock springing loose. I kneel beside her and she licks her lips. "Earn it." Is all I say, staring down at her, waiting to see what she does.

She stares right back. There's a flash of challenge in the blue of her eyes before she opens her mouth. I ease my cock into her mouth and let out a groan as her warm throat closes around it. She gets to work, drawing me in, running the tip of her tongue down the bottom of the shaft, and I reward her, bringing the toy back over and reaping the benefits when it makes contact. She moans when I slip it back inside her, mouth opening wide, allowing me to thrust into the back of her throat.

Rory gags around me and I pull back, allowing her a breath before hammering into the back of her throat again. This time, she's ready for me. The more I move the toy in and out, the wider she opens for me, taking every inch until I can't hold back my release, coming down her throat.

I pull out, giving her my full attention. Throwing my arm over her hips, I pin her down while I play with her. Making her howl and scream each time I shove the toy deeper. With her movement restricted, she's unable to escape the building sensations, and she squirms helplessly in my hold, whimpering for mercy she won't get.

She's close.

Tentatively, I press lightly on her backdoor. Her body tenses, but she's too lost in the other sensations to do much about it. I slide my pinky in, stretching her while increasing the pressure on the toy. She loses it. Arching her back off the mattress, her body erupts into violent shakes while screaming out my name.

Slowly, I remove my finger, but continue to pump in and out of her as the orgasm rips through her, more intense after my repeated denials. Each pulse of my hand elicits a full body tremble until finally she goes limp.

Removing the toys, I rise. Hands on each of her sides, I push her further up the mattress, creating slack in the chains. Her eyes fly open. "What are you—"

I flip her, propping her up on shaky knees. She nearly collapses down on herself before I prop her up again, smacking her ass hard enough to sting my palm. Rory lets out a surprised squeak.

"Ass in the air, princess." I remove the hand that's holding her up, and this time she stays how I want her. I nod in approval. Her head and chest pinned down by her arms crossed beneath her, held still by the chains. She can't see me from this position.

When my fingers graze her ass again, she jumps. "That's it, just like that, baby." Climbing onto the bed, I gently nudge her knees apart, spreading her wider. Rory lets out a whimper of anticipation, body trembling—but this time it's not in fear.

Lining myself up, I rub her with my fingers. She shudders, the nerves still incredibly sensitive from the violent orgasm I just ripped out of her. "You gonna come for me again, ice princess?" I slip two of my fingers inside and curl them. She answers me with the most delicious moan I've ever heard.

Replacing my fingers with my cock, I slam into her, none too gently, but she leans into it. pressing back into me for more. So responsive, I can feel her spasming around me like a ticking time bomb. Quickening my pace, I take a fistful of her hair in my hand and tug, forcing her head up and arching her back. She squeezes around me and my eyes roll back in pleasure, and I groan, "Damn baby, you're making it real hard for me to remember why I shouldn't keep you chained to my bed." She lets out a little whimper of pleasure that nearly does me in.

On the verge of climax, I reach for the little toy. Finding it, I press it hard against her clit while I continue to pummel into her. She explodes, falling from her knees to the mattress, squeezing down hard on my cock, and I let out a groan, coming with her.

I reach up over her and free her hands before collapsing down on the mattress beside her.

She works to catch her breath, fully sated and limp in my arms, and I tug her toward me. My little fallen angel curls into me, her head resting against my chest, tracing the dark ink along my ribs with her fingers.

I don't know what turns me on more: the memory of what we just did, or the fact that she trusted me enough to do it.

62

THAT'S GOOD HOCKEY

AIDAN

"You know, the sight of you in those hockey skates makes me want to lay you out at the first opportunity." I shoot Rory a devilish grin, and she pretends to roll her eyes in annoyance.

It took some convincing—okay, *a lot* of convincing—to get her back out on the lake, and now that she's here....

Dressed in leggings and the Breakers hoodie I gave her—*the one with my number on the back*. She wears Liam's old hockey gloves and holds Reagan's stick. She's the only righty out of the four of us. And God, the sight of her—it's a distraction. I can barely track the puck she's practicing with at her feet.

"I never thought I'd see the day when the ice princess traded in her toe-pick for a pair of hockey skates."

"It's not like I had much of a choice—you don't have any figure skates lying around." She moves forward a little, deftly handling the puck between her stick. I stand up a little straighter. "Don't get too excited—I'm just desperate for a little ice time."

I lean forward on my stick, grinning. "Oh, I'm already excited. You're about to learn what *real* skating is all about."

She snorts, "Please, I was landing axles before you were tying your own skates."

I laugh. "Sure, you can spin in circles and look pretty, but I'm not sure you can handle the game. Hockey players are just built tough."

Rory stops skating, angling her head a bit to the side, considering me. I let her see the smirk on my face. Narrowing her eyes, they flicker between the puck at her feet and then back to me. Determined. A mischievous glint in her blue eyes. My dick twitches at the sight.

My smile falls when she winds up the stick and slaps the puck at her feet. I don't have time to move out of the way before it crashes hard into my shin.

Wincing, I curse, rubbing the area that's stinging like a mother... "Damn ice princess, way to go Tonya Harding on my ass."

"Whoops," she says with faux innocence. "My bad. It's not too late to get your pads. Looks like you might need them." She glides backwards on her blades. The hockey skates on her feet do not make her any less graceful, even on the rough surface of the lake.

I lean forward, picking up the puck with my stick, maneuvering it in front of me. "Enough talk, little lion. Let's see if you can actually score on me." I pass her the puck. She catches it easily. Lazily skating back and forth, sizing me up like a predator would prey. Coming alive with the challenge. The gray in her eyes glitter in the daylight sun.

"Ready?" I call out, gripping my stick tighter, keeping my eyes locked on hers.

"Always," she quips right back, rushing me with the puck. Stick-handling with surprising finesse, she comes straight for me, as if meaning to skate right through me—like a frozen game of chicken. But at the last second, she dekes left. My arm shoots out, fast as lightning, catching just enough of the puck to throw it off course and out of her control. She skids to a stop.

"You're fast," she huffs, out of breath.

"And you're sneaky." I skate up beside her until I'm in her personal space. She doesn't back up. "I like it."

That's when she twists out of my sight, disappearing around my backside and swiping up the abandoned puck I'd left feet from the goal. I tear after her, but it's too late. She skates it in with ease, scooping her stick under the black disc and landing a goal—top shelf. At the clink of the puck hitting metal, she grins, circling around the net, laughing at me.

"That's cheating."

"That's good hockey," she challenges, and I can't help but smile.

My phone buzzes in my pocket. I let it go a few times before removing my glove and reluctantly pulling it out. Seeing my coach's name on the caller ID, I motion to Rory to give me a second and turn around to take the call.

"Coach."

"O'Rourke." I can already tell from coach's tone, I'm not going to like what he has to say. "Listen, I talked to the board and they won't approve your leave from play, seeing as it's not injury-related."

I sigh, running a hand down my face. I knew this was a possibility. We're in the height of the season and the Breakers' record puts us in third place overall.

372

"I can excuse you from tonight's practice, but you're expected in Toronto with the team the day after next."

My eyes find Rory watching from a distance, concern in her eyes seeing my mouth pinch tight.

"Okay, Coach. Let me see what I can figure out."

"Be sure you do, O'Rourke. You're on thin ice as it is. The past few weeks have helped, but it can just as easily fall apart," he warns.

"I understand."

I slide my cell back into my pocket, skating to meet Rory.

"You have to play the Toronto series?" She's already two steps ahead.

I mess with my hair before tugging my hockey glove back on and shrug, "That's what they said."

Her eyes narrow, "Aidan, you have to play. If you don't, the Breakers could drop you..."

"I know." I look at her, pulling her close to me, both hands on her hips. "But some things are more important. I need to keep you safe."

She's already shaking her head, "One of us already set their career on fire." There's a flash of pain in her eyes that feels very much like a knife to the gut. "There's no reason we both have to."

I consider her. She thinks her figure skating career is over... She had the choice to either follow her father's plan or abandon her dream. She chose freedom at the expense of everything she's worked for. My mind reels with other plans.

"What if you came with me?"

"Came with you?" she raises an eyebrow, "To Toronto?"

I pull her closer, the plan in my head already formulating, "You heard me."

"Is that allowed?"

"Fuck anybody who says it isn't." I scoop her up and she wraps her legs around me, my gloves resting under her thighs. I skate us slowly back to the house.

"Well, I guess we better go pack." The sight of a smile on her face has my heart constricting in my chest. *This fucking girl.* I lean forward, claiming her mouth aggressively with my tongue. The soft moan she makes has me instantly hard.

When I pull back, she stills, hungry for more.

"Aidan—" she starts, but doesn't have a chance to finish before I toss her into the large snowbank behind the goal.

"Hey!" she huffs, brushing off the snow clinging to her, a few flakes on her hair and cheeks like crystallized freckles. "What was that for?"

"Cheating," I grin and skate off, laughing at the string of curses I hear thrown at my back.

63

WATCH THE GAME

RORY

*A*idan and I barely catch our flight to Toronto after the hours-long ride back to Logan Airport. Irish soldiers met us before we entered the city, handing off Aidan's hockey equipment to him before escorting our SUV to the airport.

Flying with a professional hockey team certainly has its perks. We practically bypass security with a quick private check before exiting right onto the tarmac. Aidan keeps hold of my hand the entire way, keeping me right next to him.

On the plane, no one seems surprised to see me, and if they are, no one asks any questions. Aidan must have worked something out with his coach prior to our arrival. Coach McIntyre gives me a little salute before nodding to my *husband* in approval.

We reach our row, and Aidan motions for me to slide in. I'm pleasantly surprised to find Liam grinning like a fool in the window seat.

I plop down next to him.

"Mrs. O'Rourke," He grins, and I punch him in the shoulder hard enough that he winces.

After storing our carry-on bags, Aidan swoops into the seat next to us. "C'mon man, you couldn't at least give her the window seat?"

Liam stretches out. The Breakers' private plane offers far better seating options than any commercial flight I've ever flown. Plush, roomy seats that recline with leg space for days. It's like the entire cabin is first class. "I thought the only thing you'd want her looking at is you."

I snort, and Aidan scowls.

"I'm fine right here," I assure them, as I settle into my seat.

"Before I forget," Aidan reaches into his backpack, pulling out a shiny new cell phone. He slides it to me across the tray of my seat. "I know you had to leave your old one behind."

I eye the device with both wonder and suspicion, feeling Aidan's eyes on me, reading my expression. "It's got GPS tracking in it, but that's it. No one's monitoring your communications. You're free to talk to whoever you want."

I nod slowly, picking up the phone, "Thank you."

He just shrugs, "It's a long flight." He places a brand new pair of headphones on the tray, too. "I preloaded some of your favorites, or well," he tilts his head thoughtfully, "what I think are your favorites, based on what you listen to at the rink..."

My heart swells as I pick up the bluetooth headphones, black with little skulls on them. I scroll through the music selection Aidan added, finding both the heavy metal rock I love and the bubbly pop music I secretly love. I turn to look at him, but he's busy talking to one of his teammates across the aisle.

Choosing a song, I reach over and link my fingers with

376

Aidan's. He tenses, with the contact, but continues his conversation.

Taking a deep breath, I close my eyes, content for once in my life.

Since the Breakers are away, the friends and family section for the team is much smaller than it would be if we were back in Boston. And it's within the actual stands, with no extra security for protection.

I stick with the team right up until their final pre-game walk through the tunnel. I wait outside the locker room until the Breakers emerge, led by their starting goalie West Cavanaugh. West holds up his glove to fist bump me as he passes. Caught off guard, I scramble to raise my fist in time. And then, one by one, the rest of the team does the same until I spot Aidan, bringing up the rear, trailed only by the coaching and athletic staff.

Unlike the rest of the team, Aidan stops when he reaches me, an uneasy expression on his face, his attention all over the chaotic underbelly of the arena. He's distracted.

Reaching up, I grab hold of his helmet and tug his face down to mine.

"Go," I urge, staring into those deep emerald pools, "I'll be fine. Focus on the game and go kick some Canadian ass."

"Stay in your seat. Don't leave for any reason. I'll send someone to escort you back to the locker room after the game."

I smile, "Code word: Offsides."

His eyes flash and the way his jaw works sends a little thrill through me. "Save *that* word for after the game." There is still a little uncertainty in his eyes as he backs reluctantly away, keeping his eyes on me until the very last second, as he turns to head up the tunnel.

Letting out a deep breath, I pull off the thick sweatshirt I have on, hiding the #19 O'Rourke jersey I wear proudly—the one that caused a fight between Aidan and me on the plane. He thought it was too risky for me to wear his number here. Not only are we in Toronto territory, but it makes me stand out like a sore thumb to any Russians or Italians looking.

Not going to lie, part of me wants to wear the jersey to support Aidan and the Breakers, but the other half only wants to wear it because he told me not to.

All the bravado in the world still doesn't hide the fact I'm nervous. I take the stairs two at a time to reach the general concourse, eager to get to my seat, knowing Aidan will be distracted for a fair bit of the game trying to keep an eye on me. With everything going on back in Boston, Koen couldn't spare another guy to fly up with Liam and Aidan. With both of them gone, he was already down his two best men.

For the Breakers, it's all hands on deck tonight since Colt King won't be on the ice. He's been out of practice all week, following a nasty knee injury in the last game.

The Toronto fans are already eager for a fight when both teams take the ice. I have to push through the thick, boisterous crowd on my way to my seat, ignoring a few whistles and catcalls, trolling me for my jersey. The white and green away colors stick out amongst a sea of crimson red.

It's a relief when I finally find my section and collapse into my seat. Aside from an older couple a few rows up, I'm alone. My eyes scan the busy rink full of players to find *my* player.

He finds me first. It's easy to spot the only hockey player

staring right at me. I wave, grinning when our eyes meet, making a circle motion with my fingers trying to redirect him to focus on his warmups.

Aidan lifts his stick to me and then turns around, soaring around the arena to pick up one of the practice pucks, and sinking it with brutal force into the empty net.

The horn sounds and the teams circle off. The Zamboni comes out to clear the ice one last time before puck drop.

I don't notice the guy until he crashes into the seat next to mine, spilling a bit of his beer on me.

"Hey!" I jump up and instantly cringe at the telltale rosy cheeks and glazed-over eyes on the frat boy who's slid his ass into the seat directly to the right of mine. He takes a long swig of his beer, draining it nearly half way—though he's likely already quite a few beers deep.

"My apologies, gorgeous," Blondie tries.

I stare hard at the ice, sinking back into my seat. Aidan's focus is still on the game, in the middle of a crucial Breakers power play after Toronto came out swinging. Rolling my eyes, I sit back in my seat, hoping if I ignore him—maybe he'll take a hint.

But Blondie persists, leaning in closer, the scent of stale beer and cigarettes filling my nose, "You here all alone?" His words slur slightly as he scans the empty row beside me.

I could tell him no, but it'll be obvious in a few minutes when no one else shows up. My eyes flicker between the drunk frat boy and the ice—the last thing I need is for Aidan to notice this exchange.

The Breakers vs Thunderhawks is set to be a great game and it's sold out. Deciding to take my chances seat hopping, I move to get out of my seat. I'm barely out of it when sweaty fingers grip my wrist, yanking me back down.

"Don't go," Blondie whines, close enough so I can smell the alcohol on his breath, "we only just met."

I open my mouth, half-prepared to claw this goof's eyes out when a heavy arm wraps around my shoulders, pulling me away from frat-boy. My attention snaps to the left, finding the seat to my left is also no longer empty.

"Back off, asshole." The deep voice beside me is both familiar and not, with a dangerous edge to it that means business.

Blondie, with my wrist still trapped in his grip, blinks a few times before finally releasing it. I rip it back from him with a glare, sending myself further into the chest of the guy whose arm is still draped around me.

I turn my head, needing to tilt my chin to make out the face of the newcomer.

"Oh my God, aren't you Colt King?" Blondie slurs out behind me.

He might be drunk, but Blondie isn't wrong. Colt King himself does indeed sit next to me, a baseball cap pulled low over his face, which is doing little to hide the murderous expression in his icy blue eyes. His gaze is locked on the frat boy, as if daring him to make one more wrong move.

"Who I am is none-of-your-fucking-business and if you don't get the fuck out of this section right now, kicked-out of this game is your best-case scenario," Colt flashes his teeth, reminding me of a wolf, before I turn away to check Blondie's reaction.

Frat boy's eyes go wide and his hands go up in defense, spilling the rest of his beer all over himself as he scrambles to his feet. "Hey man, no need to get all worked up. I was just saying hi, is all." He stumbles away.

Colt's glare follows him all the way back to the section he came from and then, and only then, does he remove the arm he had wrapped protectively around me.

Meanwhile, the Breakers huddle up for a time-out at their bench, and I catch sight of Aidan's eyes on us from ice-level.

"Thank you," I breathe out, Colt and I have known each other a long time, but I'm still nervous, since I know he and Aidan hate each other's guts.

I watch my defenseman warily, half expecting him to shoot off the ice and come up here skates and all to kill Colt for daring to breathe the same air as me. I *really* hope he didn't see Colt with his arm around me.

"Anytime," Colt grunts out. Folding his arms across his chest and sinking into his seat, eyes on the ice.

When he doesn't leave, I anxiously glance sideways at him as the Breakers line up again for the face-off. "Don't take this the wrong way.." Colt lets out a grunt of amusement, but lets me continue. "I'm grateful for the save and all, but if Aidan sees you sitting next to me..."

Colt's eyes never leave the ice, following the forward's play on the first line. "Who do you think sent me?" He nods slightly toward the ice.

My eyes widen and I look between the Breakers' injured center and my defenseman husband. Aidan returns Colt's nod before dialing back into the game, checking Toronto's right wing off his feet. "He—what? I thought—you guys hated each other?"

"We do. Your husband's a right ass at the best of times," Colt shrugs, his lips curving up into a heartbreakingly beautiful smile that I can't help but return. "But he told me some-one's out to get you... *hurt* you." His dark eyes, blue like midnight, flicker my way for half a second before going back to the ice.

"So, you're going to watch the game with me?"

He pats his knee, "Not like I got anything better to do." His expression sours.

I cringe, "How bad?"

"Bad," He grunts and my heart constricts. As athletes, we are always one wrong pivot away from a potential career-ending injury.

"I'm sorry," I tell him.

"Nothing you did," his face softens slightly before a mischievous spark lights up his eyes, "now, let's see how much of a mess Aidan's game is without his number one center on the ice, making it easy for him."

I laugh, unable to help it. "Let's do it."

I offer him some of my popcorn. He growls at it before reaching in for a handful only a few seconds later.

I smile victoriously.

"Watch the game," he grumbles before reaching in for another handful.

64

CONSEQUENCES

RORY

The door to our hotel suite clicks shut behind us. I barely have time to turn around before he's on me.

"What the hell were you thinking?" His voice holds a dangerous undertone.

I open my mouth to answer, but his hands are already at my waist, pulling me toward him. The oversized jersey I wear —*his jersey*—bunches under his grip. I'd worn nothing underneath, knowing full well the effect it would have on him.

"Did I not specifically tell you *not* to wear my jersey to this game?" He growls, his hands tightening on the fabric. "Did I not go over the risks?"

"You did," I nod in confirmation, biting my lip. Heat pools in my belly under the intensity of his gaze. The two of us alone, in this hotel room... "I just wanted to support you."

"Support me?" Aidan laughs, but there's no hint of amusement in his eyes. "Wearing my name, my number, in the middle of their fans? You made yourself a target. Anything could have happened to you."

"I..." I start, looking away, overwhelmed by the look of pure anguish in his eyes, bleeding through his anger. But his fingers at my jaw stop me, tilting my head back so I have no choice but to look him in the eye.

"Do you have any idea what went through my head every time I looked over and saw you surrounded by them? Toronto's fans are notoriously unpredictable. They could have hurt you! And for what? You're lucky Colt was around."

"I'm sorry," I whisper, realizing just how upset I'd made him.

"Sorry isn't good enough." Aidan's expression darkens as his thumb brushes over my lower lip. "Not tonight."

He steps back, his eyes raking over me, over his jersey. "Take off your shoes." Aidan's fingers curl under the hem of his shirt, pulling it off and revealing those sinfully dark tattoos.

My breath hitches, but I obey, guilt facilitating my obedience, kicking off the sneakers I'd worn to the game.

"Pants too."

I comply, sliding my panties down with them until I'm standing before him wearing only his jersey.

"Now get on your knees."

I hesitate for a second before slowly sinking to the floor. The position making me feel vulnerable, exposed... and by the way Aidan's eyes darken... that's exactly what he wanted.

He steps closer, his fingers tracing the edge of the jersey where it drapes over my shoulder. It sends a shiver straight to my core. I curl my toes in.

"You want to wear this? You want everyone to know who you belong to?"

"Yes," I say, my voice barely above a whisper. The air thick with anticipation.

"Then you're going to prove it." His hand slides under my chin, tilting my face toward him. "No more games. No more risks. From now on, when it comes to *safety*, you do exactly as I say or there will be consequences." His hands go to his belt, unbuckling it and slowly dragging it out.

I nod. My pulse is pounding in my ears. Distracted by the leather belt in his hands. Nervous, but I'm choosing to trust Aidan.

"Good girl," he murmurs, his thumb brushing over my lip again, slower this time. "Now show me you understand." He drops his pants and the full length of him springs free, already hard at the sight of me kneeling at his feet, wearing his name and number. He loops the belt in his hands, sliding it around my neck.

I let out a gasp when the belt catches, the leather tight around my throat. Aidan holds the other end in his hand. He gives me a dark smile before he gives it a tug, dragging me toward him.

The air between us crackles with tension as I follow his direction, leaning forward, resting the palms of my hands on his thighs. My movements are tentative at first, but the look in his eyes tells me there's no room for hesitation.

By wearing his jersey tonight, I claimed Aidan as mine and tonight, I am his—completely and utterly his—and there is no mistaking the consequences of defying him again.

I run the tip of my tongue along the edge of my bottom lip before I part them. I surprise him by taking him deep right away. The belt around my neck tightens when Aidan throws his head back with a groan, "Fucking hell, Rory"

A smile pulls at my lips, and I busy myself licking and sucking, rocking back and forth on my knees as I work him, turning myself on. I squirm at the pressure building between my legs. Sliding one hand down to find relief, I let out a moan of pleasure when my fingers find my already swollen clit.

Aidan's fingers run through my hair before he fists it, forcing me still. His cock is deep in my mouth when my eyes flick up to meet his. His jaw flexes before he clicks his tongue, "Hands behind your back, little lion."

I release a growl of frustration but reluctantly drag my hand away from my clit, lacing my fingers behind my back. Aidan smirks at the vibration in my throat.

"Show me what a good girl you can be, and maybe I'll reward you." He tugs me forward again, loosening his grip on my hair, but not releasing it entirely, pushing me harder, deeper.

I let him, determined more than ever to show him just how far this former angel has fallen. He may have me on my knees, but he'll be the one at my mercy. I lift my eyes to his, holding his gaze as I suck hard. His body goes taut with tension and I have to readjust my grip as my body fills with need, letting a little whimper escape. The sound contracts my throat and sends Aidan spiraling over the edge. His fists my hair and the belt tightens as he pushes deep into my throat, finding his release. I take every drop.

He relinquishes his grip on both my hair and the belt when he pulls out, gazing down at me. But instead of satisfaction, there's a feral gleam in his green eyes. He picks me up. My legs wrap around his torso instinctively as he carries me across the room, setting me down on the empty desk. Aidan kisses me hard before turning his attention to my neck, freeing me from the belt and leaving soft kisses before sinking in his teeth, his hand sliding between my legs, eliciting a scream when he finds my center.

He withdraws his teeth, giving me a knowing look before his head disappears beneath the jersey. I brace myself against the desk as he too dives right in. The scrape of his teeth is a brand new sensation that I decide immediately I need more of. I squeal and sway my hips, gripping his hair to keep myself from sliding off the desk.

He chuckles. His hot breath between my legs sets my entire body on fire. I'm near desperate for release and Aidan knows it, picking up the pace. One of his hands finds my breast and I arch into his palm, begging. He finds one of my nipples, palming it, rolling it between his fingers before pinching hard. The sharp pain coupled with what he's been doing with his tongue consumes me like wildfire, and I submit to the blaze.

I come hard, but Aidan doesn't ease off the pressure. Holding me down even when I try to squirm away, the sensation is just too much. His fingers curl inside me, drawing out my climax to the point of torture.

I'm still a trembling mess when he slips his considerable length inside me, rocking the desk into the wall with powerful thrusts, fucking me relentlessly. Building back the pressure he'd just released. My breath quickens. I wrap my legs around him and lock my ankles, clinging to him as I chase that second orgasm. His mouth finds my neck and my body convulses, not fully past my first orgasm, before crashing into my second.

I tighten around him in the wake of the blinding rush ripping through me, and he groans, taking my mouth. His kiss fierce and possessive until he too shatters, raw and unrestrained, until we're both panting and shaking, our foreheads pressed together.

"Mine," he breathes, his eyes holding mine captive.

"Yours," I give in, wrapping my arms around his neck.

He picks me up, carrying me over to the bed. He sets me down gently before fetching a warm towel to clean me up, wasting no time before climbing in beside me.

I move to slip off the jersey, but Aidan's hand on my arm stops me.

"Leave it on." He lands a light kiss just behind my ear, brushing my hair away from my face. "Everyone will know Rory O'Rourke is mine."

65

THE IRISH PRINCESS

AIDAN

The flight home is a far different affair from the flight there. After we crushed the Thunderhawks in their own stadium for three straight games, the team is practically vibrating with celebratory energy. The series win is huge for the team and our season. Everyone is riding high.

But us kicking some Canadian ass sure didn't make Rory too popular in the stands. Dressed in my jersey each night, her honey gold hair falling in messy ringlets over my name, looking like absolute perfection. The memory of what she did in that jersey made it extra difficult to take my eyes off of her long enough to play.

Her celebratory shouts each time Liam or I sunk a puck into the net still made me nervous. I didn't even celebrate the first couple of goals... Toronto's crowd can be volatile at the best of times. But under my scrutiny, it was clear Colt had it locked down.

No one dared challenge the six-foot-two miserable hockey player glued to her side; Rory's personal scary dog privilege.

I'd never tell him to his face, but I can't wait for that fucker to be back on the ice. The dude may be a right ass, but he's an ass who can play fucking hockey. We definitely felt his absence in the first line despite our ability to pull out those wins.

Even our plane getting delayed right before takeoff can't dim my spirits. I crack a few beers with my teammates, talking and laughing with the guys in a way I haven't done in a long time. But I draw the line when a group of our rowdiest players break out in an awful rendition of Sweet Caroline, a Boston classic.

Rory fits in with the guys in a way I never would have expected.

The self-proclaimed "hockey hater" is laughing and joking with West and Rhodes, our two goalies. I smile to myself when she even forces a smile out of Colt himself. Celebrating the little victory with a little shake of her hips and throwing her fists into the air. Her pretty blue eyes search for mine, and her smile grows once she finds them.

I remind myself it's only temporary. Telling myself I'm playing the part. And so is she.

This thing between us could be gone before I know it.

"You okay?" Rory asks as I pull the last of our bags from the airport carousel, swinging her duffle over my shoulder with the rest, despite her bitter protests.

"Yeah, fine," I say, reaching down to take her hand as we step out into the busy parking lot.

"You were pretty quiet the whole flight..."

"Just tired," I tell her, though I'm not sure she's buying it from the look in her eye.

When we're almost to the car, I reach into my pocket to switch on my phone that I'd switched off for the flight. It immediately starts ringing. I don't even have a chance to say hello before hearing Koen's frantic tone on the other end. It gets my full attention.

Rory slides into the passenger seat, unaware of the call. I stay outside, muscles tense.

"Where the fuck have you been? I've been calling you for over an hour," my brother barks.

"The plane was delayed," I reply, concerned over what could have Koen this ruffled... "What's wrong?"

"They took her."

My eyes find Rory's, watching me through the car window, blue eyes bright with worry. But I know Rory is not who Koen is talking about.

"I need you."

"I'm coming." I wrench the driver's side door open and rocket myself into the car, putting it into gear before I've fully shut the door. I spot Liam on his way to his own car and pull up beside him, motioning with my eyes to get in. He hops in the back without question. Koen's still on the line, the phone pinned between my ear and my shoulder. I can feel Rory's eyes on me. She braces herself as I take a sharp turn out of the parking garage without slowing.

"How?" I growl, shifting into high gear, merging onto the highway.

Koen sighs, "I don't know. I thought we had everything locked down. One minute she was here and the next she was just—gone."

"The cameras?" I ask.

"Nothing." Koen swears, and the distinct sound of his fist hitting something hard comes through the line. "I don't know how they did it. Alex was watching. They had to find a blind spot, they had to know where the cameras were, they had to—"

"We'll get her back." My jaw clicks, thinking about my sister in the hands of those Italian or Russian savages. Koen is right to be panicked. Through everything, the most important thing was always the family. *Keeping the family safe.*

"How far out are you?"

I glance at the speedometer, pushing well past 100mph, then look for the next exit to get a sense of time. "Ten minutes."

"Good."

66

I MUST NOT TELL LIES

RORY

*K*oen's pacing the length of the living room when we arrive. The flash of relief in his eyes at the sight of us is gone in an instant, replaced with a hardened expression. Alexei sits as still as stone on the couch. Liam's beside me, clenching and unclenching his fists. I can practically feel the violence emanating off of him.

Aidan filled me in on the ride over. Somehow—someway, the Russians got Reagan.

Still holding Aidan's hand, I squeeze it. His body is deathly still and hard. Gone is the sweet boy who just wants to play hockey. Only the Irish's deadliest enforcer remains. I can't help but feel like this is all my fault. If the Irish weren't protecting me, Reagan wouldn't be in danger right now.

"It's not your fault," Aidan's voice pulls me out of my mind, reading my thoughts. "We all chose this life. We know the risks. We accepted them," his jaw tight. A quick glance about the room shows all four brothers' eyes on me, guilt and concern on their faces as they all give me various degrees of reassuring nods. It doesn't make me feel better, but my heart warms in my chest.

Aidan directs me to the couch, and I take a seat near the end before he turns his attention to the Irish boss.

"Any contact?"

"We're about to," Koen holds up his phone. His grip is so tight I'm surprised by the thing's durability. Koen hits the call button, switching it to speaker and the resounding rings echo throughout the high ceilings of the near silent loft.

"DeLuca." I sit up straighter at the sound of Cole's cool voice coming through the other end of the phone.

"Where's my sister?" Koen growls.

There's a pause on the other end before Cole responds, his voice devoid of all emotion. "Koen, always a pleasure...Where's my cousin?"

I freeze at the mention of Matteo, my eyes darting back and forth, torn between watching Koen and Aidan's reactions. Aidan joins Koen by the phone, making it easier to watch them both.

"Do you have her? Or was it that son-of-a-bitch Kostalov?"

Cole hums lightly, sounding amused, "The Russians don't have your sister."

Koen's grip tightens on his cell, his knuckles turning white. "Stop fucking around DeLuca. What do you want?" he bites out. Aidan listens intently, his arms crossed, the muscles in his arm flexing.

Cole just laughs. The bastard knows he holds all the cards here. "I think it's obvious what I want, O'Rourke. I'm owed a particularly pretty Russian bride." Koen's eyes meet Aidan's. "I want the girl back. *Aurora*," he purrs, his Italian accent rolling over the r's in my name.

Violence flashes in Aidan's eyes. There isn't a moment of hesitation before Koen responds, "Not going to happen."

"Fine," Cole doesn't even sound surprised, "Then I want your brother. Your hockey star little brother killed my beloved cousin. Blood pays for blood. That is, if you don't want your little sister paying that price. It would be a shame," he clicks his tongue in disapproval, "such pretty green eyes..."

"No," I whisper, fear ripping through my chest and squeezing it so tight I can't breathe. Liam looks ready to lunge through the phone to strangle DeLuca himself.

Aidan steps forward, taking the phone out of Koen's hands, "If any harm comes to my sister, there won't be a corner of this world where you can hide."

"No need for threats Ace, I'm a man of my word. I won't hurt your sister."

"When?" is Aidan's only response, his dark eyes finding mine.

"One hour, at the pier."

"Done." He hangs up the phone, handing it back to Koen.

Liam rises, "You know it's a trap, right?" He looks between the brothers, "You can't seriously be considering this." They're not just going to beat Aidan, they're going to *kill* him.

Aidan shrugs, a far off expression on his face. "They have Reagan, Liam. If they want me, they can have me. So long as Reagan and Rory are safe."

Tears well up in my eyes and threaten to spill down my cheek. I wrap my arms tightly around myself as if they can hold me together. "They'll kill you." I take a few steps toward him.

Aidan's eyes soften. "Give us a minute, guys." He takes my hand in his and tugs me down the hallway toward his bedroom. I can hear Liam continuing his argument with Koen as we go.

As soon as the door shuts, I lose my self control and tears coat my cheeks. Aidan says nothing, just swallows me in a hug, clutching me tightly to him. "The Irish will protect you. That won't change, even if... you will be safe." He swallows hard and I peek up at him.

"They're going to kill you." There wasn't a doubt in my mind about that. Cole might want to just teach Aidan a lesson, but my father won't.

"Probably." The corner of his lip ticks up, finding amusement even now.

I shake my head, my tears drying up and anger finding their place. "Take me with you."

Aidan's face hardens, and he pulls away, "No."

"You heard Cole. They want *me*. Give me back and all of this goes away. Reagan will be safe and you'll stay alive."

"But you won't!" Aidan shouts, and I reel back. "Do you think the Italians will let that little insult slide? Your father?" I wince, and he nods arrogantly. "No. This is the best plan. And you'll finally be free of them. Once things calm down, Koen will set you up somewhere safe, and you can move on."

He catches me shaking my head, and I shake it harder as he continues through his tirade. "No... No."

"Why, Rory? You don't even like me."

"Not true."

"Sure it is. It was only just last week you tried running away, wishing somebody would come and save you from me."

"I don't need saving from you!"

"And why's that?"

"Because I love you!"

Aidan stares back at me, his eyes widening before they narrow into a glare. "Take it back," he growls.

I glare right back, defiantly lifting my chin. "No."

He stalks closer, eyes dark. Reaching out, he grips my chin as he walks me backwards until there's nowhere left to go, my back pressed against the wall. "*I said,* Take. It. Back."

"I can't." Shivering in his grip, my nerves are shot with him so close. "That would be lying."

A flash of emerald is all I see before his lips slam into mine, full of passion, fire, and—goodbye. I don't realize I'm crying again until I taste the salt of my own tears on my tongue.

Aidan lifts me up and I cling to him. My arms wrap around the back of his head, letting him own my mouth. He holds me closer, deepening the kiss as he moves us through his room. My eyes close, savoring every bit of him, inhaling his scent—committing it forever to memory.

After what seems like an eternity, he pulls away, breaking the kiss. I peer up at him through my lashes, his face a mix of awe and regret. "I love you too." The heart threatens to beat right out of my chest, warmth filling my body at Aidan's words:"But I made a promise to keep you safe, and I always keep my promises."

Confused, I open my mouth, but it's too late. He tosses me. I let out a surprised grunt when I land on a soft heap of fabric, searching for Aidan, demanding an explanation.

My entire body goes rigid when I realize where I am... Too distracted by Aidan's kisses, to notice where he was bringing me—the guest room closet.

Aidan stands in the doorway, a tortured expression on his face.

Having already wasted too much time, I scramble up, tripping over myself in my haste to reach the door, but it's too late.

With one last forlorn look my way, Aidan slams the closet door shut just as my body crashes into it. The telltale sound of a lock clicking sends me spiraling, screaming, banging up up against the door, kicking it with my boot, but it's no use...

Aidan's already gone.

And I'm too late to stop it.

67

BLADES & BETRAYAL

RORY

*A*fter about ten minutes of fruitless banging and throwing myself into the closet door, to no avail, I realize Aidan's same bag of old hockey equipment is lying feet from me. He must have thrown it back in here after I left. Digging through it, I find my favorite pair of old hockey skates.

Gripping the skate tightly in my hands, I go savage on the closet door, the thick wood taking the brunt of my rage and the pent up frustration that has been building for weeks. I focus my attention near the doorknob, working to create a hole big enough for me to reach through and unlock it from the other side, when the door suddenly opens.

Mid-swing, I fall through the open doorway, both Liam and I screaming as he lunges to catch me while avoiding the blade I'm bringing down like a hammer.

We land in a heap on the floor.

"Goddamn girl, Aidan said you were crazy but—"

"Where is he?" already halfway to my feet, skate in hand, ready to fight.

"He's already gone," Liam sighs, "and Alex and I are under explicit instructions to keep you here."

I reel on him, the skate already out of my hands, flying over Liam's head while he ducks dramatically before it lodges itself into a framed picture of Aidan skating in his Breakers uniform, glass shattering to the floor, fury drowning out the hurt.

Liam straightens, twisting behind him to catch sight of the skate half stuck in Aidan's head before whipping back to me, "No need to draw the claws, little lion, just following orders." He holds up his hands, feigning innocence as he scans over me, searching for the second skate I might have hidden behind my back.

Ignoring him, I sprint to the elevator and skid to a stop in front of it. A familiar keypad pops up when I hit the bottom and I let out a screech of frustration, turning to find Alexei watching me calmly from a few feet away, one eyebrow raised.

Liam appears, looking a little rough for wear, exchanging a look with Alexei.

"Open the door," I demand, staring them both down.

"You know we can't do that, Rory," Alexei says, while having the audacity to look apologetic.

"Open the fucking door!" I slam my hand up against the keypad and the lights flash, but the door remains shut tight.

"He's a big boy Rory, he's made his decision..."

"He made the *wrong* decision. It should be me we're trading for Reagan. Me," the last word breaks on a sob.

Alexei steps forward, braving my fury and dodging my fists to drag me into a hug. I cry into his hard chest.

"Let me go after him," I plead, my voice cracking.

"No can do, Princess," Alexei says, trying his best to soothe me by running his hand down my hair. "He'd kill us."

I pull out of his grasp, staring up at him with red-rimmed eyes. "He can't kill you if he's dead."

"Oh, he'd find a way," Liam grumbles, dismissing me as a threat and plopping down in a heap on the sectional. "He'd come back from the dead just to flay my ass."

I roll my eyes before cracking a little smile, knowing Aidan would do just that. And then the hurt sets in again. I shove out of Alexei's arms.

I storm back down the hall I came from. "Leave me alone," I warn over my shoulder when I sense Alexei following me, my tone cold but broken.

Once out of their line of sight, I double over, hyperventilating and trying to pull myself back under control. After what takes embarrassingly too long, I finally catch my breath. Finding myself outside of Reagan's door, I straighten, twisting the knob, and slipping inside.

Reagan's room is neat and tidy, decorated with warm wood, creams and golds. *And cold.*

Seriously, it's freezing in here.

I rub my hands over my arms, feeling a cool chill against my skin. Following the draft leads me to the window. *The open window.*

No way. I peer out and see a winding fire escape that twists and turns all the way to the ground.

Immediately, I turn, eyes scanning over the room. *No signs of a struggle—no one heard anything...* The made bed, the dresser, the desk...

I make my way toward the closed bathroom door when something on the light pine desk catches my attention.

401

Lifting the note with delicate fingers—as if it might disintegrate—my eyes scan over the words, heart pounding with greater intensity the further down I go. Cold trails up my spine when the realization sets in.

Cole DeLuca never had Reagan.

Because Reagan ran away. Climbed right out her own window. Tired of suffocating to death in her brick tower. Which means... Aidan is about to sacrifice himself for nothing...

Cole lied.

Frantically, I tear into my pocket, fumbling for my cell, and dial Aidan's number. My hand covers my mouth when it goes straight to voicemail.

All this time and *nobody* thought to check her room. *Fucking men.*

Clutching the letter tight in my hand, I storm back out of the bedroom only to freeze at the chaotic scene I find taking place in the living room.

Armed men, dressed in black, fill the previously quiet space. Broken glass from the shattered windows glints up against the fading sunlight, spread all over the hardwood, crunching under the men's boots.

I linger under the archway. They haven't seen me yet. My eyes scan the scene, spotting Liam and Alexei, both bloody and on their knees, hands bound behind their backs. A large blonde Russian has Alexei's shirt tight in his hold, the muzzle of his gun digging into his skull.

"I swear to God, if you don't tell me where my fucking sister is, you're going to experience pain beyond your worst nightmare. You thought we hurt you before," he laughs, the sound dark, "that's nothing compared to what I'll do to you this time. And when I finally allow you to die, it will be the sweetest relief you've ever known."

"Niko," I breathe out. My voice is a sharp mix of shock and reprimand.

My brother's head shoots up, his icy eyes locking onto me. He looks me over from head to toe before dropping Alexei roughly to the ground. With his hands bound behind him, he lands painfully, on his face and I wince.

"Sestrichka! *Little sister.*" Niko rushes forward, embracing me. He pushes me back again until I'm at arm's length, checking me over for any sign of injury, any hair out of place. He cups my face, and I'm all too aware of the gun he still holds in his other hand.

"Brother," I reply to him in Russian, "what are you doing here?" My gaze trails over Liam and Alexei. One of Niko's men shoves Alexei's shoulder after Alexei spits near his shoe. Liam's eyes are on me.

"Rescuing you," Niko replies, his eyebrows rising at my perfect Russian. A half a breath later, he seems to remember where he is, stalking back over to the Irish, and without warning, pistol whipping Liam.

I shout out in protest, hurrying over to intervene. Niko's jaw is tight with rage as a blue fire blazes in his eyes. "The fuck are you looking at, mick? You don't look at her."

"Niko! Stop!" I worm my way between Niko and Liam protectively. Niko's men step forward, guns raised but hesitating, eyes flickering to their boss before touching me.

My brother's furious eyes shift off of Liam and onto me.

"They didn't take me Niko, I came to them. They protected me from Papa—from Matteo." Reasoning with him, "They kept me safe."

Trusting Niko is still too new and I watch him warily, uncertain what he'll do—always a wild card. Slowly he looks between me and my two Irish brothers-in-law. How I put myself between him and them. Confusion clouds the fury in his eyes. "You married one of them?" His gaze hardens, glaring at Alexei again. "They made you."

I place both hands on his chest, trying to push him away from the very vulnerable Irish at my back before he takes them both out in a blind rage. Shaking my head, I try to pull his attention back down to me, "No, no—they didn't. I chose—I did. I wanted to marry him." My brother is still trying to nudge me gently out of the way so he can get to Liam and Alexei, but I dig in my heels, refusing to budge. "Niko, listen to me." He's half past me already. "Niko," I'm desperate now, my tone frantic as I catch him raising his gun, "YA lyublyu yego!"

My brother stills.

The room is so silent you could hear a pin drop. Nobody moves. I swallow nervously, keeping my eyes on my brother as he slowly turns his gaze to meet mine. "What did you just say?"

"I love him." My voice shakes, but there is a certainty to it. I stare deep in his eyes, forcing the truth into his thick skull. "Aidan," I add, in case there were any question, ignoring Liam's slacked jaw, dropping to the floor over my brother's shoulder.

Niko's eyes narrow. But I've run out of patience with the situation. I reach for his gun, intending to disarm him, but he simply lifts his hand out of my reach. I jump pathetically, still intent on grabbing it.

"Jesus Christ, Sestrichka." Shaking his head, "Did no one teach you the proper way to disarm a man?" He lowers his hand back down, gun facing straightforward, though not directly at me. Niko grabs hold of my wrist and forces my hand around his. "You hold the wrist and grab the gun at the same time. Try it." He releases my hands but leaves his gun in the same place.

I blink up at him in confusion.

"Aurora," he huffs impatiently.

I move quickly, slamming one hand down on his wrist and swinging with my right to twist the gun out of his grip. The ghost of a smile appears on his lips and he nods approvingly. "Khoroshi. *Good.*"

I'm too busy admiring the gun I've wrestled out of his grip to prepare for him plucking it right back out of my hands, taking it back.

"Hey!"

"We'll work on that." He considers me before holstering his gun at his waist and nodding at his men to stand down. For the first time since I'd caught sight of them, they lower their weapons, relaxing their stance.

Reality catches back up to me and I remember the letter I'd stuffed into my pocket. I grab hold of my brother's arm. "Niko! You have to help me. Aidan's on his way to meet Cole DeLuca. I have to warn him... It's a trap."

Niko regards me for a moment before admitting, "It is, but it's too late to warn him. The Italians already have your— husband." He arches a brow at me skeptically, still searching my face for any sign I'm lying. "They shot Koen and took Aidan."

"The Irish boss lives," Niko adds quickly as both Liam and Alexei give a start at his words. "They both do."

"For now," he adds with a shrug.

"Fuck," I say, half under my breath.

"What about Reagan?" Liam practically begs.

"Who's Reagan?" Niko asks, turning.

"Fuck you, Niko, I don't have time for games. Just tell me Reagan is okay."

My mouth twists uncomfortably as I start to open my mouth, Reagan's letter burning a hole in my back pocket.

Niko's deep in thought, "The O'Rourke, girl?"

"Yes," Liam growls impatiently, "our sister. Is she alive? Where is she?"

Niko shrugs noncommittally, "I don't know. We never had her."

"The Italians did?"

Niko shakes his head, "Nyet. It was a bluff."

I dig the now crumpled stationery out of my pocket and hold it up. "I found this. No one took Reagan, she just wanted some space. She left..."

Alexei looks to the ceiling and Liam gives me a blank stare, but I don't have time for them. I turn my attention back to my brother.

"Where's Aidan? Tell me he's still alive, Niko, please." I plead with him and his blue eyes cloud with concern at my distress. "Last I heard, yes. He's alive but—" he looks at me, his face tight.

"But what..." I urge him on.

"He's at the mansion. Adrik has him."

68

WE'LL KILL YOU FOR THIS

AIDAN

The glamour and perfection of the Russian mansion do not extend to the shadowy depths of its basement. No, the Russian Lion has himself his very own private dungeon and torture chamber where he can delight in torturing his enemies within the confines of his own home.

It's freezing. There are no windows, but a cold draft has somehow found its way into the dark room, wrapping around my bare chest, my shirt was the first thing to go when they shackled me to an ice-cold metal chair, the feet of which are bolted to the floor. A familiar drain is cut into the stone.

I should consider myself lucky to have scored the chair. A variety of chains decorate the dirty and blood stained walls. A wall of *instruments* comprises the entire far wall. The Russians sure seem to enjoy prolonging death in the most gruesome ways imaginable.

"You dumb fuck," Petr mutters from where he stands under the rack of various sharp tools, picking up a hammer and looking it over. The tool is still coated with someone else's dried blood.

I test my restraints for what is likely the hundredth time; the ropes have already cut into my skin. Blood leaks from the raw wounds, dripping down to the floor.

Petr clicks his tongue, setting the hammer back down and picking up a dull, rusty knife. "Should've known better than to mess with the boss's plans." He turns back to me, running the dirty blade between his fingers. "We thought we could leave you boys alive after, you know, killing your father." Petr's icy blue eyes flash maliciously and I grind my teeth. A dirty white rag cuts deep into my lip, keeping me silent.

A cruel smile graces the Russian consigliere's face as he reaches out and grabs hold of my jaw, wrenching it up so I'm forced to look at him. "Still crying over daddy Ace? Wanna hear how we made him go boom?" His smile widens when he sees my eyes flash with a mixture of rage and pain.

He drops my jaw, moving his hand down and slashing his knife hard against my chest. Again. I bite down on the gag and lift my chin, breathing hard but refusing to scream out from the pain of the dull blade cutting through my skin.

"That's my specialty, you know?" Petr holds up the knife, watching my blood drip off the tip with delight. "Car bombs."

I glare back at him. A promise of death.

"They were all the rage back in the day. Maybe I'll bring them back into style. One car bomb at a time," he laughs, enjoying this. He sets his knife back down on the table, trading it for a thick metal rod. "This would be a fun toy to use on your little girlfriend."

I tense in my seat, and Petr notices. Excitement is his expression grows at my obvious distress. He looks me in the eye as he thrusts the rod suggestively in his closed hand, a wicked grin on his face.

My fists tighten, putting further stress on my already abused wrists as my knuckles go white, losing feeling in my fingers.

"Adrik has to give her to Cole," Petr drawls, coming closer, "but she's embarrassed him, so I'm sure Cole will give us the green light to punish her. Teach the little bitch to mind her place." He whips the rod back before driving it hard into my side, probably crushing a kidney. I let out a groan of pain and work to catch the breath the hit stole from me.

"Or maybe we'll scare her a little first. That first car bomb wasn't intended for her—she was supposed to be somewhere else—but maybe this time we'll make *her* the target."

Petr continues on, but I stop listening, wondering what he meant when he said, "*The first car bomb wasn't meant for her?*" A car bomb killed Rory's mother. Rory had been too close, was thrown back hard from the impact. It fucked up her head and almost ended her ice career... Her *life*.

My eyes lock on Petr and I see him notice when I connect the dots. "I'll end her dreams for real next time." I lunge for him, only to collide viciously with the ropes binding me, and I'm thrown back in my seat, heaving.

Petr erupts in laughter. Succeeding at his goal to rattle me.

The sound of the steel door wrenching open interrupts our lovely little chat. The large menacing frame of Nikolai Kostalov fills the doorway.

"Petr, you're needed upstairs," Niko cocks his head toward the hall, snapping his fingers like he's commanding a dog.

Amusement fades from Petr's face, his expression darkening. His hold tightens on the metal pipe for half a second before he simply lets it fall at his feet. The clanging of metal against stone is nearly deafening in the small space.

"Da, Nikolai," Petr mumbles before stalking past him.

The Russian heir doesn't bother stepping out of his way, making Petr squeeze around him to exit the room.

As Petr's footsteps fade away, Niko turns his attention to me.

I lift my chin, breathing in deep as stormy blue eyes inspect me, locking me in. I can't look away. The color so similar to his sister's—my heart constricts at the reminder of Rory.

Niko's hands slip into his pockets as he moves casually into the room, looking over the selection of torture tools hanging on pegs along the wall. He turns to face me, staring into my eyes for a long second before stepping forward, pulling a wicked-looking knife out of his pocket.

Niko Kostalov has a reputation for the things he does with that knife.

I sit still, refusing to look away as he approaches. I swear there's a slight flash of amusement in his eyes before it's gone, making me think I imagined it.

He brings the sharp knife up to my face and I feel the warm metal scrape against my cheek. I let out a breath, and with it, the dirty white cloth falls from my mouth.

Stunned, I stare at the fabric, now strewn on the concrete floor, before looking back up at Niko. He's retreated a few feet. Watching me intently, he leans up against the cell's wall.

"What's your game with my sister?"

Whatever it was I expected him to say... that was not it and so I hesitate for a second before I respond, "I'm not playing any games when it comes to *my wife*."

Niko's eyes narrow at my choice of address for Rory, but I just glare back at him.

"Why didn't you give her back this time?" The Russian heir uncrosses his arms, absently playing with the knife in his hands. "Like last time... could've saved your own skin." He points his blade at me, "We'll kill you for this."

"I know," I clip out, "but I made her a promise, and I intend to keep it." Testing my restraints again while Niko watches.

"And what promise is that?"

"To protect her." My eyes flash. "To keep her safe... to keep her far away from you," I scowl at him.

"You think she needs protection from her family?" Niko growls out, circling me. The sound of his boots echoes through the dark space.

"I know she does."

"Tell me where she is." He stops circling me, blue eyes gleaming.

"No." My jaw locks and I watch fire ignite in Niko's eyes. The same way it does in his sister's when she gets angry.

He steps toward me, leaning in. Bringing his knife—not to my throat—but to my stomach, threatening to gut me and leave me here to die—slowly. "You'd rather die than tell me where she is, puck boy? Give up all those hockey dreams, leave your brothers and sister behind?"

My jaw ticks at the mention of my family, but I trust Koen with their lives, even if I'm not around to help. "Looks like it." I steel my spine, keeping my eyes on the Bratva underboss as he digs his knife in between two ribs and I feel blood pour from where the tip has broken skin.

"Last chance," he mutters, frustration breaking through his icy fury.

I snap my jaw shut and bring my eyes up to his. Calmly waiting for him to push in the rest of his blade. To gut me like he's been dying to do for years. *Stormy blue... so much like his sister's.* But the cut doesn't come. Niko doesn't remove the blade from my abdomen, either.

Instead, he looks pissed off, staring down at me in obvious frustration. When he finally moves, he moves quickly, slashing at the ropes binding my wrist. One pass tears the rope clean through and he moves on to the other side.

Confused, I watch him warily. My eyes flicker back over to the display of torture tools but then Niko pockets his knife.

"She loves you too, you know."

I don't say anything, looking between Niko and the open door behind him, wondering what the fuck is going on...

Niko sighs, "C'mon, let's get you out of here."

I stare at him, my mind working. *He knew.* There was only one way for Niko to know what's between Rory and me is real. My blood turns to ice and I lunge for him, slamming him up against the stone walls, my arm up against his windpipe.

"Where is she?"

"Where is my wife?" I demand, my jaw tightening... already knowing the answer before he sighs, opening his mouth...

"Upstairs."

69

THE RUSSIAN LION

RORY

THIRTY MINUTES EARLIER

*N*iko escorts me through the mansion until we're standing in front of the closed doors of my father's study. The muffled drone of male voices is audible through the heavy oak.

"You're sure you want to do this?" My brother asks, something like worry showing in his eyes when he looks over at me.

But I am resolved and focused, "You know what you need to do."

His gaze lingers on me for another half a second before he nods. Another breath passes, and he straightens, throwing back his shoulders and knocking loudly. The voices inside fall silent just before someone wrenches open the study doors.

My brother's hand finds my upper arm, shoving me roughly over the threshold. I shoot what I hope is a convincing glare back at him before taking in my surroundings.

My father sits behind his large, ornate desk, like a king holding court.

Cole DeLuca's cool and measured stare finds me and I try not to wince, not expecting the Italian Capo to be here...

A handful of men occupy the room. Some I recognize as my father's soldiers and I guess the rest are Cole's.

"Aurora, Mona doch', *my daughter*, you're home!" My father steps around the desk, coming towards me and it's all I can do not to take a step back. The last thing I want is to be within striking distance of my father... Adrik eyes Niko before embracing me in a quick hug for the show of our guests. "I'm so glad you are safe!" He turns to my brother, "Where did you find her?"

I chance a look at DeLuca, who's watching the exchange with rapt attention.

"With the Irish," Niko replies coldly.

My father nods, a flash of glee on his face. *He might just get away with it.* Pinning this whole thing on the Irish... "The Irish bastards will burn for this. We'll start with the one downstairs." He reaches out and pinches my cheek hard between his fingers.

It's a warning.

"No one touches *my* daughter." He turns back to Niko, "Why don't you go down and let Petr know to go ahead and get started?"

A muscle works in Niko's jaw and I know he's reluctant to leave me alone with our father, but I need him to save Aidan. I dip my chin ever so slightly, a subtle nod my father doesn't catch, but Cole noticed, judging by the look in his eyes.

I ignore him.

"Yes, Pakhan," Niko gives our father a curt nod before

turning on his heel, stalking out of the room without another word. The relief I feel is short-lived.

Adrik lifts his chin, addressing the rest of the men in the study, "A moment, please. I must speak with my daughter." He puts a firm hand on my shoulder, holding me to him lest I get any ideas about bolting.

The men nod, faces expressionless as they silently rise, buttoning their suits before exiting stoically from the room.

But DeLuca doesn't move a muscle.

The sight of him lounging by the window sill elicits a slightly miffed expression on Adrik's face, but even he doesn't dare to say anything to the Italian Capo. When it's just the three of us, Adrik gestures for me to take one of the leather bound chairs in front of his desk but I shake my head, "No thank you."

Adrik frowns, "Have a seat, Aurora. I insist."

Again, I shake my head, shifting my weight on my feet, needing to buy Niko and Aidan time. "I'd rather stand, thank you."

My father's face grows red, fighting the urge to step towards me. "Very well." A somber expression replaces the anger. "I'm not sure if you were aware during your time in Irish captivity, but your dear fiancé is missing—" he throws a glance in Cole's direction, but the Italian Capo still has his dark gaze trained on me.

I try not to tremble under the awareness. "—presumed dead. God rest his soul," Adrik continues. "That being said, you're a bride meant for the Italians. To unite our two families." He thrusts out his chest with pride and it's all I can do not to cringe. "So, after this meeting, you will go with Signore DeLuca and he will find you an acceptable match by week's end," my father finishes, quite pleased with himself. All of his carefully laid plans falling into place.

"I will do no such thing," I inform him, clenching my fists where I hold them at my side. "I'm not going anywhere with DeLuca over here," gesturing in Cole's general direction.

"No offense," I mutter at the sight of his single raised eyebrow.

Oh, I've done it now. My father strides forward, the back of his hand rising. I lift my chin and take the hit hard, the force of it throwing me to the side.

He moves to hit me again, but that's the moment Cole chooses to speak up. His dark, velvety voice fills the office with an air of command, "Once was enough." To my shock, his words stay my father's hand and his eyes shoot me a dark promise before he drops his hand to his side.

But I'm not done. Pushing myself back up to my feet, I use the back of my hand to wipe the blood from my lip. "What's the matter, father? Afraid what might happen if I don't go with Cole tonight?"

Cole's eyes flash a warning, his protection only going so far as my father gapes at me, shocked by my sudden insolence. "Aurora, Angel, you going with the Italians is in everybody's best interest—"

"Everybody's best interest?" I cut him off and his eye twitches, "Or yours?" I dig deep for the inner rage I keep buried, drawing it up to give me the strength to continue.

My father stutters, unprepared for my defiance and grappling with Cole's already expressed displeasure at him for my physical punishment. "I don't—what are you—"

"Volkov."

My father's mouth snaps shuts and I know without having to look I have Cole's full attention.

"Did you think I didn't know about your business with the Volkov Bratva, Papa?"

Adrik pales and a couple beads of sweat appear on his brow, "I won't hear this nonsense. You do not know what you're talking about... just a silly little girl." He rushes forward, wrenching me by the arm, dragging me toward the door. Just before he reaches the door, someone slams it shut in our faces.

Both of us turn to find Cole's dark expression glaring down at us. "What about Volkov?" His tone is dangerous and I lose a little bit of my nerve staring up into his dark eyes. My father seems torn between trying to force his way out the door and knocking me out to keep me from running my mouth.

I clear my throat as best I can, but my voice still comes out with a rasp, because of my nerves. Banking only on the hope that when I finish, Cole will let me live—a small mercy, I start, "My father got into business with Volkov." Everyone knows the merciless and volatile Russian gang currently wreaking havoc over in Russia and, most recently, New York.

Cole looks to my father, who appears to be recovering from his initial bout of panic. "I did. Of course I did. It was smart business sense."

"But, it wasn't—" I counter, "because you didn't deliver. And now you owe them. Which is why you *have* to sell me."

My father's eyes glint with malice, "I won't hear any more of this. These are the words of an insolent daughter."

I go to open my mouth, but my father cuts me off, continuing, regaining his arrogance with every word, "Aurora, let's make one thing very clear. You are a daughter of the Bratva. Being a daughter of the Bratva means you have certain obligations. You don't get to choose. *I choose.* I own you until *I* decide who to give you to. Do you understand me?"

I grit my teeth at his words, especially the ones claiming he "owns" me.

"You will have everything," a smug smile appears on his face, "Just as soon as you marry a man of Cole's choosing," He waves a hand like we can be done with all of this. "I've heard enough. You will not weasel your way out of this marriage. Again." His glare laced with violence.

Instinctively, I inch closer to Cole—not my best survival tactic—considering, Cole is far more dangerous than my father.

"I'm not marrying anyone. I can't!" My voice rises, tired of being overrun by my father.

"And why not?" his voice booms with rage.

"Because I'm already married!"

Silence.

My father's face slackens before it twists into anger. "Who —?" he demands, before his eyes widen, answering his own question, "The O'Rourke boy?" He seethes, "A fucking Irishman?" He takes a menacing step towards me and I retreat.

"Suka," My father spits at me, but then he laughs, "You thought that would save you?"

I tense.

"You think that's a *problem*? Can't be married to two men, can you now?" My father's anger has reached a level never before seen, and he's spiraling, a maniacal look in his blue eyes. "Not a worry. I'll take care of that *problem* right now. You'll be a widow by the hour's end!" A malicious smile twists my father's face as he leans forward, "Wouldn't want it to be too quick..."

418

He takes one step toward the door. And then another.

All sound cuts out and the only image playing in my head is one of my father killing Aidan. The image of his blood on my father's hands has me seeing red. I spin, lightning fast like on the ice, grabbing hold of Cole's gun, ripping it out of the holster just inside his jacket.

The Italian Capo lets out a shout, caught off guard, reaching for his gun, but I knock his hand away like Niko showed me this morning.

Spinning, I cock the small handgun, locking in on my target. My father's hand is already on the door, on his way to murder *my* husband. I can feel Cole's arms closing around me, my window of opportunity down to nanoseconds.

My father spots the gun in my hand, but it's too late.

I return his cold smile, "Das vi danya, Papa." And I squeeze the trigger. *Goodbye.*

The recoil of the gun jolts me back hard into Cole's chest with a grunt. He catches me, wrenching the gun out of my hand before wrapping an arm around me, pinning my arms to my sides.

Both of us stare down at my father's lifeless body. A trickle of blood spills out of a single wound, right in the center of his forehead.

The Russian Pakhan dead... at my hands.

70

HOME GAME

RORY

"You better start talking," Cole growls in my ear.

"He deserved it," I whisper, still in shock. *He was going to kill Aidan.*

Cole spins me slowly, turning me from the sight of my father's body. His gun is in his hand, but he doesn't point it at me. Not yet...

"I killed him." *Is this shock?* The sound of the gunshot is still reverberating in my ear. Emotionally, I'm cut off and my head is spinning.

"You did."

Cole's gaze is as cold as an icy tundra, but there is a hint of indecision in his eyes as he carefully studies my face. Probably deciding whether or not to kill me. *Get in line, DeLuca.*

His hand holding the gun raises and, like pulling a trigger, words erupt out of me in an endless string of panic, everything Matteo did, everything he said. "They were expanding the skin trade in the city... It was only a matter of time before they betrayed you..." Cole DeLuca was one of the most dangerous men in Boston, but they say he drew a hard line on selling bodies.

Cole's eyes narrow on me, his dark eyes suspicious. I keep mine trained on his gun, the one he still hasn't put away... "That's not possible."

My cheeks heat, supercharged emotions flooding in, and so I snap at him, "Don't be an idiot, DeLuca." Not the best sense of self-preservation, but it is what it is at this point...

The Italian's brow raises at my audacity.

"You knew something was up. I saw the way you were watching him. Adrik betrayed the O'Rourkes, had Declan killed when he discovered what Adrik and Matteo were up to."

If Cole's surprised, he doesn't show it, his face stony and cold—*but still listening.*

"Adrik betrayed me. He betrayed my *mother.*" My voice breaks when the puzzle pieces finally click together and I know without a doubt that Adrik had had a hand in her death. *She'd been trying to save me from him.* "What makes you think he wouldn't betray *you?*"

Cole's quiet, his gaze impossible to read.

"And why should I believe you?"

My face falls, seeing the doubt in his eyes.

"How do I know you're not making this up just to save your own skin?" His gun clicks, but I meet his eyes, holding his gaze despite every instinct screaming at me to run. I wouldn't make it two steps...

I let out a breath, an eerie sense of calm filling me. "That's easy. I'm standing here, unarmed, telling you the truth, because you should know. Certainly, Matteo wasn't the only one in your circle involved," I hedge.

There's a dangerous glint in Cole's eyes, a warning, but I press on.

"I don't care if you kill me, Cole. I'm just asking you not to kill Aidan. He killed Matteo *for me*. To protect *me*. I'm the reason your cousin is dead. And I'm not sorry." I lift my chin defiantly, "Blood pays for blood. And this debt is *mine*." My eyes darken, threatening to haunt the Italian capo's ass from the grave should he not listen, "This is between you and me. Leave the Irish out of this."

We enter a tense standoff, neither one of us breaking eye contact.

The door crashes behind me. I momentarily forget where I am, putting my back to the cold-blooded killer behind me. I feel his hand curl around my arm, tugging me backwards. As I come face to face with the horrified expressions of my brother and my—husband.

"Aidan," my voice breaks on his name—at the sight of him. Dried blood cakes the side of his face, his shirt missing. His chest is streaked red from various cuts across his chest.

He doesn't hesitate, lunging forward and grabbing hold of me. I protest, screaming in panic, certain Cole is about to blow Aidan's head off right in front of me. My husband rips me out of Cole's arms, but before I can get my bearings, I'm thrust into Niko's chest with Aidan in front, blocking me entirely from Cole's sight.

"No one touches my wife, DeLuca," Aidan growls menacingly.

Cole's gun is high, pointed right between Aidan's beautiful green eyes.

"No," I squeak out, trying to get back in between them,

but Niko holds me back, despite my best efforts to escape his grip.

"You killed my cousin," Cole snarls.

"Aye, I did," Aidan admits, chancing a glance behind him, finding my eyes. I choke out a sob and he shifts his body again to better block me from Cole's view. Turning back to face the Italian Capo with a smile, "Do you want to hear how he cried before he died?"

I'm shaking, the fight ebbing out of me as fear takes hold of my body. Cole will *never* let Aidan live after this. Niko seems to realize this at the same time as me and starts for the door. Not wanting me to see what's about to happen.

There's a tense silence before Cole finally speaks.

"Good."

The room stills.

To everyone's surprise, Cole lowers his gun. "It appears I owe the Irish a favor."

Cole holds out his hand to Aidan and all three of us blink at him—stunned. Aidan recovers first, taking Cole's extended hand and shaking it hard.

The Italian Capo holsters his gun, his dark gaze passing over mine before leaning in to tell Aidan something only they can hear. Aidan's eyes follow Cole's to mine.

Then Cole straightens, moving around Aidan and heading for the exit, casually, as if he wasn't just about to kill all three of us seconds earlier. He stops on the threshold, looking back at the three of us.

"Hold on to this one," he nods his head in my direction, "If you can." The corner of the Italian's lip quirks up. "And give me a call when she gets you into trouble again."

Niko lets out a snort, and my eyes narrow on DeLuca. Giving him what I hope is a death glare, I notice the corner of his lip only ticks further up in amusement. He slides his dark gaze back to my husband, "I never had your sister... As far as I know, no one did."

Aidan nods solemnly.

"But I'll put every available resource into finding her."

"Thank you," Aidan gives Cole a nod of respect before wrapping an arm around my shoulder and pulling me close, looking pointedly in the direction of Adrik's dead body.

Cole laughs, and he shakes his head. "Oh, that wasn't me. That was all your lovely little wife here."

I wince when Aidan looks my way, eyebrows raised.

"Don't piss that one off," DeLuca winks at me and disappears into the hall.

Aidan doesn't waste any time. The second Cole's gone, I'm in Aidan's arms and he's checking me over for injuries, his gaze lingers on my cheek. "Are you okay?"

I let out a shaky breath, not having to pretend in front of him. "I think so, I—" I look over to where my father lies. Niko stands over him, arms crossed.

"It was a good shot," Niko looks up at me, but I can't read his expression. "Looks like you're a Kostalov after all." He gives me a little smile, and I return it. I'm a little shocked, not having realized his face could do that...

Niko straightens when his gaze slides to Aidan, his body angled slightly between my brother and me. I realize with my father dead, Niko inherits the Russian crown, making him the new Pakhan.

My brother and my husband size each other up.

"Take care of my sister, O'Rourke. I think you know the

consequences if you don't." Niko's eyes darken before he extends his hand, "Truce?"

There's silence for a beat before Aidan takes Niko's hand. "Truce." Relief sweeps through me and with it comes all the pain and exhaustion my adrenaline was hiding.

Niko sees it on my face and points toward the door. "Why don't you get my sister out of here? I'll take care of this mess." He peers down at our father's body, curling his lip in disgust.

"Thanks, Niko." Aidan laces his fingers through mine and leads me out of the study after exchanging a meaningful look with my brother that I don't understand.

Out in the hall, it's just Aidan and me. I follow him around a dark corner before he catches me by the waist, leaning me up against the wall. "Are you sure you're okay?" His hands reach up to cup my face, eyes searching and full of worry.

"No," I admit, still feeling the effects from the shock and trauma, "but I will be." I give him a reassuring smile.

"You should rest. Do you want me to bring you up to your room?" I look up at him and he drops his hands from my cheeks, raw vulnerability shining in his eyes. We stand in the Kostalov mansion. My father gone—my engagement... off.

I shake my head slowly, and he turns his head ever so slightly to the side, questioning.

"I just want to go home."

There's a flash of hope in his dark green eyes.

"With you."

Aidan leans forward and kisses me, a soft lingering promise of everything to come. Sweeping my legs out from under me, he carries me out of the mansion.

Taking me home.

71

EPILOGUE

AIDAN

*T*he ice arena buzzes with excitement and anticipation, but this time, it's not for hockey. With every seat filled, all eyes are on the rink as Rory skates to center ice, sliding gracefully to a stop. Her gaze is fixed straight ahead, calm, focused, *ready*.

I'm the complete opposite; a mess of nerves, feeling everything she isn't. This is the moment she's worked for—years of training and sacrifice and overcoming challenges no one else in this arena could possibly understand.

Liam elbows me excitedly from my right, but I don't dare take my eyes off the ice for a second. "This is insane!" My brother exclaims, marveling at the sheer magnitude of it all.

I wish Reagan was here to see it. She would have loved this... but no one's heard from her. A few days after everything went down, Koen got a text from our sister telling us *not to worry* and that *she'd call when she was ready*...

Her last pinged location showed New York. Just before her phone went dark...

We tore that city apart looking for her, but it's a big place and Volkov territory. And if Reagan doesn't want to be found... the little menace could pull that off.

Alex stayed back, continuing the search. But the longer she's gone, the more I worry. The silence is unnerving.

Rory waits patiently for her music to start, about to perform her much anticipated long program on the Olympic stage. Flags of every color decorate the arena ceiling above her. Her short program was already next to flawless. The competition is hers to lose and even I'm feeling the pressure. I grip the railing in front of me tighter.

"Any tighter and you might just tear through metal," says a cool voice in my ear, cutting through all the surrounding chaos. I steal a peek at my white knuckles and loosen it a tad, rolling my eyes at my older brother watching the performance with his arm in a sling. The Irish boss, just a little out of place in the colorful crowd.

Rory's music begins and she starts strong, hitting each mark with fluid precision. Her skating dress is very similar to her old one. Except instead of all white feathers, they're tinged in black, like the fallen angel she is.

Rory launches into her first jump with explosive power and speed. She's barely landed before she draws herself into a tight spin with a graceful transition into the complicated footwork section.

I catch a glimpse of her face as she twirls and spins and switches from back to front and back again. Her blades move in intricate patterns while the rest of her body makes it look effortless.

"C'mon, c'mon." I clench my fists, urging her on as she

comes into the most difficult section of her program: the triple-triple.

She rounds the far end of the rink, digging deep for speed, and launches herself into the first jump with an intensity that sends a roar of delight through the crowd. Three tight rotations and she's landed it! I hold my breath as she brings her skate back with force, jutting herself back into the air and pulling in tight.

"Yeah! Baby Kostalova, get it!" Liam shouts from beside me, clapping his hands together.

I shove him without looking, growling out, "It's O'Rourke, asshat."

Still, his support and cheers puts a small smile on my face. I can feel Koen beside me watching with the same cool intensity he watches most things. His body tenses each time she launches herself into the air, silently willing her through it.

When Rory lands the last jump, her concentration breaks for but a moment. Her smile takes up her entire face. Excitement bubbles in my chest and I lean forward. *This is it.* With the hard parts done—if she finishes the rest out clean...

Rory glides across the ice, her leg high above her head in a crowd pleasing spiral before throwing herself down across the ice into an artful lunge. Perfectly timed to the most dramatic section of the song, arching her back as she slides across the ice on one skate, coming to a stop right in front of the judges.

The music stops, and the arena erupts in cheers.

She's breathing hard, her eyes on the crowd—searching—looking. Her blue eyes are bright in the spotlight when they find mine and her smile widens, pointing right at me, shouting me out.

In response, I raise my hand, pointing right back at her. She did this. It was all her.

I know without needing to check, the cameras have found me. The announcers are likely eating up this moment up for everyone back at home: "Hockey star Aidan O'Rourke here cheering on his wife, Rory O'Rourke on the Olympic stage."

Rory's eyes lock on mine and for a moment, and everything fades away.

I raise my hands, clapping furiously. A loud whoop sounds out from my left and I turn in shock to witness Koen with both hands over his head shouting out Rory's name.

He throws his good arm around me, pulling me close. "That's your girl right there."

I nod in agreement, "That's my girl."

He gives me a little shove, "What the fuck are you waiting for? Go get her, Ace."

I move past him and make my way down to ice level. My all-access pass gets me through security to the skaters and coaches staging area.

It's crowded and busy as the competition continues, but I'm looking for one skater in particular.

She's giving an interview to a reporter when I find her and I slow my pace, wanting her to have her moment. But the second she sees me, she bolts, racing over and leaping into my arms. I catch her, spinning her around, eyeing her blades cautiously and relaxing when I see she's got her guards over them. Setting her back down, I tug her in close for a kiss.

"What you just did out there was magic." I brush a stray hair out of her face.

She smiles, and it's one of genuine delight and happiness,

one I'll hold close to my heart for the rest of my life. "It felt like magic."

The staging area is a blur of excitement and noise. Rory's coach draws her away from me for the score announcements. It's no surprise to anyone when she takes gold.

I stand at the side of the rink, beaming up at her on the podium.

She's practically glowing.

As soon as the award ceremony is over, Rory comes skating off, heading right for me. I'm shaking my head in disbelief and awe. This beautiful creature is all *mine*.

When she's within striking distance, she swats me in the face with her bundle of roses and I'm reminded there's still a little brat in there somewhere.

"You did it," I tell her, my heart swelling with pride.

"We did it," she corrects, "together."

She's referencing the last several weeks we both spent training, bleeding, sweating and *working*.

Rory for the Olympics and me for the tail end of the season. Keeping up the eight game winning streak the Breakers are currently on moves the team up into the second place spot going into playoffs.

The board is happy. Next week, I sign a four-year extension, keeping Rory and me in Boston and close to my family and her brother. Though I've taken a step back from my role as the mob's enforcer, letting Koen establish his rule with the help of the newfound truce between the Irish, Italians and the Russians, for however long it lasts.

I can leave the Mafia business in my brother's more than capable hands and just focus on Rory and hockey.

In that order.

There are no more promises to be made and no certainties to cling to. Whatever comes next, Rory and I will face it.

Together.

AFTERWORD

Dear Reader,

Thank you for joining me on this wild ride of hockey, mafia intrigue, and love that defies the odds. Writing this book has been an incredible journey, and I hope you fell as hard for these characters as I did.

You can absolutely expect more books in this series! We have to find out what happens to Reagan after all!
If you enjoyed this story, I'd be so grateful if you could take a moment to leave a review. Reviews are a powerful way to help authors like me connect with new readers. Whether it's a few words or a full essay, your thoughts mean the world and make a huge impact.

Sharing your review not only spreads the love but also helps this book find its way into the hands of others who might need a little escape into a world of danger, desire, and redemption.

Thank you for your support, your time, and your love of stories. I can't wait to share more with you soon.

With all my gratitude,
Aj

P.S. If you want to stay updated on my future releases, behind-the-scenes looks, or just chat about your favorite parts of this book, you can find me on social media at @ajwildingbooks. Let's stay connected!

Amazon - No Promises, No Lies
Goodreads- No Promises, No Lies

ACKNOWLEDGMENTS

Writing this book has been an unforgettable journey, and I owe so much of it to the people and moments that made it possible:

To my family, thank you for your endless love and patience throughout this journey. Through all the late nights, takeout dinners, and the mountains of unfolded laundry—you never once complained (too much) and always cheered me on. Your unwavering support means everything to me, and I could not have done this without your understanding and encouragement.

To my grandmother, who took me to the bookstore for every birthday, good report card, and *just because*. Thank you for fostering my love of reading and filling my life with stories. Your encouragement shaped the writer I am today.

To my amazing editor Nicole, whose insight, guidance, and meticulous attention to detail have elevated this book beyond what I ever imagined. I'm so grateful for your belief in my work and for pushing me to make it the best it could be. This book wouldn't be what it is without your hard work and support. Thank you for everything—you are truly a rockstar!

To my incredible beta readers, you are the unsung heroes of this story. Your feedback and excitement for this book gave me the courage to polish it into what it is today. I'm so grateful for your time and your belief in my characters. And you can thank them for the wedding scene!

To Kayla, Shonnah, Ivory, Saundra and Nancy your advice and edits were invaluable! I am forever grateful!

To my amazing street team and ARC readers: Thank you for your unwavering support and enthusiasm. Your excitement and tireless efforts to spread the word about *No Promises, No Lies* means more to me than words can ever express. You've not only helped bring this story to life, but also reminded me why I love sharing my worlds with readers like you.

To Margret, Brittney, Cody, Kayla, Amanda, Melissa, Courtney, Taylin, Jessica and Richel: Thank you for your early enthusiasm and belief in this story. Knowing you were in my corner gave me the confidence to bring this book to life. Thank you for your encouragement, your kindness, engagement and messages and for being part of this journey from the very start.

To Rebz, I'm so grateful to have you in my corner. Thank you for always hyping me up, and for always encouraging me to follow this dream. Your belief in me has meant the world, and I'm so lucky to have you by my side.

And finally, to you the reader, whether you devoured this book in one sitting or took your time savoring every word, I'm so grateful you chose to spend your time with these characters. I hope they made you laugh, cry, and maybe yell at a page or two. Without you, this story would just be words on a screen— thank you for bringing it to life.

With all my love,

Aj

ABOUT THE AUTHOR

 Aj lives in New England with her husband, two sons, two dogs and two cats (yes, it's chaos).

A dedicated hockey mom, she spends an unreasonable amount of time in cold rinks, fueled by coffee and a deep appreciation for warm blankets.

When she's not writing, Aj enjoys sipping coffee, reading, spending time with her family and friends, and digital art. Though nothing beats the thrill of crafting a story that makes readers feel something. Whether it's a moment that makes your heart race, a line that makes you laugh, or a scene that lingers long after you've turned the last page, that's the magic she strives for in every book.

JOIN THE WILDING STREET TEAM!

Did you love No Promises, No Lies?
Consider joining "Aj Wilding's Street Team and ARC Readers": A private group on Facebook

https://www.facebook.com/share/g/182Cjtrjvx/

This is our cozy little corner to connect, share, and gush about all things books (and maybe a little behind-the-scenes magic).

As a member of this group, you're not just helping me get the word out about my stories—you're part of the journey. I'll be sharing:

📖 **Exclusive sneak peeks** and bonus chapters.

✏️ Behind-the-scenes look into my writing process.

🎁 Fun challenges, giveaways, and rewards for your support.

📖 Advanced Reader Copies (ARCs) of my upcoming releases!

www.ingramcontent.com/pod-product-compliance
Lightning Source LLC
Chambersburg PA
CBHW010651100726
47901CB00012B/2508